T H E   F A L L

T H E

F A L L

R. J. PINEIRO

Thomas Dunne Books
St. Martin's Press New York

This is a work of fiction. All of the characters, organizations, and events portrayed in this novel are either products of the author's imagination or are used fictitiously.

THOMAS DUNNE BOOKS.
An imprint of St. Martin's Press.

Designed by Molly Rose Murphy

ISBN 978-1-250-05214-8

For Lory,

Loving wife,
Devoted mother,
Best friend,
Soul mate.

Thanks for holding my hand in the tunnel.

And,

For St. Jude, saint of the impossible,
For once again making it possible.

THE FALL

1

A WORTHY CAUSE

*The credit belongs to the man who is actually in the arena,
whose face is marred by dust and sweat and blood; who strives
valiantly; who knows great enthusiasms, the great devotions,
and spends himself in a worthy cause.*

—Theodore Roosevelt

What goes up must come down, thought Jack Taylor as his gloved hands gripped the
handles framing the oval-shaped exit hatch of his windowless capsule.

He loved the adrenaline rush, riding atop the booster that had shot him off
the Florida peninsula like a cannonball, giving him the gut-wrenching, suborbital ride of a lifetime for the past few minutes.

And that was the easy part.

The stereoscopic image painted on his helmet's polymer faceplate, slaved to
the external cameras, displayed the rocket booster's fall to Earth as he rapidly
decelerated while approaching the apogee of his programmed sixty-two-mile
ballistic flight, skimming the Kármán Line, the official threshold where space
began above sea level.

But Jack was far more engrossed in the splendor and magnificence projecting beyond the spinning booster as it vanished in the vast carpet of mountains
and plains dotted with dozens of lakes and meandering rivers stained with vivid
hues of orange, red, and yellow-gold by the looming sun's wan light.

He flew temporarily weightless now, as his ballistic flight reached its zenith
high above glaring mirrors of infinite shapes and sizes surrounded by forests,
agricultural crops, mountain ranges, cities, and grids of roads and highways—
all framed by endless coastal plains, by the eastern seaboard projecting far north
into the darkening curvature of Planet Earth and the stars beyond.

The soft whirr of his suit's environmental control and life support system broke the silence of space, the dead calm that Jack enjoyed as much as the cold and wonderfully refreshing pure air sprayed gently inside his helmet from the suit's liquid oxygen supply.

The familiar aromas of plastic and sweat filled his nostrils as Jack inhaled deeply, his gaze gravitating to the west. Tropical storm Claudette, which had moved up his launch schedule, gathered strength over the warm Gulf of Mexico, bright flashes of cloud-to-cloud lightning trembling across hundreds of miles as it twisted its way north.

"Stay the fuck away," he mumbled, glaring at Claudette's swirling clouds.

"Phoenix, KSC, we didn't quite copy that. Say again."

Shit. "Ah, nothing, KSC. Just enjoying the view," he replied to Pete Flaherty, his boss and longtime friend, who was acting as capsule communicator, or CapCom, for this mission down at Kennedy Space Center.

Jack heard a slight pause, probably Pete trying not to laugh, followed by a lively, "Copy that. Sixty seconds to Kármán."

"Roger," Jack replied, scanning the myriad displays projected all around the periphery of his helmet, marveling at his wife, Angela, the genius behind this amazing piece of hardware that he hoped would bring his ass down through sixty miles of hell in one piece to a smooth touchdown in a designated grassy field northeast of Orlando.

The Orbital Space Suit, nearly six years in the making, had his wife's ingenuity written all over it, from the amazing helmet displays, to the retina-controlled systems, integrated stability jets in the gloves and boots, a closed-loop oxygen system to eliminate the need for large tanks, and multiple of layers of titanium, Nomex, nylon, Mylar, and graphite to keep the intense heat from reaching the sensitive inner layers—all packaged in an incredibly light and flexible one-piece jumpsuit. The OSS just flowed. It was elegant, clean, and highly intuitive, minimizing the time it would take the wearer to grow familiar. Plus Angela had designed it with full modularization so it could be mass-produced for a new generation of American fighting forces.

And all courtesy of the slice of the DOD's extensive budget that Pete had managed to channel to this project.

"Thirty seconds to Kármán."

"Roger, KSC. All good up here," Jack said, glancing at the video projecting a vast void below him, feeling the reassuring mild stiffness of pressurized oxygen inside the suit.

Trapped inside this tiny pod hurtling at more than five thousand miles per hour to reach an altitude two and a half times as high as the well-advertised jump by "Fearless" Felix Baumgartner a few years earlier, Jack couldn't help but wonder if he had gone just a bit too far this time. This was not one of the relatively easier jumps from the Stratosphere that Baumgartner and USAF Colonel Joseph Kittinger before him had accomplished. Jack was at the official edge of space, deep in the unforgiving thermosphere, about to reach the exact height where Alan Shepard flew *Freedom 7* back in 1961, marking America's entry into the space race with that historic fifteen-minute suborbital flight.

Yeah, but Shepard stayed inside the capsule, Jack.

He shook the thought away while tightening his grip on the handles, becoming hyperaware that everything sounded right. Inside his suit, sound was a primary sense, and Jack's trained ears listened to the whirring pumps not only feeding oxygen into the suit but also dumping exhaled carbon dioxide to keep his blood oxygenation at the proper level. Their constant—and reassuring—humming mixed with the occasional sound of nylon creaking as he inched closer to the exit hatch.

Just a walk in the park, he thought, remembering his prior job as a federal contractor for the U.S. government, testing gear and tactics before they became plans of record for SEAL teams, Army Rangers, and other elite fighting forces. The assignments had taken Jack from desert sands to icy mountain peaks, from the depths of the ocean to stormy heavens while pushing prototype equipment to the breaking point. From the latest skydiving rigs to leading-edge underwater gadgets, rappeling equipment, and every conceivable type of weapon, Jack was the Pentagon's leading test warrior, wringing out the kinks of prototype hardware and tactics for the benefit of America's fighting forces.

And this assignment was just another stepping stone in Jack's uniquely dangerous career. Pete had wasted no time signing him up for the elite Project Phoenix.

NASA hoped to breathe new life into its dying operations by proving to the Department of Defense the immense value of space jumps. If NASA perfected orbital jumps, the Department of Defense could have soldiers jumping from so high up that the enemies of the United States would never detect them in time.

And this suborbital flight was the first step in the process. Angela was already finalizing the computer design of a suit that would allow a true orbital jump directly from the International Space Station—an assignment that Pete was already hard at work lobbying to fund.

But first, Jack had to succeed today.

Everything depends on it, he thought, activating the suit's BIST—Built-in Self Test—an algorithm developed by Angela to have the suit's master computer system test every module of the OSS, displaying the results in Jack's faceplate as well as in one of the large monitors in Mission Control. His primary concern was damage by the Gs he had endured during the ascent phase.

"All systems in the green, Phoenix," reported Pete from the Cape.

"Roger," Jack replied.

The press, which was under the impression that NASA was simply testing an early prototype suit designed to help astronauts abandon the International Space Station in case of emergency, was certainly having one hell of a field day with his latest stunt. From passing out and failing to open his chute to breaking up when hitting the speed of sound, or—Jack's favorite—his eyeballs and heart exploding while burning up in the atmosphere, the pundits were going crazy with their—

"Ten seconds to Kármán, Phoenix. OSS looking good."

"Roger that."

Focus, Jack, he thought, scanning the telemetry displayed on his visor, confirming that the OSS—the single-most compact and complex piece of equipment ever made by NASA—was fully functional, making this mission a go.

"Five seconds . . . All systems nominal."

His tactile gloves clutching the handles flanking the exit hatch, his power boots pressed hard against the Velcro floor pads, Jack watched a single bead of sweat momentarily floating right in front of his eyes before the suit's recirculating system sucked it away.

"Three . . . two . . . one . . . Kármán."

Point of no return. Jack took a deep breath as he watched, completely devoid of sound, the oval-shaped hatch blasting into space courtesy of a dozen explosive bolts in a pyrotechnic display of oranges and reds that ironically matched the myriad hues from the tunnel-like image of Earth beyond the pod's large opening.

Right up to Kármán, Jack had the ability to abort the mission and use the capsule's heat shields to return to Earth safely, just as Shepard had done decades before. NASA had built the pod as Plan B in case of a suit malfunction during the ascent phase. But just as Cortez burned the ships when conquering the New World to force his troops inland, NASA had also technically just burned Jack's ship. There was now no other way down but to jump.

"Well, good thing the suit's holding up," he said, before thinking, *Thank you, Angie.*

"Roger, Phoenix. All looks good down here as well . . . hold on."

Jack dropped his gaze at Pete's last two words.

"Phoenix, this is General Hastings."

Really, dude? Right now?

The Pentagon had decided to place the entire operation—just twelve damned hours before the jump—under the direct command of General George Hastings, a senior member of the DOD overseeing committee who had never set foot at the Cape before. Jack had nearly lost it when he'd arrived at Kennedy Space Center last night to find an entourage of dark SUVs packed with a small army of soldiers and a couple of scientists from Los Alamos. Then an hour later, as NASA technicians were going through the process of getting him inside the multiple modules and layers of the OSS, Hastings made his appearance and had gone straight into a discussion about changing the descent profile, in direct conflict with Angela's instructions. A heated exchange followed between Hastings, Jack, and Angela.

No offense, General, but she's got the MIT Ph.D., not you, Jack had finally told him, prompting the general to storm out of the suit-up room to call the Pentagon. But in spite of clashing personalities, there was simply too much at stake, and there was no one else skilled enough—and perhaps crazy enough—to make this jump. So after a ten-minute conference call between the Joint Chiefs of Staff, the White House Chief of Staff, Hastings, and Pete, it was decided that the jump would go on as planned but with the reprogrammed descent profile requested by Hastings, and that Pete would find a way to keep Jack on a leash.

"General?" Jack finally said.

"Jack, you must accept the reprogrammed Alpha-B profile when you reenter the atmosphere. It is critical that . . ."

Jack tuned the general out while watching the Earth below him, leaning forward into the abyss, freeing his boots from the Velcro straps on the floor while still holding on to the exit handles, trying to listen to his suit rather than to Hastings. His mind focused on the job ahead, letting the general continue to rattle off the same garbage he had spewed back in the suit-up room.

This is the precise reason why so many well-planned military operations turn to shit, General.

But Jack held his tongue, trusting his wife, deciding to accept whatever descent profile appeared in his display.

Instead, he gazed at the nearly surreal view beyond the capsule as he waited for the timer to start the jump countdown sequence. It was one thing to view the world painted on his faceplate display by exterior cameras. It was an entirely different animal to actually see it from this altitude with his own eyes. No camera could capture the incredible depth and colors of planet Earth as he swung forward as much as he could while still holding on to the handles, projecting half of his body beyond the opening, milking the moment for as long as he could.

Even Claudette looked amazing from this altitude, its angered clouds alive with pulsating lightning resembling balls of light arcing across its twisting mass, trembling wildly in a rainbow of colors contrasting sharply with the bluish hues of the Gulf of Mexico as it slowly turned east towards the middle of the Florida peninsula.

Although seldom easily impressed, Jack took it all in, enjoying his very own fireworks show, filling his lungs, savoring the moment before his jump window opened, listening to his suit, to the droning pumps keeping the OSS's internal temperature at 70 degrees Fahrenheit, to the light beeps made by the master computer system as it ran yet another diagnostic, and even to the sound of his own breathing as he became nearly hypnotized by the view.

Somewhere in the background, Hastings was still talking, still dispensing orders.

Jack continued to ignore him, his eyes scanning his faceplate displays, confirming proper operation of all his systems, before returning to the cloud-to-cloud lightning, framed by the ocean and the Florida peninsula. Beyond it a sea of stars outlined Earth's delicate curvature, countless points glittering against the darkness of space.

A green numeral 20, projected in the middle of his faceplate, disrupted his cosmic sightseeing.

Lock and load time, he thought.

As the timer turned red and began the critical twenty-second countdown before the jump window closed, Jack remembered Alan Shepard in *Freedom 7*, recalled what later became known as Shepard's Prayer in the aviator's community thanks to the movie *The Right Stuff*.

"Dear God, please don't let me fuck up," he said, interrupting Hastings's monologue.

Then Jack lowered the heat shield over his visor and jumped into the abyss.

"He'd better know what in the *fuck* he's doing, Flaherty!" hissed George Hastings, the oversized Army general, while standing next to Pete at the CapCom station in the relatively modest Mission Control Room, occupying the second floor of an old space shuttle–era building recently refurbished for Project Phoenix in Launch Complex 39. In this windowless room, eighteen mission specialists sitting in three rows of six monitored every aspect of the launch. If successful, the next Pentagon grant would allow Pete to expand this Mission Control Room, add a second one at the Johnson Space Center in Houston, Texas, and add an OSS Launch Module to the International Space Station, where America could house its first platoon of orbital jumpers ready to be deployed to any location on the globe.

"I thought you were going to keep him on a leash, dammit!" the general snarled before stepping back and crossing his massive arms while looking at the large displays monopolizing the entire front of the room.

Dr. Angela Taylor, sitting at the far end of the last row, shook her head while sipping her third energy drink in two hours, finishing it, and tossing it over her head and directly into a waste basket just five feet from the growling general with the blazing orange hair and freckles. The can banged loudly against the other two she had previously deposited in the same trash can.

That's another three-pointer, Grumpy.

Angela felt his stare on her as she loudly popped the lid of a fourth drink while glancing at her short fingernails, painted black to match her lipstick, before shifting her gaze between Jack's vitals, the descent profile display, and the suit's hundreds of internal monitors—telemetry that was broadcast through two passing satellites and one in geosynchronous orbit right above the jump as backup. In addition, the pod's final task was to shoot off in a parallel descent path to Jack's while providing them with high-resolution imagery for the first few minutes of the jump, before it burned up on reentry at around mile thirty. Then the cameras aboard a dozen high-altitude balloons parked along his planned route would pick up his epic fall right up to his final chute deployment, when ground cameras and several spotting helicopters would be waiting to record the final descent.

Everyone in that room—with the exception of Hastings and his annoying crew—had a specific task to handle, from managing the capsule's trajectory and tracking satellites, to the incoming weather system, the high-altitude balloons, distance to all other orbiting objects, and even working real-time with central Florida's air traffic controllers to create a twenty-mile-wide temporary flight restriction around Jack's planned descent path, also known as the "pipe."

On top of all that, the Air Force had a dozen fighter jets hauling high-frequency transmitters meant to keep all birds away from the pipe. The stakes were high, and the last thing NASA and the Pentagon needed was for Jack to hit a chunk of space debris or a damned seagull on his way down. But even the finest rocket-scientist minds couldn't anticipate every possible thing that could go wrong with a project of this complexity, and that very, very small—but still very, very real—probability of something going wrong kept Angela's heart rate high and her throat dry.

Come home to me, Jack, she thought, feeling immense pressure building up in her chest, just to realize she had stopped breathing.

Slowly inhaling through her nostrils and exhaling through her mouth, Angela took a sip of her drink and tried to control her growing heart rate, for a moment feeling ashamed that Jack's was actually lower than hers. But then again, Jack had always been in superb physical shape, which over the years meant that Angela also got in shape to keep up with him, from long runs, mountain climbing, and ocean kayaking to becoming his official self-defense training partner at home, an activity that typically ended in the bedroom. In return, Angela taught Jack to ride Triumph motorcycles and even got him to get a tattoo to match hers.

She grinned, glancing at the burning Triumph Bonneville T140 flanked by American and British flags on her right forearm, half covered by her lab coat.

The knowledge that Jack had one just like it up there somehow helped her steady her breathing.

You are some smooth operator, she thought, amazed that he could calm her down even from outer space.

But just as Jack could calm her down, he could also really push her buttons, bringing out the worst in her.

Their relationship hadn't been easy the past two years, with Jack signing up for every high-adrenaline military mission while she developed space suits for NASA.

What happened to us? she pondered as the countdown sequence ticked down in the upper left corner of her display. The glimmer in his brown eyes last night, as they shared homemade pasta while reviewing the various phases of his descent and last-minute adjustments to his space suit, had reawakened long-dormant feelings in Angela.

But you came along, you little fucker, she thought, glaring at Claudette in one of the large screens at the front of the room, remembering the cell phone vibrating on the dinner table, Pete informing them that an incoming weather system had moved up the jump. A car was already on the way to get them both to the Cape.

Angela sighed, recalling the feelings rekindled during their interrupted dinner—feelings long absent in their busy lives.

Two damn years, Jack, she thought, frowning. That's how long it had been since they'd really connected, since the fire of their initial years of marriage was quenched by the realities of their almost separate lives, driving a deep wedge between them, resulting in Jack sleeping more often on the couch than in their bedroom.

But there had been something there last night, a spark of years past, and a part of Angela was hoping to pick up where they had left off.

But first you need to do this jump, she thought, as Jack separated from the pod and instantly assumed the planned initial descent profile, opening his arms and legs as if he were flying, stretching the titanium alloy webbing from his waist to his elbows and in between his thighs. The idea, which had earned her another patent, came to Angela by watching sugar gliders jump from tree to tree.

"Phoenix, KSC. Jump plus five seconds. Looking good. All systems nominal. Pod ignition started. Ten seconds to drone deployment," Pete said while sitting back down at his station in the middle row as General Hastings stepped aside to confer with the pair of Los Alamos physicists he had brought down with him along with a dozen military personnel, which he called his "security detail."

"Roger that. Phoenix's good up here."

Hastings said something to his head of security, Captain Riggs, a steroids-enhanced brute who had come close to attacking Jack after last night's heated exchange with Hastings.

My money would have been on Jack, she thought with a grin, taking a sip while sizing up Riggs, who looked as if he ate rocks in his morning cereal. The man was certainly solid, with tight muscles visibly pressing against his dark uniform.

In fact, he looks too perfect, she thought, with his closely cropped blond hair, hard-edged features, and very fair skin—certainly a fine specimen of Aryan descent. And interestingly enough, all of Hastings's men had that look. Some had dark hair. One was Asian. Another black. But they all looked as if they were grown in the same place, like little toy soldiers, seldom making eye contact, and not one of them ever looked in her direction.

Maybe they're gay, she thought.

Or maybe the good general cuts off their balls like they used to do in the old days.

Riggs saluted the general, did a perfect about-face, and proceeded to direct his team of eunuchs to cover all entrances to Mission Control before approaching NASA's press coordinator in the back of the room.

She exhaled slowly, reminding herself that the brass was footing the bill. But if NASA could pull this off, perhaps Hastings, his pit bulls, and his pair of gurus would crawl back to whatever shithole they had come out of and let the real pros continue to drive this program.

She gave the Alamo scientists a furtive glance while biting her lower lip. The male one was in his sixties, bald, and a bit hunched over, with round glasses perched at the edge of his thin nose. The female was much younger, perhaps in her forties, rail thin, with ash-blond hair, light-colored eyes behind thick glasses, and a pasty complexion that suggested she probably didn't get outside much.

Maybe Hastings is doing her, she thought with another grin, finishing off her drink and executing another perfectly loud three-pointer.

She had never seen either one of them before last night, when she caught them in the suit-up room with their noses deep in the electronic guts of her baby, the product of nearly six years of painful design and redesign. Jack had to literally restrain her when Angela had instinctively reverted to her biker upbringing, turning into a junkyard dog about to mangle the visiting physicists, who scrambled out of the room.

She hoped she wouldn't see them ever again after today.

Angela had no clue yet, why there was a need for a pair of tablet-armed nerds sticking their noses in her project and scrubbing through the OSS computer network but she intended to find out. An alarm in the back of her head told her that the Pentagon brass didn't pull last-minute stunts like this one without a powerful motive.

But the cyber-sword cuts both ways, she thought with a slight grin. The same VIP accounts that allowed the Los Alamos scientists to connect their tablets into the OSS network had allowed Angela to load up a nice little virus into their portable devices, creating back doors that should give her access to their networks.

You get to see mine but I also get to see yours.

As soon as this jump was over, she would find out who they were and why they wanted to modify Jack's descent profile during the reentry phase from Alpha-G to Alpha-B.

She had gone over the data and it didn't make any sense. Alpha-B would increase the angle of descent by two degrees, keeping Jack supersonic for fifteen more seconds than planned, which could potentially set him off course by as much as three miles from his designated touchdown site northeast of Orlando. The Alpha adjustments, from A to K, were created to compensate for the winds aloft during reentry and keep the jumper on a mission-specified vertical track. Part of Project Phoenix's deliverables was touchdown accuracy to within ten feet of the intended target.

In the end, NASA had caved and agreed to program Hastings's Alpha-B descent profile. But just before the launch, Angela had used her secret back door into the OSS descent control algorithms to reprogram it back to Alpha-G while still keeping all systems reporting that they were set for Alpha-B.

It's my husband you're fucking with, General, not one of your eunuchs, she thought, glad that she had listened to the hacker in her and programmed multiple back doors into every system in the OSS network.

"Jump plus ten. Pod burn complete."

"Roger."

Pete looked over to Angela and gave her a reassuring thumbs-up. His soft features contrasted sharply with a pair of blue eyes gleaming with bold intelligence under a full head of dark hair.

He turned back toward his monitor. Pete's dark skin had the handsome damage of countless weekends sailing or skydiving with Jack. Those two went back to high school in New Jersey. Although Pete was captain of the chess team while Jack led the football team, they developed a deep friendship. Then Pete got an academic scholarship to Stanford's prestigious School of Engineering while Jack played football for Rutgers before joining the Navy, where he eventually screened for BUD/S, Basic Underwater Demolition/SEAL Training at Coronado. That led him straight to SEAL Team 3, followed by five years of missions in the Middle East's hottest spots and another two years with SEAL Team 4 in South America. When a mission in Colombia went south due to faulty combat gear, Jack signed up to test prototype military equipment for the Pentagon, feeling that he could best serve his country by working out the kinks in high-tech weaponry and gadgets before they became plans of record for America's fighting forces. Pete, on the other hand, accepted a contract with the Pentagon to develop America's next generation of weaponry, which led him to NASA and Project Phoenix, where he wasted no time in recruiting Jack.

Angela watched the ends of her lips curve up on her reflection on the flat-screen monitor, remembering the first time she laid eyes on the clean-cut Jack Taylor, rapidly deciding he was definitely not her type. Angela had grown up among the tough biker crowd that hung around her father's motorcycle shop in Cocoa Beach. The former SEAL, albeit ruggedly handsome and quite free-spirited, didn't trigger any feelings in her. And besides, she was too damn busy developing the OSS to give Jack's advances any serious thought. But somewhere along the way, he had turned her around, and before she knew it they were married.

Angela forced those thoughts aside while focusing on the data displayed on her monitor, confirming proper functionality of all systems. Everything was as it should be, including her secretly reprogrammed descent profile.

She pinched the bridge of her nose, seeking comfort by remembering Jack's final words just before he'd left the suit-up room. Beaming with confidence, he'd looked her in the eye and gave her the same damn line he'd always given her before going on a mission: *Relax, honey. I'll be right back.*

She took a deep breath, glancing around the room, trying very hard to keep it together while her husband dropped out of the sky like a fucking meteor.

Come home to me, Jack. Please come home.

Jack plummeted to Earth, at least according to the altimeter reading next to the mission timer. One mile down and sixty-one to go, but all he felt was a serene sense of floating in space as outside temperatures read 100 degrees Kelvin or about minus-280 degrees Fahrenheit.

Pretty damn cold, he thought, reaching almost five hundred miles per hour before the drone deployed. It wasn't really a parachute but more of a small wing-like appendage to increase stability for a cleaner entry into the speed of sound.

Jack kept his profile steady now as he approached six hundred miles per hour, the mission timer shifting to red, which indicated he was almost supersonic.

"Seven hundred miles per hour and fifty-eight miles high, Phoenix. Looking good."

Jack was about to reply but felt a slight buffeting that couldn't be due to air molecules. He was way too far up for any of that.

"KSC, Phoenix, there's a slight—" Jack stopped. The buffeting vanished as quickly as it had appeared.

"Congratulations, Phoenix. You are Mach one point oh and climbing."

Well, I'll be damned. He had just punched through the sound barrier with little fanfare.

"Roger that. Phoenix is supersonic," Jack replied, limbs still stretched, keeping the tension in the stability webbing as he shot past eight hundred miles per hour at mile fifty-six.

The stars slowly dimmed as a violet halo-like glow extended radially around him.

Weird.

But he ignored it as Mach two came and went, as he dropped below the thermosphere and into the ionosphere while the suit kept him completely isolated from the harsh environment.

One minute and fifty-three miles to go, he thought, enjoying a deep breath of pure cold oxygen while reading the mission timer as his speed continued to climb due to a lack of an atmosphere. And that also meant no sound since there were no air molecules to carry sound waves.

Jack breathed in the refreshing air again, listening to the pumps while watching the rapidly expanding Earth almost as if he were in some sort of silent video game.

Systems remained in the green, the multiple layers of the OSS and its insulating gels holding his body temperature at a nominal 96.7 degrees Fahrenheit as he accelerated beyond the fastest fighter jet. The violet halo intensified, enveloping him in its dazzling glow.

"KSC, Phoenix. You guys see that purple haze around me?"

"Ah, negative, Phoenix. The pod's camera shows you bright and clear. Looking good through Mach three."

Jack decided to let that go, focusing on his instruments, staring at one of the many retina-controlled icons on his faceplate display and blinking once, releasing the titanium-alloy winglet while getting the OSS ready to fire his boot and glove jets to increase his angle of descent as prescribed by what he hoped would be the Alpha-G profile that Angela had preprogrammed in the suit's directional algorithms, preparing him to reenter the atmosphere and get bombarded by the air molecules that would slow down his descent, in the process creating an air pocket in front of him that would heat the air to incandescence.

But to reenter the atmosphere safely, Jack had to transition from his current skydiver attitude to a near-vertical profile to create the smallest possible cross-section to the incoming compression wave of thermal deceleration. Angela had designed his oversized helmet—which reminded Jack of the elongated head from one of those old *Alien* movies—and extra-wide shoulder pads as the suit's primary ablative shields, designed to take the brunt of the direct reentry heating.

Following engineering principles that dated back to the 1950s showing that the greater the drag, the lower the heat load on the object reentering the atmosphere, Angela had designed the OSS's helmet and shoulder sections to be blunt rather than aerodynamic. In doing so, air molecules wouldn't be able to get out of the way fast enough, acting as an air cushion to push the heated shockwave layer forward and away from him. Since most of the hot gases would no longer be in direct contact with Jack's suit, the heat energy would stay in the shocked gas and simply move around the OSS to later dissipate into the atmosphere above him.

Jack's primary job was to keep all of his mass hidden behind these critical blunt shields made of the same reinforced carbon-carbon material previously used for the nose of the space shuttle and designed for temperatures above 1300 degrees Fahrenheit. The rest of his suit's outer shell, like the chest and waist plates, were fabricated from the coated L-9000 silica ceramics used in the space shuttle's belly, while his limbs were shielded with layers of flexible insulation blankets used by the space shuttle for temperatures below 1200 degrees Fahrenheit.

Jack frowned, unable to avoid thinking about the tragic fate of Space Shuttle

Columbia burning up during the very unforgiving reentry phase back in 2003 due to damage to its thermal protection system under one wing during the launch phase, exposing its inner skin to the blazing inferno. Hot gases had breached the wing structure through a hole in the TPS, leading to the rapid disintegration of the shuttle.

If his outer shell cracked due to the reentry stress, the OSS would be breached, just like *Columbia*, with disastrous results.

"KSC, Phoenix. Jets firing," he reported, listening to the bursts and confirming readings on his faceplate display as he slowly shifted from a horizontal pose to near vertical, tucking his arms against the built-in recess points on the sides of his suit while closing his legs and engaging the magnetic locking mechanisms to keep his limbs from shifting during reentry.

Jack quickly assumed a bulletlike profile behind his blunt shields, getting a green icon confirming achievement of the Alpha-G angle.

I guess Angie won, thought Jack. He blinked and accepted the descent profile.

"Phoenix, KSC. Copy that. Mach three point two and holding. Forty-six miles high."

That's almost 2,500 miles per hour, he thought, realizing that he had broken every record in the books for the fastest speed without a spacecraft. He could only hope that would be the only thing he broke today, as he plummeted into the stratosphere like a silent meteor.

But the peaceful fall didn't last long the moment air molecules began their attack, slow at first, just a few pings against his armored shields, before rapidly increasing their intensity, pounding him like invisible bullets, like millions of shotgun pellets striking the protective layers on his helmet and shoulder pads. The noise reminded Jack of being trapped inside an RV on a rock-climbing trip in Arizona with Pete eons ago during a massive hail storm. The pounding was deafening.

"Phoenix, KSC, TDRSS in fifteen seconds."

Jack grimaced, barely hearing his friend. "Copy that!" he shouted through the noise.

Jack stared at an icon in the shape of a satellite on the upper right side of his helmet display and blinked once, engaging the tracking and data relay satellite system. Created during the space shuttle era to solve the dreaded reentry communications blackout caused by ionized air from the compressing atmosphere around the decelerating vehicle, TDRSS allowed the shuttle to maintain communications by relay with a tracking and data relay satellite through a hole in the ionized air at the tail of the craft created by the shuttle's shape. Angela had basically accomplished the same thing at a much smaller scale, incorporating the relevant shuttle contours into the shape of the Orbital Space Suit to punch a similar hole through the ionized envelope and keep tabs of her husband's whereabouts all the way to the ground.

Jack activated the stiffeners around his neck, anchoring the long helmet to the frame of his suit as he felt the G-forces accumulating, as the building pressure on his upper body intensified, as the shockwave compressed the stress-absorbing materials of the suit's titanium and carbon fiber skeleton. But contrary to popular belief, shock-layer heating wasn't caused primarily by direct air friction but by the heating of air molecules within the increasing compression wave.

Jack focused on the graphics of his first ablative shield, which provided protection on two levels. The outer surface began to char, melt, and sublime in the rising heat, while the remaining ablation material underwent pyrolysis, an irreversible thermochemical decomposition at elevated temperatures in the absence of oxygen, expelling the product gases and keeping all layers beneath it quite cool.

Jack watched as the blunt ablation shields worked their chemical magic, lifting the hot gases away from the shield's outer wall, creating a cooler boundary layer as he dove into a wall of fire that always remained a quarter of an inch away from him, before washing away in the slipstream, caressing the sides of his suit's flexible insulation material.

But the thermal shields could do little about the noise, which continued climbing to an ear-piercing crescendo as the atmosphere put up a fight.

Jack tightened his jaw muscles as his near-vertical mass continued to punch through the resisting thin air, turning the sky around him into a blinding, incandescent white stained with that weird violet haze that now started to pulsate in stroboscopic waves.

Jesus Christ, he thought, as the G-meter read 8.5 and continued to climb.

He increased the pressure of the suit's gel to counter it, to force more blood to his head, to fight the growing light-headedness, receiving visual confirmation through the faceplate display and feeling the squeeze action on his legs.

"Phoenix, KSC. Looking good at forty-three miles high."

Jack tried to respond but the arresting pressure on his chest prevented him from articulating a single word, though he could still read the displays, could still see the firestorm rapidly consuming his first ablation layer.

Forty-two miles high now.

Mach 2.3.

Outside temperature a dash over 1,000 degrees Fahrenheit.

Jack narrowed his eyes as he scanned the telemetry, blinking once at the okay icon that Angela had incorporated into the helmet display for precisely this kind of situation.

"Phoenix, KSC. We read you're okay. Looking good at forty-one miles. Eject first heat shield."

The compression wave slowing him down chemically blasted away at his thermal protection system, reducing his first micro honeycomb ablation layer to ten percent in fifty seconds. He focused his eyes on an icon, blinked, and the spent layer of reinforced carbon-carbon on his helmet and shoulder pads jettisoned off with a burst of compressed helium, vanishing in the scorching slipstream, exposing the second ablation shield.

"Phoenix, KSC. First shield is off."

Jack blinked okay while mustering savage control to focus on his deceleration stats.

Thirty-nine miles high.

Mach 1.9.

Temperature soaring to 1,100 degrees.

G-meter at 10.2.

The laws of physics were certainly at work as his speed plummeted, turning vertical velocity into the charring furnace that chipped away at his new set of shields.

Energy can be neither created nor destroyed, only changed, he recalled Angela telling him as he struggled to stay focused, to keep his mind frosty. But despite his forced concentration, thoughts slowly gravitated to the periphery of his consciousness.

Jack fought vehemently for control, to remain awake, refusing to let the autopilot take charge of this mission.

He jammed the suit's gel pressure control into the red, feeling the compression against his legs where swelling bladders fought to deliver precious blood to the capillaries lacing his brain.

Just hold on a little longer.

Thirty-four miles high.

Mach 1.5.

Temperature 1,150 degrees.

G-meter at 10.9.

Shields at forty percent.

The forces pummeling his body were approaching the G-suit design, threatening to breach his physical limits, pushing him to the brink of his endurance through a dazzling violet halo that increased in intensity as he continued to fall, plunging at a maddening speed.

"Phoenix, KSC, pod video terminated. We're picking you up on the balloons now. All systems nominal."

Nominal my ass, he thought, nearly paralyzed now, unable to even blink the okay icon.

"Thirty miles high, Phoenix. Switching to feet."

The same forces that had smoked that four-ton titanium and silica capsule were starting to put a serious dent in Angela's masterpiece.

Altitude 150,000 feet.

Mach 1.3.

Temperature almost at 1,200 degrees.

G-meter at 11.6.

Ablation shields at ten percent.

The blinding violet light swallowed his thoughts, his mind, engulfing his very core as Jack started to lose consciousness, but he managed one final reading of his instruments, somehow managing to blast off his scorched second set of reinforced carbon-carbon shields in a burst of helium while hoping—praying—that his third and last set of thermal protection would see him through this.

Altitude 130,000 feet.

Mach 1.24.

Temperature 1,180 degrees.

G-meter at 11.6.

Ablation shields at ninety-eight percent.

The Earth and cosmos seemed to swap places somewhere in a remote corner of his mind.

That's impossible.

Jack tried to regain focus. He couldn't be tumbling, not now, with soaring temperatures and while still supersonic as he careened down to Earth like a blazing comet right through the altitude where Felix Baumgartner had jumped in 2012.

Confused, disoriented, his mind rapidly becoming as dark as the space above him, Jack reached deep into his reserves and pushed his body to perform one final task, staring at the autopilot icon and blinking once as atmospheric forces overwhelmed him.

But just as he dropped below 120,000 feet—just as the G-meter displayed 12.0, outside temperature reading 1200 degrees, and the Mach meter reported 1.2, the heat, the pressure, the blinding glare and deafening noise all faded away, and Jack felt engulfed by the most amazing, comforting, and warm violet haze.

His display began to flash that last set of readings in bright red to the rhythm of the vibrating light that had engulfed him.

MACH 1.2
G-METER 12.0
TEMPERATURE 1200 DEGREES
ALTITUDE 120,000 FEET

What . . . is . . . happening?

The violet haze enveloped him, infusing him with warmth while propelling him through a labyrinth of colors. Dazzling. Blinding.

Intoxicating.

"Phoenix, KSC, how do you copy?"

Pete's voice suddenly seemed distant, echoing lightly inside his helmet.

Jack found the okay icon and blinked on it.

"Phoenix . . . how . . . copy?"

Wondering why they couldn't get his response, Jack blinked on the icon again as he fought for control in this surreal world, where up and down had no meaning, no significance.

"Phoenix . . . copy . . ."

He tumbled over and over again, unable to restore his descent profile, unable to use his suit's thrusters to arrest the spin while his display continued flashing the same readings.

MACH 1.2
G-METER 12.0
TEMPERATURE 1200 DEGREES
ALTITUDE 120,000 FEET

But that was impossible.

Jack could sense his rapid fall, could feel the vertical drop in his gut.

"Phoenix . . ."

Pete's voice was a mere whisper now as Jack continued to drop out of the heavens while he scanned his displays, searching past the stubborn telemetry, finding his emergency icon, the one Angela had incorporated in this design in case of extreme disorientation.

He blinked on it, trying to activate the emergency gyro to recover from his uncontrollable fall while signaling to Pete that he was in trouble.

But he got no reply from KSC as he plunged into what looked like a storm, alive with sheet lightning.

And then it hit him.

Did I . . . drift . . . to the . . . storm?

Realizing he was dropping right on top of Claudette, Jack closed his eyes a second before impacting the pulsating bolts of lightning, thunder crashing around him as he felt immense pressure against his chest, his head.

Unable to breathe from the force squeezing his pressure suit, Jack struck what felt like a layer of gel, stretching under his downward momentum, arresting his fall like a tri-dimensional bungee cord while the pressure peaked.

Colors exploded in his mind as the membrane crushing him trembled and extended like a soft trampoline, forks of lightning gleaming under the stress before bursting as he finally punched through.

And in the same instance, his telemetry stopped flashing red, returning to normal.

MACH 0.7
G-METER 4.3
TEMPERATURE 350 DEGREES
ALTITUDE 108,000 FEET

What the . . . fuck . . . just happened?

Confused, still disoriented, on the edge of blacking out, Jack tried to figure out how he could have dropped that much that fast, but the sunlight . . .

He placed a gloved hand against his faceplate as blinding sunlight gleamed around him, clouds and blue skies magically replacing the storm.

But how . . . is that . . . possible?

He closed his eyes, momentarily drifting away, before shivering back into consciousness, his eyes blinking to remain awake, focusing on the telemetry.

MACH 0.52
G-METER 1.8
TEMPERATURE 185 DEGREES
ALTITUDE 65,000 FEET

Feeling nauseous, light-headed, Jack tried to speak, to call out to the Cape, but his body had been pushed beyond endurance as his thoughts gravitated to the periphery of his mind, and he faded away again, only to force himself back into consciousness, if only to read his telemetry one more time.

MACH 0.3
G-METER 1.5
TEMPERATURE 167 DEGREES
ALTITUDE 32,000 FEET

Time passed.

Then somewhere in this state of semiconsciousness, Jack felt the autopilot deploying the main canopy, snapping and tugging as it blossomed above him, breaking his fall, jerking him skyways.

And that was the final straw, the final shove that propelled him over the edge as Jack heard the suit automatically venting into the atmosphere the moment it reached ten thousand feet, but he could control nothing—could say nothing. The wild ride had paralyzed him, like the frozen icons on his faceplate display.

But the autopilot is still operational, he thought, dizzy, disoriented, his mind blurring before everything turned black.

Angela's vision tunneled to the middle of her flat-screen display, which no longer showed her husband descending through the ionosphere.

"Phoenix, KSC, how do you copy?" asked Pete Flaherty for the tenth time in his best attempt at a controlled voice.

Silence. Nothing. Just like the clear image of the ionosphere captured by the high-resolution cameras.

"Phoenix, KSC, how do you copy?" he repeated.

"Phoenix, how do you copy?"

A few seconds later, Jack's vital signs via the TDRSS link flat-lined with a chilling high-pitch alarm that froze Angela's fingers to her keyboard.

This is impossi—

"Could someone tell me what the hell is going on?" Pete continued while General Hastings stood behind him but remained eerily calm, exchanging whispers with the two Alamo gurus consulting their tablets. Captain Riggs stood behind him stoically, skin glistening like a marble statue, hands behind his back while his men guarded the doors in similar military style.

"Are the cameras malfunctioning?" Pete shouted.

"Negative, sir," replied a woman two rows ahead of Angela. "Just ran diagnostics on the video equipment. All balloons report nominal readings."

"Confirming loss of vitals," reported the flight surgeon, a middle-aged man to Pete's right.

"Looks like a major malfunction," replied the descent controller sitting next to the flight surgeon.

"Concur," replied the TDRSS controller in the front row. "We have a mishap."

Jack, what the hell? Angela thought, tuning out Mission Control as her fingers miraculously began to move again, almost on muscle memory, pulling back the replay from the closest high-altitude balloon, showing Jack in perfect vertical pose, diving through 120,000 feet one instant and gone the next. He had just expelled the second set of heat shields before engaging the autopilot, an action that told her he had been right on the edge of succumbing to the pressure and heat.

But then again, the G-meter was pegged at twelve. This prototype version of the OSS was designed to keep the wearer conscious up to eleven Gs. Beyond that, it was up to the jumper's physical resistance. Jack had tested well up to thirteen Gs in simulated drops, but when you compounded the stress factors of the real thing, Angela wasn't that surprised that he hadn't reached the simulation level.

But that didn't explain why he had vanished. The OSS's autopilot was designed to take him down the rest of the way, and again, the imagery showed him in a perfect reentry profile well within the suit's design specs.

While Hastings continued his eerily calm observation of the flurry of activity in Mission Control with Pete at the helm going through various equipment checks while trying to make contact with Jack, Angela rewound the high-resolution video on her screen again and advanced it frame by frame, watching the ablation layer jettison in a puff of compressed helium, followed by dozens of frames showing Jack descending through the ionosphere, shields glowing.

Before simply vanishing.

She stared at the last two frames in disbelief.

That's . . . impossible.

From one frame to the next, Jack was gone. He didn't burn up in the atmosphere. He didn't lose control and enter a potentially deadly supersonic tumble, like Felix Baumgartner did during his jump. And the OSS certainly didn't fail. Had the latter been the case, the frame-by-frame would have shown Jack turning into a fireball before dissolving into thin air.

Jack had just disappeared. There had been no fireball, no explosion, no breakup, no reentry burn-up like Space Shuttle *Columbia.*

Angela felt pressure on her wrist and realized that General Hastings had just grabbed her and was slowly but quite firmly lifting her light frame from her seat with incredible ease. His massive freckled hand covered her wrist and almost half of the Triumph tattoo on her forearm.

"Hey! Let me go!"

"Where is it, Dr. Taylor?" he asked in a low and calm voice, nearly whispering, eyes narrowed beneath his thick orange eyebrows. "Where is my damned suit?"

Angela burned him with her stare. "*Your* suit, General? You want to know what happened to *your* damned suit?" she hissed, turning her wrist and pulling back to break his hold, just like Jack had taught her.

The red-haired general blinked.

Before he could react, Angela took a step back, turned sideways to him, and got ready to kick him in the balls if he got near her again. "*Fuck* the suit, General. What about my *husband?*"

Hastings leered at her as the Alamo scientists approached them. Everyone in Mission Control was silent and looking in their direction.

But all Angela could notice was how the two gurus also didn't seem alarmed, almost as if they had expected this. The man readjusted the glasses on his nose while speaking in a low voice to the woman fingering her tablet computer.

What the hell's going on?

The woman then nodded at Hastings, who returned the nod before signaling to Captain Riggs, who came over along with two of his men.

Paranoia triggered alarms through her system as the military detail converged around them and drew their sidearms.

Pete materialized from somewhere and jumped in between Angela and Hastings's posse.

"Whoa! This is NASA, folks!" he proclaimed, arms in front, palms opened as he faced Hastings and the wrong end of three shiny black pistols, which Angela recognized as 9mm Sig Sauers Model P229, similar to one of Jack's. "We're scientists. Let's put the weapons away now."

"Wrong, Flaherty," said Hastings with a composure that only fueled Angela's rising state of anxiety. "This is a national-security-level military operation that happens to be supported by NASA. I'm in command, and I need you to manage this mess in here while I have a little private chat with the doctor. Then you and I are going to figure out how to handle the press downstairs before calling Washington. Until then, Riggs will see to it that no one in here talks to anyone."

"General, guns were not in the deal."

"That's right, Flaherty. The deal was Descent Profile Alpha-B." He looked over to his gurus and added, "My people tell me that this little lady here took it upon herself to hack into the mainframe and reprogram the descent back to Alpha-G while making us all believe it was still an Alpha-B jump. Isn't that right, Dr. Taylor?"

Angela just stared back.

"That's what I thought," Hastings continued. "So, Flaherty, from now on, we do it *my* way and under the supervision of *my* scientists." Turning to Angela, Hastings added, "See, Dr. Taylor, I may not have a Ph.D. but I *own* plenty of them."

"Fine, General," replied Pete, "but none of this changes the fact that we have a big problem to solve, and I need my complete staff of experts to do it, *including* Dr. Taylor. She designed the suit, remember?"

"Who's stopping you from solving the problem?" said Hastings, nodding to Riggs, who promptly holstered his sidearm. His two wingmen did the same. Raising his light-colored brows at Pete, Hastings added, "There. Happy? Now, why don't you put all of those engineering degrees of yours to good use and go do your fucking job while I go do mine. And I need Dr. Taylor for five minutes."

Pete blushed as he hesitated. Angela gently nudged him aside before removing her lab coat, revealing a black AC/DC T-shirt. "It's okay. I don't mind having a word in private with the general. Why don't you go find out what happened to my husband . . . and the OSS. Start with the video feed. It doesn't make sense. There was no reentry burn-up or visible suit malfunction. Jack just vanished."

Hands on his waist, Pete took a deep breath, looked at Angela as she reached for the black leather jacket on the back of her chair, then at Hastings and his guards. Slowly nodding, Pete backed away.

"Okay, people," he announced to the onlookers while pointing back at the monitors. "The problem is *that* way. Back to your stations and let's walk through the telemetry."

"Shall we, Dr. Taylor?" Hastings said as he started for the door that led to the stairs going up to the private offices on the third floor.

"Just three things, General," she said while donning her riding jacket before pocketing her mini tablet computer and her smartphone.

Hastings stopped in mid-stride and turned to face her, dropping his gaze at the skull and bike patches on her jacket. "Only three, Doctor?" he finally said.

"First, don't touch me again," she said, running a hand through her short hair. "Second, don't touch me again. And third, don't ever, *ever* fucking touch me again."

The general took a deep breath, freckles dancing on his pulsating high cheekbones while he stared down at her before exhaling heavily. "Fine, Doctor. Now, shall we?"

Hastings led the way with a reluctant Angela in tow, followed by the ever-present Riggs. The general used the VIP master key card that Pete had given him the night before to get through the thick door, leaving behind the controlled chaos inside Mission Control. The trio proceeded in silence up the concrete steps under the grayish glow of fluorescents, reaching the third-floor landing, where he used the key again to gain access to a square foyer lined with offices, including Pete's, Angela's, Jack's, and also the visiting VIP office, which Hastings had the honor of occupying since last night.

The general tapped his key against the reader by the door, disengaging the magnetic locks, and went straight for the chair behind the empty desk by the large windows offering an unimpressive view of the parking lot. Large framed and signed prints from old shuttle missions covered the other walls. He pointed to the chair across from him.

Angela took her seat and looked over her right shoulder at Riggs standing at attention behind her, eyes straight ahead.

"Where did you find this guy, anyway?" she said. "Steroids-R-Us?"

"So, Dr. Taylor," Hastings began without making eye contact, crossing his legs and glancing at his wristwatch. "Tell me why you chose to commit an act of computer terrorism against the United States of America."

Angela just glared at him.

"See, Doctor," Hastings continued, still not looking her in the eye but at the tips of his manicured fingers. "Last time I checked, treason carries an automatic death sentence."

Angela also crossed her legs and began to play with her black fingernails, which she was proud to notice didn't look nearly as manicured as his. "General, I have no idea what you're talking about."

Hastings kept his gaze down as he said, "You reprogrammed the descent algorithm against my direct order. *That* is treason."

The hacker in Angela couldn't think of a way that even the Alamo gurus could have traced the change back to her, so she decided to stand her ground. "I still have no clue what you're talking about, but tell me, why the interest in Alpha-B, General?"

Hastings's eyes finally gravitated to her. "*That* is classified."

Not for long, she thought, glad that she had loaded up those viruses into their tablets.

"I not only have top secret security clearance, General, but I'm also *read-in* for Project Phoenix. There is *nothing* you can't share with me about this program," she replied, referring to the sensitive compartmented information clearance—commonly referred to simply as "read-in"—she held as lead scientist in the OSS project.

"Well, you may be read-in for Phoenix, but you're not cleared for this, Doctor. And since this is the United States military, I don't need to explain anything to a civilian employee. You work for me and you didn't do what you were clearly directed to do."

"This is a highly scientific program, General. In fact, it is probably the most scientific program of our times, and in the scientific world, data trumps everything, even the opinions of people with higher pay grades than mine," she replied. "From my *data-driven* point of view, Alpha-B would have placed Jack at least two miles off the planned target, and dangerously close to the outside of the safety pipe. Not only would he have missed the target, but he could have struck a bird or another foreign object. I just don't get why you would insist on a descent profile that would had added unnecessary risk to the mission."

"If your Alpha-G profile was so *data-driven*, Doctor, then tell me, why did the mission fail?"

Angela frowned. "I don't know yet, but I do know it had nothing to do with Alpha-G. It was still the best descent profile."

"So you do acknowledge changing it without my authorization."

"No, I'm trying to tell you that what happened had *nothing* to do with Alpha-G or Alpha-B, or any of the other descent profile options for this jump. The telemetry strongly suggests that this was not a descent-profile-triggered event, and we need to figure out what happened. My husband vanished into thin air. There was no reentry burn-up. The OSS didn't fail. We need time to dig through the telemetry and piece together what happened, where he went."

Hastings shook his head. "*Where he went?* Doctor, I hate to break this to you, but your husband's gone." He made a fist before stretching his fingers. "Poof! Gone. Dead. And *you* are responsible. You're not going to get out of this one so easily. You disobeyed a direct order in a military mission, resulting in disaster. You committed treason, Dr. Taylor, and I will see that you pay for it. And you're not even a first-time offender. With your prior, you're definitely getting the death penalty."

"What prior?"

"Really, Doctor?" Hastings grinned while slowly shaking his head. "Does the name Anonymous ring a bell?"

She glared at him for a moment.

Angela had been raised by her father, Miguel "Mickey" Valle, a hardcore motorcycle mechanic and first-generation Cuban American, after her mother died during child labor. But disaster struck again when she was fourteen. Mickey Valle had lost his battle with lung cancer from a lifetime of smoking, and shortly afterward Angela had gone rogue, joining Anonymous, a group of hackers dating back to 2003, where she quickly became one of their best "Black Hat Hackers." Within a year, Angela made the mistake of hacking into the FBI for bragging rights, got caught, and was offered a deal: work for the Bureau at an undisclosed cybercrime facility in Orlando for room and board until finishing high school, or go to a Florida juvenile detention facility.

Some choice, she thought, remembering how she had reluctantly gone for the former, becoming a "Gray Hat Hacker" for Uncle Sam, helping the Bureau fight cybercrime during nights and weekends while finishing high school, and returning to her dad's old bike shop on the day of her high school graduation. Her dad's partner and his fellow mechanics, who had taken over the business and had pretty much adopted her, pooled their funds to send her to FIT in nearby Melbourne, where she got her degree in computer engineering before her grades earned her a scholarship to MIT.

"I was *fourteen,* General, and I *paid* for it. In return, my record got cleared, purged. And the FBI assured me that event would be locked away forever."

"Do you think I don't have access to *everything?* Besides, you know what they say, Doctor?"

Angela didn't reply. She was angry at herself for letting this asshole get to her.

Hastings continued. "Once a hacker, always a hacker. You can't help it. It's who you are. You committed a criminal act at fourteen and you have now graduated to high treason at forty. I'm taking you down."

"In that case, General, I know my rights. I want my lawyer."

"Terrorists have no rights," he retorted. "You sabotaged a military mission. Plain and simple. You destroyed highly classified and valuable American military technology, setting us back *years*—not to mention the murder of a highly skilled and unique military contractor."

"Is *that* what you're calling Jack now? Last night he was a dog on a leash."

"I should have Riggs shoot you right now for gross insubordination, and I would be well within *my rights* as leader of this Pentagon-sanctioned military operation."

"Then do it, General," she said, calling his bluff. "Have your oversized eunuch put a bullet in my brain."

Hastings slowly leaned forward, looked over Angela's head, and nodded slightly.

She surprised herself at how at ease she felt when hearing Riggs draw his weapon and press the barrel against the back of her head. Perhaps that was one of the benefits of growing up among rough bikers at her father's shop and the local bars.

Angela and Hastings locked eyes.

"Nice knowing you, General," she said in a steady voice that also surprised her. "And best of luck finding your fucking suit or designing the orbital version," she added without breaking her stare, referring to the next generation suit that Angela was starting to design to jump from the International Space Station. "Most of the key details of building it are locked in the little brain that you're about to splatter all over this office."

For the second time since Jack vanished, Hastings blinked, leaned back, and waved a hand at Riggs, who put the gun away.

"Now, General, do you have any important questions for me, or can I get back to trying to figure out what happened to my husband?"

Hastings rubbed his eyes and exhaled heavily. "Doctor, I don't seem to be getting through to you. There are very, *very* technically valid reasons that I couldn't share with you—and still can't—that justified the change in descent profiles. The mere fact that I was sent down here the evening before the launch with a pair of federal scientists should have been enough to accept the change. But instead of getting with the program, you chose to sabotage a *military operation* and caused this mess."

Hastings stood and added, "I'm going to consult with my guys and then I'll be back, and I can promise you that our next chat won't be nearly as pleasant." He looked at Riggs. "Keep one of your men outside this door. No one comes in or out without my permission."

"Yes, sir," Riggs replied, following Hastings out the door and locking it from the outside with the card.

Alone, Angela took a deep breath while staring at the gray metal door, wondering how the hell things had gone so bad so fast.

Jack, where are you? she pondered, going through what little information she had, trying to find an explanation for his disappearance right in clear sight of a high-resolution camera.

And what's Hastings's problem anyway? Treason for changing the descent profile back to the original plan, which was backed by carefully collected and analyzed data?

It didn't make sense. Hastings and his Los Alamos friends hadn't provided her with any technical explanation for the change. She did what she did because all of her data told her this was the safest descent profile for this version of the OSS. Alpha-G was the smoothest of reentries, one that guaranteed Jack would remain within reasonable velocities and in the middle of the planned pipe down to the target area northeast of Orlando. Alpha-B would have kept him supersonic for longer, putting the OSS through more stress than she would had liked, and Jack would have missed the target by nearly two miles.

On top of all that, Hastings's approach was in direct conflict with NASA's crawl-walk-run philosophy.

Alpha-G was a "crawl" in the learning process. Alpha-B certainly fell deep in the "walk" territory.

And again, with no technical explanation.

But something had gone terribly wrong, and the reality of the situation started to inject doubt in her self-confidence, making her question her actions. What if she really had screwed up? What if Hastings and his experts knew something she didn't and had valid technical reasons to back up their request for a different descent profile—reasons they just simply couldn't share with her due to valid security reasons?

Did I blow this?

Did I just kill my husband?

She bit her lower lip as she stood and crossed her arms, staring at the walls, feeling trapped, and not looking forward to the next round with Hastings, especially if he was right.

I need to get out of here.

I need time to think.

Slowly, Angela's gaze shifted to the large windows behind the desk.

2

LEVELS OF CONSCIOUSNESS

*No problem can be solved from the same level of consciousness
that created it.*

—Albert Einstein

She crawled out of the third-story window, grateful that it faced the rear of the building, opposite from the press and the public anxiously waiting behind the barricades out front.

The sun was low over the horizon, casting long shadows against the redbrick structure. It would be dark soon.

One hand on the windowsill, she reached for the round copper drainpipe running down from the roof, and tugged it, testing its anchor to the brick structure.

Hoping for the best, Angela let go of her grip around the window and brought her second hand over while swinging her body off the ledge, her face now an inch from the green patina layering the aging copper pipe, the soles of her motorcycle boots pressing against the rough surface of the bricks, creating enough friction, just like Jack had shown her during their rock-climbing trips.

Slowly, with caution, she brought one hand beneath the other and began her descent, taking only thirty seconds to reach the bushes below, jumping the final few feet, landing in a half crouch amid waist-high shrubbery and instantly breaking into a run for the rear parking lot connecting the building to Flight Control Road.

The sun's waning light gleamed over the blacktop as she pushed her legs to go faster, waiting for the shouts she expected from the building behind her at any moment.

But none of Hastings's men came after her as she reached the bike parking area in the front of the lot and hopped on her vintage black 1979 Triumph Bonneville T140 motorcycle. When it came to bikes, Angie was a purist, not only restoring "Bonnie" herself, but she had picked the 1979 model because it was the last one before Triumph added an electronic starter.

If you can't kick-start a bike, you shouldn't ride, she thought, reaching behind her, and grabbing her open-face black helmet, which had a pair of clear riding goggles snugged around the top. She strapped it on before kick-starting the British-made bike, which roared to life as its two cylinders fired in perfect synchronization.

Gotta get away.

Buy time to think this through.

The thoughts flashing in her mind matched the intensity of the rumbling bike as she put the Bonneville in gear with the toe of her boot and released the clutch while twisting the throttle.

She rode around the back of the building, past the line of dark SUVs— Chevrolet Suburbans—monopolizing the VIP section of the rear lot, adjacent to the dozens of vans from the media and the press. Three of Hastings's eunuchs stood by one of the dark vehicles but didn't look in her direction.

Accelerating toward the Samuel Phillips Parkway on the eastern border of the Cape, Angela glanced at her rearview mirror and caught a glimpse of one of the drivers reaching for his cell phone, answering it, and immediately becoming agitated.

Crap.

She lost sight of them as she rode past the security checkpoint, waving at the guards, who waved back as they let her through, the adrenaline racing through her system, heightening her senses.

The Triumph roared toward the parkway, away from the sea of reporters waiting to get word on the jump. An even larger crowd awaited Jack's descent northeast of Orlando.

What a mess, she thought as she worked the gears, formulating her next move, her scientific mind scrubbing her options, zeroing in on her best choice.

She needed information and she knew how to get it.

The cybersword cuts both ways.

Angela accelerated, lowering the goggles as she entered the parkway and headed south, away from the place she had called home for too many years—a place she intended to return to after she figured out what the hell had happened to her husband.

She checked her mirrors.

Clear. No dark Suburbans in pursuit.

Yet.

Soon everyone would be looking for her. She needed a place to hide, and fast.

Her home was out of the question. She might have gotten away but knew Hastings's posse would be on her trail soon, and based on his reaction, Angela wouldn't be surprised if she saw her picture on the evening news. It was obvious to her that the good general would likely do everything within his power— which she guessed was quite extensive—to bring her into custody.

But for what?

The wind in her face and the sun in her eyes, Angela accelerated to the one place she felt she might be temporarily safe while her mind continued to—

Her phone started to vibrate in the breast pocket of her leather jacket.

The phone!

Damn!

She grabbed it. It was Pete.

Angela frowned and thought about pitching it over the bridge going across the upcoming Intercoastal Waterway, the body of water separating the Cape and Cocoa Beach from the mainland, but quickly decided against it. Knowing that Hastings could use the phone to track her could be useful later on.

She powered it completely off and shoved it back in her jacket.

Sorry, Pete, and fuck you, Grumpy.

She glanced at the fuel gauge. Half a tank. Enough to get her a hundred miles away from the nasty general.

Why was he so angry at a change in a descent profile that anyone with a brain could quickly deduct had nothing to do with Jack's disappearance?

Unless . . .

Angela realized she was speeding. Switching to the right lane, she slowed down while settling in between an eighteen wheeler and a UPS delivery truck. The last thing she needed was to get pulled over. In this day and age, it would only take a minute for Hastings to send out a nationwide alert to every law enforcement agency.

Crossing the bridge over the Intercoastal Waterway, she drifted all the way to the right side of her lane while the faster traffic sped by as she kept to the speed limit on the parkway.

The problem with this arrangement was that she couldn't see anyone approaching from the left lane until they were right on top of her.

Slowly, she edged the T140 to the middle of her lane, checking the left rearview mirror, and inched the bike a little more to the left of the lane until she could barely see the upcoming traffic and—

A dark SUV, headlights gleaming in the twilight of early evening, was speeding in the left lane at the other end of the bridge, just exiting the parkway. From this distance, she couldn't tell if it was one of Hastings's Suburbans or not, but she had to assume it was.

She quickly shifted back to the right, completely out of sight.

How did they track her so quickly? It'd been less than two minutes since Hastings had left her in that room.

Angela weighed her options. She could simply swing over to the left lane and punch it. Her well-tuned Triumph could easily do 120 miles per hour, certainly more than enough to get away from them, especially in traffic.

But what if they didn't know where she was? What if Hastings had simply dispatched his SUVs in every direction to try to spot her before she reached the mainland, where her avenues of escape multiplied? In fact, the accelerating SUV could be doing just that, trying to flush her out so they could radio ahead. And what if this wasn't even one of his vehicles? Accelerating well beyond the posted limit would bring unwanted attention.

Angela made her decision and remained put, steering the T140 just enough to the left to keep an eye on the right front fender of the SUV so no one inside could see her.

The vehicle, which she now recognized as a Suburban, grew larger in her mirror, and she caught a glimpse of Riggs in the front passenger seat, a mobile phone in his right hand as he spoke with agitation while making brusque hand gestures to the driver, who gunned the engine, accelerating even more.

Damn, they're fast.

She waited, biding her time, knowing she would only get one chance at this. The bridge had a narrow shoulder—too narrow for a car.

But not for me.

Just as the front grill of the black Suburban reached the rear of the UPS truck,

Angela drifted onto the shoulder and twisted the throttle just enough to bring the Bonneville in between the massive rear tires of the eighteen wheeler and the waist-high guardrail.

The road noise from the rig was deafening as she matched her speed to her moving shield, its wheels roaring over the concrete, kicking up dust and debris, but masking the sound of her bike's muffler.

Fortunately, neither driver, in front or behind, made any sudden moves in reaction to her little stunt, but just continued riding down the bridge as the first exit for the mainland neared.

The SUV lurched forward, speeding.

Angela could see its tires spinning past the eighteen wheeler, just as they all reached the first exit.

Angela thought about taking it but decided to stick to her original plan, accelerating just enough to reach the front of the rig, a foot beneath its massive rearview mirror, where she watched the Suburban hurtling away, on the hunt for her.

Good luck with that.

She grinned while watching it disappear from view in the left lane as she approached the I-95 exit a minute later. As luck would have it, the eighteen wheeler began to flash its turn signal. Her shield was headed south on I-95, and so was she.

Angela downshifted, also gently applying the brakes to steer the T140 before waving to the UPS driver, who continued on the same road.

That was close, she thought, following the large truck around the curved entrance to the busy north-south corridor, her mind regaining focus.

There had to be a logical explanation for Hastings's lack of alarm when Jack vanished, followed by his over-the-top reaction to a minor change in a jump profile that clearly had nothing to do with her husband's disappearance. Hastings had gone from cold to hot in seconds, and there was nothing in her data that could offer insight into his strange behavior. And of course, she also couldn't explain why Hastings had shown up in the first place with those scientists.

Angela pressed on, thoughts converging in her mind as the sun began to set, shaping an initial plan of attack. Darkness would soon fall over central Florida and that suited her well.

She settled in the right lane while staying just under the speed limit, right hand on the throttle, left hand on her lap. The Triumph was a pretty maneuverable machine, but at high speed, it was quite steady, easy on the rider.

She inhaled the cool coastal air and reviewed everything that had happened, forcing herself to think it over again, to see if there was anything she might be missing, finally confirming her chosen approach to finding out what had happened to Jack, whom she strongly suspected had to be alive.

Somewhere. Somehow.

And if Jack Taylor was indeed alive, Angela swore at that moment to use every skill she knew—every asset at her disposal—to track him down while making Hastings and his crew of misfits pay dearly for what they had done.

But for any of it to work, she needed to pay a visit to an old friend.

Someone she hadn't seen in a long, long time.

Someone she desperately hoped—prayed—would help her figure out where in the world her husband had gone.

Darkness floated above him, swirling, before resolving into a bright field of stars as Jack opened his eyes, blinking rapidly to clear his vision.

There were stars, all right. Tons of them surrounding a moon in its third quarter.

He took a deep breath, filling his lungs with cool air and exhaling slowly, letting consciousness take over his senses.

He inhaled again, wondering what had happened to the cloud coverage, remembering the weather forecast. The tip of tropical storm Claudette was scheduled to cloud the skies over central Florida by sundown, before the storm hit Tampa by morning—the reason for moving the damn jump up to this morning in the first place.

Yet, it was nighttime and the skies were clear.

Weird, he thought . . . just like the jump.

Briefly closing his eyes, he remembered the violet glow that had engulfed him in the ionosphere, followed by that strange lightning storm he thought was Claudette, before he punched through some sort of membrane into clear skies.

Did I dream that?

He narrowed his gaze and frowned while staring at the star-filled sky, at the moon.

Insects clicking, birds chirping on unseen trees, his tired mind did a quick calculation and decided it was impossible. Unless some drastic meteorological event had taken place while he was falling from the sky, the skies over central Florida should be not only completely overcast, but winds should have picked up by now in anticipation of—

Wait.

Where the hell is everybody?

Sitting up with effort, he looked around, shaking his head, trying to clear his mind, his throat dry, his mouth pasty.

A field of short grass surrounded him.

He heard a noise to his right, and for a moment saw the outline of trees backdropped by the very dim glow of passing lights.

A road.

Probably rural, explaining why he could see so many stars. He was away from city lights, which washed out the night sky.

He stared at his gloved hands and exhaled heavily, not understanding why he was alone in the middle of nowhere when just about half of the United States military, the FAA, NASA, Florida State Troopers—and even the frickin' Boy Scouts of America—were tracking his jump and were supposed to be here to greet him.

Something had gone terribly wrong.

Giving the stubborn skies another glance, Jack realized he wasn't wearing his helmet, only to figure out a moment later that the autopilot had ejected it when he landed to keep him from suffocating. After all, the enormous helmet weighed almost half as much as the entire suit.

Looking around again, he spotted its elongated silver shape next to the parachute, which the autopilot had also disconnected from his suit upon landing.

Angie had certainly thought of everything.

Everything except for this, he decided, trying hard to suppress the anger that always welled in the pit of his stomach whenever he wasn't in control. And at the moment, Jack was anything *but* in control, from the time of day, the landing spot, the lack of a crowd—even the lack of Claudette, which allowed him to see that damn third-quarter moon glowing in the sky.

Is it possible that I drifted that much off course because of the jump profile change that Angie programmed instead of the one Hastings had demanded?

Seemed pretty unlikely.

If there was one thing he would bet his life on it was his wife's smarts. In fact, he had just done so by jumping off that orbital pod.

Another vehicle went by the road, engine rumbling, lights forking through a silhouette of trees before fading away.

He frowned again as his mind continued to wake up, reminding him of the multiple GPS beacons that Angie had built into the OSS to ensure his constant tracking. If he had drifted off course, NASA would have known it and diverted the rescue crews to his landing spot. On top of that, the OSS had two independent emergency locator transmitters, or ELTs, one on his helmet and the other on his lower back, designed to transmit a signal as a pair separated by twenty-four inches—something Jack always thought of as a bit of NASA dark humor. If the spacing between the ELT emissions increased, it would immediately tell controllers that his head was separating from his shoulders on reentry.

He lifted the heat shield on his left wrist, exposing a small control panel—a backup to the retina-controlled systems on his helmet display—to check on the status of his emergency beacons.

The panel was dark.

Upon closer inspection, he saw that the suit's built-in batteries, designed to last up to forty-eight hours, were exhausted.

Surprise, surprise.

No batteries meant he couldn't tell if the ELTs, which had their own batteries for redundancy, were operating. But again, since he was all alone, it was a pretty good assumption that nothing was working. The OSS, which was designed to remain fully operational for almost two days, was completely shut down.

But if that was the case, then how did the OSS eject the helmet and the parachute upon landing?

Add that to the growing list of shit that doesn't make sense.

There had to be an explanation for all of this.

But you sure as hell aren't going to find it here, Jack.

Standing with some effort, he stretched his legs, then his back, working out the kinks.

The media must be having a field day with this, he thought, deciding that people probably thought that Phoenix had burned up on reentry since he hadn't landed where he was supposed to and his suit couldn't broadcast his location.

Walking over to his helmet, Jack leaned down, picked it up, hoisted it over his head with some effort, and lowered it over the round neck ring of his upper suit's structure, locking it in place while hoping for the best. Angela had included another set of batteries in the helmet as additional redundancy, but the thing was as dead as the rest of the suit.

What in the world drained all of these batteries?

Annoyed at the lack of answers, Jacked pulled off the helmet and dropped it by his feet before removing his gloves. Reaching under his left armpit with his right hand, he unzipped the side of his reinforced carbon-carbon upper plate, the third and final layer of his ablation shields. He did the same to his right torso before releasing the ring around his waist that connected the upper and lower sections of the OSS.

Pulling off the silvery vestlike shield over his head, Jack folded this ultra-light but amazingly strong piece of engineering that had kept him from turning into a well-done steak, for a moment remembering how skeptical he had been the first time Angie had shown it to him. All of the heat shields he had seen up to that point, including the space shuttle's TPS, were composed of very thick silica or reinforced carbon-carbon tiles. While the main ablation shields on the shoulder pads and helmet stacked to almost two inches at the start of the jump, the rest of this upper shell was less than a quarter of an inch thick, and it was all designed to be folded along with the gloves and stowed inside the large and elongated helmet. And the whole apparatus had a pair of built-in straps that Jack pulled out from their Velcro-secured niches so the jumper could wear it like a backpack.

Disengaging a second inner ring from his waist, Jack dropped the lower outer suit to his ankles and stepped out of it. Made of flexible insulation blanket materials laced with gel-filled capillaries, it resembled a pair of waders, boots included. Again, he folded it almost on automatic, just as he had drilled endlessly at NASA, also stowing it in the helmet before donning the high-tech backpack that made him look as if he were hauling an alien artifact.

He inhaled deeply, actually enjoying the cool air that now streamed through the one-piece camouflaged undergarment made of breathable compounds laced with Kevlar fibers, designed to keep the jumper comfortable but armored, ready for combat.

He frowned, realizing that the only thing in his possession that qualified as combat equipment, besides the suit, was his old trusty SOG knife from his SEAL days, which Jack had insisted on strapping to the battle dress clip on his left thigh especially made for it. He touched the handle of the sheathed seven-inch blade, verifying it was properly secured.

Giving his parachute a parting glance, Jack started for the distant tree line, feeling the soft ground beneath the spring-action soles of the carbon-fiber and rubber-compound boots integrated into his battle suit, which Angela had designed per Pentagon specifications to be worn by the jumper for the ground mission that would follow a real insertion into hostile areas.

He glanced at the sky, feeling dehydrated, wondering again what had happened, but also wishing to just be home, to be with Angie.

Jack approached a wall of tall pines separating the field from a dark road, one lane going in each direction divided by a narrow grassy medium.

Slowly, cautiously, he crossed the twenty-some-feet of forest, amid waist-high bushes, stepped onto a gravel shoulder, and just stood there staring at the dark road, trying to decide which way to turn. Since he landed just northeast of Orlando, that meant Cocoa Beach was to the south. But he lacked a compass or a working GPS.

When all else fails, you still have the stars.

Glancing back at the heavens, he ignored the moon and looked for the Big Dipper, spotting it high up in the northern sky and nearly vertical with the bowl at the bottom pointing to Polaris, the North Star, which formed the very tip of the handle of the Little Dipper, also vertical but with its bowl at the top. Tonight everything looked about the same as last night, when he had stared at the stars on the way to the Cape, though for some reason he thought that the stars had shifted a bit more than normal for just one day's difference.

Maybe it's just my imagination.

Or . . . maybe I really did drift way off course.

And that could at least explain the lack of cloud coverage.

He remembered dropping out of the sky into a blanket of lightning resembling Claudette. Could it be possible that he caught the leading edge of the storm and somehow got caught in its southerly winds in the stratosphere?

But where did it push me? Miami?

He shook his head. This certainly didn't look like Miami or the Everglades.

What if it pushed me farther south . . . like, to Cuba?

That would explain why there was no one here greeting him and why he could see the stars and the moon. Claudette's track kept it clear off Cuba and the tip of Florida.

Shit!

He stared at the road again, but with different eyes. There was a chance he was no longer in the United States but perhaps in Cuba, wearing this damned high-tech suit.

At least you didn't splash down in the middle of the ocean, he thought, deciding to look at the bright side of this surreal event. Besides, he had been in far more exotic destinations during his years with the SEALs, from deep in the Colombian bush taking out drug lords, to the mountains of Afghanistan smoking Taliban commanders.

His SEAL training took over, forcing him to accept the undeniable meteorological facts while ignoring the gastronomical chaos in his stomach.

He retreated to the safety of the tree line, fingers brushing the handle of his SOG knife, still secured to his left thigh, but suddenly wishing that this jump had included some of the high-tech weaponry that the DOD was developing to arm the new generation of orbital soldiers.

Jack needed to reassess his next move while further inspecting the road, looking for any sign that would tell him where he was.

But he saw nothing. Just an empty, dark road.

He waited, remembering the passing lights of vehicles. Sooner or later, another car would—

Headlights pierced the darkness, grayish beams of light washing out the asphalt and surrounding trees as the road turned.

Jack remained in the shadows, waiting. The vehicle finally appeared around the bend, a large truck . . . no, a motor home, a very large one with a diesel engine in back towing a small vehicle.

A diesel pusher, he thought, having seen lots of them in Florida from all over the northern states, especially in the winter months, when the "snow birds" migrated south to get away from the cold.

He watched as it drove down the road, engine rumbling.

Slowly, in a deep crouch, Jack stepped onto the gravel just as the gray and black motor home sped by, his eyes focusing on the license plate on the back of the rig and also on the towed compact sedan.

And right there, as clear as day, he read the bottom of both plates.

NEW HAMPSHIRE.

And above the license numbers, LIVE FREE OR DIE.

He retreated to the cluster of pines.

New Hampshire?

So he wasn't in Cuba but still in Florida, and south enough to be away from Claudette? But then why wasn't anyone here? Cuba, as complicated and unpleasant as the place would be for him, at least offered some semblance of an explanation for the absence of a welcoming committee.

Jack took several deep breaths, settling his system, regaining his focus. There had to be a logical explanation. There always was.

Just as the motor home vanished around the curve, another vehicle approached in the opposite direction. Jack dropped to a crouch, his eyes narrowed, his mind racing.

The car, which Jack recognized as a Toyota sedan, had Florida tags.

Over the course of the next five minutes, he spotted three more Florida tags, two from Georgia, one from Alabama, and three more from northern states.

He finally sat at the edge of the gravel, his back against the rough bark of a pine tree, the reality of his situation taxing his trained, logical mind.

How could he be in Florida when there was no one here to greet him? The whole world was tracking his jump.

Go home, Jack. Go home to Angie.

The words flashed in his mind, washing down his anxiety. He needed to retreat, to reexamine, to think this through, and he needed Angie to help him process this.

Jack decided to just start walking. He was obviously in Florida. He had landed where he was supposed to, but the same world that was tracking his epic jump with overwhelming interest as he had leaped off that pod had somehow vanished.

The stars told him this road ran east-west, so he turned east, toward the ocean, walking on the gravel, left hand up in the air and thumb out every time a vehicle went by.

Sooner or later, he would reach an intersection, a crossroads, a roadway sign—something that would show him the way home.

Or maybe, just maybe, someone would be crazy enough to pick up a lone hitchhiker walking in the middle of the night wearing a camouflaged skin-tight battle dress and hauling a silvery backpack in the shape of the head of an alien.

3

PROBLEM-SOLVING 101

When a truth is necessary, the reason for it can be found by analysis, that is, by resolving it into simpler ideas and truths until the primary ones are reached.

—Gottfried Wilhelm von Leibniz

The old hacker sat back in his weathered reclining chair and pet the black cat sleeping on his lap. He smiled and took a sip of coffee, listening to his feline companion purr while letting his scripts perform the heavy lifting.

They were works of art, really, designed to penetrate, carefully but firmly—and most important, systematically—the traditional firewalls of cookie-cutter IT security systems such as the one protecting the online dating service that had just rejected his application.

"Who do they think they are, Bonnie?" he asked the cat who had wandered onto his front porch as a kitten some years back in search for food.

The feline looked up, shook its head, and went back to sleep while its master's code did its magical work, stripping away defenses created by corporate programmers, people who followed industry-standard rules.

Rules that made them quite predictable . . . and vulnerable.

He sighed. There was a time long ago when he had been one of them, IT professionals with titles such as systems analyst, data modeler, Web master, and database administrator. He had developed his foundational skills in that environment until his desire to be different conflicted with the predetermined programming guidelines of the corporate world.

He was good. In fact, his last supervisor had told him that he was one of the best programmers on their floor.

Brilliant, was the word he had used.

But they were letting him go.

His methods to develop and refine algorithms, albeit quite efficient and elegant, clashed with the company's well-established processes. In other words, his skills were too good for them.

But that had been the party line. In reality, his job—as well as the jobs of many of his colleagues—had gone to India for a fraction of their U.S. salaries, plus they didn't need to provide benefits. All in the name of controlling cost.

Arturo Zepeda, a second-generation Cuban American, became Art-Z that day, on his way to his rented studio apartment in South Florida to develop some of the most elegant code ever written—code that allowed him to enter public and private networks completely undetected and siphon just enough funds to pay the bills, own his small home, his modest car—and the finest hardware and software money could buy.

The hacker smiled at his companion and scratched her gently behind the ears while the code continued to bore into the firewall, like a digital drill. Most hackers chose handler names that had no resemblance to their real names. But then again, most of his brothers-in-arms also strived for fame and glory, boldly breaking into financial institutions, corporations, and government agencies to prove something, to wreak havoc, or steal millions. And then they even had the stupidity to claim responsibility in some chat room or blog.

Not me, thought Art-Z, proud of the elegance of his techniques as well as of his handler name, which allowed him to operate anonymously while retaining some semblance of his identity, of his heritage. In addition, unlike his fellow hackers, Art-Z conducted his online activities right below the level where it was not financially justifiable for his corporate victims to devote the resources required to track him down—assuming that they could actually find someone good enough to do so.

That philosophy had allowed Art-Z to stick it to The Man while safely living off his dark trade by the progressive use of a "rounding-down" technique, custom codes secretly inserted into the networks of targeted institutions to round-down bank deposits and transfer the excess funds into temporary accounts. Five hundred dollars from a bank in Laredo, Texas, with questionable affiliations to the Mexican cartel. A thousand from an exports-imports firm in Canada doing business with Cuba. Fifteen hundred from an insurance company in Western Michigan connected to the UAW, which Art-Z held responsible for bringing down Detroit. And even two thousand from the R. J. Reynolds Tobacco Company.

The trick to long-term use of this age-old hacker technique, however, was in keeping the level of these temporary accounts quite low before closing them and transferring the stolen funds to one of three accounts in the Bahamas, Ontario, or the Cayman Islands via a globally mind-boggling maze of connections guaranteed to give the finest government agencies an unforgettable cyber migraine. But again, each of his actions always remained below the level of interest from authorities on the hunt for bigger fish to fry.

Art-Z browsed through his arsenal of algorithms, programs written and rewritten through a lifetime of hacking for the sole purpose of accessing data, information.

Which is far more valuable than money, he thought. Once spent, money was gone, but data could be used again and again to get more money.

The hacker leaned forward the moment his code broke through, creating a narrow, protected conduit into the heart of the couple-matching algorithm of the dating service.

"There it is, Bonnie," he said, staring at the network's core, beating with activity as nearly a third of its 23,456 registered members, ages eighteen to ninety-three, actively checked their daily matches.

The cat looked up, stared at him with round hazel eyes and meowed once, before resting her head back on his lap.

With the precision of a surgeon, the hacker injected a homemade digital potion tailored to alter the company's crown jewels: its matching algorithm. Designed to connect couples based on common backgrounds, career interests, age groups, degree of sexual and romantic passion, spirituality, education level, and dozens of other attributes, this company claimed that its mathematical algorithm had resulted in over seventy percent of its customers entering long-term relationships, with forty percent of them leading to marriages.

So let's change that a little, he thought, as he guided his cyber poison across the network, altering results, creating matches where there shouldn't be and vice-versa.

In addition to getting even for his rejection, Art-Z took pleasure in the fact that this Web dating service was owned by a U.S. subsidiary of a Shanghai conglomerate.

Second to sticking it to The Man, Art-Z loved doing it to the Chinese.

Bastards think they own the world.

It only took a few minutes before the e-mails began to pour into the site's administrators. An eighty-three-year-old widow from Milwaukee was complaining about her last three suggested matches, men in their early twenties who had registered the highest sexual passion preference. One of the e-mails was from one of those men complaining about being matched to the old widow, who was simply looking for elderly companionship. A homosexual man in his early sixties complained about being matched to a dozen different girls, all eighteen and fresh out of high school. A recently divorced thirty-five-year-old mother of three was being matched to six men in their late eighties and four college freshmen. And so it went, until the network administrator took down the site a few minutes later.

Art-Z grinned and logged off, having had enough fun for the—

A knock on the door.

He sat upright and the black cat jumped off his lap, landed on all fours with grace, and vanished in the dark hall leading to the bedroom.

Art-Z stared at the front door, not expecting company tonight.

In fact, he *never* had company and even went through the extra trouble of keeping a P.O. Box for his online purchases to avoid home deliveries.

He pressed a function key across the top of his keyboard and a window materialized on the lower left side of his screen, linked wirelessly to six Web cams covering every angle of his house.

A grin formed again under his beard as he magnified Web cam number five, providing a clear view of a woman standing on his front porch, arms crossed, while looking back to the street and then straight at the camera, raising her fine brows.

Well I'll be damned.

Art-Z was very seldom surprised. He had spent most of his adult life making sure that surprises, like the day he was terminated from his one and only job, were the exception to the rule.

He shut his eyes and opened them wide before staring at the image on the screen once more.

Incredible, he thought. Tonight was certainly an exception.

Nearly spilling his coffee as he set it down next to the keyboard, the hacker stood and walked over to the foyer with an energy he hadn't felt in years, sandals flopping over dusty hardwood floors.

He paused by the door, then opened it.

Right there, like a ghost from the past, stood a short-haired woman wearing dark lipstick that matched her biker attire, down to the boots and fingernail polish. Those amazing lips that he remembered from long ago turned into a little frown as she tilted her head and raised her right eyebrow at him.

"Hey, Bonnie," he said, calling Angela Taylor by her old hacker name. "Long time."

"I'm in trouble, Art."

He nodded at his former girlfriend from a lifetime ago, then said, "You were in trouble the moment you chose to trust The Man. Is he trying to stick it to you?"

She took a deep breath while looking back at the street again, where her bike was parked. Finally, she said, "Yep. Deep and hard. I'm probably all over the news by now."

"Have you been to the shop?"

"Was planning to hit them up later. I need to get some info first."

"What kind of info?"

"I think the military has taken my husband."

Art-Z slowly compressed his lips while regarding the woman who had broken his heart in another life.

"Drive around back," he finally said. "I'll meet you in the garage. Let's get that old bike out of sight first. Then we'll talk."

Jack couldn't believe it when the truck's brake lights came on, followed by its right blinker as it pulled onto the shoulder, its massive tires kicking up gravel, its diesel grumbling. It was a Peterbilt without a hitched trailer.

He ran to the side of the tall cabin, opened the door, and stepped up and into the spacious interior, where the smell of tobacco, coffee, and cheap cologne struck him like a fist.

"Come on in, son!" the driver shouted, a man well into his sixties, with thinning salt-and-pepper hair, a matching beard, and wearing faded jeans and a tank top. His arms, quite firm for his age, sported an assortment of military tattoos, including a USMC on his exposed right shoulder with an eagle perched over the Earth and an anchor through it. Beneath it another tattoo read VIETNAM ERA VETERAN.

"Thanks for stopping."

"My pleasure," he replied while chewing something Jack realized was tobacco when he smiled at him. "Where you headed?"

"Anywhere near Cocoa Beach will work," he replied with some hesitation since he still wasn't sure where he was.

"You're in luck, son. I just dropped off a load in Orlando and am headed down to the docks in Miami to pick up the next one, so I can drop you off on the way."

"Perfect, thanks," he replied, realizing that at least he had landed more or less where he was supposed to, which still didn't explain why there was no one here to—

"What are you hunting with that suit anyway, son?"

Jack gave the odd but friendly stranger his best attempt at a smile as he unstrapped the backpack-helmet and set it inside the large foot well before sitting down and closing the door. "No hunting. It's just the latest in hiking gear."

"Hiking my ass," he replied as he steered the rig back onto the road, working through the gears with practiced ease. The Peterbilt accelerated into the night, headlights washing the darkness. "But that's all right. You look like one of the good guys."

"That's good, I guess," Jack replied. "Who are the bad guys?"

"Oh," he said, briefly lifting both hands off the wheel before steering the rig around a bend in the road as he stared straight ahead, his jaw pulsating through his beard as he chewed. "That's a long list, son. A *very* long list."

"For starters?" Jack prodded him, anxious to get this guy off the topic of his suit since he was contractually obligated to keep it a secret. It was one thing to mouth off to General Hastings. It was an entirely different thing to leak highly classified military secrets. While there was no way to keep the general public from seeing the outside of the suit, the high-tech battle dress layer he now wore—considered Manhattan Project–level at the Pentagon—certainly contradicted NASA's press release about the OSS being just an escape vehicle for emergencies at the International Space Station.

"AIDS," the driver replied.

"AIDS?" Jack replied.

"Don't let anybody fool you, son. HIV was created by the government as a biological weapon. A tool for genocide. But the thing got away from them."

This guy's seriously off his rocker, he thought, but in a way, Jack found it refresh-

ingly entertaining given his surreal situation. "Really? Which part of the government's responsible?"

"Well, the CIA, of course. Them spooks are always up to no good. And not
for one second do I believe that the big man in the Oval Office didn't know about
it." He gave Jack a sideways glance, lowered his voice, and added, "I think he was
the brains behind the thing."

"Which president are you talking about?" he asked.

"Well, Reagan, of course. He was planning to release the virus on the Soviet
Union by contaminating their blood supply if the Politburo didn't go along with
Gorbachev in dissolving the Soviet Union. He was just going to let all of them
Commies die off over the course of a year or two. But the thing backfired on us.
Ain't that a son of a bitch?"

"Wow," Jack replied as he stared out the window, finally spotting a road sign
that seemed as bizarre as the brain firing inside this guy's head.

A chill gripped him as he read the sign again while starting to wonder if
perhaps *he* was the one imagining shit.

But the sign was for real, right there, on the side of this winding two-lane road.

SPEED LIMIT

75

How could it be seventy-five miles per hour? The speed limit on an interstate in
Florida was sixty-five.

"What road is this?" he asked.

"Forty-Six heading for I-95, son. Why do you ask? You lost?"

"Yeah," he replied. "Was hiking and I think I lost my bearings."

"You got lost on a clear night with all them stars up there?"

Jack tilted his head.

"Some hiker you are."

You have no idea, Jack thought, forcing a half-embarrassed shrug.

"But Reagan's ancient history," the Marine veteran added as Jack tried to piece
this mystery together. This was a side road that connected Orlando to I-95, and
if memory served him well, the speed limit on it was around forty-five or fifty.
Certainly not seventy-five.

"The one that really gets me is the Clinton body count," the driver continued.

Really, dude?

"Yeah," Jack finally said, deciding that it was best to keep the guy talking while he did more thinking. "So, how many people did Clinton have killed?"

"Oh, son, many more than the ones reported by the American Justice Federation. Many more. Many more, indeed. The man was ruthless, I tell you. Taking out Vince Foster and about sixty more of his close associates from previous business deals. Poor bastards. From suicides and accidental deaths to murders that remain unsolved to this day."

And so it went, for the next fifteen minutes, as this nameless driver continued down this dark road while covering Clinton, Obama, Reagan, the two Bush presidents, and then took off in the direction of MLK, JFK, and especially LBJ before diving even deeper into Nixon, Marilyn Monroe, Elvis Presley, John Lennon, Jimmy Hoffa, and Salvador Allende, who Jack learned was a former president of Chile.

Finally, after what seemed like a deep and nearly endless discourse, the driver paused, frowned, and thrust an open hand in Jack's direction. "Look at me. Where have my manners gone? I'm Lou Palmer," he said, offering a smile of stained teeth adorned with greenish chewing tobacco.

"Jack Taylor," he replied, pumping the man's hand, unable to think of a reason he shouldn't use his real name.

"Jack Taylor, huh?" the man replied. "Your name sounds awfully familiar," he added.

Jack was about to reply when they reached a sign for Interstate 95.

Palmer got suddenly quiet as he worked the gears while steering the Peterbilt cabin toward the entrance ramp for I-95 south.

And that's when he felt a bit light-headed as the Peterbilt accelerated down the highway and a new road sign loomed into view:

SPEED LIMIT

105

One Oh Five?

Really?

"You okay, Jack?" Palmer asked after putting the rig on cruise control, shooting him another sideways glance. "You look a little pale there, buddy."

"I get a little carsick," he lied as he looked over to the dashboard and noticed the speedometer needle pegged to one hundred.

And then it hit him.

For reasons he couldn't explain, this version of central Florida, where his greeting committee and Claudette were absent, was on the metric system. Everything was in kilometers.

Fuck me.

Palmer reached into the large center console separating them, revealing a small cooler. He pulled out a can of Sprite and handed it to him. "The carbonation usually helps."

Jack was actually hoping for tequila.

But he thanked him for the cold soda, popped the lid and took a sip, momentarily closing his eyes. The drink was cool, refreshing his core, and in a way renewing his desire to find Angie and get some answers.

He decided to simply inspect the world projecting beyond the rig's large windows. Traffic on the interstate looked normal, except for the speed limit signs.

Neighborhoods and businesses crowded both sides of the highway now, in sharp contrast with the desolate road he had walked for the half hour before Palmer picked him up.

On the surface, everything appeared normal, from the Exxon, Texaco, and Shell gas stations to his right to a Walmart sharing a parking lot with a Home Depot on the left. A large bank was next, with the current temperature displayed above its empty parking lot.

Twenty-two degrees Celsius, or around seventy Fahrenheit, meaning the temperature was also being reported in the metric system.

He tensed again when a large billboard caught his eye. A couple in swimsuits holding hands staring at the sunset below the words:

CUBA

THE HONEYMOONER'S PARADISE

He stared at the picturesque image in growing disbelief, his eyes slowly drifting back to the road ahead, his mind resigning itself to the reality of his situation, however bizarre or inexplicable it seemed.

And that reality blasted in his mind the words he had been so reluctant to accept:

It wasn't a dream, Jack.

But then what was it?

How did he end up here, back on Earth, alone, with no tropical storm overhead—and where former President Jimmy Carter back in the 1970s had apparently succeeded in transitioning America to the metric system.

At least in Florida.

He closed his eyes, wondering if he could be suffering from some sort of post-traumatic stress disorder. Although SEALs rarely suffer from PTSD, primarily because they had volunteered for combat-related duties and had gone through extensive realistic scenario training, making them better mentally prepared, Jack still contemplated the possibility, which effects varied from depression to delusions.

Am I delusional and just don't know it?

Pushing that last thought aside, Jack forced his sorry ass past denial and into acceptance of whatever it was that was happening to him. There had to be a logical, scientific explanation for what he was experiencing. There always was.

He should just roll with the punches, knowing deep inside that things always had a way of working themselves out as long as he kept his thinking cap on, as long as he followed his training and remained calm.

But what if my thinking cap is off its rocker, like this guy's?

What can I do if my senses are lying to me?

He shook those thoughts away and forced his confused mind to think of something productive, like analyzing the final moments before entering that strange storm—remembering the numbers that had flashed on his faceplate display over and over again:

MACH 1.2

G-METER 12.0

TEMPERATURE 1200 DEGREES.

ALTITUDE 120,000 FEET

The numbers. Those numbers have to mean something.

They continued flashing red while he fell, violating the laws of physics in ways that made his tired mind hurt. Energy couldn't be created nor destroyed, only converted from one form into another. And the telemetry up to that point confirmed that theory as vertical velocity was converted into heat and pressure.

But then things just froze while he continued to fall.

Was the suit malfunctioning?

Eventually the display returned to normal once he punched through that membrane-like layer full of lightning, and he reached the atmosphere.

But he also remembered fading in and out during the latter portion of the fall. Was it possible that he dreamed the part about the display contradicting the laws of physics?

His mind then jumped to Pete, recalling how he'd tried to contact him and how the transmission faded away shortly after he was immersed in that storm.

Did the TDRSS link fail? Is that why they couldn't talk to me anymore?

But what about afterward?

It was pretty obvious that he hadn't drifted away like he had originally thought. But if so, then where was everybody?

It simply didn't make any sense.

Or maybe . . .

Jack stared into the distance, pursing his lips.

Maybe I have some sort of concussion from the extreme Gs, he thought, recalling that at some point the G-meter had read almost thirteen, which was in itself unprecedented. Most astronauts experience only three to four Gs during launch and a few more during reentry. There was a case of a malfunctioning Soyuz causing a pair of cosmonauts to experience around ten Gs some time back, but he couldn't recall what became of them. Fighter pilots sometimes go up to twelve Gs, but not before their bodies have gone through a lifetime of conditioning in flight training plus lots of time in those dreaded centrifuges.

His eyes drifted back to the road, starting to believe that he had to be staring at a distorted version of reality as a result of his ride, and he could only hope that this condition was temporary.

It has to be, he thought, touching his head, ignoring the sideways glance that Palmer shot him before looking back to the road ahead. Jack pressed his fingertips all around his skull, the base of his neck, and around his temples, looking for any tender spots, bumps or other telltale signs of external trauma, but he was clean.

Sighing, he returned his attention to the world outside, looking at everything, at vehicles, at buildings, at road signs, at billboards, finding commonalities and also finding differences. Some were subtle, like the slightly darker green background on highway signs, or the more rectangular license plates, though not as wide as the ones in Europe. But then he would see bold differences, like the billboard advertising a high-speed ferry delivering you to your dream vacation in Havana, paradise for gambling, music, surf, and sand—in only two hours directly from Miami Beach.

Does that mean that in my sick mind Castro fell? Or does it mean the bastard never won that old revolution?

Another billboard appeared behind it depicting a smiling Pan American Airlines captain flanked by beautiful flight attendants welcoming passengers with open arms to their new fleet of Boeing 777 clippers.

Your mind is certainly fucking with you, Jack.

The advertisements that followed for McDonald's, Ford Motor Company, Apple Computers, and even Walgreens and Rolex all looked just like home, and so did the—

Jack suddenly felt himself being stared at again.

This time he turned to see Palmer regarding him with a narrowed gaze under his bushy brows. The man seemed to have an amazing ability to keep the truck dead in the middle of the lane while looking away from the road for more than just a second—something that even the high-adrenaline junkie in him found dangerous.

"What?" Jack asked.

"There's something really odd about you, Jack," Palmer said, his beard shifting as he frowned and returned his eyes to the traffic ahead. "But I haven't been able to put my finger on it. Yet."

"Well, this hiking suit is certainly different, Lou," he replied.

"No," Palmer said. "It ain't that. I already know that's military-issued, including that serrated SOG knife strapped to your thigh. But you've got your reasons—probably orders—not to talk about it, and I respect that."

"Look, it's really not—"

"I served for twenty years," Palmer interrupted before giving him a wink. "Did four tours in 'Nam before spending time in the DMZ. I know what I'm talking about, and you *know* that I know. But again, that's not what's odd about you."

"Okay," Jack said, deciding to go along with this strange but somewhat in-sightful man. "Then what?"

He studied Jack again before shifting his eyes back to the road.

"It's the way you're looking at everything, Jack."

"How's that?"

"Like . . . if it was your *first time*."

Angela felt her life had been defined by a series of crucial experiences, events that had transformed her thinking, her way of looking at the world around her. It started with her father's death, followed by her short but impactful time with Anonymous, where she had strayed from the straight and narrow while acquir-ing skills that placed her on the FBI's radar. But that experience, however dark at the time and certainly life-changing, had eventually forced her back onto the right path, steering her toward Florida Institute of Technology and her decade at MIT, where NASA recruited her. Then the road changed drastically again from academia in Cambridge, Massachusetts, to a government contractor living in Cocoa Beach, Florida.

And straight into the arms of Jack.

And straight back to this dungeon, she thought, sitting next to Art-Z while rubbing her eyes and trying hard to suppress a yawn.

She was tired. *Very* tired.

Her dose of energy drinks had long worn off and her body demanded the rest that her mind couldn't yet allow. The data browsing down the screen of her former mentor and boyfriend required her to stay frosty, alert.

So she drank more energy drinks while ignoring the slight shake in her hands and her increased heartbeat—though it was hard to tell if her heightened level of anxiety was chemically induced or due to the information Art-Z had man-aged to extract from the bowels of the Department of Defense's network via the hack that Angela had so masterfully done to the tablets of the two scientists accompanying General Hastings.

"Did you really have to name the cat Bonnie?"

He shrugged, and said, "Same color eyes and hair, and just as . . . tempera-mental."

Angela looked down at the dark feline and noticed the hazel eyes. "I'll be damned."

Art-Z pointed at the screen and said, "Payback's indeed a bitch. Nice hack job, Bonnie. I see you still haven't lost your touch, or your good looks. You been working out or something?"

"I'm married, Art."

"Did you get a boob job, too?"

"Art!"

"Yeah, I got that you're married and all. Just not to me," he replied, leaning back and petting the cat, regarding Angela with strange detachment.

He wore a pair of loose shorts, a Green Lantern T-shirt, and flip-flops. He also smelled a little, just like he did in the old days. And just like the old days, Art-Z was extremely pale from days—or weeks—without stepping outside. The interior of his small house at the end of a narrow road in the middle of a forgotten neighborhood in South Miami was in a permanent state of darkness. Heavy drapes kept sunlight—and outsiders—from peeking into the hardware that governed his cyber kingdom. And his lack of contact with the physical world for weeks at a time meant living off a diet of canned or frozen foods, plus copious amounts of coffee and energy drinks.

"We were kids, Art," she replied, her tired eyes taking in the information on the screen.

"Yeah. We were. That was then."

"And this is now."

"And this is certainly now," he said with a heavy sigh.

After a moment of silence, Angela asked, "So . . . seeing anyone?"

He slowly shook his head.

"You probably would if you had a better ride," she observed, remembering the electric scooter parked in the garage, quite diminutive next to her Triumph.

"Hey, it gets me around."

"I'm just saying."

"Plus it's good for the environment."

"Whatever."

He leaned forward and tapped the screen with an index finger. "I thought you said these guys were from Los Alamos."

Angela frowned, feeling foolish for having believed Hastings. His pair of mismatched nerds were actually from CERN, the European Organization for Nuclear Research and home of the Large Hadron Collider. "What can I say, Art? That's what I was told."

"Bonnie, Bonnie, Bonnie, when are you going to stop trusting The Man? Look where that's got you. Lost your husband and your career, and you're claiming that your pretty face's about to be on every news outlet labeled as a mastermind terrorist."

"Lucky me," she mumbled as she read on.

"For now it looks like you're in the clear," he said, monitoring the Florida State Trooper's Web site as well as the FBI's.

"Trust me. I'm not. I think Hastings is just keeping his little manhunt low-key to avoid attracting attention."

"Either that or perhaps you're imagining things. Maybe drank too many energy drinks?"

"Stop fucking around, Art. I'm in serious shit."

"Easy, there. Just making sure you have your head screwed on right," he said before pointing at the screen. "So, CERN, huh? That's the particle accelerator people in Europe."

She sighed. "That's them all right. They're both resident scientists there."

"So," asked the hacker, glancing in her direction. "What's that got to do with your husband vaporizing in midair and you being hunted by this general's private army?"

Angela crossed her arms and shot him a look. "If I knew *that* I wouldn't be here basking in your wonderful personality."

The hacker grinned and turned back to the screen, where they continued to read through the history of each scientist, including past patents, and current projects.

"Here," said Art-Z. "The woman, Doctor Olivia Wiltz, did spend ten years at Los Alamos, as did her older colleague, Doctor Richard Salazar, and apparently they're still associated with Los Alamos even though they spend most of their time at CERN these days. Wiltz was an associate director in the weapons physics division."

"And Salazar was the director of the weapons systems prototype fabrication division," she added.

"That's all good, Bonnie. But what's that got to do with your husband going bye-bye?"

She frowned. "Well, for one thing, the suit I'm developing is intended to be used as a military weapon. Maybe these guys are the ones who were going to take it into mass production?"

"Sure, but what in the world are they doing at CERN? That's quantum physics stuff. Particle collisions and that sort of microscopic shit."

She also didn't get that weird connection. "Let's see if we can figure out what sort of work they're doing there."

They dug into CERN's core, gaining access to the experiments, the data, and eventually the results—again, all thanks to the passwords that they had extracted from their tablet computers.

"Just a lot of particle collision experiments," she said, pointing to a window of results from CERN experiments two years earlier. "These guys were deep-analyzing the data from the detectors in the Large Hadron Collider to understand the particles created during collisions in the accelerator."

"Yep. And they were playing at both ranges of the spectrum," Art-Z said, moving the pointer to a list of experiments that used general-purpose detectors to understand the largest range of physics possible.

"Yes," she said, "while this other set of experiments focused on what they called forward particles, protons that rub each other instead of actually colliding, but transferring energy to each other in the process."

Angela read on, reviewing the data from experiments that tried to explain the link between cosmic ray and cloud formations, all using antiprotons from CERN's Antiproton Decelerator.

"My head's starting to hurt," confessed Art-Z, sitting back and rubbing his eyes. "This goes well beyond my pay grade, Bonnie."

Angela ignored him, reading about a related experiment that analyzed hypothetical particles radiating from the sun, a joint project between CERN and the International Space Station.

"Look," she said. "There are a number of experiments connected to quantum physics and sun radiation being conducted in Columbus."

"What's Columbus?"

"The research facility module for European payload at the International Space Station. It's being run by the ESA, the European Space Agency, which has pretty deep ties to CERN. They're going beyond the collider to look at the effect of particles coming from the sun."

"And our friends Wiltz and Salazar are all over these experiments, designing them, conducting them, and analyzing their results," he said.

"Well," Angela observed. "I agree with the designing and conducting part. They are really brief when it comes to results. In fact, for most of these CERN-Columbus experiments, the results section is almost nonexistent."

"Could it be because they didn't work?"

"I doubt it," she said. "Think about the cost of creating CERN and the Columbus module. Very expensive not just to build and deploy, but also to operate. Each of these experiments has to be costing them millions, maybe even tens of millions, to conduct. There has to be very tangible results from them, Art. They're just not reported here."

They continued to dig for another thirty minutes, Art-Z on one computer and Angela on an adjacent one, both connected to the same back door and also to the vast library of scripts that her former boyfriend had amassed through a lifetime of hacking. Each script was analogous to a tool in a large tool box. The right one would help unlock an entryway. The wrong code had the risk of setting off an alarm. The trick was knowing which to use, when, and for how long before switching to another one.

Slowly, as they worked their way through the guts of the European particle physics laboratory, it became evident that the information in the CERN databases didn't go beyond the particle accelerator experiments. That's when Angela stumbled upon a hidden directory in one of the tablets.

"Well, well, what have we got here?" she said.

"What is it?" Art-Z said, looking over to her screen.

"A link to another database."

"Where?"

"DARPA," she replied, referring to the Defense Advanced Research Projects Agency, the military's premier and most secretive R&D agency. "My guess is that Hastings and his gurus only used the CERN and Columbus experiments to corroborate whatever theories they were working on. After that he locked his gurus and the results in the one place he could control. We need to break into DARPA next."

The hacker looked into the distance before regarding her with his dark stare. "Breaking in isn't the hard part. CERN—hell, even Los Alamos—is a cakewalk, Bonnie. DARPA . . . man, I know guys—really *talented* guys—doing time because they hacked into the place only to have the Feds up their asses within the hour."

She put a hand to his bearded cheek. There was fear in his eyes. "Look, the last thing I want to do is compromise your location. You've been generous enough to help me. But I need to find out what happened to my husband, and the only path I see is to get some answers, and those answers, for better or for worse, are very likely hidden somewhere in those DARPA servers."

Art-Z took a deep breath and said, "There are places that no one should try to hack, no matter how good you are. You of all people should know that. I warned you last time not to screw with the FBI, and I'm telling you now not to mess around with DARPA."

"I'm already in deep shit," she said, "so it really doesn't matter if I get caught like the last time. But no one knows about you, yet. So I'd completely understand if you—"

"Shut up, Bonnie," he interrupted, gently getting her hand off his cheek before lowering his gaze to the black feline sleeping on his lap. "If you're seriously willing to put it all on the line," he added, lifting his eyes and locking them with hers, "then there might be another avenue. But we're going to need help."

"What kind of help?"

After hesitating, he said, "Between you and me, we have plenty of cyber muscle. What we lack is muscle in the real world."

For the first time that evening, Angela Taylor smiled. "And I know just the place where we can find it."

The hacker didn't return the smile. Instead, he rubbed the base of his neck, frowned, and said, "I was afraid you'd say that."

Highways gave way to familiar streets, familiar buildings, familiar sights under the glow of a moon and accompanying stars that should have been hidden by the missing tropical storm.

Jack watched this strange world go past his side window with mixed emotions, uncertain what lay ahead. He had seen enough to be convinced that something was seriously wrong with his senses, which screamed that this was not the same Earth he had rocketed from earlier that day. But that couldn't be possible.

Could it?

He shook his head, wondering what in the hell was wrong with him. How could he be suffering from a concussion when he felt perfectly fine, albeit a bit dehydrated?

And the more he thought about it, the less he felt he could be suffering from any form of PTSD, especially after what he had gone through with the SEALs. This jump was a walk in the park compared to Afghanistan and Colombia.

But he had to admit to himself that no one had ever done a suborbital jump before, and perhaps there were serious physiological consequences that only now would become known . . . thanks to him.

Jack pinched the bridge of his nose.

He could almost imagine himself hooked up to tubes, probes, and wires as scientists tried to figure out why he had gone cuckoo.

Fuck me, he thought, his mind searching desperately for a single shred of an answer to explain anything, from the absence of Claudette, to the frozen telemetry on his faceplate display when he was obviously falling, and a world that had literally abandoned him.

Stop torturing yourself.

He tilted his head at that last thought.

Torturing?

Jack suddenly realized that in a strange way, what he was experiencing was a form of imprisonment of his mind. His perception was being held hostage by whatever neural damage he had likely incurred during the fall, and his SEAL training taught him that one way to survive long periods of captivity was by forcing happy thoughts into his mind, by recalling the good times.

He chose to remember when he had first met his wife, the feisty Dr. Taylor during his initial weeks at the Cape. Angela was the only daughter of Miguel "Mickey" Valle, founder of the legendary Paradise Motorcycle Shop in South Miami, where she grew up among bikers and hackers before earning degrees in engineering from nearby Florida Institute of Technology and a doctorate from MIT. It had not taken very long for the slender brunette and former criminal hacker with high cheekbones, light-olive skin, and amazing hazel eyes—and who seemed to live on energy drinks—to get under his skin. And what made it impossible for him to give up the hunt was the way Angela tried to hide it all by minimizing makeup, keeping her brunette hair very short, wearing faded jeans, black T-shirts, and riding boots and jackets. But even her tomboy-biker tough looks couldn't hide a natural beauty that Jack found simply irresistible. And his persistence paid off in the end. After a long courting period, the couple was married on the beach among a colorful collection of characters from Angela's side of the fence, from bikers to hackers. Across the aisle, the groom's side was limited to Navy personnel, mostly his SEAL brothers, plus Pete, who stood as best man for the short ceremony. Following an adrenaline honeymoon rock climbing El Capitan at Yosemite National Park in California, the couple settled into a little bungalow-style house in Cocoa Beach, just minutes from their work at the Cape.

Jack reminisced while looking up at the moon and the stars, which instantly reeled him back to his screwed-up reality.

Sitting in the passenger seat while Palmer calmly steered the rig down Highway 528 through Cocoa heading for the bridge leading to Cocoa Beach and the Atlantic Ocean, Jack got the sudden urge to punch someone—and have someone punch him back very, very hard. Maybe that's what he needed instead of some happy fucking thoughts: a good old-fashioned bar fight to get his head screwed back on.

"You okay there, buddy?" Palmer asked. "You've been awfully quiet."

"Do you ever get the feeling that things aren't the way they should be?" Jack asked before he could stop himself.

It only took a microsecond before the conspiracy theorist nodded and said, "All the time, my friend. All the damn time. I'm telling you, nothing, absolutely nothing is really as it seems. Everything, from the water we drink and the food we eat to the clothes we buy and the girls we date, is carefully controlled and watched by big brother up in the sky. There's really no place to hide. And the Internet only made things worse."

"How so?"

"It proved that people are quite willing to trade off their privacy in return for things like free Facebook accounts, giving Uncle Sam even more insight into our personal lives."

"So, what can you do?" Jack asked, choosing to keep stoking this guy as a way to disengage from the reality of his situation. Though in a way, Jack's current altered state of mind only helped give Palmer's view of the world a certain degree of credibility.

"Well, of course you go on," Palmer replied matter-of-factly. "You keep doing what they're expecting you to do, every day, week after week, year after year. But you do it with full knowledge that the world as you know it is nothing but an illusion created by those in power."

"An illusion?" The word struck a chord in him.

"That's right, my friend. You see, there ain't no accidents, Jack. Everything, stock market swings, oil prices, and even the news is centrally controlled and managed. Sometimes things gets away from them, shit like 9/11 cybercrime, and AIDS, but eventually Uncle Sam manages to un-fuck its fuck-ups and keep the machine rolling forward."

Palmer steered the rig from Highway 528 onto A1A at the end of the bridge as it reached Cocoa Beach and the entrance to the Kennedy Space Center off to their left.

"So it's still there," Jack mumbled, for a moment wondering how his altered mind would see the Cape. But it looked just as he had left it this morning, and for a moment he almost told Palmer to drop him off at the security checkpoint. Walking straight into NASA with his suit in hand would be one quick way to get answers.

"What's still there, Jack?"

"Ah, nothing," he replied, but Palmer had already caught him looking in the direction of the brightly lit KSC. "Take a right at the next light," he added, guiding the truck driver toward his home and his wife—at least according to his confused mind.

"You're one strange man, Jack Taylor," the trucker replied, shooting him another glance before steering the rig onto the right lane as they approached the intersection. "But I still think you're one of the good guys."

"What makes you think so, Lou? You've known me for less than an hour."

Palmer shrugged, put on his blinker, and made the turn. "I may not be the smartest guy on the planet, Jack, but I'm a pretty darn good judge of character."

"Keep down this street for about a quarter of a mile. Take a right on De-Leon Road. It's right before we get to the Cocoa Beach Junior High," Jack said, before asking, "So, why am I strange?"

"For starters, you're full of contradictions."

"How so?"

"Well, you're genuinely fascinated by the sky, especially the moon. You've been staring at it most of the way here, like you haven't seen it before. Then you're staring at roads, billboards, and buildings with almost childlike interest. Some signs even make you close your eyes, like their mere presence is shocking you. So that suggests that you're either not from here or haven't been around in quite a while, which contradicts the fact that you claim to live in the area. But you do seem to know where you're going, at least based on the directions you're giving me. And then there's this futuristic suit you're wearing and your comment about the KSC still *being there*." Palmer made quotation marks with his fingers, returning his hands to the wheel and adding, "Weird, Jack. You're just one very weird dude . . . but still a good guy."

Although he found it amusing that Palmer was calling him weird, Jack didn't want to engage this guy any more, chastising himself for having been that transparent. But he couldn't help it. So much just didn't make sense. Why were some things the same while others had changed, and quite drastically? Why was he alone at the landing site? Where had Claudette gone?

"But I respect your privacy, my friend," the trucker continued, taking a left on DeLeon. "Everyone's entitled to their secrets. I sure have plenty of them."

Jack's heartbeat kicked up a notch the moment Palmer turned onto his street. In this part of Cocoa Beach, city streets resembled fingers surrounded by the calm waters of the Indian River, the body of water in between the city of Cocoa and Cocoa Beach. The houses on either side had backyards facing the water, where homeowners kept their boats and other water equipment with ready access to the river and the Atlantic Ocean. Jack and Angie owned an old but reliable thirty-two-foot Boston Whaler with a pair of outboards, their weekend getaway with a long enough range to get down to Miami or even the Bahamas for scuba diving.

"That one," Jack said, stretching an index finger toward a white house with blue trim and a detached two-car garage to their right, about halfway down the block. Relief swept through him as he added, "Home sweet home."

"It's been a pleasure," Palmer said, stretching an open hand.

For the second time that evening, Jack shook the trucker's hand before reaching in between his legs for his backpack.

"Really appreciate what you did, Lou," he said, opening the door.

"I hope you find what you're looking for, Jack," Palmer replied, producing a business card and handing it over.

LOUIS PALMER

INDEPENDENT TRUCK DRIVER

"If you need anything, don't hesitate," he added. "I spend my life traveling between Miami and Orlando, so I'm always in the area. Good guys need to stick together. Especially in uncertain times like these."

Jack narrowed his gaze at this very odd man before pocketing the card, thanking him again, and closing the door.

He waited for Palmer to turn the Peterbilt around and drive off before facing his home, which looked eerily just like the place he had left last night, when Pete interrupted his dinner with—

Get on with it, Jack.

Taking a deep breath, ignoring the increased pounding of his heart against his chest, Jack took a step toward the house. The lights were off, which was no surprise given that it was close to one in the morning. He stared at the garage, which he hoped had their five-year-old Honda and two Triumphs.

Walking up the driveway and onto the small front porch, Jack looked toward the line of bushes hugging the front of the house, spotting the one dead shrub that Angie had been on his case to replace for weeks now.

Jack rang the doorbell, his heartbeat now hammering his temples.

Steady, Jack.

A light went on in the bedroom, then another light in the living room, before the foyer light came on and a half-asleep but edgy female voice shouted, "There had better be blood or broken bones to ring my bell at this fucking hour!"

Jack grinned. "Hey, it's me. Open up."

He heard the door unlock as she said, "Pete? What the hell are you doing here at this hour?"

He frowned.

Pete?

Jack was about to reply when the door swung open.

Right there, in front of him, stood Angela. Only her hair was no longer short and dark but long and blond, and she now had a little chocolate freckle just above the right corner of her lips. On top of that, Angela wasn't wearing one of her oversized MIT T-shirts as her nightgown but a long pair of silk pajamas.

Sleep rapidly vanished from her hazel eyes as they grew wide, staring at him as if he had three heads. Her lips parted but nothing came out as she pointed a trembling index finger at him.

Before fainting right into his arms.

4

CONSPIRACY

The world is in a constant conspiracy against the brave. It's the age-old struggle: the roar of the crowd on the one side, and the voice of your conscience on the other.

—General Douglas MacArthur

Dawn in southern Florida.

The warehouse's window panes trembled to the roar of another F-16 on final approach to Homestead Air Reserve Base, home to the 482nd Fighter Wing, reminding Angela of years gone by. There was a time when she had been scared of the rattling glass under the corrugated tin roof of Mickey Valle's Paradise Motorcycle Shop as Air Force jets from another era took off and landed at this base, once America's first line of defense during those dreaded days in October 1962. Back then the world had been on the brink of war after discovering that the Soviet Union was installing medium-range nuclear missiles in Cuba, just ninety miles away, giving it an unprecedented offensive capability in the Western Hemisphere.

Angela closed her eyes, remembering her father's harrowing stories of Castro's Cuba, including his own gut-wrenching escape at just fifteen years old in 1961 aboard a leaky rowboat, drifting north for almost a week before a U.S. Coast Guard cutter plucked him out of a stormy sea a few miles from Key West. Her father had gambled death at sea for a chance at freedom, however small. Anything was better than growing up under the unyielding fist of communism. So he had stolen a weathered dingy from a marina in the middle of the night and rowed north until he couldn't row anymore, finally passing out from exhaustion and exposure. But the winds and the currents had been merciful, carrying him away from oppression and delivering him to the home of the brave. And he had worked harder than hard in this land of opportunity, climbing his way from a mechanic apprentice to shop owner in just ten years—an impossibility in a country where his parents were labeled *gusanos*—worms—and imprisoned for simply complaining about long food lines.

Angela took a deep breath, filling her lungs with the sweet aromas inside the old shop, with the smell of the ever-present WD-40, which brought her back to endless nights rebuilding engines and transmissions. Her nostrils also detected rubber, gas, and paint. But none came close to the amazing fragrance in the motorcycle world of burnt pre-mix, the residue of two-stroke engines that conjured images of the legendary Mickey Valle in oil-smeared coveralls, tools in hand, face deep in the guts of a Harley.

She had been a kid back then, never once expecting that this amazing world of chrome, rumbling engines, grease, tattoos, and leather jackets would meet such an abrupt end when her father died, triggering some of the strangest years of her short teenage life.

But she had survived them and gone on to become one of America's top scientists.

Only to lose her husband, her career, and now be hunted by the very same people she had devoted her life to serve.

But this is far from over, she decided, opening her eyes and breathing deeply again, but this time filling her body with her father's strength, with his unyielding resolve to fight for what is right, to risk it all for just one chance at a better life.

Now it's my turn, she thought, surveying the interior of the bike shop once more before settling her gaze on the heavily inked man standing next to a half-disassembled Harley atop a red hydraulic lift and wearing a pair of worn-out jeans, riding boots, and an open denim vest that exposed his muscular arms and chest. A heavy silver chain hung from a bull neck supporting a well-tanned square face sporting a contrasting white goatee and an intense pair of green eyes beneath closely cropped hair hidden by a Stars-and-Stripes bandanna.

Born Daniel Goodwin and known in the Florida biker community simply as Dago, Mickey Valle's former right-hand man and current owner of the Paradise Motorcycle Shop crossed his massive arms while regarding Art-Z with a look that could cut the aluminum frame of the Harley on the lift.

"You have some nerve showing up here, asshole," he said in a tenor voice custom-made for his six-three and two-hundred-fifty-pound frame. Even pushing sixty, Dago still commanded respect. The man was as formidable now as the day he nearly tore off Art-Z's head when the FBI arrested Angela on hacking charges. "Maybe I'll finish what I started twenty years ago."

"He's helping me, Dago."

"He left you holding the bag, Angie," he replied in a much softer voice, his eyes warming up, even glistening a little as he stared at her with parental concern. After all, it was Dago who had fought like hell to gain custody of the orphan, just as Mickey Valle had stipulated in his will, only to lose her to the FBI on technicalities. Three years later, upon her release from the Feds, it was Dago who'd brought her home from Orlando, given her time to decompress, and taxed the shop's bank account to send her to college. Dago had been there when she graduated from FIT, helped finance her years at MIT, funding the room and board not covered by her scholarship, had stood and clapped when she'd earned that Ph.D. diploma, and had even given her away at her wedding.

Dago's gaze became frosty again as he shifted it to Art-Z, his tone regaining its edge as he added, "This no-good weasel took you from us, taught you to be a criminal hacker, and then ran for cover the moment the Feds showed up. The world would certainly be a better place without him, and I'll be happy to do the honors."

"I told you I shouldn't have come," Art-Z said to Angela, taking two steps back while rubbing his neck. "I think I like my head exactly where it is."

"And I can think of a warmer place to stuff it," Dago replied, cupping a fist into the palm of his hand.

"Stop it, you two!" Angela snapped. "If you care one damn iota about me, you *will* put your differences aside and help me find my husband! Have you been listening to me? My face may not be in the evening news, but I promise you that I have one hell of a military posse on my ass, and they are *armed and dangerous!*" She stopped and pinched the bridge of her nose, closing her eyes, feeling a headache coming, then added in a calmed voice, "I'm . . . deeply screwed, Dago, and I need your help."

The veteran biker, arms crossed again, looked away while leaning against the hydraulic lift and exhaling heavily, dropping his gaze to the oil-stained concrete floor. "Angie, I promised Mickey I'd always take care of you. I love you like the daughter I never had, and you know I'd do *anything* for you."

Angie walked up to him and wrapped her arms around his wide chest.

"All right, Little Hacker," he said, returning the hug while patting her on the back. "What do you need old Dago to do for you?"

"What I *need*, Flaherty, is any information that will tell me where she may have gone," fumed General Hastings while pacing in his VIP office on the third floor of Project Phoenix's Mission Control building.

Pete shifted his gaze to the large windows, through which Angela had made her amazing escape.

It was midmorning now, and the press was already aware of the mission's failure. Social media had gone viral with stories about Jack vanishing during reentry and presumed dead. Unlike Columbia, whose large mass could be seen burning up across the skies of Texas and Louisiana, Jack's reentry burn-up would have resembled little more than a brief shooting star. Fortunately for all involved in Project Phoenix, the news quickly shifted to tropical storm Claudette, scheduled to make landfall within the hour and rip across Central Florida with winds up to seventy miles per hour. Preparations were already underway at the Kennedy Space Center to get the facility ready for the storm, including exiting all nonessential personnel, even the media.

Pete just *wished* that included one General George Hastings and his damn entourage.

Pete regarded the strapping general, his freckles dancing on his face as he tightened his jaw in obvious anger. This man, like so many of America's top brass, was quite used to getting his way, and he was *especially* accustomed to stomping on anyone who dared challenge his authority. Angela had managed to give the general's attitude right back to him and get away with it—at least for now.

Fucking bully, he thought, staring at Hastings.

Pete, who used to get picked on in high school for being smart, had spent a lifetime dealing with assholes who loved to steamroll over anyone they considered weak. Fortunately, he had gotten help along the way, first from his blue-collar father, who taught him how to box so he could at least put up a fight, and later on, from Jack who showed him a trick or three about self-defense, SEAL style.

People like Hastings, however, had elevated bullying to a fine art. The general belonged to a class of bastards who cared about nothing except their own personal agendas, directing traffic from their comfortable Pentagon offices and control rooms while people like Jack risked everything out in the field.

Unfortunately for Pete, the powers that be had decided that Hastings would be part of Project Phoenix's overseeing committee, making him his superior. That, however, didn't mean that Pete couldn't fight back.

Though never overtly.

Although Pete had learned much from Jack in the art of hand-to-hand combat, he also learned to think and act *covertly*.

"General, I've already told you she turned off her phone and didn't go home," Pete finally replied in his best professional voice while mustering savage control to keep his tightening fists from delivering a quick hook followed by an uppercut—though he wondered how much damage he could really inflict on the general while Riggs stood at attention three feet away.

"We *need* to find her."

Pete looked away for a moment, before scratching the back of his head and asking, "What I don't understand, General, is why she fled in the first place. What would make my chief scientist—one of NASA's finest—climb out of a three-story window, hop on her bike, and drive away like a bat out of hell? I mean, the woman has more patents to her name than the rest of my scientific staff, *combined*."

Hastings shrugged, his face awash with innocence. "I was just having a conversation about the incident. I was simply trying to get her to admit that she changed the descent profile, and then I was going to cut her loose back to you to work the problem. God knows we need her to help us solve this mess. But I got called away in the middle of it, and when I returned she was gone."

Pete just stared back, his training preventing his emotions from betraying him.

Had the good general paid closer attention to the detailed monthly billings of Project Phoenix—like he was supposed to as chair of the overseeing committee— he would have noticed the million-dollar closed-circuit monitoring system installed in this building six months ago, which included hidden Webcams in every room linked wirelessly to his workstation in Mission Control, as well as the computer in his office, and the one in Pete's study at home in nearby Melbourne.

Pete had seen the way Hastings and Riggs threatened Angela at gunpoint, and he also had been delighted and relieved to watch her escape. He had quickly downloaded the entire video file to a flash card currently tucked away in one of his socks before deleting it from the servers to keep Hastings from knowing he had witnessed this gross act of harassment.

Pete almost grinned as he wondered how the joint chiefs would react to the video, which he planned to release if things got out of control.

"General, I'm not sure what to tell you except that Dr. Taylor just lost her husband." He paused for effect, then lowered his voice a couple of decibels while adding, "Look, I was close to them. They were in love, sir. She has to be devastated—in shock. I'm wondering if your conversation, however well-intentioned, could have been misinterpreted."

Hastings crossed his arms and nodded. "I think I see your point."

"Maybe try the local bars?" Pete offered. "I think they used to frequent the Mai Tiki over at the Cocoa Beach Pier. Maybe she just needed a couple of drinks and some time alone to mourn her loss."

Hastings considered that for a moment before glancing over at Riggs, who took off in a hurry.

That should buy some time, he thought, not certain what to do next. They had combed through the telemetry and basically had nothing. Jack was gone, and with him Project Phoenix and any hopes of resurrecting NASA.

And then there's Angela.

Pete was certain that she was anywhere but in a bar. He would put his money on one of the biker or hacker hangouts in the Miami area, but he wasn't about to tell Hastings that, especially after seeing the way he had treated her.

No, the general would have to figure that one out all on his own.

Let him put his so-called military intelligence to the test, he thought, trying to figure out a way to reach Angela, whom he felt was central in solving whatever happened up there.

Jack's disappearance didn't make any technical sense. Angela had already deducted as much by reviewing the video feed before Hastings scared her away. Jack had not only vanished, but the event had taken place just as he'd reached a very strange harmonic to the numeral twelve.

Hastings's mobile rang. He pulled it out of his coat pocket, looked at it, and waved Pete away.

Pete left the VIP office and stepped into his own just two doors down, closing the door and quickly settling behind his computer, where he logged into the video monitoring system and pulled up the feed from the Webcam in the VIP office.

A window appeared in the middle of his screen, showing Hastings looking toward the parking lot while holding the encrypted phone to his ear.

"... *she's still missing, but we may know where she is ... I've already given the order to my* *people in Miami ... she changed the descent profile ... but that worked to our advantage. I don't* *think she knows how much she's helped us ... all right, I'll call back again in a few hours.*"

So he knows about Miami, Pete thought, watching him leave the office and killing the feed in case Hastings was heading his way, but the general went back down to Mission Control.

Pete logged back in and pulled up the very last and very strange telemetry reading from Jack's jump.

MACH 1.2

G-METER 12.0

TEMPERATURE 1200 DEGREES.

ALTITUDE 120,000 FEET

There's the numeral twelve.

But what does it mean?

In addition to a natural tendency to think and act covertly, Jack had also ingrained in Pete the stark reality that there were no such things as coincidences. There was a logical reason for everything—*everything*—and that included this weird set of numbers that could explain what happened to his best friend.

The key was knowing how to make sense of them.

And that key resided in the mind of Angela.

Pete had seen the gifted MIT doctor at work over the past few years and knew that there was never a technical challenge that she couldn't overcome given enough time and data. From the mind-numbing difficulties of miniaturizing NASA technology to fit it all in that incredible suit to developing new insertion algorithms and even solving the complexities of delivering jumpers one-hundred-percent combat-ready the moment they landed, Angela had not only solved problem after problem, but had done so with technical elegance. And the enabling catalyst was Pete providing her with plenty of experimentation resources and lots of time to iterate, learn, and improve.

Time and data.

At NASA, Pete became adept at giving her both while he handled the impatient and temperamental Pentagon brass, blocking and tackling so she could focus on the technical aspect of this cutting-edge program. This division of labor,

plus the fearless but highly intuitive nature of Jack's ability to become a very con-
sistent and tireless guinea pig, had been the magical combination that allowed
this project to make progress at the pace it did.

Time and data.

The question now was how to provide them to Angela while she was on the run.

After considering his options, Pete made a decision that could very well cost
him his career—and even imprisonment—if he got caught.

But I owe Jack that, and then some, he thought, running a hand over the scar tissue
on his left thigh, which got mangled during a rock-climbing accident in Colorado eons ago. He had nearly bled out while Jack carried him for two miles on
his shoulders down that mountain to the nearest park ranger station, where they
airlifted him to Denver.

Pete logged into the system and invoked a back door installed by Angela to
communicate preliminary project results before they made it to official reports.
This was a bit of a safe haven to allow open communications of experiments
between him and Angela, especially those that didn't work, without having any
government personnel looking over their shoulder. Jack had thought of the concept to keep a covert communications channel between them without the risk of
being overheard, especially by those who didn't understand the highly experi-
mental nature of the scientific learning process.

Pete finished his short message and logged off before reaching for the
bottom drawer in his desk and retrieving a small Taser X2 secured to an ankle
strap, a gift from Jack last Christmas.

Pete strapped this compact insurance policy to his right ankle before turning around in his swivel chair and staring at the heavy cloud coverage over the
Cape.

The KSC weather system reported winds already reaching thirty miles per
hour as Claudette's edge embraced the western portion of the Florida peninsula.
The downpour over Tampa had topped five inches of rain and winds in excess
of sixty miles per hour.

Pete stared at it while thinking of his best friends.

Wherever they may be.

In his forty years of life, Jack thought he had seen everything. From that devastating car accident that took his parents when he was seventeen, to joining the

Navy and entering the BUD/S training program at Naval Amphibious Base Coronado.

Jack had clicked with the SEAL culture from the moment he'd stepped into the starting phase of BUD/S designed to eliminate those who didn't belong with this elite fighting unit. He'd entered the grueling sixth week of training, also called Hell Week, with plenty of steam left in his inner engine, and pushed on to the finish line, graduating at the top of his class. Soon after graduation, Jack was given an assignment with SEAL Team 3 and was deployed to the Middle East.

He spent the following five years giving the Taliban a taste of its own terrorist medicine, conducting dozens of operations, mostly of the "doing a hit" variety, SEAL speak for eliminating HVTs—High Value Targets. Jack then took a transfer to SEAL Team 4, operating in the South and Central American theaters—a duty that inserted him deep in the jungles of Colombia hunting drug lords.

It was there, during a special reconnaissance mission south of Bogotá, where the failure of brand-new surveillance gear telegraphed their position, resulting in the slaughter of his SEAL team at the hands of surprisingly well-equipped Colombian cartel militia. Only Jack had escaped, using every trick he knew to slog through four miles of jungle to his extraction point while being hunted like a dog.

That same evening, as he'd sat alone on the deck of that Navy cruiser on his way home, Jack stared at the vanishing Colombian coastline beyond a turquoise Caribbean sea and made a promise to his fallen warriors: he would honor their deaths by doing his best to keep faulty equipment from ever reaching the front lines. And that promise led him to become the Pentagon's premier tester of leading-edge combat gear.

But all of his training, his experiences, his missions—even dropping from the sky like a comet into this surreal world—couldn't prepare him for the folded American flag and the three shell casings on the mantelpiece next to the framed condolence letter handwritten by the Secretary of the Navy to Angela. In honor of Jack's death.

Five years ago.

What. The. Fuck.

Feeling light-headed, Jack held on to the back of the sofa, where he had just deposited Angela, still passed out.

Breathing deeply, his eyes converged on the framed photo on the cocktail table. It showed Angela holding hands with none other than Pete Flaherty.

Slowly, Jack sat down at the edge, by her feet, breathing deeply, looking around the room, his hands feeling the fabric of the very same sofa where he had spent countless nights these past two years.

But how could it be the same sofa? How could this be the same living room? When he left last night for the Cape, he was pretty sure he was alive and breathing.

And he was damn sure his wife wasn't dating Pete!

He briefly closed his eyes, listening to the voice deep in his gut telling him not to buy the PTSD or concussion theories. There was no way he could be imagining this.

But if he wasn't delusional, then how could he explain what his eyes were projecting deep into his confused brain? How could he have been dead for five years? How come there was no one waiting for him at the landing site? How could a tropical storm just vanish from sight? And how in the world did Angela's hair become blond and grow several inches in one day?

The room started to spin, as confusion led to vertigo.

Jack closed his eyes again and took several deep breaths, hands gripping the bottom cushions of his sofa.

But the same voice told him it wasn't his sofa, and this wasn't his living room, or his house, or . . . even his wife?

But it *was* Angela. He stared at her features as she slept peacefully next to him. Aside from the hair and that new freckle, she certainly looked like the same woman he'd married.

Am I imagining her long hair?

Jack reached down and felt it, running his fingers through it.

Nope, that's real.

The hair was real, the chocolate freckle was real, the letter from the Navy was *very* real, and so was everything else he had seen since waking up alone in that field. His SEAL training, ingrained in his DNA, told him to trust his instincts, his senses, especially that sixth sense that had kept him alive for longer than he probably deserved. That inner voice had gotten him through extremely rough and gory times in the Middle East and South America, especially during his last mission, keeping him frosty, thinking, always one step ahead of that ruthless Colombian posse shouting at him across the jungle how he would be fed his own genitals and eyeballs when captured. But the voice had kept him going, kept him ignoring the threats, kept him anticipating, striking, and evading, even after he'd long run out of ammunition, until he reached his extraction point with nothing but his SOG knife, its partially-serrated steel blade stained with Colombian blood.

Jack felt the handle of the same weapon that had saved his butt in that nightmarish mission, gripping it, curling his hand tight around the deep finger grooves until his knuckles turned white. And that same voice shouted at him now from the deepest corner of his mind, noisier than the loudest gunfire, that this world, as he saw it and felt it, was very, *very* real.

So the next question that suddenly flashed in his mind was—

"*Jack?*"

He let go of the handle and turned toward her, not knowing what to say.

"Oh, my God!" she screamed, sitting up, throwing her arms around him, hugging him tight, burying her face in his chest like she used to do long ago. "Oh, Jack! Oh, my God! You're *alive!*"

Emotions boiled inside of him as he returned the embrace, kissing the top of her head, smelling her hair, reawakening feelings long dormant in their relationship.

She pulled away, gazing at him with wet hazel eyes, taking him in, lips quivering as she mumbled, "It . . . it *is* you."

Angela clung to him again, and all Jack could do was hug her back, his mind in turmoil.

"I . . . I always wondered . . . hoped, even *prayed*," she said, face still pressed against his chest, before looking at him again. "But the mission . . . in Afghanistan . . . they had eyes on you . . . Pete was there . . . but they never recovered your body . . . I . . . oh, Jack."

"Angie, look, I need to tell you—"

"I imagined this," she said, hugging him hard again. "I dreamed about this moment. Prayed that you managed to survive . . . somehow."

Jack pressed his lips together, searching for the right words. Unlike Angela, he'd had some time alone to start processing this, to digest the clues and slowly get past denial and into reluctant acceptance of this unbelievable reality, though he still had no explanation. Angela, on the other hand, had been hit cold and hard across the face by his sudden appearance, coming back from the dead. Yet, he had to tell her that things were not quite as they seemed. And the sooner the better.

Gently, he pushed her away and held her at arms' length, fighting hard to stay focused as his eyes drifted to that chocolate freckle. She put a hand on his face, fingers running over his lips, his chin.

She was obviously still very much in love with him, while the Angela he had left at the suit-up room had probably been one fight away from filing for a divorce. Still, he needed to come clean with her and perhaps they could figure this out, together.

"Listen, Angie," he finally said, mustering enough strength, deciding there was no easy way to say this. "I'm not sure what's going on . . . and although I can't explain it, I may not be the same man you married."

Surprise gave way to confusion as she dropped her eyebrows at him.

Jack continued. "I was in a—"

"*Honey,*" she interrupted, a hand on his cheek. "I don't care what happened out there . . . what those motherfuckers did to you. I just care that you made it back to me."

"No," he replied, hands on her shoulders. "It's not *that* . . . look, I need you to listen to what I'm saying. And I need you to trust me. Okay?"

She swallowed, slowly regaining her composure before giving him a slight nod.

"Yesterday morning I left you in the suit-up room at the Cape and climbed aboard a capsule on top of an Atlas Five rocket that injected me into a suborbital flight for the purpose of testing an Orbital Space Suit." He pointed an index finger at his chest. "A suit that *you* designed." Angela stared at his battle dress before narrowing her gaze and running her fingers over its smooth surface.

"Carbon fiber laced with Nomex and Kevlar," she mumbled.

He smiled. "It's your design, Angie. This is the combat battle dress. The outer layer that got me through reentry's over there." He pointed at the silvery shape in the foyer.

She looked over to it and back to him. "Jack, I stopped working on it after . . . after you died . . . *five years ago.* How is it possible that you—"

He gently pressed a finger over her lips.

"I have no way to explain that," he said. "All I know is that yesterday morning I climbed into a capsule, got shot sixty miles up into the sky, jumped, and after a very, *very* weird ride, I ended up pretty much where I think I was supposed to touch down, in a grassy field northeast of Orlando. But there was no one there to greet me, and believe me when I tell you, the whole world was watching this jump. NASA had cameras mounted on the capsule, which followed a parallel reentry to capture me heading down. And after it burned up, high altitude balloons picked me up. The FFA had issued a TFR over the area. The Air Force had helicopters and jets all over the place scaring off seagulls and waiting for a visual on my parachute. Even the Boy Scouts of America were tracking me. And yet, I woke up all alone a couple of hours ago."

Angela closed her eyes, a finger stabbing the middle of her crinkled forehead. "That's . . . the strangest story I've ever heard."

He gave her a half smile and said, "And that's not even the strangest part."

"You mean weirder than showing up here after five years?"

Jack tilted his head. "When I left the launchpad less than twenty-four hours ago, tropical storm Claudette was about to make landfall and rip through central Florida. That's why NASA pulled in the launch schedule by twenty-four hours. But the skies are clear out there."

"There are no storms in the forecast, Jack," she replied, twisting her lips and putting a hand to his forehead.

He gently took her hand in his while looking into her eyes. "I'm *not* feverish. I'm *not* sick. I'm *not* delusional. Yesterday morning you had short auburn hair and slept in an oversized MIT T-shirt. Yesterday morning I got into this suit and jumped from a capsule as high as Alan Shepard's flight and landed two hours away from here. I'm not making this up."

She stared at his suit, then back at the foyer, before asking, "All right, Jack. What else is different?"

He tilted his head and said, "You've transitioned to the metric system."

"Yep. Back in the seventies. Ancient history."

"In my world, Jimmy Carter couldn't get America to transition. We're still using miles, gallons, and pounds."

"What else?" she asked, the look on her face matching his altered state of mind. But in some way he felt a bit relieved to be sharing it with her.

"Well, there's Cuba," he said.

She took his hands and placed them on her lap as she sat cross-legged in front of him. "That's where we went on our honeymoon."

Damn, she's gorgeous, Jack thought, having forgotten just how wonderful Angela could make him feel.

She added, "Did we also . . ."

"Um, no. We went mountain climbing in Yosemite National Park. Cuba fell to Fidel Castro in 1959 and has been a communist state ever since."

"Really?" she said. "Now *that's* screwed up. Castro did win the revolution, but he was ousted from power during the Bay of Pigs invasion a couple of years later, and it became a U.S. territory, like Puerto Rico and Guam."

Jack shook his head. "That mission failed. JFK didn't provide the invading troops with air support. Poor bastards got stranded on the beach and couldn't drive inland."

She made a face. "You're talking about John F. Kennedy?"

"Yes, of course."

"Oh, well, here Kennedy did win the election in November of 1960 but was assassinated before he could take office. LBJ became president, and he overwhelmed Castro and his communist regime during that invasion. The place's been a paradise since, Jack. It's got some of the world's most beautiful beaches, great music, shows, gambling, boating, rain forest retreats. You name it, they got it there."

"Well, in my world, your dad escaped from that hellhole in a rowboat when he was seventeen and made it to Miami, where he built a life for himself," he said, spending a few minutes telling her about her upbringing, her father's death, her hacking years as well as those with the FBI before heading to college and eventually NASA, where they'd met.

"Well, everything except for Dad escaping from Cuba matches. He started a motorcycle shop in South Miami and he died from lung cancer. After hacking and the FBI, I also went to FIT and MIT and worked at NASA, where we met and married," she said, still holding his hands in hers. "I was in the midst of developing the OSS, as well as finalizing the weapons systems when Pete was pressured by General Hastings to perform an actual field test of the combat gear."

Jack made a face.

"What?" she asked.

"Nothing. Just hoping that Hastings didn't exist here."

"He does, and he put the screws on Pete to test the gear in a real scenario. Up to that point you had run a bunch of combat drills following HALO jumps at the Cape as well as in the Arizona desert and the jungles of Cuba. But it was time for the real thing, and you . . . you kept insisting that you needed to run the first field test yourself. So you and Pete headed for Afghanistan. But only Pete came back."

"What happened?"

She shrugged, glanced over at the mantelpiece, and said, "You know the Pentagon. They gave me the bullshit line that you'd died in a training mission, never mind that you were my husband and were wearing the combat suit that I designed." She paused, then added, "But Pete told me later. You performed a HALO insertion over the mountains northeast of Kabul to join your old buddies in SEAL Team 3 in an operation underway. Pete was accompanying them as the official NASA observer. Apparently the winds shifted and you ended up on the wrong side of a ridge and came under heavy fire. The battle dress protected you for a while, but the Taliban overran your position before the SEALs could get to you."

She dropped her gaze while lifting his hands and pressing them against her chest.

"I . . . damn, I was *devastated*, Jack. I felt I'd let you down. I should have designed the suit better . . . stronger."

"Angie," he said. "That wasn't your fault. That's the nature of military operations."

She nodded slightly, then said, "Well, in any case, I couldn't work at NASA anymore. Everything about that project reminded me of you. So I retired and eventually took a teaching job at FIT."

Jack had no idea what to say. *How could this be really happening?*

"But you came back," she said, staring at him just like she used to during the early years of their marriage. "You came back . . . to me."

She embraced him again while rubbing her face against his chest. The emotions twisting inside of him nearly made him wince in pain. A part of him wanted to take her right here, on this damn sofa where he had been relegated to spend the last two years sleeping alone. But his inner voice told him that doing so would be cheating on *his* Angela.

How can I cheat on Angie with Angie?

He just hugged her back, and they remained like that for a few moments, in silence.

"Jack," she finally said, pushing away, her eyes drying up as the scientist suddenly emerged. "Tell me everything that happened after you jumped."

He looked over to the foyer. "It was a suborbital jump, from sixty-one miles high. Pete was CapCom. The goal was to test the integrity of the suit during reentry, in particular the ablation layers on the outer shell. Up to that point we had performed several HALO jumps to test most of the suit's systems, but the highest had been from twenty-seven miles, so not much reentry heating to deal with."

"Big difference going from twenty-seven miles to sixty-one," she observed.

"Yep," he said, getting up and retrieving the packed-up suit, before sitting back next to her while pulling out the upper and lower sections of the outer shell from inside the long helmet. "You designed it to be worn like a backpack after landing."

"Interesting." Angela retrieved the upper shell, leaning forward while inspecting the collapsible titanium ring around the neck that served as the base for the helmet. "Keep talking, Jack," she said. "I'm just looking."

He sighed. That was one of the things that annoyed him most about his wife. She could hold a perfect conversation while doing something else, and without making eye contact.

Clearing his throat, he continued. "There were a series of descent profile options, which you designed to compensate for the winds aloft. The idea was that a jumper would first check the winds in the projected pipe and select the right profile to reach a specific landing zone with an accuracy of ten feet."

"I remember that. The Alpha adjustments," she said, running her hands on the inside of the suit and extracting various modules almost with practiced ease, which she brought up to her eyes while squinting before snapping them back into their respective slots. "It's all modular, for easy assembly and field maintenance. Interesting."

"For this jump, you'd selected Alpha-G, though there was some controversy with Hastings about changing the profile to Alpha-B."

She looked up. "Come again?"

"General Hastings. He showed up at the Cape the night before the jump accompanied by a military detail as well as a couple of his own scientists from Los Alamos and—"

"What do you mean his *own* scientists?"

"Yeah. Like I said. There was some heated words exchanged, and you actually went ballistic when you caught his two gurus with their little snouts deep in the electronic guts of this suit."

"Good," she said. "They had no business being there. But about the Alpha adjustments—I had it programmed for Alpha-G and Hastings wanted Alpha-B?"

"Yep. That was the main issue."

She looked into the distance and said, "If I remember correctly, and I'm pretty damn sure I do, the adjustments went from A to K, and they just had to do with the angle of insertion when hitting the atmosphere, with Alpha-K offering the most gentle ride and Alpha-A the roughest—but all still well within the design limitations of the suit. I'm sure that for the first suborbital jump, I would have selected something on the more gentle side, and then let the computers determine where you would have landed, and use those calculated coordinates as the landing site. You know, crawl, walk, run. So, what was Hastings's reasoning for the change?"

"You're going to have to ask him that. In the end—and I'm not sure how you pulled it off—the system instructed that I used Alpha-G, which I accepted at around mile forty-six."

"Oh," she said, the hacker in her grinning. "So, what happened next?"

"I became supersonic pretty quickly, peaking at around Mach three point two, and that's when things began to heat up—literally."

"Energy exchange," she said.

"Right," Jack said. "There was also this purple glow. I think it began back at around mile fifty-three, right after I went supersonic."

"A *purple glow?*"

"Yeah, shaped like a halo all around me. I asked the guys on the ground but no one could see that in the cameras from the descending pod, which was programmed to adopt a parallel path to my pipe until it burned up."

"I have no idea what that could have been," she said, before biting her lower lip, something she always did while thinking or worrying.

Unfortunately, that had a way of triggering something completely different in Jack. Now that action was compounded by that damn chocolate freckle shifting over her lip.

But he quickly pushed those thoughts away as he said, "Neither do I, but the halo never went away. It actually intensified as I dropped, almost washing out the stars. The fall got nasty at around mile forty-two, when the G-forces shot above nine and I couldn't talk anymore."

"Could you blink?" she asked, pulling up the helmet now and looking at the miniature projectors of the faceplate display.

He nodded. "I blinked my ass off for the duration of the drop, at least while still communicating with Mission Control."

Angela pointed at the small rear-facing antenna on the back of the elongated helmet. "You lost comm? What happened to the TDRSS link? I designed it to keep tabs on you all the way down, even through the ionization phase."

"That's the problem. TDRSS worked just fine. But things began to get really bizarre at mile thirty, when we switched to feet to report altitude. The violet haze became almost blinding, swallowing even the incandescence of the reentry heat. When I reached one hundred and thirty thousand feet, I jettisoned the second set of ablation shields because they were already down to ten percent. That's when I entered a tumble."

"A tumble?"

He nodded.

"But you were still supersonic and heavily depending on that third set of shields to protect you. The OSS would have burned up in an instant," she said, holding the lower section of the suit. "This is flexible insulation blanket material, Jack, and just a quarter inch of it. Not good for any prolonged exposure to direct reentry heat."

"I know, I know," he said. "That's what's so strange. The Earth and the stars were swapping places, over and over, while outside temp was well beyond the rating of anything but my last remaining set of ablation shields on my shoulder pads and helmet. But the suit was never breached, and then the most bizarre thing happened when I reached one hundred and twenty thousand feet."

"What?"

"I'm not sure. The telemetry turned red and began to flash the same readings again and again just as the purple halo increased in intensity and became a sort of entrance into a very strange electrical storm."

"Okay. Slow down. First, are you saying that the telemetry stopped giving you readings?"

"No. I'm saying that it kept flashing the same numbers, even though it was pretty obvious that I was still falling."

"What numbers?"

"Hold on." Jack got up and went to the kitchen, where he pulled open a drawer and retrieved the pen and paper they used to keep their grocery list. As he returned, he realized what he had just done.

"Jack, how the *hell* did you know where that was?"

He paused, then said, "Because that's where we keep it . . . at least as of the moment when we left for the Cape."

"Damn," she said, leaning back on the sofa as he sat down.

"Yeah," he said, "welcome to my little party."

He wrote down the numbers and placed them on her lap.

MACH 1.2
G-METER 12.0
TEMPERATURE 1200 DEGREES
ALTITUDE 120,000 FEET

"I hope you can figure out what this means," he added while she stared at it. "They continued to flash as I dropped down this bizarre storm that was pulsating with sheet lightning. And that's when I started to lose comm with Mission Control. I heard Pete a few times trying to make contact, and I was blinking the okay icon in return, but it was obvious he couldn't hear me."

Angie held the piece of paper in her hands while looking away, lips pressed together. Then she said, "What happened next?"

"That was probably the most unusual thing. I kept falling and reached the bottom of this storm, which was also vibrating with bolts of lightning. But when I struck it, it felt more like a membrane, like something elastic that extended beneath my vertical momentum, stretching, before bursting open, letting me through. And then all systems returned to normal, though I'm not sure how much time passed because by then I was fading in and out. But I do recall the very first readings when the system returned to normal . . . at one hundred and eight thousand feet."

"*One hundred and eight?* What happened in between? That's twelve thousand feet unaccounted for."

He shrugged. "Tell me something I don't already know. But there's the chance that I may have imagined it all. Maybe I passed out from pulling so many Gs and dreamed the whole thing."

"You didn't pass out, Jack," she said with conviction while holding the upper section of the OSS's outer layer. "And you certainly didn't dream this."

He cocked his head at her. "How . . . how do you know that?"

She pointed at the shoulder pads. "The third ablation shield."

"What about it?"

"It's barely touched. When you jettisoned the second layer, at least according to this piece of paper, outside temp was twelve hundred degrees, which should have taken a good bite out of this honeycomb material. But it didn't. That means that whatever happened between one hundred and twenty thousand feet and one hundred and eight protected you from the final stage of reentry heat. And as for the tumble you reported, that's also impossible. There is no damage to the flexible insulation material. For reasons that I can't explain, you didn't experience any reentry heat during that time."

Jack stared at the shoulder pads before also looking at the top of his helmet, confirming that the third ablation shield was intact, as was the rest of the suit. But how could that be when outside temperatures were still . . .

"Angie . . . what does this mean?"

"It means exactly what it means, Jack. You entered something different at that upper altitude and you exited it at a lower altitude. And in between, you didn't experience any reentry heating."

"And when I did come out of . . . whatever *that* was," he added, "I arrived at a world that wasn't quite the one I left at the launchpad."

They leaned back on the sofa in unison and just stared at the ceiling for a while.

"This is beyond my pay grade," Jack said first.

Angela reached over and took his hand.

"So . . . does this mean what I think it means?" he asked.

"I'm a scientist, Jack," she said, sitting up sideways and crossing her legs again while facing him. "And the scientific process is very straightforward. First observe, then hypothesize, then experiment to prove or disprove your hypothesis, and keep iterating until you reach the answer. In this case, my first key observations is that the laws of physics, especially those that concern the conservation of energy, were violated during those twelve thousand feet."

"What do you mean?"

"I mean there was no energy transferred from vertical velocity to heat, Jack.

The energy that you lost while falling for twelve thousand feet, or over two miles didn't turn into heat—and I gotta tell you, giving your supersonic speed, that's one *hell* of a lot of energy. This ablation shield should have been consumed, at least down to fifty percent."

"So where did the energy go?"

"Don't jump into any hypothesis yet. That's just the first observation. My second observation is you, Jack. You sitting right here next to me violates every law of physics of the classical mechanics world—the world governed by the forces of gravity, by the engineering disciplines, from aeronautical and mechanical to electrical, thermal, computer, chemical, and even biochemical. None of the laws governing those areas can explain why you are here breathing next to me instead of being a pile of bones buried in some cave in Afghanistan."

She paused, then added, "*Third* observation is your description of the world you left behind. There are mostly similarities, even down to the location of that pen and paper, but there are also critical differences, like the missing storm, Cuba, the metric system, my hair, and probably dozens more that you'll notice in the days and weeks ahead."

Jack was going to mention the freckle but knew better than to interrupt her while she was on her scientific roll.

"The fourth observation is this," she said, pointing at the numbers on the piece of paper. "The numeral twelve, which is also how many unaccounted thousands of feet you dropped, has a ton of significance in many disciplines, from mathematics to science, time, and even music."

"For example?"

"You're jumping ahead again, Jack. But at the risk of violating my own scientific process . . . take music, for example, the numbers remind me of an octave harmonic."

"What's that?"

"In music, an octave is the interval between one musical tone, or pitch, and another with either double or half its frequency. In some instruments, such as the guitar, this perfect octave is achieved by touching the harmonic of a note *twelve* frets above any open or fretted note."

"I never knew you were musically inclined," he said.

"I'm not. It's still just physics, Jack. Sound waves, in this case, but those same harmonic laws apply to all waves in the electromagnetic spectrum, from gamma rays at the upper end down to very low frequency waves. The observation here is that the number twelve has a lot of significances in several fields, but we're going to get to that later."

"Okay," he said. "What else are you including in your first round of observations?"

"Just one more for now. Something you mentioned before. Hastings and his scientists showing up at the eleventh hour and requesting a profile change, which apparently I managed to overturn. But the real observation here is that the Pentagon brass wouldn't inject itself into such a critical project at the last minute without a very powerful motive."

"Agree," he said. "Now what?"

"Now we come up with a hypothesis that best fits those five observations," she said, before inspecting the suit again. "But first I need something to drink, though it's way too early for a Red Bull."

"How about some coffee?" he said.

"Yeah. Why don't you go make us some while I take another look at this suit? I get the feeling that you know where everything is in that kitchen."

Jack got up and stood there for a moment, just watching her hands move over the lower section of the outer shell, fingers on the micro helium boosters in the boots, checking valves and hoses with obvious expertise before checking straps, attachment rings, and the internal wiring backbone connecting the central computers in the helmet to the rest of the suit.

He shook his head and did as he was ordered, going into the kitchen and finding everything just as he remembered, from the filters, coffee, and the same damn Mr. Coffee in the corner of the countertop, under the roll of paper towels hanging from the underside of the cabinets. He stared at it a moment.

Just roll with the punches.

Jack moved almost on automatic, taking all of five minutes to produce two cups of steaming coffee, which he set on the table, right next to the framed picture of Angela and Pete.

I guess her scientific process is eventually going to get to that, he thought, before saying, "I'm assuming you still drink it black?"

She looked up from the inside of the upper outer shell, where she had her fingers wrapped around a purple-looking device that he never recalled seeing before.

"Yeah. Black is good . . . Jack, what's this?"

He sat down and leaned closer. It looked like a round piece of purple glass the size of a quarter under a Velcro strap, which not only hid it from view unless you were performing a close inspection but the inside was laced with some sort of film of the same color as the glass. "I've never seen that before."

"Strange," she said, biting her lip again for a distracting instance before adding, "Everything else I recognize, though some modules are far more refined than my original design, like the helium boosters, the magnetic locks to keep your limbs from moving, the faceplate projectors, and the TDRSS antenna, even the suit's black box, which we should look at later . . . but still, I know basically what they are—what they do. But this . . . let's just call it my *sixth* observation for now, because I have no clue what it is."

Jack leaned forward for a better look. "It looks like some sort of crystal, but it also has something in it."

She brought it up to her eyes. "A microchip . . . it's embedded in the glass."

"Definitely not seen it before," he said, reaching for a cup and handing it to Angela, who held it backward, running her hand through the handle and closing her eyes before smelling the coffee just like she always did.

"Any ideas?"

She slowly shook her head.

"Now do we get to theorize?" he asked. "Because I have one."

"Not yet," she said, before taking a sip. "First, it helps to arrange the observations in chronological order. So, the first one is Hastings and his gurus showing up the night before the jump. Next is the telemetry going crazy at the instant when all critical energy readings—altitude, speed, temperature, and G-forces—reached this mysterious harmonic of twelve."

"The third," Jack added, "is the telemetry returning to normal after twelve thousand feet with a mysterious loss of energy, as shown by the unused third ablation layer of the OSS."

She nodded. "The fourth observation is the changes you've noticed after exiting this . . . energy-loss passage, which leads to you arriving here. The fifth one is this strange device hidden in the OSS. And the last one is you being here."

Jack took a sip of coffee and decided to wait and see were she went with all of this.

"I think I can state with scientific certainty that something out of the ordinary took place during those twelve thousand feet," she started. "I'm not sure at the moment why it never happened before, given the hundreds of times that space vehicles have reentered Earth since the space program began in the sixties. To answer that I would have to review their reentry energy transfer profiles, but my educated guess is that it has something to do with those harmonic of twelve energy readings. And I would venture to say that none of the prior reentries hit that sequence of numbers in unison, which I think is part of the key to opening this . . . I'm going to use the word *portal* for now."

Jack nodded. "Works for me."

"All right," she said. "Once you entered this portal, the laws of physics of classical mechanics stopped working, so we can't go there for answers because none of the laws of gravitation, or electromagnetism, or any other traditional science were in motion."

"So, where do we go for answers?"

"There are three other fields of physics besides classical mechanics," she said. "And my guess would be that what took place could be explained with one or more of those fields, though I have to admit that my knowledge is quite superficial because they are beyond my areas of expertise. The first field is called quantum mechanics, and it helps explain the really small things at the subatomic level. The second is Einstein's theory of relativity, which covers the other end of the spectrum, the really big things. Now, the problem is that each of those two polarized fields, while working almost perfectly for their respective realms, have very serious problems when confronting each other, and the mathematics break down. This is where the third field, string theory, comes in, reconciling the mathematical conflict between those two fields of physics. But, like you said earlier, this is where it goes beyond my pay grade. However, I know a professor at FIT and one at MIT that might be able to help."

"Fine," he said, "but the fact is I did go into this *portal*, as you call it, and I did enter a state where the traditional laws of time and space stopped working. And I was in there for a little while, losing almost twelve thousand feet of altitude, before literally bursting back out."

She exhaled, placed her cup of coffee on the table and did the same to his, before once more holding his hands. "That's right, and when you did, you arrived here, to a place where not only some things are quite different, but where you also died five years ago."

"So what *is* this place?" he asked. "Because unless I'm suffering some sort of delusion as a result of the jump, it sure as hell isn't the same place I left at the launchpad."

"I'm not sure. Up to the moment I saw you, I knew it as planet Earth, the third planet in the solar system, which is part of the . . ."

". . . Milky Way galaxy," he completed. "Just like where I came from. But then again, it isn't the same place. It can't be."

"That's because it isn't," she said, bringing his hands to her lips and kissing them. "The world you left when you got aboard that rocket is not the same as the one you are living in now. That much is for certain. And what's also pretty obvious is that the transition took place during those twelve thousand feet. The key question that remains is . . . how did it happen."

"And *why*," he added. "I'm a SEAL, Angie. I'm trained to never believe in coincidences, so I refuse to believe this was an accident, otherwise I'm pretty certain we would have seen it in prior reentries. But what's even more bizarre, is that the purple halo began well before the portal sucked me in. I first saw it just as I became supersonic, *miles* before I reached this harmonic of twelve. While I'm sure that the portal and the harmonic of twelve may be related, that doesn't explain why I saw that haze well before everything else, and it also doesn't explain why Mission Control couldn't see it."

"All I can go by are the observations, Jack, and the main differences between prior reentries and yours are three. The first is Hastings showing up. The second is this strange harmonic of twelve. The third is this glass token with the embedded computer chip."

"We need to figure out what it is," he said. "Maybe that'll give us another clue how I managed this . . . jump to another . . . dimension? Is that what this is?"

"Something like that," she said, still holding his hands, her eyes filling again. "Call it another dimension or a parallel world of sorts. At this moment, however, the reality is that you are *here*, Jack. You found a way to come back to me."

Jack briefly closed his eyes, feeling a headache forming behind his temples, unsure how he could explain this one to his wife back home—assuming, of course, that he could actually figure a way to return to wherever home was. For all he knew, he could be stuck here forever.

And suddenly, as he opened his eyes and stared at this version of Angela, he realized the degree of devastation that his wife back home must be going through at this moment, thinking that he'd burned up on reentry, probably blaming herself, just as this woman felt five years ago for not having built the OSS strong enough to protect him. It didn't really matter that they were on the verge of a separation, lacking intimacy for so long. She still had to be shattered at his sudden death.

You gotta get back, Jack.

You have to——

Angela drew him closer, and he chastised himself for lacking the strength or the desire to resist, to hold back, to tell her that he couldn't go through with it. He knew it was wrong, but it'd been too damn long since they'd shared a moment like this.

As he stared at the chocolate freckle, Angela bit her lower lip.

Emotion won.

He gave in and went to meet her halfway.

But Angela stopped, pulled back, and said, "I've been seeing Pete."

Jack blinked, frowned, and pointed at the photo. "I'd gathered as much already."

"I'm so sorry," she said, looking away, then at him, and finally at the photo again. "I was a mess for the first three years, Jack. I couldn't be around people, much less *see* anyone. Pete was there for me from the start, holding my hand, helping me along, fighting hard to maximize my government pension, and even nudging me toward the job at FIT. We became . . . a bit more than friends about six months ago."

"Angie . . . I . . . I understand," he lied, jealousy filling his gut.

But why are you jealous, Jack? She isn't your wife.

"Pete's a great guy," he added, forcing the words. "He was there for you. I know he'll make you very——"

"Jack. Stop. You really don't get it, do you? You're the love of my *life*. Always were, always will be. And although I've developed feelings for Pete, it's *nothing* compared to what you've just reignited in here," she said, stabbing her own chest with an index finger. "You're my *husband*."

"But, Angie . . . we just figured out that I'm not——"

"Shut up, Jack. Now it's your turn to listen and trust me."

Taken aback, he slowly bobbed his head once.

"I lost you once," she began, a hand back on his face. "For a long time, I would have given anything—*anything*—for a chance to hold you just one more time." She took a deep breath, adding, "And here you are. Call me selfish. Call me whatever you want. I don't care how you got here, or where you came from, or even how long you'll be around. At this moment, you *are* here, on my planet. And *that* makes you *mine*."

Jack stared at her long and hard. Angela always had a gift not only for words but also for calling things exactly as she saw them.

Before he could reply, she slowly pulled back the right sleeve of her night-shirt, revealing her Triumph tattoo.

He shook his head and smiled in sheer disbelief at this strange reality unfolding before him, finally unzipping the battle dress's right sleeve from wrist to elbow, exposing his right forearm and the matching tattoo there.

"See," she said. "A tropical storm may have vanished, your Cuba may be a communist state, and your version of America may still be in the British system of weight and measures. But you and I are still destined to be together, in *any* world."

Jack continued to combat his confusion, feeling torn between the very real needs of this very real Angela in front of him who had suffered so much, and who obviously still loved him a great deal—and who made him feel so damn good—and the Angela back home who'd sent him to sleep on this couch for the past two years.

But last night had been different. Last night Angie had—

"However," she said. "As much as I want to be with you, I first need to talk to Pete. I've developed feelings for him, Jack, and I owe him that much after all he's done for me. He'll understand, especially when he sees you."

"He still with NASA?"

"Sort of."

"What do you mean?"

"A lot of things have changed there, especially after you died and I quit the program. The OSS, if you remember, was NASA's way to inject new life into the space agency."

He nodded. "Project Phoenix."

"Right. The program stalled a few months after I resigned. Too many technical problems that couldn't be resolved. Believe it or not, we made a pretty irreplaceable team. I came up with possible solutions to problems, and you were my tireless guinea pig while Pete handled the Pentagon and kept the funds flowing. Well, Pete could never quite find replacements for you and me, and the Pentagon eventually lost interest in the OSS, especially after the dramatic field failure in Afghanistan. Rumor is that Hastings has basically turned the space agency into its own R&D facility for military satellites and classified weapons programs. But that's just a rumor. I lost my clearance long ago. Pete still heads everything."

"And I take it that he doesn't tell you how his day's been at the office?"

She shook her head. "The man's a vault, just like you and your top secret SEAL missions. Anyway, he lives just down the road in Melbourne, and he's probably in the best position to help us understand what happened to you. And as much as I hate saying this, Pete might also be able to help you . . . get back home."

5

TIME AND DATA

Information is the oxygen of the modern age. It seeps through walls topped by barbed wire, it wafts across electrified borders.
—Ronald Reagan

The skies over central Florida pulsated with sheet lightning, its stroboscopic flashes streaking across the boiling cloud base of tropical storm Claudette as it slowly lost its punch near Orlando. Winds at the Cape had reached thirty-five miles per hour, and forecasters predicted they would continue to increase, though nowhere near the punishing gale that had whipped Tampa eight hours ago.

Sitting in the back seat of Hastings's SUV, Pete watched the approaching storm while accompanying Hastings to a strip mall in nearby Melbourne, where his contacts in the NSA had not just pinpointed the location of Angela's mobile phone, but also had confirmed a credit card purchase at a drugstore.

Damn, Angela, he thought. *I know you're smarter than that.*

Wearing a finely pressed uniform, General Hastings sat across from him in the club-seating backseats of the large Suburban, quietly fingering his fancy encrypted phone, a tiny pair of reading glasses balanced on the tip of his nose.

Captain Riggs and three of his men drove the SUV in front, leading the three-vehicle caravan speeding down I-95 while another SUV with four more soldiers covered the rear, which Pete could see clearly from his rear-facing seat. They rode in the center lane slightly above the speed limit, as allowed by highway traffic a bit heavy for this early evening hour, probably people escaping to the clear skies of the Miami area, which Claudette had missed completely.

"General?"

Hastings briefly lifted his bloodshot gaze from the glowing phone screen as thunder rumbled in the distance, before lifting an index finger while returning to his reading.

Like Pete, no one had slept much in the past thirty-six hours, putting everyone on edge, which only added tension to an already stressful situation. The general's scientists plus Pete's own team, had combed through everything from the moment Jack Taylor left the launchpad to his vanishing, and they had nothing.

Not one damn thing.

All of the existing science couldn't explain what had taken place in the ionosphere. The only clues were the strange set of telemetry numbers plus Jack's weird comment captured in the communications transcript as he'd punched through Mach three.

KSC, Phoenix. You guys see that purple haze around me?

Pete slowly shook his head. There was no such thing as a purple haze that high up, well before Jack reached any air ionization. But then again, nothing made any sense, including this damn military posse that the general personally led. Generals *never* led field operations *in* the field. That was the whole point of lower ranks, which did the dirty work while the top brass directed traffic from air-conditioned war rooms. Yet, Hastings refused to get his oversized ass and his entourage of expensive SUVs back on that C-17 military transport jet still parked at KSC's massive runway and return to Washington, even after his secured satellite phone kept ringing for the past day. Unfortunately for Pete, Hastings must have smelled his surveillance because after that call in his VIP office, the general had held the rest of his conversations, including those with his scientists, inside his SUV.

And when he wasn't talking, Hastings was constantly texting, eyes glued to that little phone, which probably held more answers than all of Project Phoenix's servers combined.

"General?" Pete insisted. "A word?"

"What is it, Flaherty?" Hastings replied, rubbing his tired eyes before looking at him.

"Sir, I'm just wondering again if it might be a good idea to contact the local authorities and bring them in on what we're doing."

"Can't do that," he said as lightning gleamed over the horizon, accompanied a few seconds later by muffled thunder. "This is a military operation and it's delicate enough as it is. The last thing we need is to bring in civilians. You of all people should know that."

"But, sir," Pete pressed on. "We got the NSA call ten minutes ago, and it'll be another ten before we get there. The local police could have secured the area for us already. I know them well, sir. They've been quite helpful in the past during NASA events."

"Sorry, Flaherty."

"I'm just worried about Melbourne PD, a county sheriff, or even a mall cop confusing Riggs and his team for something else. It could end badly sir."

"Flaherty," he said, removing his reading glasses and using them as a pointing device. "If you really want something to worry about, then worry about finding my fucking suit, and let *me* worry about securing Dr. Taylor. And *that's* an order."

Hastings perched the glasses back on his nose and returned to fat-fingering his phone.

Secure her my ass, he thought, by now pretty certain of the general's intentions if he'd ever got his hands on Angela. Besides, how could he be working the problem when Hastings had pretty much kidnapped him to come along? And besides, his Alamo scientists had already bailed from Mission Control, rushing off an hour ago in one of the SUVs to who-knew-where.

Pete looked out the window, expecting Hastings to have reacted the way he did, but doing his best to come across as cooperative in the hopes that the general might let him in on what was really going, so he could pass it along to Angela via their backdoor communications channel.

Though she never replied to my first warning message, he thought, hoping like hell that she had received his last one, which he'd taken a huge risk sending right after the NSA reported picking up her mobile phone.

His eyes focused on the traffic behind them. No rain yet, but that would soon change as the storm continued its slow but steady march toward—

A biker approached the caravan from the right lane, single headlight cutting through the twilight of early evening, engine grumbling, washing out the distant thunder. Another biker came up from the other side, followed by three more, their mufflers deafening, even inside the SUV.

It all happened very fast. The biker on the right lane, a large man with a white goatee and a Stars-and-Stripes bandanna wearing faded jeans, an open denim vest, and dark sunglasses, throttled his Harley right up to the side of the SUV. His helmeted passenger, features hidden behind a tinted visor, turned in their direction while holding what looked like an oversized smartphone, its screen glowing.

Pete narrowed his gaze at the muscular biker, for a moment remembering Jack and Angela's wedding.

What was his name?

The passenger, whom he now realized was a woman, typed furiously on the phone with one hand while holding it steady with the other.

Angela?

She finished in a few seconds, tucking the phone inside her leather jacket and tapping the man's right shoulder, before tipping her helmet at Pete and giving him the biker wave.

The Harley roared, along with the ones on the other side of the SUV, leaping ahead, past Riggs's vehicle, squeezing in between two lanes of traffic, accelerating into the night.

"Crazy fucking bikers," mumbled Hastings, flashing a glance at the departing motorcycles before returning to his texting or whatever he was doing.

I'll be damned, Pete thought as the Harleys vanished from sight.

Angela removed her helmet and jumped off the Harley the moment Dago steered it into Pete's garage and parked it next to her Triumph and Art-Z's little scooter.

She quickly lowered the door before rushing inside the dining room, where they had set up their temporary base of operations twelve hours ago, after Pete had told her that Miami was compromised and urged her to hide here, also telling her about the extra key hidden in the back porch and giving her the passcode for his alarm system.

The rest of Dago's little gang from Paradise had made camp at a nearby motel to avoid bringing attention to Pete's house.

"Tell me it worked," she said, snagging a Red Bull from the six-pack on the table, next to an open bag of Cheetos, before grabbing a chair and sitting shoulder-to-shoulder with Art-Z and three laptops arranged in a semicircular pattern glowing with scripts.

She popped the lid and took a sip as the hacker pointed at the left one. "This little piggy got the data from the hijacked phone and it's parsing through it now.

Hopefully we can find something useful to hack into DARPA. Now, *this* badass little piggy," he added, index finger shifting to the center laptop, "will do the actual deed and has been configured to look like a server in the Solomon Islands with a further link to Geneva, pointing to the compromised tablet of the Wiltz woman, one of Hastings's scientists, sending them on a circular wild goose chase if they manage to follow the hack. And this little piggy, the meanest of them all, is filled with my finest brew, to be released when we're finished . . . my way of covering our tracks while sticking it to the big, bad wolf."

"The good, the bad, and the ugly," she said.

"They're all ugly, Bonnie. Ugly and mean. Don't try this shit at home."

"Was it encrypted?"

Art-Z nodded.

"Did you break it?"

"*Please,*" he replied, eyes glued to the left screen. "One of these days The Man's gonna wake up and smell the coffee. Shitty salaries gets you shitty talent, which gets you shitty encryptions."

"Watch it. NASA's part of the government."

"Right," Art-Z said. "And . . . *remind* me why we're here?"

Dago stepped into the dining room before Angela could reply. "Did it work?"

"Yeah," she said, shooting the hacker a look before removing her jacket. "We'll know in a moment if Hastings kept anything useful in it."

"What's this shit?" Dago said, pointing at the energy drinks.

"Fuel for the mind, man," Art-Z replied.

"You didn't get any beer?"

Art-Z made a face. "Oops. Want some Cheetos?"

"Christ," the biker replied, stomping away toward the kitchen. "Your NASA friend better have some in the fridge."

"That didn't win you any points," Angela said, watching the left laptop as the scripts scrubbed the sixty-four gigabytes of data in the phone's internal memory. It had only taken Art-Z thirty seconds to break through the encryption. In her prime, it would have probably taken her a couple of hours.

"I forgot," Art-Z replied. "Besides, I never touch the stuff. Tastes like piss."

"How do you know what piss tastes like?"

"Found some!" Dago proclaimed from the kitchen.

"Almost there," Art-Z replied, pointing at the screen as Dago walked back in the dining room holding a longneck.

"Never figured you as the Corona type," Art-Z said.

"That's funny. I *always* figured you as the little scooter man," Dago replied, pulling up a chair and straddling it behind them while sipping his beer.

"Hello, little SIM," Art-Z said, smiling, displaying the data on Hastings's SIM card, which was basically a small computer, complete with a processor, memory, and even its own operating system.

And that meant it could be hacked.

First thing he did was break into the encrypted EEPROM, the SIM card's electrically erasable and programmable read-only memory, basically a secured space where mobile payment apps could store their customer's sensitive banking data, primarily account numbers and routing numbers, plus log-in IDs and passwords.

It took his scripts ten seconds to break the Triple EDS encryption and another two seconds to download it.

"Here you go, Bonnie," he said, running a finger across the touchpad of his laptop, shifting the file over to Angela, who started dissecting it in the middle laptop.

"What are you doing?" Dago asked Angela.

"Ripping into Hastings's personal life," she replied.

"And you're next, Corona man," Art-Z commented as he started to dissect the much larger flash memory of the phone, where everything else was stored, from applications to e-mail and text messages.

Angela pulled up the data file and began to deconstruct it, aligning user IDs with their respective passwords—at least those that the general had the laziness to keep in his phone for quick access instead of entering them each time. But she wasn't that surprised. Most high-security sites required very complex passwords, which were hard to memorize, encouraging users to let their devices remember them.

Which worked just fine for Angela. In another thirty seconds she had access to Hastings's bank accounts, at least the ones stored in this file. But she wasn't immediately interested in Hastings's financial data, nor did she care much about the water, gas, and electric bills for his Bethesda, Maryland, home—or even his monthly cable TV bill.

Angela quickly converged on a user ID connected to a set of three passwords, each thirty-two characters long to be entered in sequence at five-second intervals. A small script embedded in the file managed the process. And from the looks of it, Angela guessed this was the way Hastings had received the phone from his IT staff.

Interestingly enough, there was a fourth password, but it was not linked to the first three, making her guess that it would be required after logging into the system, where users would be kept in a bit of a holding room, like a cyber foyer, for a limited period of time—usually a few seconds—until they entered this final password and were allowed into the main house.

Although the user ID or passwords in themselves didn't reveal the access site, the complexity of the login strongly suggested a high-security network, and one that she had never seen before in all her years dealing with NASA and the Pentagon.

Time was now of the essence. Although the phone hijacking had been successful, it was just a matter of time before somebody—probably some bored Pentagon graveyard shift IT technician—noticed a usage pattern change in the general's phone and flagged it. Just like credit card companies monitored client credit or debit card usage searching for anomalies, so did some of the highly sophisticated IT security systems. And contrary to Art-Z's perception about government scientific talent, the Pentagon seldom cut corners where it really mattered. It was one thing to hire second-rate IT contractors to pull together government Web sites such as the Affordable Health Care Act site. It was a very different ball game when it came to agencies in charge of America's defense—whose umbrella also included the NSA, the FBI, the CIA, the DIA, the FAA, the Secret Service, Homeland Security and, for better or for worse, even the IRS.

"I'm going in," she said, launching the script. "We may get shut down at any moment."

"Got it. Just cracked the flash, and I'm in download mode."

"What's going on now?" asked Dago, sipping his beer.

"We've got a small window of opportunity," Angela explained, watching the script go through its sequence. "I think I found Hastings's access to DARPA, but the moment we log in we run the risk of getting caught if we navigate the site in a way that's different than how Hastings typically does it."

"Or if he attempts to log in while we're in," added Art-Z.

"Then what?" Dago asked.

"Then all hell breaks loose," replied Angela as the screen turned dark, followed by the words,

PROJECT SKYLEAP
ENTER PERSONAL ACCESS CODE NOW.

SkyLeap?

A timer came up at the bottom of the screen.

Ten seconds.

Angela keyed in the last password, a long string of letter and numbers.

A wheel spun in the middle of the display before changing to a menu of options superimposed on a star-filled background.

TRAINING
SUITS
TECHNOLOGY
PROGRAM MANAGEMENT

She almost clicked on the Technology tab but kept her index finger hovering an inch over the touchpad.

What would Hastings do?

Slowly, she shifted the pointer to Program Management and clicked it once.

And she stopped breathing.

Jack inhaled deeply while Angela dialed her cell phone and put it on speaker mode, holding it at shoulder level between them as they sat on the sofa. Dawn was still a few hours away, and he couldn't help but wonder what new set of strange findings the day would likely bring.

But one thing remained constant. Angela was certainly Angela. Her hair might be longer and blond, her clothes might be different, and she wore a bit more makeup, but those hazel eyes regarding him with the same warmth from their early years hadn't changed one bit.

The phone rang twice before a sleepy voice came on the line.

Pete.

"Angela?" he said, before coughing and adding, "What . . . what time is it?"

"Almost three," she said.

"Is . . . everything all right?" he asked, coughing again.

"Ah, no. That's why I'm calling at this hour. Something's come up and I need to see you right away."

There was a rustle in the background, like papers being shuffled, before he cleared his throat and asked, "Okay, sure, sure . . . what's it about?"

She looked at him and lightly bit her lip before saying, "It's . . . about Jack."

There was a pause, before Pete asked, "What about Jack?"

"Well, there's no easy way to say this," she said, raising her brows. "Jack's right here with me."

Another pause, this one much longer.

"Pete, are you still there?" she asked.

"Angela, yes," he said, slight condescension replacing grogginess. "You know I'm *always* here for you. Did you have another nightmare?"

"No dreams, Pete. He's sitting next to me in my living room, flesh and bones, and we need to see you right away."

A heavy sigh came clearly through the speaker, followed by "Angela, look—"

"Hey, Pete," Jack said. "It's me."

"It's . . . wait a minute . . . who's *this?*" Any trace of sleepiness vanished.

Jack grinned at Angela and said, "Your best buddy."

"That's . . . *impossible.* I watched you . . . Angela, what the hell's going on?"

She was about to reply, but Jack put up a hand. "I carried your sorry ass for two miles to a park ranger station in Colorado while you screamed like a girl after one of your stupid aluminum alloy carabiners failed, and that's *after* I told you, dumbass, to stick to steel. Remember?"

He looked at Angela and then at the small phone in her hands, noticing that this version of his wife also had long fingernails painted red.

"*Jack?*" Pete finally said. "How . . . how did you . . . *survive?* Your position got overrun . . . we saw you taking fire . . . no one could have—"

"It's a long story," Jack interrupted, "and better told in person."

"Jack," Pete insisted. "What happened? How did you not die from that . . . *fusillade?* Those bastards were right on top of you unloading their AKs."

He sat back a moment and looked at Angela, who nodded.

"All right, man," Jack replied. "As weird as it sounds, I'm from another version of Earth."

Silence, then, "Come again?"

"Yeah, I know how it sounds. I still have a hard time believing this, and so does Angie. In my version of Earth, she finished the suborbital suit, and I executed a jump from sixty miles high, but I somehow went through some sort of passage during reentry that brought me down to your Earth."

"*My* Earth? Jack . . . there's only *one* Earth."

"The events I've experienced in the past several hours certainly challenge that view."

"Okay. Hold on, Jack. Start from the beginning."

Jack did, taking just a couple of minutes to give him an abridged version of what happened.

When he finished, the phone was silent for a moment, though Jack could hear Pete's heavy breathing at the other end.

"So . . . let me get this straight," Pete finally said, "you just woke up in the middle of a field near Orlando?"

"Yep. And I hitched a ride to my . . . to this house."

She leaned over and whispered in his ear, "Jack, this *is* your house. You even know where the damn coffee is."

He put a hand on her face, the tip of his index circling her freckle. She smiled and kissed his finger.

"Okay," Pete said. "Who else have you spoken to?"

"Just Angie and now you."

"Jack, listen very carefully. Don't move. Don't call anyone else. I'll be right over. We'll sort this out."

Angela put her phone away and said, "I'm sure there's a way to explain all of this. We just need to get the right data in front of the right people."

He sighed and nodded, looking at their matching tattoos. "So we still have the bikes?"

"Yep. Just changed the cylinders on yours. Runs like new."

"And the boat?"

"*Dark and Stormy.* Still in the boathouse out back. I work on it now instead of the marina guys. Gives me something to do on the weekends, plus I continue to scuba dive."

He grinned. They had named it after Jack's favorite drink during his SEAL days, made with Gosling's Black Seal rum.

"Do you enjoy teaching?"

"It's different, and I don't have to think too hard. After you died, I had difficulty concentrating for very long."

"I'm sorry," he said.

"You're here now," she said. "That's all that matters."

Jack cleared his throat, realizing he was quite dehydrated. "Do we still keep vitamin water in the fridge? I'm thirsty as hell."

She laughed and took him by the hand to the kitchen, where she snagged a couple of bottles from the refrigerator.

Her back against the sink, she twisted the cap off and brought her bottle up to his, tapping it and saying, "Here's to 'Relax, honey. I'll be right back.'"

Jack gave her a half laugh and took a long swig before asking, "Was the body ever recovered and brought home?"

She shook her head. "Why do you ask?"

He shrugged. "Ah . . . it's nothing."

"No," she said. "What is it?"

"Forget about it."

"Jack, dammit. We have a deal . . . or at least we did in this world. We *always* spoke our minds, so get it out."

Raising an eyebrow, he said, "All right . . . it's just . . . just what Pete said on the phone about no one surviving that fusillade. What I've gathered so far is that they saw the Taliban firing in my . . . in Jack's direction." He paused, frowning at how weird that sounded, before adding, "But did they actually *see* him die?"

"No, but the reports said that—"

"Hold on," he interrupted. "Was the body shown off by the Afghan rebels? Maybe on some Web site?"

Angela put her bottle down, crossed her arms, and slowly shook her head. "Where are you going with this?"

Standing in front of her, Jack also put his bottle down and placed his hands on her shoulders. "Look. I just know how those Taliban motherfuckers think," he said. "I fought them long enough. To them it's all about promoting their cause, and one of the ways they do it is by parading any semblance of a trophy they can get their dirty hands on. Bragging rights is a huge part of their mission. If they shoot down a Predator, next thing you'll see is a video of them chanting to Allah around the smoking wreckage. Every time they kill one of ours and manage to take the body, you'll see it displayed on some Web site. Bastards even like to execute our people on video. So, if they really did kill Jack Taylor wearing a version of this futuristic suit, I would bet my government pension they would have paraded my carcass all over the Middle East."

"But they didn't," she said. "There was nothing but that damn letter on the mantel . . . plus what Pete told me."

"Well, I can promise you one thing, Angie. We *always* take our wounded and our dead," he said. "It's our code. We do it not only out of respect for a fallen warrior and his family, but also to take away the enemy's bragging rights. And when we can't take our dead with us, we make damn sure there's nothing left behind . . . like I did in Colombia."

Angela made a face. "*Colombia?* You . . . Jack never went there."

"I did . . . after Afghanistan, for about a year. This particular mission turned out to be my last one with the SEALs."

"What happened?"

Jack looked away. Those memories still stung.

She put a hand to his cheek and gently turned his face toward her. "It's all right. You can tell me anything, remember?"

He certainly remembered a time when he could.

Taking a deep breath, he said, "It was supposed to be a routine recon to track down the location of this big-shot drug lord. But the damn surveillance gear malfunctioned, and we lost our cover. It turned very quickly into a turkey shoot. Everyone on my team was dead within a couple of minutes. The only reason I survived is that I sat them all up holding weapons so the incoming militia would think we were still alive, and then I booby-trapped them with everything we had, from Claymores to C4. I heard later that the heat from the blast was picked up by satellite. Not only did I vaporize my team—plus a few dozen bad guys—but such an unexpected and over-the-top bloody counterstrike has a way of stripping the enthusiasm right out of the most determined enemy. It bought me time to escape while the fuckers were trying to figure out which head went with which asshole."

He paused, then added, "My *point*, Angie, is that even in that extreme case, there was nothing left behind to be paraded around."

She just stared at him. "So you think that he may have survived the . . ." Her voice trailed off as she bit her lower lip and her eyes filled rapidly, a tear running down her cheek, wetting the freckle.

He instantly regretted bringing that up, chastising himself for being so insensitive. It was probably hard enough for Angela to wrap her head around him literally dropping out of the sky five years after his reported death. The last thing she needed was to fuel that confusion with false hope dispensed by the same man who had shocked her an hour earlier.

"Look," he continued, searching for the right words. "I seriously don't believe that anyone could have survived the fusillade that you've described. But my point was that Pete has a hell of a lot of explaining to do because in both worlds, Jack hauled his delirious ass and his mangled leg for two miles, while he was incoherent, talking shit. Pete *owed* Jack a trip home to his wife, even if it was in a body bag."

"But like you said, there was no body displayed by the Taliban, and you're right. It would have made for an excellent trophy," she said.

It was obvious now that he had opened Pandora's Box. Angela wasn't going to let this one go so easily, so he tried a different tactic.

"Maybe they realized the value of the armored battle dress technology, which was top secret at the time—and still is—and decided to put a lid on the whole thing and not advertise the killing so they could sell the suit to the Chinese or the Russians. I'm sure that money would have easily trumped the short-term press they would have gotten by parading another dead American. Look, I'm sorry I even brought it up. I don't think he's coming home, especially after five years."

Still holding his hands, Angela pulled him toward her. "But . . . that's the thing . . . he did . . . *you* did. You made it home, Jack. You still made it home to me. You *found* a way, and that's all that matters."

"Angie, I—"

She hugged him, and Jack didn't resist. He simply returned the embrace, his body responding when feeling her chest pressed against his.

"When you lose someone you love," she finally said, still clinging to him, "it doesn't really hit you until later, after the initial shock passes. The military funeral, the shiny uniforms, the volleys of shots fired, the jets flying overhead, and even the damn folded flag and those shell casings . . . all of that came and went in a flash. But it was later, Jack, when I had to go to bed alone, when I woke up alone, when I ate alone—hell, even when I walked into the garage and saw your bike and had to go riding alone. That's when it hit me, and it kept hitting me as I saw you in everything I did. Even in that orbital suit that I couldn't stomach to look at anymore. And that's why I couldn't stick around NASA. I couldn't breathe in there. It was truly suffocating. I had to get the hell out."

"Well, that suit's the reason I'm here," he said.

"No," she said, walking back to the living room and sitting on the sofa, where she inspected the strange glass token. "Not just the suit."

Jack took his seat next to her. "What do you think it is?"

"I don't know . . . but I do know someone who . . ."

Jack saw the glow from incoming headlights forking through a gap in the drawn living room curtains, and he raised a hand. "Don't make a sound."

She stared at him as he narrowed his gaze, shifting it to the foyer, listening to a sound that didn't belong. The sound of . . .

"Something isn't right," he whispered.

But before she could reply, Jack was already on his feet, killing the lights in the foyer, in the living room, racing toward the curtains, peering through their narrow gap into the darkness beyond, staring at three Humvees driving slowly down the street.

Car doors swung open followed by seven soldiers scrambling over the pavement, taking positions across the street at either side of the house. Pete finally emerged from the center armored vehicle holding a radio to his lips.

What are you up to, buddy?

"What is it?" she hissed from the living room.

"Your boyfriend," he replied, waving her over. "He's decided to play soldier."

"What are you talking about?"

"He's brought armed men with him. I don't get the feeling he's here to help us sort things out. I think he's here for *that*." He pointed at the OSS by the sofa. "And after he gets it . . ." He ran the tip of his thumb across his neck.

"No way. Something's gotta be wrong, Jack. I know him," she said, grabbing her mobile phone and speed-dialing him.

A moment later they watched Pete reach for his phone with his free hand and read the screen, obviously realizing it was Angela.

"Hey, I'm on my way," he answered.

"What's taking so long?" she asked.

"Traffic. I'll be there in a couple of minutes. Hold tight."

She hung up and said, "Jack . . . I don't understand what's going on. Why is he lying? What are those soldiers doing across the street?"

"I don't intend to stick around long enough to find out," Jack said, considering his options, and finally asking, "Angie . . . my arsenal . . . did you hang on to any of it?"

She looked at him, understanding flashing in her eyes as she said, "Yes, *all* of it."

"They're *all* going to have to be modified," Angela commented, popping the lid of a Red Bull and taking a swig before adding, "Idiots."

"Here's to trusting The Man," Art-Z said, also holding a can and tipping it in her direction.

Angela ignored him while she browsed through screen after screen of complex production timelines reminiscent of the space shuttle era, when suppliers from all over the globe provided the primary contractor, Rockwell, with every component required to assemble a shuttle, from the thermal protection system to zero-G toilets.

"Looks like there's quite the operation already underway," Art-Z added while she read through Project SkyLeap's production schedule for orbital space suits. The Pentagon procurement division had been busy conducting top secret biddings from every possible supplier—many of them companies that she had collaborated with over the years to develop the various prototypes—and had created an assembly line at an undisclosed location.

Angela frowned, realizing that she shouldn't be that surprised. After all, the objective from the very beginning had been to create a weapon, and that meant that at some point in time the military would have to take the OSS from NASA's R&D labs into a production facility just like every other military weapon in operation today.

She'd simply expected to have been part of that process, and not just because of professional pride, but because of precisely what had transpired. The screen glowing with data in front of her indicated that the Pentagon was already producing something that wasn't ready for prime time yet. She had warned Pete on multiple occasions about tempering Washington's enthusiasm for productizing a program of this complexity too soon. Something with this many moving pieces—and most of them state-of-the-art—required careful testing at the component level, followed by the module level, and then through various integration steps.

Crawl. Walk. Run.

Hastings, just like his push for Alpha-B, was definitely running again, and in doing so, he was jeopardizing the entire Project Phoenix. But even when a program was launched successfully, like the original space shuttle, the level of complexity of space operations required careful adherence to scientifically derived rules—rules, which often conflicted with schedule pressures, and which could result in disaster, as was the case with *Challenger*.

But still, nothing that she saw in this Web site so far told her anything new, anything that could explain what had happened to her husband.

"These guys already have over one hundred suits made," Art-Z said, pointing at the production schedule. "Plus twice as many in various stages of assembly."

"Yep, they're definitely going to have to modify all those suits—or maybe even scrap them," she replied. "But what I still don't get is why the hurry to productize this particular suit. The current version of the OSS is only good for suborbital jumps. It can't withstand the stress of a true orbital jump, like from the International Space Station. That version's still in the drawing board and up here." She touched the tip of her index finger against her temple.

"So what do you think he's trying to do by building so many suits that can't be used from orbit?" asked Dago.

"Not sure. Maybe they've figured out a way to use them . . . I don't know yet. At the moment it all looks like a huge waste of money."

"In that case, here's to my tax dollars at work," Dago replied, lifting his Corona. "At least the beer is free."

"And we still have no idea how your husband vanished," Art-Z added.

"Nope," said Angela.

"So, what do we do now?" asked Dago.

"Now we browse through another section of their Web site. But the more sections we open, the bigger the chance of getting caught," she answered, before asking Art-Z, "You've got everything you need from the flash card?"

"Not quite," he replied. "The general used a military version of Invisible Text, so reading his text messages will be a little tricky."

"What happened?" asked Dago.

"Hastings has a safety feature in his phone that basically deletes text messages after he sends them," Angela explained. "And it also deletes the ones he receives after he's read them. That, plus the fancy encryption algorithms, keeps the average phone hijacker from reading his private conversations."

"But we're far from average," Art-Z said.

"You're certainly far from something," the biker commented.

"So, Art, can I get in there or not?"

The hacker gave her a thumbs-up before using another finger to reply to Dago.

"See what you can learn, Bonnie," Art-Z added. "I've replicated the flash content in this machine," he said, pointing at the third laptop on the table that contained their getaway potion. If something goes wrong, I'll pull the plug and release this bad boy to cover our tracks."

Angela returned to the Web site's main menu and stared at it again.

TRAINING
SUITS
TECHNOLOGY
PROGRAM MANAGEMENT

If she assumed that an alarm would be triggered by opening another section—meaning she may only get a quick look at it before having to unplug—which should it be?

She felt she had a pretty good idea of the contents in the Suits directory given that she had designed the prototype, and she also felt that Training would reflect what Jack had gone through to get ready for the jump.

Slowly, she ran her finger across the touchpad and brought the cursor over to her original choice, Technology, and clicked on it.

The screen dissolved and changed to a set of menu options that made her blink.

"What's this, Bonnie?"

"I'm not entirely sure," she said, reading through what looked like more particle collider experiments, though they weren't conducted at CERN.

"I don't get it," said Art-Z. "I thought that CERN is the big kahuna of particle acceleration and collision."

"They are . . . except that these experiments aren't using copper as the conduit, but . . . *glass* . . ."

"You lost me there."

"All right," she said, recalling her limited knowledge of quantum physics. "A modern accelerator, like the one in CERN, consists of a large number of cavities through which particles, normally electrons, are accelerated by alternating the voltage in the cavities to either repel the electrons with negatively charged cavities or attract them with positively charged cavities. The object is to switch the voltage of a cavity just as an electron passes through it to accelerate it. Each cavity, therefore, injects more energy into the electron, kicking it faster. In the case of CERN, the particles get accelerated through its entire circumference, which has a diameter of around five miles. Higher frequency of voltage flipping, combined with a higher electric field, and smaller cavities packed together one after the other, translates into faster speeds, which in the case of CERN, can get close to ninety-nine percent the speed of light."

"That's pretty fast," said Art-Z

"Yeah, but it takes this mammoth of a facility, and a hell of a lot of electricity, to accomplish it. These cavities are surrounded by a conducting metal, which in this case is copper. The problem with copper is that it puts a ceiling on the amount of frequency and electric field levels it can take before melting. Now glass, which last time I checked was still on the drawing boards, has the potential to take the particle-acceleration game to a new level because the alternating electric field can be supplied by light, which is electromagnetic radiation, and that means much higher operating frequencies. While copper can probably handle about one gigahertz, glass allows frequencies in the *thousands* of gigahertz."

"That's *tera*hertz," commented Dago.

Angela and Art-Z looked over their shoulders at the large biker calmly nursing his Corona.

"What?" he said. "You don't think Harleys are pretty high-tech these days? I'll have you know I've got an associate's degree in electronics."

"From where?" Art-Z asked, "Devry?"

"Fuck you, little scooter man."

Angela smiled and added, "Easy, boys. It's not the size of the bike that matters."

"Ha!" said Art.

"Right," Dago replied, taking another sip.

Her eyes went back to the screen. "Another benefit of glass is that the higher the frequency, the smaller the wavelength, which means the shorter the distance the particle has to travel. Now this place, wherever it is, claims to have run particle acceleration experiments using glass. Impressive."

"It's fifteen minutes outside of Melbourne," Art-Z said. "I've got the address."

"What . . . how do you know that?" Angela said. There's nothing on this Web site that—"

"Please, Bonnie."

"Very impressive, Art," she said, leaning back. "So, Hastings had a production operation running just down the road all this time?" she asked.

"Looks that way," Art-Z said, before looking over at Dago. "Not bad for a little scooter man, huh?"

The biker's goatee shifted up as he grinned and raised his longneck at the hacker, tapping it to his can of Red Bull.

Just like at CERN, Angela dug in, pulling up the results of several experiments, which included particle collision events using gamma rays as the accelerant, which had the highest frequency in the electromagnetic spectrum right at 10^{12} hertz.

"That's *twelve* terahertz," she mumbled to herself, recalling the last set of telemetry from Jack's jump.

What the hell does that—

"Oh, shit! Oh, shit! Oh, shit!" Art-Z screamed, typing furiously before the SkyLeap site went black.

"What just happened?" Dago asked.

"Bad shit, man. Bad shit just happened," replied Art-Z.

"Just the opposite," Angela said. "I think we've just got handed an amazing opportunity."

She stared at her friends and smiled, her mind converging on a new plan of attack while her former mentor kept cursing while working the keyboard with intensity for a few more seconds, finally releasing what had to be the most virulent piece of code she'd ever seen.

6

THE RETURN OF THE WARRIOR

But the Lord is with me, like a mighty warrior, so my persecutors will stumble and not prevail. They will fail and will be thoroughly disgraced; their dishonor will never be forgotten.

—Jeremiah 20:11

He moved swiftly, quietly, with purpose, the armored battle dress blending him with the night as he made his way across the backyard and up the side of the house opposite the detached garage.

The MK11 semiautomatic sniper rifle in his gloved hands felt right, balanced, just as he remembered, even with the QD sound suppressor also designed to attenuate muzzle flashes for the seven shots he expected to fire tonight.

One for each of the soldiers that had exited those Humvees.

Seven shots. Seven kills.

That was the SEAL way, precisely what his training—which surfaced with unparalleled clarity—commanded him to do as he advanced in a deep crouch, camouflage cream darkening his features, a black bandanna concealing his hair, hiding him perfectly with his surroundings under a blanket of stars in the wrong world.

Jack pushed those thoughts aside as he neared the corner, the warrior in him tempering the adrenaline rush, eyes focused on his prey, his hands in perfect position, shooting finger resting on the trigger casing, feeling the deep gauge bitten out of the metal by a ricocheting Taliban round a lifetime ago.

But this couldn't possibly be his old rifle, the one he had lost in Colombia.

Still, a part of him felt a strange sense of joy at being reunited with the MK11.

He paused by the front corner and dropped over the cool lawn, setting the long barrel on the Harris swivel-based bipod, eyes scanning the street through the Leupold riflescope, easily locating the first three targets, two across and one on the sidewalk just forty feet from him. Three more covered the other side with identical deployment. The last one stood by the middle Humvee next to Pete, who was on the phone. All seven soldiers were armed with standard-issue M17 SCAR-H rifles that fired the same 7.62 mm NATO rounds in Jack's twenty-round box magazine.

And that realization made him pause, reassess what he was about to do: open fire on American soldiers.

But what choice did he have? Through his actions, Pete had already telegraphed his intentions loud and clear.

This blood is on him.

And besides, what would happen to Angela if Jack was either captured or killed? She was now a liability.

Seven shots. Seven kills.

That was his best option—the only option that Pete had left for him.

Pete Flaherty.

He watched him for a moment, still talking on the phone. The retired SEAL commando had something completely different reserved for his former best friend.

Jack shifted sights between targets, for a moment wondering why they hadn't yet moved on the house. The only thing that made sense was that Pete could just be holding the area while waiting for reinforcements, even though it was already eight against two.

If so, then time was of the essence.

Jack could easily disable the closest three in rapid succession, but the other four soldiers—plus Pete—required at least one more SEAL firing in unison.

Lacking that, he needed a distraction for just a few seconds, something to keep the other soldiers from looking in the direction of their fallen comrades, realizing they were under attack, and scrambling to return fire.

He reached into a Velcro-secured pocket next to his SOG knife and produced the one gadget that was not military-issued on his persona, and lining up his closest target, he tapped it once.

The garage door started to open on the other side of the property.

All heads shifted in unison toward the source of the noise—and most important, away from his immediate kill zone.

Jack exhaled and squeezed the trigger, feeling the recoil as the semiautomatic rifle ejected the spent cartridge while chambering another round from the magazine. The bullet hit the mark on the Kevlar vest over the soldier's solar plexus at a velocity of nearly 2,900 feet per second, delivering a nonlethal but crippling blow guaranteed to knock him unconscious for several minutes.

Shifting targets before the first soldier had fallen, Jack aligned the Leupold crosshairs on the second mark, still looking in the direction of the garage.

Firing again, Jack scored another hit within two seconds of the first as the soldier also dropped from view silently.

He shifted again, firing a third round two seconds later, neutralizing the third target before bringing the soldiers at the other side of the house into view.

Lining up the one closest to the house in the crosshairs, Jack fired for a fourth time in eight seconds at a distance of roughly one hundred feet, hitting his mark just as the ground exploded several feet in front of him with the sound of thunder as muzzle flashes lit up the street.

He rolled back once, twice, retreating like a vanishing shadow, catching a glimpse of Pete jumping inside a Humvee before losing sight of his remaining targets.

Reaching for his utility belt while rising to a deep crouch, he curled his fingers around a cylindrical canister, freeing it from its pouch, pulling the safety ring, and throwing it hard around the corner, in the direction of the incoming soldiers, before hurtling back to the rear of the property.

Thousand one. Thousand two. Thousand three. Thousand—

The M84 stun grenade thundered, illuminating the street behind him like a bolt of lightning, its magnesium-based pyrotechnic guaranteed to inflict immediate flash blindness, deafness, and loss of balance from inner ear shock to anyone within a fifteen-foot radius.

He heard screams, shouts of pain, anger, and confusion as he reached the back corner, stopping, rolling into view, landing on his feet, the MK11 automatically leveled at the opposite end of the backyard, in case the soldier closest to the house had managed to escape the blast and anticipated his retreat.

But no one came.

He gave the waterfront a quick look, verifying no threat near the Boston Whaler in the boathouse, before sprinting across the back of the house, like a ghost, reaching the opposite corner and moving up to the front, in between the corridor formed by the side of the house and the detached garage.

Dropping to the ground by the front corner, behind a line of waist-high bushes, he used the MK11's barrel to part the shrubbery, spotting his remaining targets, two rolling on the ground, hands over their ears, their eyes. The third soldier, on all fours, vomited on the asphalt.

His gaze shifted to Pete in the back of the lead Humvee, a hand over his eyes, the other holding a radio to his lips.

He was about to race across the pavement to deliver a dose of up-close-and-personal SEAL justice when three pairs of headlights turned onto his street, their beams stabbing the night, exposing the kill zone.

Help. But not for Jack.

He doubled back, tapping his voice-activated throat mike three times, signaling to Angela to come out.

Looking over his shoulder again to make sure no one followed, Jack reached the backyard just as she came out dressed in black jeans and a gray halter top while hauling two large duffel bags strapped over her shoulders, filled with his choice ordnance, while clutching one of Jack's favorite weapons after the MK11: a loaded M32 grenade launcher.

"Get the boat ready," he told her, swapping weapons. "This will slow them down."

"Jack," she said, holding his MK11. "The suit. I couldn't carry it with all the ammo. It's already folded back inside the—"

"I'll get it. Start the engine. I'll be right behind you," he said.

"Please, be careful," she said, her eyes screaming, *I can't lose you again.*

"I will," he said. "But time is against us. Now go."

She kissed him on his cheek, smearing her mouth with camouflage cream before taking off in the direction of the boathouse.

Relax, honey. I'll be right back.

Inhaling deeply, he turned his attention to the street, hearing the next round of Humvees approaching, engines roaring.

Jack frowned, realizing what he had to do, hands gripping the M32, verify-

ing all six chambered M406 high-explosive dual purpose rounds, each capable
of engaging lightly armored, point, and target areas.

Rushing to the right side of the house, he lined up the M32's reflex sight on
the street a hundred feet away just as the lead Humvee shot by, followed by the
second, and the third.

Jack centered the last Humvee in the reflex sight and fired two HEDP rounds
in one second, the recoil pad of the modular butt-stock jerking twice against his
shoulder as the rounds thumped out of their chambers.

Sprinting to the opposite side of the house, he faced the long corridor-like
path between the detached garage and the brick structure once again, spotting
the lead Humvee, soldiers jumping out just as the first two M406s detonated,
their blasts shaking the house's foundation, shattering windows.

He ignored it, popping two more HEDP rounds just as soldiers jumped back
from the acoustic energy of the first two explosions, invisible fists punching them
in the chest, propelling them against their armored vehicles.

Moving away, he scurried toward the sliding glass doors, still open, trained
instincts arresting his momentum, forcing him to wait for the next two blasts,
which came an instant later, deafening, stroboscopic—deadly—buying him
the seconds he needed to retrieve the OSS, his ticket home.

Jack ran into a living room littered with broken glass, eyes focused on his
target on the sofa, the long helmet—

Gunfire erupted from the street, peppering the house, puncturing the front
door, demolishing furniture, picture frames. The dining room chandelier
exploded as it crashed over the long table beneath it.

He dove, landing on a sea of sharp glass, his battle dress shielding him as
rounds buzzed overhead, tearing into the sofa, into the ceiling, showering him
with plasterboard.

The deafening noise momentarily disoriented him as he tried to crawl to the
suit when an invisible force punched him square in the chest, the Kevlar over
Nomex fabric absorbing the impact of a direct hit, spreading it across his upper
body, pushing him back with savage force, nearly making him lose control of his
bladder muscles.

Jack landed on his back, dazed, out of breath, mouth wide open trying to
inhale, his chest on fire.

A trembling hand reached down for the M32 by his feet, clutching the weapon while the other felt his chest, verifying that the round hadn't pierced the Kevlar.

Jack made another attempt for the OSS, ignoring the agonizing pain as he crawled back to the sofa, but the earsplitting fusillade held him back, forcing him to stay low as bullets punched holes in the helmet, ripping through the folded suit inside, in an instant eliminating his return home.

Damn!

Instincts made him roll away toward the back of the house, wincing in pain as the M32 pressed against his chest on every roll, the staccato gunfire intensifying, the ceiling and the carpet swapping places again and again until his right shoulder struck something hard, unyielding, a wall by the dining room as rounds shaved wood inches above him.

He crawled on elbows and knees under the heavy dining table while shots hammered it, splinters exploding, stinging the back of his neck as he reached the other side, just a few feet away from the same sliding glass now shattered by gunfire, gloved hands still clutching his grenade launcher and its two remaining rounds.

His inner voice now screamed at him to jump, to move, to scramble from his temporary hideout, from the false sense of security of lying low inside a light structure under heavy fire.

Because the former SEAL knew precisely what would come next—knew the tactics of flushing an enemy in modern suburban warfare.

This initial volley of rounds, as intimidating as it was at the receiving end, was just the appetizer of a standard-issue U.S. Army ass-kicking meal.

The main course came a moment later, just as the firing stopped in unison.

Jack heard three popping sounds as payback skittered across the living room floor.

Something snapped inside of him, and he sprung, almost as if he were lying on a nest of scorpions, long-ingrained survival instincts propelling him toward the shattered sliding glass doors, ignoring his throbbing chest and shards of glass threatening to tear his armored battle dress apart as he kicked his legs hard and dove through, landing on the back patio, rolling into lawn chairs just as multiple blasts rocked the house.

Glass and flaming debris exploded over the backyard, tongues of flames forking through shattered windows, through the doors he had just jumped through, licking the night sky.

The acoustic wave punched him in the back, throwing him a dozen feet in the air, before crash-landing on the grass beyond the patio.

Jack rolled to his side, sitting up with great effort, wincing in pain as he did so, but grateful for his SEAL training as he stared at his hands, still clutching his grenade launcher. Just like NFL players are trained to protect the football, so are SEALs taught to protect their weapon.

Get up, Jack.

He staggered to his feet, dazed, disoriented, his back burning from the blasts. Ears ringing, he blinked rapidly, clearing his sight, tightening the grip on the M32, taking a deep breath, coughing, fighting the urge to convulse as nausea spread through his system.

Move, Jack.

Mustering strength, he forced his legs to move, to run, to cover the fifty feet to the boathouse. He didn't need to look back to know the soldiers were coming, as prescribed by their training.

Jack scrambled from the threat, flinching in pain with each step, his ribs protesting the abuse, his heartbeat rocketing, hammering his aching chest.

His vision tunneled, converging on the Boston Whaler backdropped by the water as he pushed his scourged body ahead, refusing to give up, to capitulate, to let them take him. He owed it to Angela to escape, to survive to fight another day, just like in the Colombian jungle.

So Jack persisted, lurching forward, struggling to keep his footing, resisting the urge to turn around. Timing was everything, especially with only two M406s left in his launcher.

His chest stung with every step as he stumbled, nearly losing his footing, regaining his momentum, pointing it straight at the boathouse.

Thirty feet now, where Angela awaited, twin outboards rumbling.

Dark & Stormy.

Jack continued running, the spring-loaded soles of the battle dress increasing his momentum, assisting his escape.

Twenty-five feet.

The soldiers would be almost in view now, about to reach the backyard from both sides.

Twenty feet.

Now!

Dropping to the ground and rolling once, Jack spread his legs, arresting the roll while leveling the M32 to the right of the house, where he used the reflex scope to place the first grenade, the butt-stock recoiling before he shifted the wide muzzle to the left, releasing his last round.

Surging to his feet, waiting for the blasts, Jack took off again, kicking his legs against the grass, hearing shouts behind him, threats, warnings. But his mind blocked everything, counting the seconds as gunfire erupted and the ground exploded to his left.

He cut right, then left, zigzagging in the darkness, almost by the short pier as gunfire increased, the sound of a near-miss buzzing in his left ear.

Jack ducked and kept rushing away.

Movement is life.

He cut right, then left, then right again, the terrain under his cushioned soles hardening, changing from grass to wood as he kicked harder, the boat now less than—

The first blast finally came, overarching, powerful, killing the gunfire, the acoustic blast reaching him an instant later, lifting him off his feet, tossing him in the air, propelling him forward with savage force.

And the second blast took over, ear-piercing, kicking him back up in the air as Jack instinctively let go of the M32, arms covering his head, bracing for impact as he crashed into something, disoriented, stung by the twin explosions, unable to hear, to speak, to—

An invisible force shoved him sideways now, and he tumbled in its wake, striking another wall as the world around him blurred, as engines roared, as he sensed motion, bouncing on the floor.

He heard her voice now, distant, remote, quickly fading, just as her silhouette planted at the controls, legs spread for balance, long hair swirling in the wind as the Boston Whaler leaped from its shelter.

Holding his aching chest while lying sideways on the stern, under the rear bench, Jack tried to speak, to shout, to tell her that he had failed to retrieve the suit, his ticket home, the only way he knew to return to Angela.

But . . . then again . . . he *had* returned.

Angie was right there, her slim figure steady against the night, navigating them to safety.

Jack struggled to focus his tired mind, but shock overwhelmed his last straw of resistance, draining his stamina, dragging him into unconsciousness.

The world of Dr. Olivia Wiltz, SkyLeap's chief engineer, forever changed the moment her screen flickered, then went blue.

She just didn't know it yet.

Leaning forward, readjusting her large glasses, the former CERN scientist stared at the screen in disbelief.

The servers at SkyLeap never glitched.

Ever.

They had a triple-redundancy protocol, standby uninterrupted power supplies, and it was all backed by massive generators in the basement that could keep the entire building operational for up to a month in case of inclement weather.

And Claudette was anything but inclement now, having lost its punch somewhere over Orlando.

So what just happened?

Sitting behind her desk in the R&D lab on the second floor of the two-story facility built four years ago, the Swiss-born scientist watched the system go through its reboot process, before her gaze wandered around the interior of the pristine lab, where multiple versions of the OSS hung neatly from their frames, resembling glorified coat hangers, before staring at the final design, the one Jack used two days ago.

The confirmation that Jack had jumped dimensions had validated General Hastings's decision six months ago to ramp up the production facility on the first floor. Operation SkyLeap was a Go, and with it any hopes of Olivia returning to her formal life. She knew too much about this program, and the framed photo of her ten-year-old daughter, Erika, attending a private boarding school in Orlando, served as a constant reminder to never, *ever* deviate from the instructions handed down by Hastings.

Olivia had thought about going public once, in the beginning, shortly after she had learned of Hastings's long-term plans. But before she could contact the press, the general had summoned her to his office and calmly set a photo of Erika in front of her, taken by a surveillance team just hours before.

No words had been spoken, and to this day Olivia didn't know how he had figured out her plan. But whatever thoughts she may have had about exposing the operation had ended in that office.

Taking a deep breath, trying to keep the past in the past, Olivia chastised herself for accepting Hastings's offer to join SkyLeap. But at the time it had seemed like a great opportunity. She had just lost her husband to a brain tumor, and perhaps a change of scenery from Geneva to warm and sunny Florida was just what Erika needed—not to mention the amazing opportunity to develop the next-generation, glass-based particle accelerator.

In a way she wished their technology allowed for time jumps. Olivia would gladly turn back the clock and just continue on her work at CERN. Erika would certainly be safer now.

Readjusting the glasses on her fine nose, she watched the system go through its long reboot.

The laboratory walls, made of glass, gave her an unobstructed view of the entire operation. She walked over to one end, overlooking the Class-1000 clean room below, where suits hanging from tracks moving through various stages of assembly had just stopped as a result of whatever was happening to the network. Red lights flashed across the production floor, where technicians, dressed in clean room suits to keep particle contamination below the target of one thousand per million, moved about trying to get things started again. But their handheld tablets, designed to control every aspect of manufacturing, were as dark as her screen.

Sighing, wondering what could have happened, Olivia walked over to the other side of the lab, which overlooked the massive SkyLeap module under construction, to be deployed to the International Space Station aboard an Atlas-V rocket later this year as a secret military payload. Capable of housing up to twelve jumpers at a time for a period of three months, SkyLeap promised to be the largest single module ever deployed in space.

But construction had also stopped as the half-dozen computer-controlled robot arms used for assembly hung useless from their bases around the module while the system restarted.

Hastings isn't going to be happy, she thought, returning to her monitor, sitting back, elbows on the arm rests, hands by her face, as if she were praying while her blue eyes watched the system finish its power cycle.

Only it didn't quite start up again.

The SkyLeap main menu appeared for a few seconds. The display then turned completely black before a door opened in its center, like someone entering a dark room, his dark silhouette, as black as the screen, contrasting sharply with the bright light beyond the doorway, which also cast his shadow into the room.

Slowly, from the bottom of the screen, a phrase loomed into view.

YOU'VE BEEN HACKED.

Oh, God . . . no.

Her heart stampeding in her chest, Olivia reached for the phone and stabbed the button for the IT department in the cubicle area exactly below her, wedged in between the production floor and the SkyLeap module assembly room.

"Talk to me, Rajesh," she said.

"Virus attack, Dr. Wiltz," replied Rajesh Sharma, SkyLeap's IT manager and a former hacker who Hastings had recruited to prevent precisely what had just taken place.

"What is its origin?"

"The Solomon Islands, but it's a decoy."

"I don't understand."

"My guess is that the true origin's somewhere else. We're following it from the Solomon Islands to an ISP in Geneva. We're still digging into it, but my opinion is that tracking it that way may be a red herring."

Olivia momentarily froze at hearing Rajesh mentioning her hometown, before asking, "Why?"

"Because that's what the hacker would want us to do, use up resources that could be assigned to containing the virus, which is a higher priority."

"How . . . how bad is this, Rajesh?"

"Very bad, doctor. Probably the worst I've seen . . . almost elegant."

Coming from him that was really bad news.

"How are you going to contain it?"

"The quick and easy way: we're performing a hard shutdown and re-imaging the servers from our daily backup. So all data and activity in the last twenty-four hours will be lost, but when the system comes back up, it will be one hundred percent clean. That's the only way to be sure."

"How long?"

"Thirty minutes. An hour tops."

Olivia leaned back in her chair and closed her eyes, exhaling in relief before asking the obvious question. "How did it get past the firewall?"

"It had to be an inside job, doctor."

She leaned forward, her heart skipping beats inside her chest. First he had mentioned Geneva and now someone on the inside might be responsible. Her eyes gravitated toward the picture of Erika, and the words almost got caught in her throat as she said, "Please . . . explain."

"Right before the virus struck, one of my guys ran a routine system usage log and found General Hastings's account accessing the network. First the program management site and then the Technology site. That's when we flagged it. The general never checks the Tech site. He only cares about schedules."

Rajesh was correct. Hastings hardly logged in to the system as it was, and when he did, he just checked the PM tab for production updates. To him it was all about the numbers. He wanted as many suits built as fast as the facility could crank them out. But more often than not, Hastings would just skip the Web site altogether, pick up the phone, and call Olivia or her colleague in charge of production, Dr. Richard Salazar, currently spending most of his time at a materials lab that Hastings had disguised as an old warehouse in some field thirty minutes away.

"But . . . Rajesh . . . why would he compromise his own operation?"

Silence, followed by, "We think it was probably someone using his credentials. I think his phone was hijacked because they got the passwords right the first time—all four of them. Also, there is a possibility—however remote—that the hack may have originated in Europe. The Geneva ISP. But then again, it could just be a distraction. That's how hackers like to play the game."

Olivia glanced at her tablet computer on her desk, glad that she lacked external access, as was the case with everyone at SkyLeap, except Hastings, who had insisted on being able to monitor progress from anywhere in the world. Only the general had the passwords in his mobile device to log in to the system from beyond the high-security walls of Project SkyLeap. The rest of the personnel had to be physically inside the facility to gain access to the network.

"We have to warn him that his phone may be compromised," she said, hoping that the Geneva connection was just a weird coincidence.

"We already did," Raj said. "The passwords were stored in his SIM card."

"But isn't it encrypted?"

"It is. But that doesn't mean it can't be decoded. All it takes is the right software in the hands of a talented hacker."

"Is there a way to track down who did this?" Olivia asked, feeling a headache coming.

"That's a catch twenty-two, doctor."

"Explain."

"Well, in order to figure that out, we need to leave the system as is, with production on hold and the virus replicating while we try to dissect it and extract its origin."

"How long will that take?"

"That's the thing. It could be days, or longer, and there's no guarantee of success."

"Then that's not an option. The general has been quite clear that running production is a priority," she said. "We need the network up as soon as possible."

"Then that means a hard reboot from backup, like I was planning to do, which will kill the virus but also any information we could have used to track down its true origin. By the way, that's precisely the way I would have done it if I'd tried to hack into SkyLeap. Whoever did it knew how to cover his or her tracks."

"Do whatever is necessary to get us back online, Rajesh."

"Yes, ma'am."

Olivia hung up the phone, stood, and paced her lab, hands behind her back, lips pressed into a scowl. The gamma-ray glass accelerator, Olivia's creation—along with her colleague, Dr. Salazar—monopolized almost half of the R&D floor space, though its fifty-foot diameter was nothing compared to the colossus at CERN.

She stared at it with mixed feelings. As much as she despised being held hostage to work on this project, the scientist in her was amazed at the groundbreaking achievements of the SkyLeap team.

And that's just the beginning, she thought, realizing that they had only started to scratch the surface of what was possible with gamma-ray glass accelerator technology, which had completely obsoleted CERN's copper-based accelerator. Though no one at CERN—or anywhere outside of SkyLeap—would know for some time, or maybe ever, if Hastings got his way.

It was indeed too bad that such a promising discovery was under the control of a madman. But as long as that madman had a way of hurting her daughter, Olivia would continue to play ball. Which was precisely what she did as she reached for the phone to call Hastings. But before she could pick it up, the phone rang.

"Dr. Wiltz," Raj said. "We may have something."

"Good news?"

"I'm not sure. Maybe. The fact that General Hastings is the only authorized SkyLeap individual with remote access may actually play in our favor."

"How?"

"As part of Hastings's log-in protocol, the system performs a handshake with the ISP that Hastings uses when attempting to log in. Well, as a safety feature sometime back, Hastings himself thought of having the ISP record the physical location of the access anytime it didn't originate from his phone, from his device's IP address. At the time we all thought he was just a paranoid old fart."

"Turns out he was right."

"Yes, he was. And the thing is that the hacker wouldn't know it because that isn't standard procedure, just as the hacker wouldn't know that Hastings's phone was the only device that could access the network from outside our walls."

"Okay, Rajesh, so you are telling me we have an address?"

"Yes, ma'am. But that's what doesn't make sense."

"Why?"

"Because . . . it belongs to Pete Flaherty, the head of Project Phoenix."

Olivia froze, staring straight ahead, her mind going in different directions.

"Doctor? Are you okay?"

"Yes, Rajesh. I am. I need to contact the general right away," she said, hanging up and dialing Hastings, who picked up on the second ring.

"Doctor?"

She closed her eyes and tried to keep her voice steady, under control, like the professional she was. "General, the hack into the network originated from Pete Flaherty's house."

There was a long pause, while Olivia stopped breathing.

"Are you certain?"

She inhaled and said, "Yes, sir. Your phone was hijacked and it was used to get through the firewall, but although the IP address of the offending computer is sending us on a wild goose chase across the globe, the ISP recorded the physical address where that computer resided during the time of the attack."

There was second long pause.

"Thanks, doctor. You've done well. Please go home and rest. You've earned it."

"Thank you, General."

Feeling a strange sense of relief, Olivia hung up the phone, reached for a bottle of water on her desk, took a swig, and sat back, trying to steady her heartbeat.

She finished drinking the water, threw it in the wastebasket, and yawned. She was indeed exhausted and perhaps the general was right. Perhaps what she needed above all was a good night's sleep to clear her mind.

She waited another twenty minutes for the system to come back up—time she used to return several text messages from her suppliers, including mining operations in a half-dozen countries providing them with the critical minerals delivered to the materials lab headed by Salazar, responsible for creating the gamma-ray glass accelerators embedded in every suit.

Olivia finally called Rajesh the moment everything returned back to normal, and thanked him, before gathering her things and taking the elevator for the basement parking lot.

A minute later she reached the exit gate, where two security guards opened it while waving at her.

Olivia waved back and exited the compound, rain peppering her windshield as she steered her car for I-95, taking another five minutes to reach the entrance ramp and drive the six miles it took to reach her exit.

Ten minutes later, she pulled up in front of her house as lightning glowed on the horizon, followed by thunder that seemed to last far longer than she would have expected, and continued rumbling around her, behind her.

That's when she spotted individual headlights looming in her rearview mirror, along with the roaring mufflers of motorcycles.

Lightning gleamed in the jungle, forking through thick foliage, followed by cracking thunder, so close that it shook the ground beneath him.

Through the rain, Jack watched the figures get close, their silhouettes back-lit by the storm as another flash cast a stroboscopic glow across his immediate area of interest, the narrow meadow separating his trap from the incoming militia.

"Get out . . . of here, Jack," mumbled the other surviving SEAL, who Jack cradled in his arms while pushing another Fentanyl lollipop in his mouth, delivering a second dose of the strong painkiller through the blood vessels in his mouth far quicker than with the traditional syrettes.

"You know I can't do that," he whispered to Lieutenant David Bennett, Officer in Charge of his SEAL Team 4 platoon, as they hid behind the trunk of a towering ceiba.

"I'm done for, Jack," he hissed, the lollipop shifting as he spoke. "But you . . . you got a chance . . . on your own."

Jack rubbed the rain from his eyes and tightened the tourniquet over the gauze, keeping the man from bleeding out after shrapnel blew off the bottom half of his right leg.

Lightning cracked overhead, the glow exposing the threat, the cartel guns pausing at the other end of the meadow, by the tree line.

"I'm *not* leaving without you."

"Dammit . . . Jack . . . the LZ . . . too far . . ."

Jack kept working the tourniquet, but he knew it was a losing battle. His platoon leader was shivering now, going into hypovolemic shock, even with the IV that Jack had jigged into his left forearm filled with a brew of plasma, red blood cells, and platelets.

"Go . . . Jack . . ."

He frowned.

His OIC was right, of course. He always was.

It would be quite difficult for Jack to move, to get away from the enemy while holding on to him and keeping the IV in place as well as the tourniquet. But he couldn't possibly leave him here alive, either.

"Leave . . . me . . . Jack . . ."

His free hand brushing against the holstered Sig Sauer P226 with his last five 9mm rounds, Jack peeked around the wide trunk, narrowing his gaze at the figures emerging from the bush, cautiously, spreading across the meadow. He wished he still had the MK11 sniper rifle. At this distance, he could easily take out at least half of them in twenty seconds. But he had lost it in the gunfire of their uncoordinated retreat, as the world exploded around them after the damn surveillance gear malfunctioned, telegraphing their—

"Do it . . . Jack . . . do it for me."

Jack peered through the rain, watching the soldiers, close to thirty of them, all armed with a deadly mix of machine guns, high-powered rifles, grenade launchers, and even machetes. They appeared well trained, but that wouldn't matter when the time came.

"Jack . . . I would do it . . . for you."

Reaching down his leg, ignoring the bugs crawling on his skin and the rain dripping from his black bandanna, Jack curled his fingers around the handle of his SOG knife, releasing it from its Velcro-secured strap.

The soldiers made it halfway across the meadow, approaching the dead SEALs he had left by the edge of the jungle, twenty feet away; bait to lure his prey.

Thoroughly soaked, Jack looked at his commander once more, ready to follow his orders, but instead put the knife away and hoisted him over his shoulders.

"Jack . . . what . . . the . . . fuck . . ."

"I'm sorry, buddy," he whispered. "Can't leave your sorry ass here."

Surging to his feet, his back against the wide trunk, Bennett's weight squarely on his shoulders, Jack watched the threat again, saw them poke their bayonets into the lifeless bodies of his comrades, before reaching for his remote control and starting off in the opposite direction.

The jungle became a blur as Jack raced away from the threat as fast as he could, trying to keep his balance, vines, branches, and other vegetation brushing past them as he counted his steps, as Bennett moaned, heading downhill, where a stream led to a river a mile away, until he was sure he had put two hundred feet between him and the charges.

Kneeling in the soaked ground behind another towering ceiba, his legs sinking in the deep blanket of leaves and fallen vegetation, and keeping Bennett wrapped around his shoulders, Jack pressed the detonator three times.

The jungle trembled as Claymores and C4 charges went off in unison, forks of blinding white light reaching deep into the jungle, followed by flames, by a deafening explosion and incinerating heat that set everything ablaze.

Jack jumped in his sleep, bumping his head on something hard.

Opening his eyes, he felt motion, sensed the vibration from the roaring out-boards behind him, realizing an instant later that he had passed out in the stern, Angela's silhouette still standing in front of him, at the controls.

The smell of the sea tingling his nostrils, helping him shake off the night-mare, Jack rolled from under the seat, sitting up with effort, his chest burning, his ribs throbbing, his back aching from the blasts, a headache stabbing the base of his neck.

Reaching for the nearest handle, he staggered to his feet, struggling to keep his balance as the boat bounced in the waves. Angela had the throttles fully open, probably doing almost forty knots as he blinked to clear his sight, spotting lights in the distant shoreline on the starboard side, meaning she had them on a southerly course holding parallel to the eastern seaboard roughly six or seven miles out.

The wind gusting against his face, the night, the stars, and the ocean mist—plus the fact that Angela had been smart enough not to turn on the boat's navi-gation lights—reminded him of SEAL insertions. And for some reason, it injected him with renewed enthusiasm, with energy as he stared at his wife's thin form, halter top flapping in the wind, legs spread a foot apart for balance, hands on the oversized aluminum steering wheel, charging the bow into four-foot waves.

"Hey!" he shouted over the noise of the twin 250HP Mercury engines.

"Jack!" she screamed over her shoulder, without turning around. "Glad you're up! Come over and give me a hand!"

Standing, he grabbed the stainless-steel bar running across the rear of the vinyl bench behind the controls and used it to steady himself in the choppy seas, before settling next to her under the stretched canvas canopy.

"How are you feeling?" she asked, eyes glued to the bow.

"I'll live," he said. "Thanks to your suit."

"I wish I could take credit for it," she replied, a hand reaching for the cooler under the seat and producing a bottle of vitamin water, which he gladly took, twisting the top off and almost draining it. It tasted like heaven.

Angela opened the glove compartment under the instrument panel and snagged the first aid kit, retrieving an 800 mg Ibuprofen tablet, which Jack gladly swallowed with his final swig of water.

"I checked on you right after we left, once I felt we were far away. You seemed banged up but alive."

"Yeah," he said, before adding, "now, about the rest of the OSS . . ."

"Yeah . . . I figured as much," she said, both hands on the wheel again, turning slightly to port and back to starboard to keep up with the shifting swells. "Guess you're stuck with me for a while."

He looked at her, the wind swirling that long, blond hair. The chocolate freckle as inviting as ever. "Looks that way. Where are we going?"

"Miami," she replied. "Remember Dago?"

He laughed and said, "The man's hard to forget."

"Gave him a call as soon as we cleared off and—"

"Angie, the phone," he interrupted. "It's got GPS tracking that—"

"Relax, Mr. Navy SEAL," she said, shooting him a half smile. "I made the call and then turned it off. Look around, do you see anyone on our ass?"

Jack still didn't like it. Anyone with the right credentials could access her log at the phone company and find out who she had called. But it was done and he was too tired to have an argument with her.

"Here," she said, reaching under the seat and handing him a pair of jeans, a T-shirt, and sneakers. "As much as you like your suit, I think it's time to take it off."

"Can't argue with that. Hey, these are my—"

"Yeah. Grabbed them from your closet along with your guns. They should fit."

Amazing, he thought, staring at his very own faded blue jeans, before unzipping the battle dress from neck to groin. He stepped out of it wearing a translucent thermal undergarment laced with a thousand feet of micro tubes filled with gel, which served to keep him cool during reentry and also comfortable in any weather on the ground. He also unzipped it and dropped it down to his waist.

Angela looked over, sized him up, and grinned as she said, "Everything looks about right."

Jack ignored her while dropping it to his ankles and stepping out of it, the wind chilling him before he quickly pulled up his jeans. The sneakers were also his, as was the extra-large black T-shirt sporting a subdued trident embroidered over the left breast. It fit him almost skin tight, his muscles pressing against the cotton fabric.

"Better?" she asked.

"All good."

"Great. Now you can take over. You're the sailor. I'm not that comfortable being this far out," she said, sitting back and also grabbing a bottle of water.

Jack glanced at the instrumentation, his naval mind doing some quick math. He eased the throttles by a quarter, slowing them down seven knots while keeping the boat on plane, but saving them a bunch of gas, especially since Miami was still over a hundred miles away, and the outboards had already consumed nearly a third of the three-hundred-gallon fuel tank.

Being much taller, Jack remained sitting and just placed one hand on the wheel, holding a course of one seven zero while Angela sat next to him and wrapped an arm tightly around his bicep.

"Sorry about your house," he said.

"It was yours, too, Jack."

He tilted his head and frowned. She had a point.

"But the hell with the house, Jack," she added. "I've got you."

Angela rested her head on his shoulder, hugging his arm tight, a finger tracing the outline of his Triumph tattoo.

And suddenly, at that very instant, as Angela snuggled up against him while he steered *Dark & Stormy* across a choppy ocean in the predawn darkness of this parallel universe he had fallen into, everything felt strangely right with the world.

But just as suddenly, Jack's inner voice told him the feeling was an illusion. The same instincts that had kept him alive in Afghanistan, Colombia, and back in Cocoa Beach now broadcast that they weren't alone.

The wind in his face, the hull splashing against waves in explosions of foam and mist, the roar of the outboards rumbling in his ears, Jack glanced up at the night sky, his eyes searching for any indication of surveillance, though he knew that would be futile. If the U.S. government had eyes on him, especially with all the noise around him, he wouldn't notice it until either a Coast Guard helicopter or cutter loomed in the horizon, or worse, a Hellfire missile from a drone blew them to kingdom come.

Jack felt the latter scenario to be the likely one. For better or for worse, he had fired at U.S. Army soldiers, probably even killed some. Revenge would come just as sudden and unexpected as that fusillade in his living room.

Feeling exposed to infrared surveillance, realizing how vulnerable they were in the middle of the ocean in an open boat when the enemy was armed with so much aerial reconnaissance technology, he returned his attention to the twin flat screens on his instrument panel, the right one slaved to the boat's GPS navigation system and the left one displaying engine parameters.

Jack scanned the latter one, making sure that everything from oil pressure to fuel levels remained in the green for both outboards, before focusing on the GPS map, an evasive plan forming in his covert ops mind—a plan straight out of the SEAL manual targeted at giving him the edge against a much stronger and better-armed adversary.

An adversary that Jack had angered tonight. And everything he knew told him that this bear he had just kicked would be coming back with a vengeance.

He reached for the radio and switched it to Channel 21A, a frequency of 157.05Mhz, the first of several frequencies reserved for Coast Guard operations.

"What's wrong?" Angela asked.

"Just getting a bad feeling."

She understood and jumped off the seat, standing in front of the instrument panel, shoulder-to-shoulder with Jack, and began to scan the airwaves.

Pursing his lips, Jack narrowed his gaze at the sky once more before inspecting the GPS overlay of a map of the Florida coastline, making his decision, and turning the bow thirty degrees to starboard the moment he spotted a set of red and green lights marking the entrance to the Fort Pierce inlet connecting the ocean to the Indian River.

"You mind telling me what in the world she was doing in your house, Flaherty?"

Pete sat in the same chair where Angela had been interrogated the day before, with Riggs standing behind him while Hastings inspected his fingernails, backdropped by the remnants of Claudette, which was mostly light rain and sporadic lightning.

The trip to find Angela had proved unproductive, just as he had hoped. But something had gone terribly wrong on the way back. Hastings's attitude toward him had changed just as they'd reached the Cape, after a short phone call from one of his gurus.

The three of them had come straight to the VIP office on the third floor, where Hastings had just sprung a question that Pete wasn't quite ready to answer.

"Sir, I have no idea how she got in."

"See, Flaherty, that's the thing. I can see her breaking in, but I certainly don't get how she knew the proper alarm code, as well as your wireless password."

Pete frowned inwardly, realizing this was precisely the risk he had decided to take on when making his decision to help Angela.

"I know how it looks, sir, but I have no idea how she did it. She used to be a hacker."

"Yes, indeed," he said. "And apparently she still is quite the little hacker."

Pete remained silent.

"But you," Hastings added, "are quite the lying piece of shit."

He leaned forward. "With all due respect, sir, I will *not* stand for—"

The blow was completely unexpected, and before he knew it, Pete found himself rolling on the carpeted floor, his right temple on fire.

Before he could react, powerful hands yanked him off the floor and dropped him back on the chair.

Stung, dazed, confused, the blurred image of General Hastings leaning forward and planting both elbows on the desk, Pete blinked rapidly, trying to come around, to get it together, to—

"Lets try this again, shall we?" Hastings hissed. "How did Dr. Taylor end up at your place?"

"General," Pete said, taking raspy breaths, a hand on his throbbing temple. "You are . . . completely out of line . . . I will . . . report this to—"

The second blow stung infinitely more than the first as he rolled onto the carpet again, gasping for air, hands shielding his face as a boot came into view, swinging toward him, kicking him in the solar plexus, doubling him over, sending him flying right into the wall like a football, crashing face first, bouncing, landing hard on his back.

His mouth open, Pete tried to force air into his lungs, limbs trembling, eyes flickering, staring at the ceiling, his mind at the edge of consciousness.

And Riggs snatched him up again with animal strength, dumping him back on the chair like a rag doll, his massive hands clutching his shoulders to steady him.

"Flaherty, you just pissed your pants," Hastings said. "Now, I'm going to ask you one more time . . . Dr. Taylor managed to land at your house, where she hacked into one of my classified networks and infected it with some really fucked up stuff. You are not only going to tell me how she ended up at your house, but you're also going to tell me where she's hiding—along with whoever is helping her."

Pete couldn't have told him if he had wanted to as he wheezed air in and out of his lungs, his eyes losing focus.

"Tell you what, I'm going to step out and leave your stinking ass here with your new *best friend,* who will keep a good eye on you while you think things over."

With that, the hands on his shoulders vanished and Pete collapsed on his side, landing back on the carpet, arms bracing his aching chest as he curled up in a fetal position trying to breathe, the stench of his own urine reaching his nostrils as he started to heave, to convulse, vomiting whatever little he had managed to eat in the past few hours.

Bastards, he thought, clenching his jaw, the smell of bile mixing with the coppery taste of his own blood adding to his nausea.

Fight it! Pete could almost hear Jack screaming.

Mustering strength, he held back a convulsion, blinking rapidly to clear his sight, the blur resolving into Riggs's boots a few feet away, by the door, where he stood with hands behind his back.

Still curled up, pretending to moan while rolling over, turning his back to Riggs, Pete managed to sneak a trembling hand down his right leg, curling his fingers around the Taser's handle, freeing it from its holster and holding it by his waistline.

Breathing deeply, settling his nausea, his eyes regaining focus, Pete rolled back to face Riggs, who stood tall and firm, like a damn rock, eyes front, hands still behind his back.

"Hey . . . eunuch," Pete hissed, recalling the video he had seen during Angela's turn at the barrel.

Riggs blinked and dropped his gaze at him, eyes widening in surprise.

Pete pulled the Taser's trigger just as Riggs reached for his sidearm.

Two probes shot out at nearly five hundred feet per second connected to fine wires spooled inside the unit.

The probes poked into Riggs's upper thigh and lower abdomen, delivering a series of five-thousand-volt pulses to his neural network, overwhelming normal nerve traffic.

The large man dropped unceremoniously, like a giant sack of potatoes, and to Pete's joy, it was Riggs's turn to convulse, vomit, and even urinate.

Slowly, his thumb pressing the Taser's trigger, Pete staggered to his feet, suddenly feeling tall next to this trembling bastard.

"Hey . . . best friend," he said, keeping a respectful distance to avoid getting shocked himself. "You just pissed your pants."

Pete released the trigger while kicking Riggs across the temple to knock him out, just as Jack had shown him years ago, before reaching for the soldier's sidearm, a Colt 1911, and shoving it in the small of his back.

Then, just as he had seen Angela do, Pete also shifted his attention to the large windows behind the oversized VIP desk, where he—

"Wait . . . please," Riggs mumbled in between raspy breaths.

Pete dropped his gaze at the oversized soldier, amazed he was still conscious. *This asshole has a pretty thick skull.*

He swung his leg back, getting ready to kick him again.

"There's . . . something . . . you should . . . know."

7

PRESSURE POINT

In a crisis, be aware of the danger, but recognize the opportunity.
—John F. Kennedy

The MQ-1B Predator lurked over the horizon at twenty thousand feet under a star-filled night, its Rotax 914F engine pushing the unmanned aerial vehicle, or UAV, close to its maximum speed of 135 knots.

The half-ton drone dashed over the beach ten miles south of the Kennedy Space Center, its infrared sensors scanning the ocean below in programmed grids as guided by KU-Band satellite communications via the Primary Predator Satellite Link, a ground-based dish relaying the commands from an adjacent ground control station in nearby Patrick Air Force Base.

Sitting in the left seat of the windowless Predator ground control station, which resembled the back of a semibed, Predator Pilot Major Virginia Jackson, USAF, used light finger touch to shift the right-hand joystick slightly to the left. Two seconds later, she received visual confirmation via the aircraft's nose camera of the Predator banking ten degrees left to a course of one seven nine, parallel to the coast five miles out.

"We're white hot," reported Captain Rob Quinn, the Predator sensor operator sitting in the right seat of the PGCS and responsible for target prosecution, reviewing the information gathered by the infrared camera of the UAV's Multi-Spectrum Targeting Sensor, the gimbal-mounted dome protruding beneath the aircraft's nose. He compared the scans with the geospatial location of every Coast Guard-sanctioned vessel in their current hundred-square-mile quadrant of ocean at that very instant.

Virginia, a former F-16 pilot who had long become accustomed to the lack of sensory input when flying drones from armchairs, fingered the left-mounted throttle control, trimming power to sixty percent, keeping the Predator at a steady 125 knots for improved endurance while also maximizing the time it would spend over each quadrant. The intelligence briefing had revealed that the target, runaway terrorists associated with Al-Qaeda aboard a thirty-two-foot Boston Whaler, were last reported leaving their hideout in Cocoa Beach heading south following a fierce battle with a Special Ops team, who had stormed their cell.

Where are you hiding, motherfuckers? she thought, keeping her plane steady while her colleague did the heavy lifting, processing the video feed and transmitting it in real time to a Predator operations center a mile away in the center of the base, where a team of intelligence analysts combed through the acquired imagery and relayed instructions back to the ground control station for prosecution. Three more Predators and their ground crews were deployed five minutes after Virginia's, scanning nearby grids of Atlantic Ocean under the coordination of the same POC.

The intelligence briefing had included the deaths of at least eight servicemen, drastically escalating the relevancy of the threat.

For the next twenty minutes, the Predator team continued to scrub their assigned grids in white-hot mode, meaning heat sources showed up as white against a dark background. The Coast Guard report helped eliminate most contacts, approved vessels—commercial and recreational—cruising up and down the picturesque coast.

"Got something," reported Quinn, bringing up the finding on the main flat screens hanging between them, placing the crosshairs onto a vessel fitting the description. "This one's not on the list," he added.

Virginia went to work immediately, reducing throttle while banking to the left, commanding the UAV into long, lazy circles over the target, like a true predator, fingers itching in anticipation.

"HVT confirmed as a thirty-two-foot Boston Whaler," announced the senior intelligence officer at the POC a minute later, after Quinn had zoomed in and provided them with enough close-up imagery. "I think it's trying to make a run for international waters."

"Copy that. Starting tracking," Quinn replied. "Updating coordinates real time."

Virginia stared at the screen, locating the high-value target while keeping the

Predator on a ten-degree bank at a steady ninety knots, holding altitude, allowing Quinn to paint the HVT with the laser range designator housed in the
underside dome.

"Target locked," Quinn reported.

"Coast Guard's on the way," reported POC. "ETA fifteen minutes."

Virginia reviewed the information on the screen, reading the relevant data,
including target position coordinates, bearing to target and range to target while
the ball, or dome, rotated as the Predator banked, keeping the crosshairs locked
on the target, as specified during the briefing.

"How many on board?" she asked, squinting.

"Hard to tell," Quinn reported.

She frowned. The heat from the large outboards pretty much washed away
any other heat signatures on such a small boat. On top of that, the vessel had a
fiberglass canopy in the middle, and they couldn't see through it.

If this was a daytime ops, they would be able to zoom in using the Predator's high-resolution cameras and count the pimples on their asses, but at night
they were limited.

But it didn't really matter. They had them, and as much as Virginia simply
wanted to blow the bastards back to the land of a thousand virgins, someone
with a higher pay grade had decided that they wanted the terrorists captured alive.
Besides, the intelligence briefing indicated the possibility of a hostage aboard.

Although Virginia was Air Force, her current assignment piloting domestic
drones placed her under the direct command of the Department of Homeland
Security, which had limited her rules of engagement on this mission to locating
and reporting their coordinates to the Coast Guard, while maintaining missile
lock just in case the terrorists decided to fight back.

And that's where the AGM-114N Hellfire missile, the Predator's primary
strike weapon, came into play. The Hellfire was considered a high precision
asset—meaning it was ridiculously accurate. Although it weighed in at only one
hundred pounds, placing it on the lighter side of air-to-surface missiles, it's
thermobaric warhead was good enough to obliterate a truck or lightly armored
vehicle.

Or a fiberglass Boston Whaler.

Virginia glanced over at Quinn, who gave her a thumbs-up. He was ready to
fire on command.

She contacted the Predator Operations Center, letting them know she was in a holding pattern with missile lock active.

Engaging the autopilot, Virginia did something she couldn't do back in her F-16 days: she reached for a can of soda in the small cooler under the flat-screen monitors and waited for the cavalry.

As she popped the lid and watched Quinn grab a bottle of water, she zoomed out on one of the center screens and located the feeds from the other Predators, one of which showed the transponder signature of the USCGC *Margaret Norvell*, the Sentinel-class cutter cruising at twenty-nine knots to intercept.

She zoomed in on the 154-foot long vessel packing enough firepower to blow the Whaler to pieces if the terrorists decided to get naughty. On top of that, the *Margaret Norvell* would be backed by a pair of super-fast Defender-class speed boats, each doing forty-five knots along their own intercept courses but scheduled to arrive more or less at the same time as the larger but much closer cutter.

And literally hovering above all of that firepower, Quinn was just a push-of-the-button away from releasing a Hellfire, which being supersonic, would smoke the boat in less than five seconds.

She returned her gaze to the HVT, holding just twenty knots while maintaining zero eight zero about four miles out.

Don't these guys know we have eyes in the sky everywhere? she thought, figuring that after all of the press the Predator and its big brother, the Reaper, had received during the Iraqi and Afghan campaigns, that Al-Qaeda would have gotten smarter about evasive tactics.

She frowned while staring at the Boston Whaler. Something felt wrong, but she wasn't sure what it was.

"Hey, Quinn, what's the top speed on those?"

"Close to forty knots," he replied.

"Yeah. That's what I thought. So why is this one going so slow, especially if it's trying to get away?"

"I've already thought about that," he replied. "Don't have a good answer."

Virginia shifted uncomfortably in her seat and set her drink down. "I mean, wouldn't you be hauling ass if you had just blown away a bunch of soldiers in their home turf? And where is it headed? What's their range?"

"About four hundred miles fully fueled."

"Any larger vessels in the vicinity?"

"I'm tracking a dozen freighters within their range. I'm getting their coordinates to the Coast Guard in case they make a run for any of them."

They continued to follow it for another ten minutes, zooming in as much as possible to see if they could spot people moving about, but the signature remained steady, with the outboards painting the boat white.

The cutter finally approached it from starboard and turned parallel to the HVT's course keeping a distance of three hundred feet. A minute later the first Defender boat showed up and approached the Boston Whaler.

Virginia and Quinn watched the large center screen, where the infrared camera painted all of their respective heat signatures, including that of the second Defender boat, which joined the first, flanking the runaway—

Virginia blinked and leaned back the moment the screen went blinding white.

"What the hell's that?" she yelled.

She figured it out just as the screen returned to its normal resolution, depicting only three vessels now, the large cutter still cruising at normal speed plus the two Defender boats surrounded by flaming debris that rapidly vanished as it sank.

"They blew themselves up, Quinn," she said, a heavy sinking feeling squeezing her chest. "The crazy motherfuckers blew themselves up!"

Inside the Predator Operations Center, Pete Flaherty, director of the Kennedy Space Center, watched the large center screen tracking the runaway Boston Whaler until it detonated.

"We have confirmation that none of the Predators fired, sir," said Commander Heather Vickers, assistant to the commandant of the U.S. Coast Guard, standing next to Pete by the large screens in front of a row of POC analysts monitoring their workstations. She was dressed in a standard camouflage working uniform with a matching cap partially hiding her brown hair and sporting a silver oak leaf. "The boat exploded from within. Probably suicide."

"Damn fanatics," hissed the analyst sitting at his workstation in front of them, an Air Force lieutenant, as he replayed the video feed on the overhead monitors.

Pete exchanged a glance with Heather and asked, "Did the Defenders have eyes on the occupants before the explosion?"

"Negative, sir," she replied. "Everything happened before they could train spotlights on the HVT."

"I need the whole area combed," he ordered.

"Agree," replied Heather. "Though I'm not sure how much we'll find after that blast."

"I know," he replied. "Just want to be thorough."

"I'll direct a pair of Predators to run a white-hot scan on the entire grid. And it'll be morning soon. We should be able to spot anything easily with the HD cameras the moment the sun comes up."

Pete nodded. "Good thinking, Commander. I'll mention your cooperation in my report to General Hastings."

"Thank you, sir. We're all on the same team."

"I need to get back to the Cape now. Please keep me posted."

"Yes, sir."

Pete walked off and headed for the POC's exit, his mind exploring the possibilities, starting with his strong belief that Jack and Angela had not perished in that explosion.

The man's a SEAL, for crying out loud, he thought, which meant he had plenty of options—and the training to execute them—especially when surrounded by a dark ocean.

He frowned as he walked out of the building and stared at the predawn skies over central Florida, filling his lungs with cool, humid air, trying to keep his tired mind focused.

A car waited for him to take him back to the Cape, and he walked toward it, opening the rear door and settling in the backseat while contemplating the very surreal turn of events in the past couple of hours.

He shook his head. At first he thought it had been a hoax, but as far as he remembered, only Jack knew the detail about the carabiner failure during their Colorado rock climbing trip long ago.

As downright impossible as it sounded, Pete couldn't come up with another explanation to Jack's sudden return from the dead than the one he had offered over the phone. There was no way he could have survived Afghanistan. Pete had seen Jack take at least a dozen rounds fired at close range from those Taliban rebels before the SEAL team could secure the ridge. And although the rebels had taken the body with them as a trophy, the blood-soaked sand in the same spot where Jack had fallen just minutes earlier was enough evidence to call it KIA.

But then again, Pete hadn't actually *seen* Jack tonight. He had spoken to someone who *sounded* like Jack, and who even knew details about their rock-climbing trip... but he never had eyes on him, and neither did any of the surviving soldiers, who had just reported a dark figure escaping in the Boston Whaler along with Angela. And the Coast Guard wasn't able to get close enough to identify anyone before the explosion.

But Angela claimed it was him, he thought, his mind still having difficulty swallowing the uncanny reality that had unfolded—and continued to unfold—right in front of him.

So, if he assumed for the time being that Angela actually knew who the hell her husband was, that meant that Jack had either survived Afghanistan and somehow made it back here, or...

Dimensional jumps are possible.

He shook his head again, having a difficult time accepting either possibility. But, if he assumed for the moment that the latter was true, then it meant that the technology existed to achieve that, and that further meant it had to be protected at all cost, including making sure the knowledge of its existence remained secret until he could unravel all of this.

And that technology likely resided in the carefully packed suit inside that oversized helmet he had retrieved among the smoldering remains of Angela's house—a suit he intended to thoroughly inspect the moment he got back to the Cape.

Aside from a few bullet holes, the suit had been protected from the multiple explosions by a helmet that on the surface appeared designed to survive the immense G-forces and heat of reentry.

He stared out the window as his driver approached the base's exit and turned toward the Cape.

Possession of the suit, however, wasn't enough to get to the bottom of this.

Pete also needed Angela—and even Jack—more than ever.

He continued inspecting the world beyond the tinted glass window, but in his mind he saw her hazel eyes.

Less than forty-eight hours ago, he had cooked dinner for her, and even brought up the subject of moving in together. He'd had feelings for the beautiful scientist from the moment he'd laid eyes on her years ago, during the early days of Project Phoenix, before Jack had entered the scene. But he had been too slow, too shy, and perhaps too damn professional to date an employee, allowing Jack to slide right in and steal her away. But destiny had given him a second chance after Jack was killed in Afghanistan. And he had been patient, probably far more than any reasonable man should, holding her hand, giving her a shoulder to cry on, supporting her during her long mourning period, being a friend while hanging on to the hope that one day their friendship would become something more.

And just when their relationship finally started moving in his desired direction, he had received the most bizarre phone call of his life.

He looked down and frowned.

The last thing Pete had wanted was to hurt his girlfriend and former best friend. But Jack had to be Jack, starting a firefight, attacking his men, forcing Pete's hand.

But then again, Jack probably wouldn't have gone SEAL on him if Pete hadn't appeared with soldiers and deployed them around the—

His phone started to vibrate. It was Hastings, his boss up in Washington.

"Good morning, sir," he said.

"Pete, I just got the DHS update. How are you holding up?"

"As good as can be expected. We lost a few men in the firefight."

"That's a damn tragedy. Any word on the bastards responsible for this mess?"

"DHS is launching a combined effort to search the grid and look for any debris that might give us a clue, but I'm not holding much hope for that. The blast was pretty severe, and they were already in fairly deep waters with strong Gulf Stream currents."

"How many terrorists do you estimate were involved?"

"We're guessing at least three or four to put up the fight they did at Angela's house."

"So you think we lost her?"

"I'm afraid so, sir. They took her hostage, and we have every reason to believe she was aboard the boat when it went off. I think they were after our old Project Phoenix technology. Remember Al-Qaeda got its hands on that early suit version in Afghanistan."

"Yeah," Hastings said with a heavy sigh. "Hard to forget that one."

"I'm thinking they may have wanted Angela to help them take the design to the next level. And as harsh as it sounds, given the options of her being captured alive or what just transpired, I guess from a national security perspective the latter is the lesser of the evils."

Silence, followed by, "I know, but it's still a real shame. First we lost Jack and now her. I had high hopes for that program way back, you know."

"I know, sir. So did I. They were also my friends. I only wished I would have brought more soldiers to her house after I got her distress message," he replied.

"Don't beat yourself over it, Pete. You did all you could, including dialing 911 and even getting there faster than the cops. Who knew you would be walking into a terrorist ambush. It's Cocoa Beach, for crying out loud. And who the hell would have expected them to come after Dr. Taylor five years later?"

"I know," Pete replied. "We kept a security detail on her for almost a year, finally dismissing them when we went through that project's budget cuts, plus she had already left NASA, so it became difficult to justify the expense."

"I know," Hastings said. "We had to mothball Project Phoenix and allocate resources to more promising projects. It was the right call then, and it's still the right call now. Look at how much progress we've made since on our other programs. And much of the credit belongs to you for helping us focus our limited resources to get the biggest bang."

"I appreciate that, sir."

"All right," Hastings said. "I need to run now. Let me know if there's anything we can do at this end, Pete, and I'll be down in a week to go through our standard program reviews. There's also . . . something else we need to discuss. But it's better done in person."

"Yes, sir," he said, glad that Hastings had bought his cover story, but now intrigued by the general's last comment.

He hung up and decided to put that aside for now. At the moment he had more pressing issues, including thinking through a plan to not just inspect the suit in secrecy for now, but also to locate Angela and Jack.

Pete looked into the distance, toward the ocean.

The explosion was visible even from five miles away, followed a few seconds later by a sound wave resembling distant thunder.

"Oh, my God," she mumbled in the darkness, standing next to him.

"It's done," Jack said, turning off the remote detonator before flipping the bilge blowers of the thirty-nine-foot Tiara he had quietly towed out to sea from the ranks of moored motors and sail yachts dotting the large waterway of the Fort Pierce marina.

The rest had been easy, transferring their gear, including the scuba equipment, to the larger vessel, which he hoped wouldn't be reported stolen for a few hours. Jack had then placed a C4 charge next to the Boston Whaler's gas tank and pointed it out to sea, accelerating to twenty knots before engaging the autopilot and jumping off, swimming back a thousand feet to the Tiara, where Angela was busy securing their gear to the bungees lining the port and starboard railings of the yacht's open stern.

He bypassed the simple key ignition system and waited sixty seconds to clear out any fumes from the engine compartment below, which housed a pair of Crusader 350HP gas inboards, before engaging the portside engine, which came to life with a low rumbling sound. He watched the oil pressure climb into the green before punching the button for the starboard-side engine, which caught right away.

He inspected the gauges once more while letting them warm up, confirming his initial inspection of the yacht back at the marina. The vessel was old but well maintained, with a two-thirds full 398-gallon tank, plenty to get them to their destination while the Coast Guard—and whoever else Pete had searching for them—remained distracted by his diversion.

Turning on all navigation lights, he slowly advanced the port and starboard throttles in unison while engaging the stern trim tabs, bringing the yacht to an efficient plane angle as they reached a relaxed cruise speed of twenty knots about a mile from shore.

The Tiara sliced through the waves far easier than the smaller Whaler as Jack sat back on the wide bench behind the controls and Angela snuggled up next to him again, her chest pressed against his arm. Being much longer and heavier, the yacht also gave them a much gentler and quieter ride, especially behind the controls, protected by a tall and semicircular windshield that cut down the wind noise, allowing them to hold a conversation without having to shout.

"Looks like about three hours to Miami Beach," she said, her head on his shoulder and her eyes on the GPS while he nodded in agreement before surveying the dark horizon, spotting a few vessels far out at sea, but nothing directly ahead as they followed the coastline toward the tip of the peninsula.

"Yep. And *that* should keep them busy for a while," he said, extending a thumb over his left shoulder.

"Let's hope so," she said, reaching in her jeans' front pocket. "We need time to figure out what the hell this is."

Jack glared at her hand in disbelief as she held the purple glass token.

"Angie! You got it!"

"Of course," she said. "I wasn't going to leave it behind for that son of a bitch."

Jack grinned.

"This is the one module I don't understand in that suit," she added.

"Thank you," he said, perhaps with more gratitude than he wished to show.

"I know you need to get back to your world, Jack . . . and to your wife."

"Angie, I—"

"Hush," she added. "But I also want to make sure that you understand that while you're in *my* world, you belong to *me*. Clear?"

"Crystal," he said.

"Good," she replied, tightening her grip on his arm. "First thing we need to do is figure out what this is supposed to do."

"It has to be connected to the light I saw," he replied.

"The question is *how*, Jack," she said, before biting her lower lip while staring into the darkness, thinking. The navigation lights cast an almost magical glow across her profile, narrowed hazel eyes glistening.

His emotional side overpowered all logic, making him wonder if he really wanted to go home.

Ever.

"What I don't get," Angela added, completely oblivious of the thoughts splitting through his common sense. "How can a little piece of glass like this with an embedded integrated circuit wreak such havoc on the laws of physics?"

"I know," he said, refocusing his thoughts. "But you said you knew someone who might be able to help?"

"I do," she said. "His name is Jonathan Layton, a professor of theoretical physics at FIT."

"How well do you know this guy?"

"Quite well, actually. He's in his late sixties and lost his wife to breast cancer two years ago. Very sweet old man, and very smart, too. Took me under his wing in the department when I first came in."

"Does Pete know you know him?"

"Yeah. Why?"

"Because I'm sure he's going to be under surveillance, so we're going to have to figure out a way to approach him without alerting any tails."

"How?" she asked.

"Not sure yet. Add that to the list of things we'll need to figure out," he said. "Starting with how Pete's playing this out."

"What do you mean?"

"I mean, how is he explaining all of this to his superiors? I don't think he simply told them I've come back from the dead . . . or from another dimension. But somehow he was able to gather up quite a few soldiers in no time, plus enlist the Coast Guard and probably even a few Air Force drones to track us down."

"Here's one way to find out," Angela said, reaching for the radio on the console, next to the instrumentation, and once more began to scan the Coast Guard frequencies.

"Good thinking," he said.

It didn't take longer than twenty minutes listening to conversations between Coast Guard personnel to start to paint a picture of their situation, which included her death at the hand of Al-Qaeda terrorists on American soil.

Angela sat back, fuming. "I can't fucking believe it."

"Sorry," he said.

"First he lied to me and tried to have us killed, then he blew up our house, and now the asshole's telling the whole world that I'm dead at the hands of terrorists." Crossing her arms, she stared into the distance while biting her lower lip.

He put an arm around her. "He'll get what's coming to him. Though I have to admit, the man's pretty smart."

She swung her head in his direction. "What?"

"Smart," he repeated. "By claiming this was a terrorist attack and having you killed in the process, he can now legally and quite easily freeze all of your assets, from bank accounts and credit cards to all of your investments and pension plans. That's his way to force you to the surface. It's a lot harder hiding out without funds."

"Is that supposed to make me feel better?"

"It's just how he's making his moves. Now we have to make ours."

"So you think he believes we survived the blast?"

"Probably. I mean, he knows my skills, and frankly stealing a boat while planting a remotely detonated blast in another is a cakewalk for me. I'm betting he believes you're alive and on the run with me, but he's having the whole world think you're dead via suicide bombers."

"That way he can get everybody to forget about me," she said, completing his thought.

"Right, and notice I haven't been mentioned in any of the reports, and there's also no mention of whatever he was able to recover from that OSS after the house exploded."

"Which could be quite a bit," she said.

"Maybe. But I saw it being peppered with bullets, and that was before the grenades detonated inside the house."

"Yeah, but I had packed it in the helmet, so even though it may have some bullet holes, the remaining ablation layer on the helmet would have gone a long way to protect it from the shockwaves and flames."

Jack hadn't considered that and nodded. "Well, in any case, now that Pete's got everybody looking away from us, he's free to deploy his own little soldiers and come after us again, though I get the feeling he'll be a little more covert this time around. I'm sure he wants to get his hands on you—and probably even me—so we can help him rebuild this technology, which is obviously very powerful and . . ."

Jack stopped, staring at the horizon, though his eyes weren't really looking at the sky's colors changing from black to indigo.

"What's the matter?" she asked.

"Oh, shit," he mumbled.

"What, Jack?"

"Hastings. I think I've just figured out what the son of a bitch is after."

They stared at each other in semidarkness.

"Dimension jumps," she said, her eyes widening. "That connects the observations we made at the house, from your strange fall through that storm to showing up at my doorstep five years after you died."

"Yep. That's also why Hastings appeared at the Cape and brought his gurus along to screw with the suit and incorporate whatever that piece of glass is."

She stared at him awhile and said, "Hastings has much larger plans than simply dropping down on his enemies around the globe with orbital jumpers, Jack."

"Exactly, but why use me for the first dimension jump? Was it because he wasn't sure if it would work?"

"Possibly," she said. "Maybe he needed a test run."

"Sure, but once I jumped and crossed over, I would be beyond his reach. If his intention was to send his own army of orbital jumpers to this Earth—for whatever reasons—then me being here ahead of his own team makes me a liability."

"Unless you were never supposed to make it," she offered.

"What do you mean?"

"The descent profile change. The one I . . . Angela in your world ultimately chose, Alpha-G, resulted in a convergence of the harmonic of twelve across all energy levels. Alpha-B wouldn't have accomplished such a unique alignment of energy conversions. You would have certainly reached the right altitude of one hundred and twenty thousand feet, but either the outside temperature, or the G-forces, or the vertical velocity would have been off."

Jack considered that while scanning the gauges, verifying heading and speed.

"But," he finally said, "the purple haze began well before I chose a descent profile. The portal was starting to get activated miles before I reached that energy alignment."

"And I think that's where this comes in," she said, holding the glass token. "Somehow—and believe me, I *will* figure it out—this little gadget, combined with the energy alignment of Alpha-G, did the trick."

"If that's the case, then why did Hastings plant this in my suit and then insist on Alpha-B? Did he just want me to get close enough to the dimensional jump to check his technology, but without actually doing it?"

"Maybe, but I don't have enough information to answer that," the scientist in her said. "But I believe I will after I get this into the right hands."

Jack rubbed the tips of his fingers against his sore chest and continued monitoring the gauges as the Tiara's hull fought the swells, putting more distance between them and the search vessels, buying them time to think, to theorize, to piece together how in the world he had managed to achieve what he was certain no other human being had ever done.

And as hues of orange and yellow-gold began to stain the indigo horizon—as Jack stared at his very first sunrise in this new world—his mind desperately clung to the hope that somewhere past the looming sun, somewhere beyond the span of time and space, his wife was also hard at work unraveling this mystery, applying all of her skills, her training, her experience—everything locked inside that brilliant mind of hers—to help him find a way back home.

Somehow.

Angela sipped an energy drink while staring at the clouds over central Florida from the back porch of Dr. Olivia Wiltz's home in Melbourne, which faced the woods leading to her old alma mater, the campus of the Florida Institute of Technology.

The first round with Olivia hadn't gone well. The woman was obviously scared out of her mind not just for her own safety, but for that of her daughter, Erika, and she had basically clammed up, demanding protection before releasing any information.

Problem was, Angela couldn't guarantee her own damned safety, much less that of this woman and her ten-year-old daughter.

But none of that changed the fact that she still needed answers, needed access to the information locked inside Olivia's head.

"How do you want to play this, Angie?" asked Dago as he stepped outside. She had left him keeping an eye on the Swiss scientist, along with Art-Z. And to keep a low profile, just as they had done at Pete's house, the rest of Dago's Paradise gang was back at a nearby motel.

She tilted her head and frowned.

"That lady looks pretty shaken up in there," he added.

"Still. I need to know what happened to Jack," Angela finally said. "And that pale skinny bitch knows *exactly* what went down during the jump."

"So," Dago asked, hands in front of him, palms facing up. "Again, how do you want to play this? She ain't gonna talk until her daughter's safe."

Angela turned away from him, biting her lower lip, a part of her wanting to go back inside the house and have Dago and his pals beat the crap out of Olivia until she talked.

But she couldn't bring herself to do that.

There had to be another way.

Angela looked up at the skies again, spotting a break in the thick coverage just above the horizon as the remnants of Claudette began to dissolve. She stared through the parting clouds at the early morning light shining beyond the sliver-like opening.

What would you do, Jack?

As the tip of the rising sun loomed through the widening gap, glowing down from the heavens, it suddenly came to her.

"Follow my lead," she said, making her decision and heading back inside, where Olivia sat alone in an armchair in the living room looking quite frail, her wrists and ankles bounded with zip ties to keep her from trying to run away.

Dago took a seat on the sofa next to her. Art-Z sat in the dining room doing what he did best: ignoring everyone while working on a laptop he had interfaced to Olivia's home computer and her tablet.

"You will not get away with this," Olivia warned, lifting her angered gaze, speaking in heavily accented English. "You do not know Hastings like I do. He will find you, and when he does—"

"Whatever he does to me won't be in the same league as what Riggs and his soldiers are going to do to you—*and* your daughter—after Hastings learns that you told us everything . . . that you betrayed him."

Dago shot her a puzzled stare. Even Art-Z looked up from his hacking to see where this was headed.

Olivia's thin and pale face twisted in obvious confusion. "Told you . . . ? What do you mean . . . I have not *told you* anything."

"That's the thing, Olivia," Angela said, slowly approaching her. "*You* know that, and *I* know that. But *Hastings* doesn't know that, does he?"

The Swiss scientist dropped her thick brows at Angela.

"See, Olivia, I already know about SkyLeap's production schedules and your glass particle accelerator. I know that you worked at CERN before transferring here to continue your collider experiments. I also know the location of your building."

She paused for effect, then added, "See my bearded friend over there?" She extended an index finger at Art-Z, who offered a half grin while waving once. "He already broke into SkyLeap through Hastings's phone, and we achieved that through a hack in your tablet."

"My . . . tablet?" Her eyes gravitated to her mobile system on the dining room table. "How . . . when?"

"Back at the Cape. When you and Salazar were granted access to our network, I took the opportunity to upload a little virus into your tablets. I figured that if you wanted to stick your little nose into my business, I should have the right to peek into yours. So sooner or later, the general's going to track this to you. And when he finally does . . ." Angela ran the tip of her thumb across her neck, just like she had seen Jack do for effect.

"Oh, my God," she said, dropping her gaze back to the floor.

"Olivia," Angela continued, "you look like a decent person trapped between a rock and a hard place. And I'm very sorry that you and your daughter ended up where you are. But I'm also in the same place now. My husband has vanished and I have a pretty good feeling that you know *exactly* what happened to him. The more I know, the easier it will be to expose Hastings, who I believe is working outside the purview of the government. But you need to help me, *now*. In return, I promise you my friends and I will do everything we can to help you and your daughter."

Slowly, Olivia lifted her bloodshot eyes and leveled them with Angela. "Swear to me that nothing will happen to Erika."

Angela filled her lungs and exhaled slowly, before saying, "I swear it."

Looking away, the Swiss scientist said, "Your husband . . . he is not dead. He is alive."

I knew it, Angela thought, relief washing her tired mind while looking at Dago.

"How, Olivia? How did it happen?"

Olivia opened her mouth just as glass broke behind them, from one of the large windows facing the backyard—an instant before blood erupted from her chest.

8

CONNECTING THE DOTS

You can't connect the dots looking forward; you can only connect them looking backward.

—Steve Jobs

He worked alone, aware that eventually he would have to bring others into this, perhaps even Hastings. But not yet.

Certainly not until he understood.

Sitting at a lab table on the second floor of a building that hadn't seen much use since the Pentagon shut down Project Phoenix, Pete inspected the suit he had found in Angela's house, comparing the design with the half-dozen versions he had retrieved from the storage room in the basement.

He stared at the outer shell, carefully going module by module, writing the differences in his tablet computer and complementing his notes with high-resolution photos taken with the same tablet. He photographed and jotted down all noticeable refinements from those early prototypes, from the improved helium boosters and the TDRSS antenna in the power boots to the latest-generation magnetic locks carefully stitched into the flexible insulation material to keep the jumper's legs together during reentry. He ran his index finger through the holes punched by the bullets, which actually allowed him to see the insulation and ventilation layers sandwiched beneath the quarter-inch-thick material.

He made a long list of observations, though everything so far continued to be polished versions of every component in those old OSS prototypes.

Pete moved on to the inner compartment of the outer shell, verifying the location of each module against the original design, from the suit's built-in batteries lining the top of the power boots to the electronics for communications, navigation, and finally, the OSS's black box, a matchbox-size recorder housed inside an inch-thick shell of reinforced carbon-carbon designed to survive a cat-astrophic event, like the jumper burning up on reentry.

"Hello, little one," he said, setting the black box aside before resuming his inspection, spending almost an hour on the long helmet, fascinated by its shape and its carefully packed electronics, making it the central command of the suit. At the time of the project's cancellation, the helmet had been in the drawing stage. All of Jack's jumps had used modified versions of prior NASA helmets, which were domelike in shape, not elongated, and certainly not housing this number of modular high-tech components.

He extracted them from their respective recesses along the inner section of the long tail, which unlike the front of the helmet, hadn't been damaged during the fusillade, before Pete could react and stop his soldiers from firing, ordering them to use stun grenades to flush Angela and Jack out of the house.

Again, he photographed everything and kept careful notes of the precise location of each module he removed, setting them on the large lab table with individual tags so that eventually, at the right time, his most-trusted scientists could perform a deeper analysis and reproduce this marvel of engineering.

Incredible, he thought, moving to the ablation shield layering the top section of the helmet, ignoring the bullet holes, remembering long meetings with Angela, Jack, and other scientists about the tradeoffs between a single thick thermal shield layer versus multiple thinner layers that would be ejected as they were consumed during reentry. His index finger reached the edge of the thermal protection section and felt the dozens of helium nozzles that would have ejected every spent layer.

So that's what we chose.

And he also noticed the blunt shape of the thermal protection shield, again remembering long discussions about the tradeoffs.

The more Pete inspected the suit, the more it brought him back to a happier time, to those glorious days of Project Phoenix, to Jack and Angela before Afghanistan, before the funeral and her resignation.

Before Hastings pulled him into his ranks, turning him slowly but steadily into his right-hand man, while also converting NASA into the general's very own agency to develop and deploy military satellites of every sort, from surveillance and communications to prototype lasers and plasma guns currently undergoing tests in orbit—plus the airship-to-orbit technology to deploy them all.

Pete looked into the distance, proud of this low-cost but highly efficient—and highly stealth—method of inserting classified equipment into orbit.

ATO, which was developed by a subcontractor in Orlando, took advantage of a conventional high-altitude balloon, which would lift a floating dock station and its payload up to forty-five kilometers above the ground in the middle of the night before a low-thrust rocket mounted on the dock station accelerated the payload horizontally to orbital velocity, reaching altitudes in excess of one hundred kilometers over a few days. And they had ATOs created for every size of payload, from small satellites to those who would have filled the old space shuttle's cargo compartment.

But in the process of creating and deploying Hastings's vision, Pete had to make choices, easy ones at first, minor lies to Congressional panels to secure funding, channeling tax dollars to secret projects—baby steps that strung together over a few years brought him right into the core of the general's world of deception and manipulation.

Damn, Jack, he thought, realizing how quickly and how far he had drifted from the straight and narrow after losing his best friend.

Jack's relentless conviction to always do the right thing no matter the cost had always been a strong positive influence on Pete that dated back to their teenage years growing up in Jersey, continuing as adults, even as they followed different paths after high school, but always finding a way to stay in touch, to align their vacations, holidays, to always find time for adventures, from rock climbing to skydiving.

But now his old friend was apparently back—at least some bizarre version of him—and his return also brought along disruption on other levels, from this amazing technology to his relationship with Angela.

He frowned, emotions broiling in his gut.

Just when he thought he had finally turned the corner and earned her love and trust—which had been easier to do since Angela no longer worked at NASA, allowing Pete to hide Hastings's dirty work—Jack had literally dropped out of the sky.

And for the second time in Pete's life, Jack had snatched her away.

Focus.

Pete moved to the suit's upper shell, starting with the breastplate, which was flexible and could be folded into four sections for easy stowage inside the helmet, and unlike the bottom section, it had miraculously escaped unscathed. He compared the designs, documenting all differences, though again, they were mostly refined versions from the vintage suits at the time the project was canceled.

An hour later, he sat back, frustrated.

Nothing in the suit told him—as far as he could tell—how Jack had achieved a dimensional jump.

Keep digging.

Rolling up his sleeves, Pete dove in again, spending another two hours scrubbing every square inch of the suit, inside and out, finally noticing an interesting difference he had missed the first time, and which he almost missed again had he not run a finger along a seam on the inside upper shell.

He lifted the corner of a Velcro cover about two inches square ingeniously disguised as a seam, removing it completely, exposing a round socket-like recess in the suit about the size of a quarter and about a half-inch thick.

What was in there?

He flipped the small cover and stared at its inner side, filmed with a purple substance, translucent, like a membrane.

Now that's new.

Pete looked again at the recess in the suit and back at the inside cover, noticing a circular mark matching the size and shape of the recess. Something was in there, and it somehow interfaced with—

He noticed a small black square on a corner of the small cover, and he got up and walked over to a nearby microscope, centering the membrane under a 50X lens and turning on a twelve-inch monitor next to the microscope.

The screen came on, displaying what looked like a grid embedded in the purple film. He panned around the surface, locating the tiny black square.

"A computer chip," he mumbled, noticing a pair of leads extending from one end of the chip, connecting it to the fine grid, which he now recognized as gold wires crisscrossing the membrane, in a way resembling an antenna of sorts.

He also located an optical connector on top of the chip, which he guessed would interface this antenna to the missing round module.

And he could think of only one place where that module could be.

He stood and looked back at the lab table, at the suit, realizing its possibilities, its potential if he could indeed find a way to not only get it operational but also reproduce it.

Don't get ahead of yourself, he thought, returning to the table, his eyes shifting to the reinforced carbon-carbon shell of the OSS's black box, where he hoped to find some answers.

But irrespective of what he learned from the transcripts of the conversation that took place between Mission Control and Jack, Pete knew that he would need not only Angela back but also the module he guessed she had taken from the suit before escaping the house.

Slowly, he walked to the windows overlooking Launch Complex 39, originally built for the Apollo program and later modified for the space shuttle.

Those had been NASA's glory days, when the agency led the way in technological innovation, when the best minds of the country competed for a chance at participating in the latest cutting-edge projects.

But budget cuts over the year had stripped the agency of its talent, of its punch, including the elimination of any vehicles capable of delivering astronauts to the International Space Station, forcing Americans to rely on fifty-year-old Russian Soyuz technology to reach orbit.

How far we have sunk, he thought, wondering if the technology in that suit could be a way back, the spark to reignite the dream that had been Project Phoenix, injecting new hope into an agency long hooked up to life support and forced to play Hastings's deception games just to get any semblance of substantial R&D funding.

But to achieve any of that, Pete needed the missing module back, along with Angela's brilliant mind and Jack's fearless nature.

He needed his former friends, and he made his decision to use every resource at his disposal to find them.

He had already frozen her accounts, narrowing her options, and he would follow that by planting tails with every possible person Angela would consider asking for help, starting with the last phone call she had made before shutting off her phone.

To Daniel Goodwin.

Dago.

Pete shook his head, remembering the oversized biker who never did warm up to the concept of Pete dating Angela.

He frowned, his mind focusing on the problem of finding his former friends, and doing so while keeping it from Hastings. If there was one thing he had learned from the general in the past few years, it was how to play the shell game when it came to funding, siphoning resources to special projects.

And the potential of this technology certainly qualified as the mother of all special projects.

Pete reached for his mobile phone and made a single phone call, in an instant channeling government funds to a selected list of private contractors—mercenaries—activating his covert plan to locate Jack and Angela.

He would find them and bring them in.

Wherever they were hiding.

At any cost.

He adjusted his buoyancy compensator device, or BCD, to maintain a depth of fifty feet, deeper than the standard SEAL underwater transit depth of just ten feet, but it was a clear day in very clear waters, and Jack didn't feel like being spotted from a surface vessel.

He held a course of two five zero, according to the navigation compass hugging his wrist, which he expected to take him within a thousand feet of his target by the coast of South Miami, two miles away, after adjusting for the Gulf Stream's strong northerly current.

The distance fell safely within the ninety-minute charge of the SeaDoo Sea-Scooter RS1, the bullet-shaped handheld scuba propulsion system he kept in front of him, droning at almost four miles per hour.

Although not nearly as sophisticated as the systems he had used in the SEALs, the SeaScooter provided an effective—and even relaxed—mode of underwater transportation, especially since Jack hadn't slept much in the past thirty-six hours.

But it felt good to be submerged again, especially in the waters off the Florida coast, warm enough not to need anything but the swimsuit Angela had found in the Tiara's main cabin.

SEALs belonged in this quiet world, among coral reefs and blue ocean, detached from the noisy and hectic surface and the dangers it presented.

Down here, Jack was his own ruler, hunted by none, respected by all sea crea-tures, even the pair of black-tip sharks he had seen swimming parallel to him five minutes ago, checking him out, probably attracted by the steady hum of the SeaScooter, before opting for easier prey.

Jack had thought about going deeper to make himself a harder target, but that meant taxing his compressed air supply more than necessary. Besides, he had his SOG knife strapped to his ankle for defense in case a shark decided to take a closer look.

Jack watched the black-tips vanish from view as he continued on his westerly course.

The decision to part ways with the comfortable Tiara had been easy, since Jack was convinced that by sunrise the yacht would be reported stolen, and its description passed on to the Coast Guard, which would probably search the area.

So after leaving Angela and their hardware—minus the scuba gear he would need to swim back—in the hands of a very shocked Dago, Jack had steered the Tiara out to sea and pointed it north, toward Fort Pierce, estimating that the remaining fuel in the tank would take the yacht close enough to the marina to hopefully fool the Coast Guard into thinking that the vessel might have gotten loose from its moor and drifted out to sea.

It was a stretch, especially with the empty gas tank, but at a minimum it would lessen the chance of anyone knowing where they had gone—assuming that anyone was still looking for them.

But the SEAL in him had no choice but to assume that his little blow-up stunt hadn't fooled Pete, since he was very aware of Jack's skills. And in the back of his head, Jack was still worried about the phone call Angela had made to Dago. If Pete was indeed going to any extreme to find them, he would have certainly searched her phone records by now. So Jack had Angela warn Dago about possible tails using a pay phone at the marina, and asked that he come alone and take a long route to make sure he wasn't being followed. He had waited for the biker to arrive in his truck, and after making sure he was free of any surveillance, Jack had sailed back out to sea and dumped the Tiara.

He continued along, listening to the bubbling sound of his own breathing mixed with the constant droning of the SeaScooter, trying to enjoy the feeling of weightlessness, especially since he wasn't encumbered by the bulky space suits he wore for years in NASA's training pools. This was much more reminiscent of his SEAL days, but without the bubbles. SEAL teams used closed-circuit rebreathers that absorbed the carbon dioxide of the user's exhaled breath, not only eliminating the bubbles that could signal their presence to the enemy on the surface, but also, as the name implied, rebreathing their exhaled air after carbon dioxide removal and injection of a small amount of oxygen into the mix.

He heard the distant sounds of propellers, probably a pleasure cruiser, though it would be difficult, if not impossible, to tell its direction. Sound traveled more efficiently in water than air, reaching his ears almost simultaneously, making it difficult to pinpoint the origin.

Jack looked up and around him, doing so more to keep busy than expecting to find the source since his visibility was limited to around a hundred feet.

Slowly, the ocean floor resolved beneath him as he approached the shore, mostly islands of reefs amid miles of sand. But at least he now had something to look at, including colorful fish, a variety of stingrays, and the occasional shark or barracuda, though the last two always kept their distance.

In another twenty minutes, his current depth met up with the ocean floor, and Jack continued along the bottom, skirting coral reefs for another ten minutes, until reaching a depth of thirty feet.

Time to go up.

Turning off the SeaScooter and letting it hang from the end of a lanyard, Jack inflated his BCD enough to rise to a depth of fifteen feet, his safety stop.

Over the next five minutes, he remained in place, allowing his body to release absorbed nitrogen. Although technically a safety stop wasn't required unless the diver went deeper than a hundred feet, it was always good practice after spending any time below thirty feet to eliminate the chance of decompression sickness.

He surfaced less than a couple hundred feet from the Biscayne National Park, where he swam the rest of the way, removing his fins, tank, and BCD when reaching shallow water by the narrow beach, where almost two hours earlier they had met Dago by the docks lining the entrance to the marina.

Jack was tired and sore as he stepped off the water and onto white sand, walking about a hundred feet to the parking lot, where Dago, still looking surprised as hell, waited for him next to Angela by a black pickup truck.

Angela ran to hug him.

"This is fucking surreal, Jack," Dago said in his tenor-like voice, dressed in black jeans, riding boots, and an open denim vest full of patches. "It's really great seeing you."

"Same here. Thanks for the help."

"Anything for you guys," he replied.

"No tails?" Jack asked, scanning the parking lot.

"Relax, honey," Angela said with a grin. "Besides, nobody fucks with bikers."

"Damn right," said Dago.

Jack sighed as the large biker, who stood almost six inches taller than Jack, helped him hoist his gear onto the bed, before Angela handed him a towel and his clothes. Jack walked over to the nearest outdoor shower stall and rinsed off the saltwater and sand, before walking into the restrooms, drying off, and changing.

He got in the backseat with Angela, the dark tinted glass concealing them while Dago drove, pretending to be alone.

"I was at your funeral, you know," Dago said, looking at them through the rearview mirror while Angela handed Jack his favorite pistol from the arsenal, a Sig Sauer P229 9mm semiautomatic, which he quickly checked, making sure he had a full magazine plus a chambered round before tucking it in the small of his back while glancing at the side mirror.

"I heard. Thanks."

"For what it's worth, I'm glad this little lady's back with you. Never could warm up to that Pete guy."

Angela sat sideways in the rear seat, facing Jack and slowly shook her head. "I'm never going to hear the end of that one."

"That's all right. He turned out to be an asshole anyway. At least on this Earth," Jack added, his eyes watching a white Mercedes-Benz SUV with tinted windows pull out of a parking spot at the edge of the large lot and turn behind them, keeping three cars in between.

They drove past the Homestead Air Reserve Base and reached the entrance to the turnpike, heading north.

The SUV continued to follow them.

"Speaking of assholes . . . we've got company," Jack said, looking through the tinted glass of the rear windshield.

"What?" Dago asked. "I even turned off my cell, like you asked. How can they have—"

"It doesn't matter how," Jack replied with more calm than he actually felt. "We need to lose them."

"You want me to call for help?" Dago offered.

"No," Jack replied. "The moment Angela called you, she compromised your cell phone. If you turn it on, it's just going to help them track us, even after we lose that tail."

"What do you need me to do, Jack?"

"Take us somewhere public . . . something with a big parking lot filled with cars," Jack said, thinking quickly. "Is there a mall nearby?"

"I know just the place," replied the large biker.

They continued on the turnpike for another ten minutes, before connecting to Dixie Highway and turning south until reaching 211th SW Street, which skirted the south end of the Southland Mall.

"They're still back there," Angela said.

"Good," Jack replied before instructing Dago to steer onto the mall's parking lot and continue down a row of parked vehicles close to the farther edge of the crowded lot.

Angela shot him a puzzled look.

The Mercedes slowly turned into the parking lot, keeping a respectful distance, which worked to his advantage.

"Go to the edge of the lot and turn right at the end of the row, as if you're coming back around the other side looking for a better parking spot, and slow down so I can jump off."

"Where are you going, Jack?" she asked.

"To communicate," he said, smiling, a hand on the door handle as they approached the corner.

"What?" asked Angela and Dago in unison.

"Trust me. This is what I do. They want to mess with us. I'm going to give it right back at them," he replied, opening the door the moment Dago turned the corner, momentarily losing sight of the SUV.

"Jack . . . please be careful."

"Relax, honey. I'll be right back."

Angela punched him lightly on the shoulder as Jack climbed out and closed the door almost seamlessly, watching the truck go by him as he hid behind a parked van.

The SUV approached the corner slowly, windows rolled up, hiding its passengers.

Jack dropped to a deep crouch while moving to the side of the van just as the SUV drove by, coming around while grabbing his SOG knife, fast-walking right up to the SUV's rear fender on the passenger side, banking that the driver and passengers would be more worried about keeping tabs on Dago's truck than checking their tail.

He was right.

The driver made no attempt to accelerate as Jack slashed the rear tire, the serrated edge slicing through the wall's soft rubber, followed by an explosion of air.

Jack pivoted while dropping back to a crouch behind the SUV, getting out of sight from all rearview mirrors while moving to the opposite side just as the brake lights came on, signaling the driver sensing trouble.

But it was too late.

Jack had already shifted the knife to his left hand, blade protruding from the top of his fist as he swung it hard into the wall of the second rear tire, which deflated with another burst of air, before quickly retreating to the safety of the van.

His SEAL mind quickly weighed the benefits of sticking around in the hope of capturing one of them alive as they got out versus running away, and he chose the latter, taking off in Dago's direction, catching up to the slow-moving truck halfway down the next row.

As he rushed off in a crouch, he heard the SUV doors open behind him, heard someone shout in a foreign language. It sounded . . . *German?*

The biker stopped the truck when spotting him, allowing Jack to climb back inside.

"Let's get the hell out of here before reinforcements arrive."

The truck leaped forward as Dago punched it and headed back to the highway.

"Jack," Angie said. "I'm so sorry. This is all my fault. I shouldn't have used my phone to—"

He put a finger to her lips and leaned forward, just inches from hers, before saying, "It's okay. You owe me one." He winked as she narrowed her gaze, before adding, "They've made us. Miami's no longer safe. We need a way out."

"I can get you—" Dago began.

"No," Jack said. "Thanks, Dago, but you're just as compromised as Angie and me. And anyone you contact will also become a target. Those were contractors back there."

"Contractors?" asked Angela.

"Mercenaries. There's a large international community of very sophisticated bounty hunters that government agencies can activate at the push of a button to do their dirty work and bring wanted individuals into custody, and do so very, very quietly. Discretion is just as critical as delivering results. SEALs use them from time to time in various theaters to gather intelligence on HVTs."

"High-value targets," Angela said.

He nodded.

"Those guys back there were Germans. Pete must have activated them."

"So we're HVTs now?" she asked.

"Correct."

"So, what are you thinking, Jack?"

"We need to get that glass token into the right hands, and to do that we need clean transportation," he replied, staring into her hazel eyes.

"And," he continued, "I know how to get it."

9

SURPRISE

Always mystify, mislead, and surprise the enemy if possible.
—Stonewall Jackson

Everything happened very fast.

Angela and Dago instinctively dropped to the floor as another silent round broke through, bursting through the sofa where Dago had sat a moment before.

"Art! Down!" she screamed at the hacker, who started typing very fast while trying to duck under the table.

A round punched the laptop's screen, embedding itself in the wall behind him, providing the required encouragement for the hacker, who dropped to the floor, pulling down the hardware with him.

"Passcodes . . . my phone," Olivia hissed as Angela dragged her feet first from the chair.

"Passcodes in your phone," Angela repeated as another round buzzed over-head, piercing a hole into the sofa chair. "Got it. What else can you tell us?"

"Daughter . . . please . . ."

"You have my word, Olivia. We'll keep her safe."

"She . . . has . . . nobody . . ."

"I'll look after her, Olivia. Do you hear me? I'll take care of Erika."

The scientist managed a brief smile before starting to go into shock, her limbs trembling as she began to convulse, coughing blood into Angela's face.

She wiped it off with a hand while lifting Olivia's head with the other. "Tell me where, Olivia. Where is my husband?"

"Leaped . . . he . . . leaped."

"*Leaped?* Leaped *where?*"

"Passcodes . . . daughter," she repeated before her eyes shifted toward her small purse still on the chair. She opened her mouth again but only made guttural, raspy sounds as Dago put a hand on her shoulder.

"Angela, we've got to get out of here."

More rounds cracked windows, exploding plasterboard, splintering wood.

"Where is he, Olivia?" Angela demanded, ignoring him—ignoring everything while grabbing the woman by the lapels, shaking her. "Where the hell is my husband?"

Olivia's lips trembled, blood coming out of her mouth, her nostrils.

"Tell me!"

"She's gone, Angela!" shouted Dago, trying to pull her away. "She's gone!"

Angela stared into her lifeless eyes, anger boiling up inside her. She had been so damn close to finding out the truth.

"Now, Angela!" Dago shouted again. "We need to get out of here!"

She finally let go, before turning to Dago.

"Time to hit the road, Bonnie," Art-Z said, crawling to them, dragging his backpack as more rounds buzzed inches above their heads.

"Damn right," said Dago.

Something snapped inside of Angela, and she grabbed Olivia's purse before clambering toward the garage with them, getting out of sight from the rear windows, from the immediate threat.

Dago surged to his feet, pulling Angela and Art-Z up with ease, before scrambling into the two-car garage monopolized by a large Harley, her Triumph, and a scooter.

"Don't even *think* about getting on that fucking thing," Dago warned Art-Z while Angela donned her helmet and got on her bike.

"Hop on behind me, hacker," Dago added, extending a thumb over his left shoulder to the small passenger seat on the back of his large bike.

Art-Z stared at his scooter, looking like a toy next to the Harley, which rumbled into life, and quickly obeyed.

They climbed onto the bikes, their engines deafening inside the closed garage until the door finally lifted, sliding overhead, revealing Olivia's parked car.

They sprung ahead, reaching the street, spotting two figures running down the sidewalk in their direction from their far right, almost a block away, shouting something she couldn't make out.

Angela squinted, trying to see who they were, for a moment thinking that one of them looked a lot like Captain Riggs holding a gun.

Deciding not to hang around long enough to find out, they pointed their bikes in the opposite direction, burning rubber as they accelerated, working gears and throttle, increasing the gap, drowning their shouts, though she could have sworn she'd heard her name.

But it really didn't matter.

She wasn't about to turn around, not after what they had done to Olivia— what they almost did to them.

Three armed men emerged in between two homes as she accelerated, one of them wielding a massive rifle.

The trio started to train their guns at her when fire erupted down the street, behind her.

Her back itching in anticipation of a bullet, Angela opened the throttle fully in between gear shifts, watching the three gunmen fall to the ground as she reached sixty in four seconds, shooting ahead of Dago and Art-Z.

What was that?

Did Riggs just protect us?

But she didn't look back, focused on the road, past the men bleeding on the sidewalk, shooting ahead as houses and parked vehicles blurred by, the sound of her engine and the whistling wind drowning everything, her anger, her pain, her anxiety, her confusion—her overwhelming desire to do everything in her power to bring down Hastings and his circle of murderers.

But Jack was alive.

Olivia had confirmed her suspicions, her scientific deductions—her instincts.

Jack was somewhere . . . *leaped* was the word she had used, before Hastings's guns silenced her.

She frowned inside her helmet.

What the hell does leap *mean?*

But she had Olivia's purse and her phone, which Art-Z and Angela would be able to dissect, to pick apart and maybe, just maybe, peel the next layer of this complex technical onion, of this mystery that had apparently begun well before Jack jumped from that pod, before he vanished in the upper layers of the atmosphere.

She downshifted, also remembering the promise she had made to a dying mother, popping the clutch and hitting the brakes when reaching the next intersection, leaning into the turn, steering the Bonneville to the right.

Olivia was the enemy, but not by choice. She had been coerced by Hastings in the most inhuman way, threatening her child, whom she was willing to die to protect.

Angela now needed to find a way—and pretty damn quick—to get to Erika before Hastings's people.

Dago followed close behind, catching up to her after the turn, Art-Z's arms wrapped tightly around the biker's waist, the side of his face pressed against the denim vest, eyes shut.

The sight, combined with the knowledge that Jack was alive, plus the adrenaline rush from the near miss, almost made her laugh.

Shaking her head, she throttled the engine again, the toe of her riding boot working the gears, kicking up speed as they accelerated toward the highway, away from the threat, from whoever was back there, checking her rearview mirrors, confirming that no one was following them.

Angela turned onto the entrance ramp for IH-95 with Dago and Art-Z in tow, looking straight ahead through the tinted visor, contemplating her next move, her future.

A future that for the first time since the monitors went black at Mission Control and all hell broke loose, she knew would include Jack.

Whom she missed terribly and desperately hoped—even prayed—was somewhere out there trying like crazy to find a way back to her.

Some things have to be done very carefully.

In the SEALs, Jack had learned that the success of a mission depended not only on painstaking preparations but also on improvisation, on creativity, requiring thinking out of the box to get the job done, especially when things didn't go according to those carefully crafted plans.

Today, as he broke into a weathered Ford truck parked on a tree-lined street nestled among the large free parking lots a mile from Homestead Air Reserve base, he realized that success would require far more finesse than he had originally thought.

The escape from Angela's house, the diversion of destroying *Dark & Stormy*, even the stealing of a yacht and going through the extreme of taking it out to sea and sending it back north before diving back to shore, hadn't been enough to elude the manhunt that Pete had activated.

For better or for worse, there was now a price on their heads, and Jack's inner voice told him that the standing order was to capture them alive. Otherwise he was pretty damn sure those German contractors would have terminated them in the marina parking lot, while Jack was still trying to get his bearings after the long dive.

But they didn't.

Instead, the mercenaries had followed them, biding their time, waiting for the right opportunity to spring into action, perhaps even holding back until reinforcements arrived.

Jack needed to break the link, sever the connections created by the phone call that Angela had made, triggering the chain of events that had led him to crawling under the dash of the old pickup truck while Angela and Dago kept watch.

The cabin smelled of tobacco and fried food, reminding Jack of Palmer's rig.

He had thought about calling the conspiracy theorist, whom Jack felt wouldn't have hesitated to lend a helping hand—if anything to be a part of a real conspiracy.

But he had decided to keep it simple for now, opting for a clean getaway vehicle, which he had searched for nearly an hour in this parking area, looking for the right automobile: old but not too old, easy to steal, large enough for their gear, under the cover of trees in case of overhead surveillance—and most of all, one that gave the impression it had been parked there awhile, signaling that the owner might be away. The latter had not been that hard given that this particular parking area was used primarily by personnel being deployed overseas, mostly single Army grunts.

This time around, Jack was determined to leave nothing to chance. They needed time to get away from Miami and find a safe place to regroup, to reassess, to start thinking offensively—plus Jack just needed a good night's sleep. He had been awake for more than forty-eight hours, and although his SEAL training had conditioned him to operate up to seventy-two hours without sleep, Jack wasn't that young SEAL anymore. He was topping forty and his body was on the edge of mutiny.

He pushed those thoughts aside, locating the right wires under the dash, bypassing the ignition, engaging the starter, which slowly—almost painfully—turned the engine for nearly ten seconds while he held his breath.

It finally coughed into life with a rough idle and a burst of dark smoke out of the exhaust, signaling the need for a tune-up.

This one's been sitting here awhile, he thought, checking the gauges, glad to see the gas needle pointing at the half mark.

"Time to go," he said, crawling out before he gave Dago clear instructions, which included the use of their new disposable phones to stay in touch, while Angela transferred the gear to their new ride.

A minute later they parted ways with the biker, driving up the ramp of the Florida Turnpike, heading north.

Angela slid over the long bench seat, shoulder-to-shoulder with Jack, who placed an arm around her while resting the other over the wheel as they made their way through downtown Miami, constantly checking the mirrors, making sure they were alone.

He started to relax after fifteen minutes, growing certain that they had made a clean getaway, inhaling deeply, pressing her against his side. In spite of his over-taxed body and his semi-altered state of mind, it felt great to be with her, just like the old days.

"How are you holding up?" he asked her.

"I was just about to ask you the same question," she said. "You're the one who's been abused."

He managed a short laugh, though his sternum and ribs still hurt from the gunshots absorbed by the battle dress. "I'll survive," he finally replied.

"Good," she said. "What about Dago? Will he be all right?"

"As long as he sticks to the plan," he said.

"How about us?"

"We need to stick to our plan, too."

"Which includes finding you a way back home," she said, pressing herself against his side to the point that his ribs started protesting.

Jack winced in pain but said nothing. He just hugged her tight, emotion making it difficult to come to terms with the reality of their situation. But logic couldn't justify anything but finding the quickest way back, especially after suspecting Hastings's intentions to use the OSS for dimensional jumps. And that not only meant parting ways with this amazing version of Angela but also overcoming of myriad technical challenges, starting with making a new suit—at least another outer shell.

They drove in silence, getting out of the Miami area and continuing north through Fort Lauderdale and Boca Raton. Somewhere along the way Angela fell asleep in his arms, and he slowly set her head down on his right thigh, which she used as a pillow, laying sideways on the bench seat, breathing heavily but steady, mumbling something Jack couldn't make out.

For the next two hours, he listened to local news on the radio to force his mind to remain frosty but also to check if either Angela or he had suddenly made the headlines.

But after the first hour, it became evident that Pete was planning to carry out this manhunt covertly.

Which is fine by me, he thought, scanning his surroundings, driving right under the speed limit, making sure no one was following them. Along the way he discovered new differences between this world and the one he'd left at the launch-pad. Pontiac Motor Corporation was still in business, horse racing was outlawed years ago, and there was no such thing as North or South Korea. In this reality, MacArthur had apparently won that controversial war.

Jack shook his head, glad at least that World War II had still resulted in the defeat of Adolf Hitler and that the Soviet Union had also been dissolved after the fall of the Berlin Wall. ·

He continued driving, trying to put as much distance as possible from the last surveillance contact, continuing on the turnpike, driving through Fort Pierce, making it as far north as Vero Beach before the gas needle dropped dangerously close to empty.

He exited the highway, paid his toll in cash, and pulled up into the nearest gas station, stopping by a pump near the station's convenience store, where he prepaid for a full tank in cash before also grabbing some drinks, snacks, and toiletries.

Angela slept through, and Jack lacked the energy to drive. It was just past noon, and he needed some sleep, so instead of returning to the turnpike, he drove down a strip of motels, selecting one where he could park in the rear, out of sight from the road and also in front of their room.

He paid an old lady at the front desk in cash for one night and drove the truck around the two-story building, finding a spot in the shadows.

Leaving Angela in the front seat, he hauled their gear into the room, which had a faint smell of disinfectant but otherwise seemed fine. Returning to the truck, Jack picked Angela up gently and carried her into the room, setting her down on one of the double beds before closing the door and drawing the curtains, darkening the room.

Daylight glowing through the inch-long gap between the edges of the curtains and the wall, Jack sat on the other bed and stared at the still figure for a moment, trying to decide if it would be appropriate for him to join her.

She isn't your wife, Jack.

But then again, she *was*, even down to the gift for deep sleep. Once his Angela closed her eyes, nothing short of a five-alarm fire could wake her up. And it was obvious by now that this Angela had the same knack for uninterrupted sleep, for deep periods of rest.

Rest is a weapon.

Jack slowly inhaled, remembering yet another lesson from his SEAL days. Rest was a weapon as powerful as his arsenal by the foot of the bed. Rest would make him sharper, enhancing his skills, clearing his mind, allowing him to think through options, to anticipate the enemy, to find a way to get back and stop Hastings's plans.

Giving Angela another glance, and keeping his Sig Sauer within reach on the nightstand between the beds, Jack decided to be respectful and stay on his side of the room, resting his head on the soft pillow and closing his eyes.

But sleep didn't come easy. He tossed and turned, his mind still challenging this reality, trying to catch up to the radical events of the past two days, and wondering what the next forty-eight hours would bring—assuming he lived that long.

Part of his SEAL training included being truthful about assessing situations, and at the moment, with barely a few thousand dollars in cash, the odds were overwhelmingly against him.

Just like in Colombia, he thought, deciding to take it one step at a time, to focus on the next battle, on the next challenge, like he had done in that jungle a long time ago.

For the moment, he felt they were safe, buying them time to plan their next move: getting technical answers from FIT professor Jonathan Layton.

Based on what they learned, Jack and Angela would decide their next move, including finding a way to build a new suit.

But even if she builds a new suit, how are you getting to orbit, Jack?

One step at a time, man. One step at a time.

And the next step for him was sleep. He couldn't go on without it. In fact, he wouldn't just be useless if he didn't manage at least a few hours of REM sleep—he would be dangerous. He would get careless, missing clues, reacting slowly, and risking Angela getting hurt.

And so he forced it, just as he had been taught, laying perfectly still, emptying his mind from all thoughts, and keeping his eyes closed while rolling them softly to the back of his head.

Before he knew it he was back in Colombia, back in the jungle, Bennett on his shoulders, his team vaporized by the massive booby trap that had also stripped the militia's momentum.

But soon he noticed that Bennett stopped moaning, stopped making any noise.

Jack stopped, dropping to his knees, laying his commander on the soft jungle floor, glaring at his lifeless eyes staring at the canopy overhead.

Jack knew it would be futile, but he still had to try.

So he carried him to the edge of a cliff overlooking a massive river a hundred feet below, and after mumbling a few words of respect, he threw Bennett over the edge, watching him fall into the raging waters and vanish from sight.

Jack moved on, returning to his planned escape route, racing across thick jungle, reaching a shallow ravine, splashing through ankle-deep water, climbing the opposite hill, parting branches and vines as he pushed his way through thick foliage, through razor-sharp palmettos, using his compass and knowledge of a terrain he had long committed to memory.

GPS receivers didn't work well under the double and even triple canopy of the Colombian rain forest. But sunlight did make it through in spots, forking through narrow openings, creating islands of bright sunlight surrounded by darkness, marking the start of a new day for Jack. He had survived the night, had managed to avoid capture by an enemy he had deceived and also angered, an enemy that continued its relentless chase, constantly trying to flank him, to cut off his retreat. But he persisted, using his SOG knife to silently remove any obstacle that stood in his way, losing count of how many he had killed, how many throats he had quietly slit, like a predator, surprising his victims, striking fast and retreating even faster, ignoring the shouts of anger after each body was discovered by seasoned warriors that had made the cardinal mistake of assuming superiority in numbers while operating in dense jungle.

Jack pushed ahead, step by step, finally reaching the extraction point, where help arrived shortly thereafter, holding back the militia with massive cover fire as he held on to the harness, to his lifeline with all his might, rising from the jungle, from a mission that had gone bad due to malfunctioning equipment, resulting in so many deaths . . .

He opened his eyes and took a deep breath, staring at the ceiling, checking his watch, realizing he had been asleep for almost four hours. He tried to sit up but a hand pressed down on his chest.

Gently.

"What are you doing in this bed, Jack?" she asked in the twilight of the room, kneeling next to him, her face inches away, the chocolate freckle dancing over her lips as she smiled.

He didn't know what to say.

Angela stood and pulled the halter over her head.

He tried to sit up again, but she pressed the tips of her fingers against his sternum, delicately, bringing her hand to his neck, his face, index finger tracing his chin, his lips.

Taking charge, Angela unbuttoned his jeans, sliding them off and then removing her own, walking out of them. She took his hands and placed them on her breasts before leaning down to kiss him.

It didn't take Jack long, and she smiled, tapping his nose with a finger before mounting him, guiding him slowly.

Angela moved her hips, descending on him while biting her lower lip, leaning back, then forward, then back again, hands tight on his shoulders.

Jack closed his eyes, letting it all go, forgetting about soldiers, mercenaries, and dimensional jumps as she moved faster, with increased intensity.

Until he gasped, then shuddered, before inhaling deeply, dropping his arms to his sides, opening his eyes, watching her face hovering inches from his, still biting her lower lip, hips moving slowly now, finishing.

They remained like that for a minute, perhaps more, until Angela finally collapsed on his chest, heaving, breathing through her mouth, her skin moist with perspiration, her head tucked under his chin, her breath on his neck.

They embraced for a long time, holding each other tight, something Jack had missed for so damn long, to the point of almost being afraid to let her go, running his hands up and down her back, remembering what it was like to be intimate with her.

"Your heart, Jack," she said, right ear pressed against his pectorals. "I used to love listening to it afterward."

His wife had never done that, and the comment reminded him that he had just cheated on Angela *with* Angela—if that was actually possible.

Slowly, they rolled onto their sides, facing each other, kissing some more, stretching the aftermath.

"Thank you for letting me have you, Jack," she said.

And once more Jack had no clue what to say.

Before he could think of a reply, she kissed him and then added, "And now it's my turn to help you."

"Help me?" he asked, his mind still foggy, but certainly concluding that she had just helped him plenty.

"Yes," she said. "Help you . . . get back home."

10

REVELATIONS

And you shall know the truth, and the truth shall set you free.
—John 8:32

They sat alone in the hotel room waiting for his handler.

Riggs—though that wasn't his real name—had already made the call, using a disposable phone, per protocol, signaling the need for field extraction for both of them.

The call to break cover had been difficult for the deep undercover agent, who'd spent almost three years under Hastings's rule, trying to gather evidence while working his way to become head of the general's private guard.

But Hastings had already warned him once, after letting Angela escape.

And as he had told Pete in that VIP office, *The General never warns you twice.*

Riggs's promotion, Pete had learned later—after escaping together to alert Angela of the team headed for Dr. Wiltz's house—had come at the cost of the removal of his predecessor when he had managed to disappoint Hastings twice.

"And Hastings made me . . . kill the guy," he told Pete, sitting in a reclining chair. "While I was videotaped."

Pete made a face. "He *taped* you killing someone?"

Riggs nodded. "That's the ultimate test of loyalty. After that, he pretty much owns you. And there were others I also had to . . . before I could earn enough of his trust."

"That's . . . insane," Pete said.

The large agent, who still looked as if he was genetically engineered, turned his chiseled face away from him, blue eyes staring into the distance.

"Well, it might be crazy, but it's straight out of the teachings from Hitler's *Mein Kampf* and Sun Tzu's *Art of War.* Hastings is the ultimate paranoid and has the goods on every single individual under his command, from his militia to his scientists and *especially* his politicians. And he has his own internal Gestapo-like team spying on everyone to enforce compliance."

He paused, crossing his legs, staring at his hands as he flexed them into fists before adding, "His reach is deep, Pete. Very deep. Built slowly, methodically, over many, many years. There's even word he's planted his own people in the FBI, the CIA, and the NSA. Besides owning half of the Pentagon, the rumor is that Hastings also owns people in Congress, the Department of Justice, and even the White House. That's why the man's remained in power for almost two decades, administration after administration. He's literally untouchable."

Pete shook his head, having a difficult time believing a conspiracy of this magnitude.

"What's he after with Project Phoenix?"

Riggs shook his head. "That's the thing. Only Hastings knows the big picture. After three years in his operation, all I can tell you is that the general has managed to pull together quite the team of experts to develop unheard-of technology that he believes will give him an unprecedented advantage. I heard him once comment to someone he owns in the U.S. Senate that he would eventually have the power that Adolf Hitler would have had if his own scientists could have produced nuclear ballistic missiles in 1942."

Pete just stared back at him.

"But I know little beyond that. Again, the man's very careful and trusts no one but himself."

"What really happened to Jack?"

"Like I told you," he said. "I was as surprised in that Mission Control room as you and Dr. Taylor."

"So no theories? Nothing to give you even an idea after *three* years with the man?"

"You're starting to get the picture," he said, shrugging.

"Incredible. And you are—well, *were*—Hastings's right-hand man."

Riggs managed a half laugh. "Not even close. I was just the chief of his pit bulls, and very easily replaced, like most people in his operation. Now, Dr. Wiltz, she was a top asset, and Hastings didn't even hesitate to eliminate her. That's why I had to break cover. I have a wife and a young son I haven't seen in three years. They went in protected custody the moment I made the call. They're out of his reach, and soon we will be, too."

"But don't you have enough evidence to take him down? You're a material witness."

"Again, not even close. He has far more evidence on me than I have on him. All he has to do is release one of the videos, and I would be discredited from any courtroom."

"But you were deep undercover," Pete said. "You had to—"

Riggs shook his head. "That's not how it works. We always knew that any firsthand account would be useless because it would not only be segregated, removed from the mainstream because of my limited role. And we also knew about his use of videos to quickly incriminate anyone who betrayed him."

"So what were you trying to accomplish?"

"My mission was to dig up evidence beyond my own experience, perhaps finding bank accounts, maybe proof of misappropriation of tax dollars."

Pete shook his head. "The man orders people killed for a living, like Dr. Wiltz and Angela, and the FBI was trying to get him on some sort of embezzlement charge?"

Riggs was starting to get visibly annoyed. After a heavy sigh, he said, "He operates like a mafia boss, with a lot of buffers between him and the crimes he commits, plus he owns those who commit the crimes. The concept was to bring him down like Al Capone, who also couldn't be touched for murder, finally taking him down on tax evasion charges."

"So, how do you get useful information?"

"By getting to people like Dr. Wiltz before Hastings could silence her. The problem is that the FBI used that approach before, trying to turn his best people into informants, and it resulted in suicides because he had their families under surveillance. Most people with their families on the line would rather take their own lives than risk a dead son, or daughter, or wife."

"Damn," Pete said, slowly processing this amazing revelation. "Maybe Angela was able to dig up something before Hastings attacked the house?"

Riggs raised his eyebrows. "That's a possibility. She seems to be quite . . . resourceful."

"Yeah, and you should meet her husband."

Riggs almost laughed. "We did, briefly. I loved the way he told off the general. Doesn't happen often, and those who dare don't tend to live long."

"Well," Pete said, "speaking of living long, the only way I see my friends and I surviving this, and also you and your family, is to bet that Angela discovered something in that house."

Riggs narrowed his gaze at him.

Pete leaned forward, forearms on his thighs. "Do you know anyone who has gone against Hastings and lived long enough to talk about it?"

The FBI agent considered that for a moment.

"That's what I thought. Now, let me ask you this: do you really think that your family will be safe in the long run under protected custody? You just told me that Hastings may have moles inside the Bureau."

Riggs remained quiet awhile, before mumbling, "What do you think she may have discovered?"

"I have no idea, but it doesn't really matter for us. We just need to find a way to help her. Angela has a gift, Riggs—a gift for solving complex problems, and believe me, this one is as complex as they come. But she needs time and data."

"Time and data?"

"That's right. She needs access to data, to information, and also the time to process it like a scientist. In order to enable her, we need to provide her with the access she needs and with enough elbow room to analyze the information she collects."

The FBI agent locked eyes with him before asking, "All right, what do you have in mind?"

He listened to it three times while taking notes, stopping and rewinding the recording at several key spots, replaying them again and again, until he got a good grasp of the jump, leaving no doubt in his mind that something pretty unusual had taken place.

Starting with listening to his own voice.

That was Pete Flaherty all right.

It was . . . me.

He sat back, staring at the system interfaced to the OSS's black box, which he had set up in a room adjacent to the lab where he had dissected the suit.

Pete felt a bit amazed that this very special technology had literally fallen from the skies right into his lap. And the realization only served to reinforce his initial decision to keep Hastings out of it.

Listening to the way Hastings had tried to butt in, just as Jack was about to jump from the pod—and apparently going against Angela's instructions—only helped confirm his concerns that the general would have been all over this one, perhaps to the extent of taking it over completely, like he had apparently done in Jack's world.

And besides, what value did Hastings bring?

More guns? Pete had close to a hundred mercenaries in his payroll scrubbing the state of Florida, and that was on top of over a hundred of his own men patrolling just about every road between Miami and the Cape.

More surveillance? Pete remained in direct contact with the Department of Homeland Security, who had allocated the use of three Predator teams, each consisting of four Predator UAVs with their own crews, feeding all of the data to Commander Heather Vickers at the POC in Patrick Air Force Base, who sent him hourly updates.

More intelligence? Pete had certainly learned a few tricks from Hastings over the past five years, and he not only owned people in the CIA, the NSA, and even the FBI, but had also planted his own informants in the heart of the Pentagon, very close to Hastings.

More scientists? Pete currently managed over five hundred of the best scientific minds of the time—and all loyal to him.

More money? He couldn't help but laugh at that one. The budget allocated to NASA this year alone, after all of the shell games he and Hastings played with the Pentagon's vast budget, was large enough to hide one more project among the dozens of secret developments underway.

He shook his head.

All Hastings would bring to this party would be his gigantic ego, his arrogance.

No upside but plenty of downside, he thought.

And besides, Pete had gotten word via his own moles inside the Pentagon about Hastings's secret visits to an oncologist in recent weeks. A little more probing on the results of a biopsy had yielded renal cell carcinoma. The general had cancer in his kidneys. Although it was apparently treatable, and someone with

Hastings's resources would have easy access to transplants, it still meant he wouldn't be operating at full capacity for a while.

Perhaps this is what he wants to talk to me about, he thought, remembering his conversation with Hastings yesterday.

In any case, Pete decided to continue holding this one very close to his chest, only allowing his chief scientist—someone Pete owned—to inspect not just the entire suit but also that intriguing membrane-like patch.

And speaking of that...

He walked next door, past the soldiers he had posted to protect his secret, and stepped inside the spacious lab, where the OSS was still disassembled over three lab tables.

An elderly woman with white hair pulled into a tight bun and wearing a lab coat and wire-rimmed glasses worked on a tablet computer interfaced to a large microscope.

Dr. Gayle Horton, former scientist at Rockwell during the space shuttle era before joining NASA after the program was canceled and the high-tech giant conducted massive layoffs, looked up from her screen.

"Where did you find this, Pete?" she asked, pointing at the membrane secured to the microscope's stage, under a massive 1000X lens.

"You wouldn't believe me if I told you," he replied. "What is it?"

"A very efficient antenna . . . and I think it's designed to capture energy, radiation. In the upper layers of the atmosphere, a lot of that energy is in the form of gamma rays from solar activity."

"So, it's a spectrometer?"

"Not exactly."

"Why?"

"Because of its strange composition."

"What's it made of?"

"That's the thing. I'm not entirely sure. Most modern gamma ray detectors use germanium, a semiconductor with the best properties known to date for capturing gamma rays, which basically excite the crystal lattice in the semiconductor, dislodging electrons in the outer layers, triggering conductivity of tiny amounts of electricity. This forms the basis for the spectrometers that we typically use to study solar flare activity. This material, however, is . . . different."

"Did you run a spectrum analysis?" he asked, referring to the industry-

standard technique to identify the periodic table elements making up any compound.

"I did," Gayle said, "and that's what so strange about it." She ran a finger
across her tablet and pulled up the results from a mass spectrometry analysis,
which looked like a chart. The vertical axis showed the relative abundance of
a given element while the horizontal axis listed all known elements in the
periodic table.

"See," she said, pointing at the peak for Ge, or germanium, which had the
highest presence detected in the membrane. "This material is based on germanium, but that's where the similarities end compared to modern solar detectors.
There are five more peaks."

She pointed to the right side of the chart at five more elements, with the symbols Fe for iron, Mg for magnesium, Ti for titanium, O for oxygen, and OTH.

"What's that last one?"

"Stands for *other*, meaning we don't know what it is yet. But we'll get to that
later. What's very interesting at the moment is that aside from germanium, the
known elements in these relative abundance levels—and I need to perform a more
thorough analysis to be sure—are the ones that make up armalcolite."

Pete frowned. "Armalcolite . . . that's a type of moon rock."

"Right," she said, "along with tranquillityite and pyroxferroite. All three were
first brought to Earth by the Apollo Eleven crew, and larger quantities later by
the rest of the Apollo missions."

Pete nodded. "Armalcolite was named after the Apollo Eleven astronauts,
*Arm*strong, *Al*drin, and *Col*lins."

"Correct. And it was later created synthetically on Earth. Moon armalcolite
is typically an opaque mass that appears reddish to purple in reflection. The
synthetic version is grayish. This membrane is more on the purple end of the
spectrum, which suggests a moon origin."

"But it's translucent."

Gayle removed her glasses and rubbed her eyes. "Yes, we still need to understand that difference. It may have to do with the germanium and whatever that
other element is. But what's *very* interesting is this. . . ."

Gayle removed the membrane from the microscope's stage and placed it on
the lab table before taking an LED flashlight and pointing its beam perpendic-
ular to its surface.

The membrane came alive, trembling with what looked like miniature sheet lightning crisscrossing its surface as a purple halo materialized around it.

"What the hell's *that?*" he asked.

"*That* . . . is physically impossible . . . at least with the laws of physics in the world of classical mechanics. I just bombarded its surface with a very small amount of UV radiation contained in this LED beam and the reaction, which I was able to measure using a traditional spectrometer, was several orders of magnitude larger."

"Meaning . . . ?"

"Meaning it gives out far more energy than it receives," she said.

"But—"

"This is beyond our traditional laws of physics, Pete. The only other form of reaction that comes close to yielding this amount of energy is in nuclear fission, the basis of nuclear reactors used to generate electricity."

"But this isn't that."

"No. It's not, but the energy yield is in the same class. Now, I think there's a limit to how much energy this little membrane can give out when excited by light. And like in a nuclear reactor, at some point its stored energy will be spent."

"Like the rods in a nuclear plant?"

"Yes. A kilogram of uranium-235, for example, will yield about three million times more energy than a kilogram of coal, but eventually, just like the coal, it will have to be replaced with fresh material. I think this membrane operates in the same way. It's a very sophisticated energy source. You saw what it just did when excited by a very small amount of energy. Imagine what it can do up in space, beyond the atmospheric shield, exposed directly to the UV and gamma radiation of the sun's energy."

Pete sat next to Gayle and crossed his arms, trying to piece this together.

"But the suit has its own independent battery packs to power its systems," he finally said. "This isn't connected to any of that."

"Correct. The energy is channeled directly into something else, perhaps whatever round device you indicated was missing. And whatever that is, it can handle the energy that this generator puts out, which, as I've said, can be quite significant, depending on the level of external excitation. But I need more time."

"How much longer?"

Gayle slowly shook her head. "Pete . . . I'm not sure you understand the significance of this . . . discovery."

He wasn't sure how to respond to that.

"Look. There are inflection points in science, moments when a new discovery threatens to obsolete prior technologies, even established infrastructures. The electric bulb killing the gaslight industry. Internal combustion destroying the steam engine industry. Digital photography taking down Polaroid and other film photography giants. There's the automobile, the airplane, the Internet, and so on. This one, if it turns out to be capable of being mass produced, could completely change the way we look at energy. The initial spectrometer analysis suggested that a small LED energy yielded enough power to run a couple of city blocks for a day. At the moment, I feel I'm only scratching the surface. I need to run control experiments with various light sources, from the visible spectrum to gamma rays, and measure reactions. I also need to determine the full composition of this material, including confirming the presence of armalcolite and figuring out that last missing element."

He understood, of course, but what she didn't understand was the time component. But still, the scientific process was the scientific process, and he of all people knew that fact after a lifetime in this world, from his years at Stanford and NASA.

After expressing his gratitude for her work so far and giving her full access to any equipment she needed—while maintaining secrecy due to the nature of the discovery—Pete left Gayle to her work and returned to his office, feeling that the answers were coming, but not nearly fast enough. He needed Angela and Jack, plus whatever device they had taken with them, to accelerate the learning process. The sooner he got hold of the full picture, the quicker he would be able to determine the best way to take advantage of this technology.

Unfortunately the team in Miami had underestimated Jack—even after Pete had warned them all—and allowed them to get away. Even Dago had vanished. Contractors had spotted his truck parked in front of his shop but the large biker was nowhere to be seen. And to make matters worse, five minutes later, over a dozen bikers arrived at the shop, went inside, and all came back out wearing helmets with visors, before getting back on their bikes and taking off in separate directions, making it impossible for the surveillance team to decide which to follow.

Screw the biker, Pete thought, returning his focus to Jack and Angela, who would have to surface sooner or later, especially with the number of eyes searching for them.

Pete had already accessed Angela's list of personal and professional contacts from her account at the Florida Institute of Technology, and he browsed through it slowly on his screen.

The personal list was quite short, starting with him and continuing with her biker friends already under surveillance and a few loose hackers from her days with Anonymous. The professional list, however, was quite extensive. As chief scientist for Project Phoenix, Angela had managed the activity of many subcontractors, each responsible for a specific component or technology incorporated into the Orbital Space Suit.

And add that to her contacts at FIT, he thought, browsing through the roster of professors and students.

While Pete certainly had a lot of foot soldiers, he didn't have enough to place tails on everyone on that list. So it would come down to priorities.

"Who would Angela go to for help besides Dago?" he asked his reflection on the flat screen.

And the answer came to him a moment later.

Dago followed his instructions, using the oldest trick in the book to lose his surveillance, driving with two of his guys in a large truck to a storage unit on the outskirts of Melbourne, where one of NASA's many subcontractors kept a supply of high-altitude balloons not just for the agency's experiments in low-orbital insertions but for an increasing number of commercial and industrial applications.

They reached the warehouse at night, just as Jack had told him, breaking in from the rear, disabling a lone security guard before rushing inside and making their selection, using a hand loader to haul the heavy crate, weighing close to four hundred pounds, to the open bed of their truck, before driving away.

Interestingly enough, news of the midnight theft barely made it to page six of the local paper and wasn't even mentioned in the following day newscasts.

It didn't take long.

He spotted the first sign of surveillance about thirty minutes after arriving at the FIT campus.

Wearing jeans, an FIT T-shirt, a matching baseball cap, dark sunglasses, and a student backpack he had purchased at a shop outside the university, Jack tapped his Bluetooth earpiece connected to the disposable phone in his jeans while stretching a finger toward a middle-age man reading a magazine at one of the tables in the patio of a coffee shop at the large Denius Student Center in the middle of campus.

Only he wasn't reading anything except the movements of Dr. Jonathan Layton as the elderly professor, dressed in a white button-down shirt, a light blue pair of slacks, and a matching bow tie, enjoyed a late-afternoon coffee while discussing some papers with a colleague.

Angela, also dressed in FIT attire, sunglasses, and a backpack, gave him a slow nod from her assigned spot roughly twenty feet from Jack, sitting by a bench near the entrance to the student center.

The college clothing, combined with her petite build, truly blended her with the thinning crowds of kids leaving the building. The day was almost over and students were headed for their dorms, apartments, nearby cafeterias, or the local bars. Some talked on their phones or listened to music while others chatted as they walked.

Jack also pretended to read a free student newspaper he'd picked up inside, though he made sure to avoid sudden head movements while his eyes scanned his surroundings every few seconds before returning to the opening paragraph of an article on student health stressing the need to use condoms to avoid sexually transmitted diseases or unwanted pregnancies.

He sighed.

Hopefully these kids were smarter than Angela and he had been just a few hours earlier, going two rounds of unprotected sex before it was time for a short nap followed by a shower, where they ended up going a steamy third round.

Focus.

He shook the thought away as his eyes slowly gravitated from the article to Layton, then to Angela, and finally to the tail, who seemed to be alone this late afternoon, as the sun turned burnt orange while slowly sinking toward the horizon, bathing the campus with its dying light.

Careful, Jack.

Given Pete's deep resources, he had a difficult time believing that the man wearing khakis and a Tommy Bahama silk shirt—clothes loose enough to hide a small arsenal—represented his former friend's sole team on the FIT campus, one of the obvious places where Angela would have turned up for answers.

Keep looking.

And he did, for fifteen more minutes, while Layton continued his discussion, finally getting up, shaking hands with his colleague, and heading east, presumably toward the Harris Center for Science and Engineering, where, according to Angela, he had his office and labs.

Mr. Bahama also stood, stretched, and glanced about, allowing a gap to his mark, before resuming his task, folding the magazine and tucking it under his left armpit, remaining roughly a hundred feet behind the professor.

Layton continued down a narrow walkway flanked by palmetto thickets connecting the student center to the academic quad, a large courtyard surrounded by the main library and a host of other buildings, at least according to the map Jack had memorized on the way up from Vero Beach.

He frowned. Jack didn't like corridors, limiting his options, especially when operating in hostile territory, which was exactly how he viewed this university.

Angela looked at Jack, her light olive skin glowing in the wan sunlight.

He whispered, "Show time," into his headpiece, and she started down the pathway, remaining a hundred feet behind the operative, per Jack's instructions, backpack hanging casually from her left shoulder.

A light breeze swept in from the sea, swirling her hair as Jack saw movement to his far left that seemed abrupt, breaking the pattern of students and faculty moving about.

A man emerged from the shadows of the building, fast-walking down the path, heading straight for Angela, who continued her stroll, entering the corridor-like path formed by dense palmetto clusters and the towering sidewalls of two adjacent buildings facing the quad.

A second tail.

Jack jumped into action, moving fast, but without attracting attention, keeping his head down, closing the gap to a man in his forties, shorter than Jack, fair-skinned, bald, with very wide shoulders and thick arms and legs, dressed in loose cargo pants, sneakers, and a Miami Dolphins football jersey. He resembled a pit bull, strong, moving with purpose, focused on his target.

And completely missing Jack, who reached the narrow passageway, the pal-

mettos' fan-shaped leaves swaying in the breeze, his eyes shifting from his mark
to Angela, checking his rear, making sure they were momentarily alone, before
sneaking up from behind, reaching for his Sig Sauer, and pressing the muzzle
against the man's back while tapping his headset, muting the microphone to
keep Angela from listening.

"Enjoying your walk?"

The man stopped, arms hanging free by his sides, ready.

Jack kept the pressure on the gun while risking another backward glance.

"What are you going to do?" the operative asked in English with a heavy
Slavic accent. "Shoot me in the middle of an American university?"

"No need," Jack said, glad that he was dealing with a professional, who remained relaxed.

In a single swift move, the former Navy SEAL delivered a quick and short
blow with the edge of his left hand to the upper side of the operative's neck, right
under the ear and just below the jaw line, where the carotid artery divided to
supply blood to the brain and face.

Jack instinctively shoved the gun back in his jeans the moment he felt the
palm-strike connect, using both hands to keep the heavy operative steady as
the blow stressed the vagus nerve, causing temporary inaction of the heart and
breathing organs, triggering a vasovagal episode. The muscular Slav stiffened
for a moment, before fainting right into Jack's arms, who simply shifted his
downward momentum to the right, shoving the man directly into the dense
thicket that reminded him of his time in Colombia.

An ocean of green leaves swallowed the operative, who dropped out of sight
from the pathway, among sprawling trunks, landing hard on a ground littered
with spikes and fallen vegetation.

And who would wake up ten minutes later in a world of hurt.

One down.

Jack checked his back again as the sun went down, as darkness fell across
campus, before resuming his walk, shortening the distance to Angela just as
Layton emerged on the other side of the pathway, by the quad, followed by the
operative.

Jack emerged last, passing a pair of female students going in the opposite
direction.

He forced a smile, if only to continue blending in, but kept walking without looking back, figuring that if the girls spotted the fallen operative in the thicket, he would hear their screams.

His eyes returned to Angela, now a dozen feet away, and Jack counted to thirty, the time he expected the sorority girls would take to walk past the unconscious mercenary.

All clear.

He slowed down to survey the quad, once more searching for telltale signs, scanning the benches, the clusters of kids hanging around, the ones walking alone, a dozen of them on bicycles, a girl on Rollerblades, a couple holding hands, a guy lying on a bench watching a video on his phone.

Jack looked at everyone and at no one, hunting for anomalies, for abrupt movement, for anything that suggested a break in the pattern of college kids relaxing after class.

Satisfied that they were clear, Jack got off mute. "Stop, lean down, and pretend to tie your shoes," he whispered. "Then remain ten feet behind me and keep this channel open."

She did, and Jack walked right past her, taking the lead as the first stars appeared in the indigo sky, reaching the other side a minute later, and continuing down another palmetto-infested corridor.

Jack closed the gap with the operative tailing Layton, almost catching up to him at the end of the pathway, crossing the tree-lined street, a blend of magnolias, oaks, and towering palms. He spotted the professor almost a full block ahead of them, walking toward a parking lot separating this part of campus from the science buildings to the east.

Night descended, streetlights flickered and came on, forking through branches overhead, projecting ragged shadows across the street, obscure crisscrossing shards on the pavement that often merged into pockets of near-darkness among the dim yellow glow.

Jack checked both sides of the street, squinting.

Darkness was a SEAL's best friend, but it could also be a double-edged sword, which for the moment worked to his advantage as he closed in on the operative, who occasionally checked his surroundings while Jack moved from shadow to shadow, like a ghost, his mind on automatic now, measuring his advance.

Twenty feet.

Jack dropped to a deep crouch, accelerating, pointing his momentum straight for the middle of his target's back.

Ten feet.

The operative continued his stroll, the loose clothing betraying him in the evening breeze, his shirt lifting above his waistline, revealing a black semiautomatic tucked in the small of his back.

Jack charged, closing the remaining distance in two seconds, the edge of his right hand aimed at the vagus nerve.

The operative shifted at the last minute, turning sideways to Jack, who managed a slight adjustment of his own angle, but his hand missed the sweet spot, striking the ear instead.

"Jack!"

He shifted his gaze from his quarry, who had now produced a small knife, clutching it like a professional, with the blade protruding from the bottom of his fist as he turned sideways to Jack, like a cobra, ready to strike.

A third mercenary, huge, like a massive linebacker, had grabbed Angela from the back ten feet away, picking her up with ease, an arm around her chest and the other clamping her mouth as he turned around and started carrying her away. She kicked and fought to break loose to no avail.

The operative grinned at Jack, before shifting to the right, then the left, faking with his knife hand before throwing a punch with his right toward Jack's solar plexus.

Jack blocked it with his left hand while driving the palm of his right hand straight up the man's nose, pushing cartilage and bone into his head.

The operative shuddered, stunned, but still held on to the knife as Jack finished him off, clapping his palms hard over the man's ears in unison, creating a sudden increase in pressure inside the inner ear canals, bursting the tectorial membranes, shocking the basilar system, inducing spasms.

But Jack didn't hang around, rushing around the man as he fell to his knees, charging after Angela, reaching for his SOG knife, closing the twenty feet as she continued fighting, trying to break free.

The man, almost a foot taller than him, turned around as he heard Jack, dropping Angela on the pavement before kicking her in the gut to keep her from running off.

As she rolled on the ground by his feet, clutching her stomach, heaving, the mercenary reached for a massive blade with a serrated edge with his right hand, almost as large as a Colombian machete, which he held incorrectly with the blade protruding from the top of his fist, limiting his ability to strike blows to forward slashes.

Amateur hour, Jack thought, his training forcing him to ignore Angela, focusing on the threat, seeing him clearer now, stepping out of the shadows, arm muscles pulsating with tension, his face tight, nostrils flaring.

Jack stopped a few feet from him while turning sideways, keeping most of his weight on his rear leg.

The man struck first, as Jack had anticipated, slashing the knife in a semicircle aimed at Jack's abdomen, trying to gut him. Jack shifted his rear leg back, easily getting out of the way, letting the blade pass a couple of inches from him before stepping forward, right hand grabbing the man's wrist and twisting it, extending the elbow into a horizontal line, which he palm-struck with all his might, pushing his body into the blow, driving the heel of his hand hard into the exposed joint.

The elbow's ligaments gave, snapped, dislodging the joint as the man grunted in pain, dropping the knife, disbelief flashing in his eyes while staring at his arm twisted at a sickening angle.

Jack held on to the wrist and forced the dislocated elbow behind the man's back, forcing him into a deep crouch. He was about to palm-strike his neck to knock him out, but stopped. Instead, he dropped his gaze to the operative's exposed right knee.

This one's for Angie, motherfucker, he thought, pulling back his front leg before snapping it sideways, heel first, toes pointing down.

The side kick landed on target, striking the side of the knee, which also snapped, cracked, ligaments bursting, followed by another grunt.

Jack finally let go as the large mercenary collapsed, before shifting to the front and kicking him straight across the right temple, knocking him out.

He paused, eyes searching for more surveillance, finding none, before leaning down to pick up Angela, cradling her, before taking off after Layton, still walking into the large parking lot, unaware of what had just happened.

Jack increased his step as Angela inhaled in short, raspy breaths, trying to get air into her shocked system. They reached the edge of the parking lot, ignoring the looks he got from a pair of students a half block away emerging from one of the buildings.

"Professor Layton," Jack said as he got within ten feet of the man, who turned around and froze, staring at Jack, then shifting to Angela in his arms, and back to Jack.

"Please help us," Jack added as he walked up to him.

Layton looked closer, recognition flashing in his eyes. *"Angela?* Is that you?"

"Hi . . . Jonathan," Angela said, before inhaling deeply again and coughing.

Slowly, Jack set her down, keeping an arm over her shoulder for stability as she swallowed and coughed again. She was slowly coming around, a hand on her abdomen as she winced, obviously in pain.

"Are you okay?"

"Yeah," she said. "I just need . . . a minute."

"And who are you?" Layton asked, inspecting Jack.

"He's. . . . he's my husband."

"Your *husband*? I thought he died years ago."

Angela slowly shook her head. "So did I, Jonathan. So did I."

The process was similar to the one they'd used to mine the information from Hastings's phone.

Only easier.

Olivia's phone wasn't as sophisticated.

First they'd disabled the GPS locator, doing it while on the run, before finding a motel in Jupiter, a small town south of Melbourne, far enough to give themselves some breathing room after their recent close encounter.

Next, they retrieved the address for the boarding school in Orlando, and Dago dispatched two of his guys to fetch Erika, who was now in danger.

Armed with a six-pack of Red Bulls, Art-Z and Angela dug in, using the two surviving laptops plus Olivia's table to break into the phone's SIM card and the flash memory, working systematically, byte after byte, extracting contacts, calendars, bank accounts, passwords, texts, and a host of other private information, some of it locked in a collection of security apps, which Art-Z cracked in seconds.

"Damn," said Dago, once more sitting behind them, though this time drinking a Budweiser, which Art-Z had acknowledged as a more appropriate beer for the man. "I use one of those apps to protect my personal data."

Art-Z exchanged a glance with Angela and slowly shook his head.

"Where did you get the app?" asked the hacker.

"Well, the app store, of course. Where else?"

"How much did you spend on it?"

"Wasn't free, if that's what you want to know. It was five bucks. Not cheap."

"You know what really amazes me, Bonnie?"

Angela shrugged while working one of the laptops. "Surprise me."

"People spending five dollars on some security app for their phones to safeguard the passwords to their life savings. Think about it. You get what you pay for."

"So how do you protect your stuff?" asked Dago.

Art-Z looked over his shoulder. "When this is over, I'll show you how to really protect yourself from . . . people like me."

"Fair enough," replied Dago. "And when this is over I'm going to teach you how to ride a real bike."

"Please," Angela said, ripping into the SIM card. "First you want to kill each other and now it's a fucking lovefest."

"Speaking of lovefests," Art-Z said, pointing at the screen, which displayed the contents of the phone's internal flash memory. "Looks like the general's been busy enticing foreign investors into his network."

"As if pilfering the taxpayers' coffers wasn't enough," Angela replied, reading through Olivia's text messages with a half-dozen foreign financial firms, most of them in Russia, Africa, Mexico, and the Middle East.

"I'm not sure he's after their cash, though," said Art-Z, also reading through the messages, which focused on access to mines owned by the financial institutions.

They counted four mines in the messages, which Angela pulled into a list.

Mwenezi District Mine—Zimbabwe
Mina del Toro—San Luis Potosí, Mexico
Jagersfontein Mining—South Africa
Pripyat Swell—Ukraine

They spent the next thirty minutes reading through hundreds of lines of text from Olivia's interactions with suppliers, including the operators of the mines. Although each mine produced multiple minerals, Art-Z found one that was common to all, and which was mentioned by name multiple times in the messages.

"What's armalcolite?" Dago finally asked, sipping his beer and planting his face in between Angela and Art-Z while reading the screen.

"A type of moon rock," Angela explained after doing a quick Internet check to confirm her recollection. "Originally brought home by the crew of Apollo Eleven. And it was also found later on around the Earth in these mines."

She stared at the images before asking, "But what's that got to do with the OSS? There's no armalcolite in my design."

"I don't know, Bonnie," Art-Z said, reaching the end of the text messages, which focused on the delivery aspect of securing the mineral and shipping it to SkyLeap, but without any indication of what Olivia or anyone else did with it.

"But," the hacker added, pointing to the data in the SIM card, which included an encrypted supply chain tracking system for items considered critical to the project. "The armalcolite wasn't delivered directly to SkyLeap. It first went right up the street, to this location."

"What's there?" she asked.

Art-Z pulled up Google Earth and zoomed into the GPS coordinates.

"Looks like a warehouse in the middle of the woods ten miles away."

Angela stared at the tin roof of this very nondescript building surrounded by what looked like a tall chain-link fence, though it was hard to tell from the satellite image.

"I think we just found our next target," she finally said, staring at the image, hoping like hell that within those walls lay the next clue to the whereabouts of her husband, whom she now knew was still alive, still breathing, still *existing*.

"This isn't supposed to exist," said Layton, looking at a flat screen connected to a microscope in the rear of a lab on the second floor of the F. W. Olin Engineering Complex building, where they had retreated after their skirmish with the mercenaries that Pete had dispatched to keep an eye on the professor.

Jack had objected about hanging around the campus, but Angela had insisted since they not only needed the professor's help but also the lab equipment to decipher the glass token. They had finally reached a compromise by coming here instead of Layton's building over at the Harris Center for Science and Engineering several blocks away.

Still, Jack had made them wait almost thirty minutes, circling the parking lot of the engineering building in their stolen truck until he was convinced that they were clear. Interestingly enough, they never heard any sirens for emergency vehicles—meaning a containment crew had come and extracted the disabled operatives.

Finally, Jack had driven them to the front of the building and let Layton and Angela out before circling the parking lot for another ten minutes, convincing himself that perhaps it was a reasonable risk.

"Where did you find it?" he asked, looking over at Angela.

"Long story, Jonathan. What is it?"

"A glass particle accelerator—something still on the drawing boards."

She made a face. "That small?"

"Amazing, isn't it?" he said, pointing at the screen. "Here's the narrow channel between two glass plates, each three centimeters in diameter. Both plates have these lines of teeth, six hundred nanometers wide and spaced by six hundred nanometers."

Jack got close to the screen, deciding it resembled rows of fine teeth along lower and upper jaws.

"The way they're positioned creates tens of thousands of microscopic cavities arranged in a circle, like a miniature version of CERN's Hadron Collider, though that one uses copper, the current standard for making particle accelerators. But while the smallest distance between copper cavities is around thirty centimeters, with glass, as you can see, we are exponentially smaller. In addition, copper cavities require large amounts of alternating electrical current to change the polarity of the cavities to accelerate passing particles. Glass cavities, on the other hand, can use light, which is electromagnetic radiation."

"An electric field and a magnetic field leapfrogging each other at high frequencies," she said while Jack tried to keep up.

"Correct, Angela. But the size of the cavity and its distance to the next cavity determines the type of light required to achieve optimum acceleration. In this case, a wavelength of twelve hundred nanometers—the six hundred nanometers for each tooth and another six hundred nanometers of distance between them—is required so that the phase of light, and its associated electric field, would rotate one hundred and eighty degrees as it passes through each cavity, switching the voltage from positive to negative, just like in a traditional copper accelerator, but at a much higher frequency and with a microscopic footprint."

"Jack," Angela said. "There's the number twelve again. A wavelength of twelve hundred nanometers is required to achieve a harmonic synchronization with the cavities in the glass."

"Which is the frequency of gamma rays," said Layton.

Angela nodded and added, "And which show up as violet or purple in the electromagnetic spectrum."

"That's great, Angie," Jack said, "but I still don't get how it all fits. The altitude, the temperature, the G-meter, the vertical velocity, the weird electrical storm, and now this. How does it all work together to allow a dimensional jump?"

Layton stood abruptly and blinked. "A *what?*"

Angela sighed and motioned the physics professor to sit back down before saying, "I think it's time we tell you a little story."

11

MISGUIDED MEN

Our scientific power has outrun our spiritual power. We have guided missiles and misguided men.

—Martin Luther King, Jr.

It had happened by accident.

Like so many scientific breakthroughs.

In 1928, upon returning from a month-long vacation, Scottish biologist Alexander Fleming discovered a strange fungus on a culture he had left at his lab—a fungus that had killed all of the surrounding bacteria in the culture. Penicillin was born that day, and modern medicine would never be the same.

In 1944, American engineer Percy Spencer walked in front of a magnetron while working at Raytheon and noticed that the chocolate bar in his pocket had melted. A year later, the microwave was invented.

In 1938, DuPont scientist Roy Plunkett was searching for less toxic refrigerants to replace ammonia, sulfur dioxide, and propane. When opening a container of one of his samples, he noticed that the gas was gone, leaving behind a strange, slippery surface with high resistance to heat. Teflon.

And the list went on, from Velcro, electricity, and radioactivity to vulcanized rubber, smart dust, the Big Bang, and even Coca-Cola and Viagra.

And now Salolitite, thought Dr. Richard Salazar, inside a Class-1000 clean room in the Materials Science building of Project SkyLeap.

He stared at a new sample of the germanium-armalcolite-dolomite compound he had accidentally created the day his furnace thermostat malfunctioned, nearly doubling its interior temperature, damaging the furnace's dolomite lining and fusing a dozen germanium-armalcolite samples he and Olivia were annealing in search of a more energy-efficient alternative to copper in the manufacturing of particle accelerators.

But as Olivia cleaned the interior of the large furnace to replace the charred dolomite—a heat-resistant mineral composed of magnesium, calcium, carbon, and oxygen—Salazar had noticed a purplish film coating the bottom, beneath melted glass and other charred compounds, and was surprised by the way it had reacted to her flashlight, pulsating in a way that almost resembled sheet lightning.

At first they thought that the furnace had short-circuited and was damaged beyond repair, but upon closer inspection, the former CERN scientists noticed that it wasn't the furnace reacting to the light.

It was the crystal substance lacing its interior walls.

And just like that, salolitite was discovered, a compound with the ability to generate orders of magnitude more energy per cubic millimeter than uranium-235, but without the deadly radioactive side effects.

Salolitite was a clean energy source, easy to handle and manufacture, and capable of truly changing the energy landscape much in the same way that electricity had modernized our world.

Assuming Hastings allows it to see the light of day, he thought as he used a pair of long pliers to handle the sample, a glowing cylinder twelve inches long and an inch in diameter.

Beyond agreeing to name it after Salazar and Olivia, Hastings had pretty much controlled every aspect of the discovery, letting in only a selected few at SkyLeap in a need-to-know basis.

And the number of insiders had just decreased by one.

News of Olivia's tragic death—a home burglary gone bad—had reached Salazar just an hour ago via a text from Hastings.

A fucking text message.

Salazar fed the salolitite cylinder, or ingot, to a machine that would use a laser to slice the thin wafers that formed the upper and lower sections of the diminutive particle accelerators for a new batch of tokens for this week's quota of Orbital Space Suits. The day before he had retrieved another batch, which he had atomized over a dozen Velcro pouches laced with gold micro wires used to protect the tokens as well as to act as a solar antenna, boosting the energy level

of the token to achieve the desired harmonic level for optimum particle acceleration.

He entered a code on the digital pad of the front of the large laser, starting
the day-long process, which in addition to slicing several pairs of matched upper
and lower halves, would also etch twelve thousand teeth in a circular pattern to
form the cavities, each six hundred nanometers long and spaced by another six
hundred nanometers.

He made his way back to his office. It was nine o'clock at night and he had
been at it nonstop for almost sixteen hours. Another downside of Hastings's zealous control of the discovery meant a lack of technical personnel to assist him
in these critical steps, which he hoped would be automated just like the assembly of the suits and of the ISS module back in SkyLeap's main building. But
for now he had to handle the salolitite himself, and with Olivia dead, it probably
meant that Hastings would also make him handle the suppliers of raw materials,
including the relationship with the owners of the armalcolite mines.

He sighed as he approached the front of the lab.

The materials building wasn't that large actually, just two floors of labs and
offices housing a half-dozen scientists and twice as many security guards. In fact,
it seemed that anything associated with SkyLeap had a similar ratio of brains to
brawn.

But who was he to complain? As with Olivia and so many other scientists
lured to work on Hastings's pet projects, the general was quick to develop leverage in the form of threats to the well-being of loved ones. Olivia had her daughter. For Salazar it was his elderly parents, living in comfort in nearby Vero
Beach courtesy of Hastings's arrangements with a premier ocean-front retire-
ment community.

For as long as I do my job right, he thought as he reached the exit and pressed his
right thumb against a small screen while looking into a camera, which scanned
his retinas and matched the results to the thumbprint, releasing the magnetic
locks and automatically opening the doors.

Salazar frowned, having never in his life seen a building that was so incredibly high-tech on the inside, yet appeared like a weathered, decrepit warehouse
on the outside.

Leave it to Hastings and his obsession for secrecy, he thought as he continued down a long hallway, where multiple cameras connected to a guard station on the first floor monitored his movements.

There was really no place to hide, not even in the bathroom stalls as Hastings had also installed cameras there to make sure his scientists remained loyal to him even while taking a dump.

Salazar shook his head as the elevator door opened automatically for him at the end of the hallway, taking him down to the first floor, right next to the guard station, where six soldiers as big as the now-missing Captain Riggs sat behind their stations monitoring all activity in the building, including the small parking lot and surrounding woods.

News of Riggs had also reached Salazar via text, but he hadn't given it much thought. Salazar had never liked the oversized bastard anyway, and couldn't care less what happened to him.

He waved at the guards before walking to his office, where another door automatically opened for him, revealing a spacious office with a private bathroom, a single bed, and a small refrigerator, a microwave, and even a small flat screen hanging on the wall.

His home away from home.

Although he owned a nice condo just ten minutes away in Cocoa Beach, Salazar seldom spent time there during the week, and not just because of the long hours, but also because he actually had no personal life, and he wasn't sure he wanted one while working for Hastings.

But as much as he deeply despised the general, the scientist in Salazar absolutely loved the cutting-edge work he was allowed to do. The technology being developed under Hastings's watch was nothing short of groundbreaking, revolutionary.

The discovery of salolitite had the potential to open technological doors that until his furnace malfunctioned belonged in science fiction novels. Many fields, from Einstein's theory of relativity, to quantum physics and string theory now had the concentrated energy to be tested, to be developed, to be applied. And the latter, applied physics, was the world that ignited Salazar's passion.

As revolutionary as it sounded, dimensional jumps based on salolitite crystals was just the tip of this amazing and quite deep iceberg. If reaching the right harmonic allowed a jumper to leap from one dimension to another, it was just a matter of more experimentation before the physics of salolitite could be applied to time and space, enabling the rest of Einstein's concepts. Traveling to other worlds, or even other galaxies, could become a matter of a jumper achieving the right harmonic, obsoleting the need for expensive spaceships and new propulsion systems.

And the same principle could apply to the always-elusive but real—at least according to Einstein's theory—time travel.

In many ways, salolitite was in as much an infant state as was electricity and magnetism for William Gilbert, the physician who served Queen Elizabeth I in the 1600s and whose pioneering experiments and publications inspired countless scientists and engineers in the decades—and centuries—that followed, applying the properties of electricity and magnetism to develop our modern society.

Gilbert had triggered an inflection point in the human race, and once world leaders grasped the power of electricity, there was no going back.

And that, of course, was the reason Hastings kept this technology so damn close to his chest. It explained the ratio of guards to scientists, the secrecy, the internal police within his ranks—the ruthlessness with which he governed his operation.

History was full of instances when technological superiority resulted in world domination, giving nations an unfair advantage over their neighbors. From gun powder to the nuclear bomb, those who possessed the technology thrived while those who didn't withered away or were assimilated.

And salolitite provided a revolutionary new platform to trigger a technological revolution as profound as the industrial revolution of the late 1700s.

As he sat behind his desk with a can of soda and opened his e-mail, Salazar wondered how far he would see this technology evolve in his lifetime.

Just as salolitite was discovered by accident, so was the harmonic that enabled the leap to a parallel dimension. Using the glass accelerator, they'd managed to get objects across, but the size of the transport was directly proportional to the energy level required to achieve the leap. And that energy level was proportional to the frequency of the light exciting the salolitite compound.

They had started at the midrange of the spectrum, using microwaves and infrared light as the stirring agent, before moving up to the ultraviolet and X-ray range, progressively increasing the ability to transport larger objects, including different types of recording devices, dropping them from various altitudes to document their journeys before they vanished. After a while, they learned to control the energy levels to bring their data probes to the very edge of the portal, getting a peek into the beyond, before cutting off the power source to pull the devices back for analysis. The images were stunning, depicting what looked like a parallel world beyond the intense lightning flashes of an electrical storm.

But the real inflection point came when the experiments reached the gamma-ray range, and the even faster cosmic-ray end of the spectrum, the world of the twelfth harmonic.

Their ability to miniaturize the portable accelerators to control events grew exponentially, allowing them to immerse data probes across the edge and bring them back with regularity, recording this fascinating parallel world with detail, with precision, laying the foundation for Project SkyLeap, for the glass accelerators now being mass-produced for the Orbital Space Suits.

Salazar frowned, disappointed in the loss of their last probe, whose primary objective was to record the physiological effects of the leap on a human being.

But Dr. Taylor had altered the descent profile, sending the glass accelerator, along with the OSS and its wearer, fully across the dimensional boundary, past the point of no return, beyond their ability to throttle back the energy level and pull him back.

Still, all of the data collected up to the leap strongly suggested that the jumper had made it across, albeit in a state of semiconsciousness, according to the vitals they were gathering right before the dimensional change. And assuming that the automatic parachute deployed properly, Jack Taylor probably even made it to the ground in one piece.

But Salazar wasn't sure about Jack's odds after landing since he carried nothing with him but literally the suit on his back.

Hastings's jumpers would bring along the means to set up an infrastructure, from new identities, bonds and currency, to—

The room suddenly went dark, including his computer screen, before an emergency light came on above the door.

"Something's wrong," Riggs said as he stared at the warehouse from the edge of the forest. The lights atop the chain-link fence beyond the long meadow separating the compound from the surrounding trees blinked once and went off.

"You're sure this is the place?" Pete asked, lowering his binoculars. "Doesn't look like much."

"That's the point. I came here once with the general to pay a visit to Dr. Salazar, who's in charge of the building. But never got past the front lobby."

"What do you think's in there?"

"Based on the security I saw, my guess is that Hastings is keeping something pretty important in there. But like I told you before, we can't touch it . . . legally. In fact, we're not even supposed to get this close. We're technically trespassing."

Pete frowned and slowly shook his head at Hastings's reach. The man owned people everywhere, including a number of Florida politicians and law enforcement chiefs.

"But that doesn't seem to matter much to whoever's screwing with them," Riggs added, when the lights inside the compound also flickered and went off, replaced a few seconds later by emergency floodlights.

And that's when they noticed a shadow rushing across the meadow.

Riggs saw it first and an instant later Pete said, "Holy shit."

"Talk to me, Art," Angela said, speaking into her earpiece while running in a deep crouch toward the back of the compound, just as Jack would, dressed in black, her face smeared with grease, eyes scanning her surroundings.

But that's where the similarities ended.

Unlike Jack, Angela didn't have a weapon.

At least not in the traditional sense.

But that didn't mean she wasn't ready for this particular fight. Angela carried enough high-tech weaponry in her backpack to start a small cyberwar.

The meadow was quiet, almost peaceful, secluded, away from highways and towns, under a blanket of stars. A thin layer of early evening fog hovered a foot above the ground.

Angela cruised through it, approaching the fence slowly, with caution, measuring her steps, her eyes inspecting the outer perimeter, the security cameras that Dago and his gang had just disabled the old-fashioned way: by breaking into a nearby power substation and shutting down the grid for a three-square-mile area encompassing this warehouse and a handful of farmhouses.

She reached the chain-link enclosure, strong, tall, like those securing prison yards, but topped with coiled barbed wire angled outward instead of facing in, signaling that the compound was designed to keep people out. In addition, the chain-link itself was secured to metal posts via large glass insulators, meaning it was electrified.

At least as of a moment ago.

Reaching for her backpack, Angela removed an amp meter, which she clamped to the fence, punching the red power button, and verifying that Dago's guys had also managed to disable the secondary substation used for emergencies.

"In place," she said.

"All set, Bonnie."

Silently thanking Olivia for providing them with so much information via her phone, Angela placed a gloved hand on the rear gate spanning the width of the driveway leading to the shipping and receiving dock.

As expected, it was disengaged from the chain mechanism, allowing it to be opened manually in case of emergency, per local building codes. Hastings might be powerful, but fire safety was still fire safety, and that also included registering the blueprints with the Brevard County Department of Building and Zoning.

The building was vulnerable. At least for the time it took local utility workers to undo the damage.

But Angela didn't need much time, plus her target was just past the loading dock connecting to the shipping and receiving area inside the back of the building, which she hoped to be deserted this late at night.

And on top of all that, she also had an additional distraction in the works courtesy of the Paradise Shop gang.

She slid the gate open just enough to get her slim frame through, before hurtling across the hundred feet of driveway to the single loading dock along the rear of the warehouse, a single yellow floodlight casting a dim glow over the weathered structure.

Weathered my ass, she thought, reaching the dock, breathing heavily, her back pressed against the corrugated metal wall just as the sound of Harleys reverberated in the night.

Right on time.

Angela grinned, hoping that the noise of Dago and his guys gunning their machines by the front gate would be enough to hold the guards' attention long enough.

She tested the heavy double doors, and again, they were unlocked.

Counting to three, she tugged one open and snuck inside, facing a long corridor, as shown on the blueprints she had retrieved from the county's databanks two hours ago. But the plans didn't detail the quality of the interior, and this one was as high-tech as the best NASA development center, including stainless steel walls, raised tile floors, security cameras, and retinal-thumbprint door access. All in sharp contrast with its deceptive and dilapidated exterior.

She went straight for the fourth door on the right, past shipping and receiving, and tugged on it. As with the rest of the doors, it was unlocked, the power outage bypassing the fancy security system.

And just like that, Angela found herself in the building's server room, the core of Hastings's operation.

She stared at three rows of floor-to-ceiling server racks, routers, and touch-screen panels that were still operational, thanks to a local standby power supply humming along in the corner of the room, and which typically would last for about an hour—long enough for technicians to restore power.

Angela scanned the servers, quickly locating the one of immediate interest.

She unzipped her backpack and removed a small black device the size of a pack of cigarettes with a foot-long Ethernet cable coming out of the top. She plugged the standing end into one of the Ethernet receptacles on the back of the server, and then applied a strip of double-sided tape to the gadget, securing it firmly to the rear of the frame, out of sight from anyone inspecting the server room.

"It's in," she said.

"Testing now," he replied.

Angela waited while Art-Z checked the hack into the system's firewall, which was basically a byproduct of Network Address Translation. NAT simply blocked any incoming connection attempt that lacked a matching outgoing connection. The gadget that Angela had just plugged in would create an outgoing connection for them, tricking the firewall.

"We're good, Bonnie," he said. "Inject and get out."

She removed a USB stick and plugged it into the back of the same server, introducing a malware brew that, among other things, would bypass the cryptographic protocols that assigned session keys to authorized users, giving them undetected access to the network once they got past the firewall.

Angela zipped up her backpack and headed for the door, inching it open and—

Shit!

She closed it swiftly but quietly.

Two guards were emerging from the other end of the hallway, flashlights in hand.

"Got company," she mumbled, her heartbeat thrashing her temples, her throat going dry, her mind going in ten directions as she hid in the rear of the server room, behind a couple of stacked boxes of spare parts.

"Need to haul ass before the power comes back up, Bonnie," Art-Z said.

"No shit," she hissed. "But there's a pair of guards coming this way in the hallway. Is there another way out of this room?"

"Hold on."

Angela swallowed, trying to control her breathing, inhaling through her mouth and exhaling slowly through her nostrils. It wouldn't do anyone any good if she started to hyperventilate.

"Bonnie. On the side of the room, by the floor, I see an AC return duct. Looks big enough in the blueprints."

Angela crawled on all fours while staring at the door, hearing nothing but the hum of the equipment, unable to tell if the guards were still down the hallway or about to open the door.

There.

Just where he said it would be.

"Found it," she mumbled, unzipping her backpack and pulling out a small flathead screwdriver, which she used to remove the top two screws, taking less than thirty seconds, amazed that her hands were so steady.

"Hurry, Bonnie."

"Almost there," she replied, removing the last screw and lowering the cover, which was hinged at the bottom.

Good thing I'm not claustrophobic, she thought, crawling in and closing the cover behind her, before unzipping the backpack and using a long strip of double-sided tape to hold it in place.

"Now what, Art?"

"Okay . . . head straight back until you reach a split, then go left . . . no, go right . . . no wait, I'm reading it backward . . . it's left. Yes. Go left."

She sighed and began to turn around in the cramped space, also glad that she was petite enough to maneuver in this very tight—

The door to the server room opened and the guards walked inside.

She froze.

". . . so I told her that she had to either get her kid to straighten up or I was out."

"Don't blame you, man. Bad enough you're putting a roof over their fucking heads. You shouldn't have to take shit from a stupid brat that's not even yours."

Angela licked her lips, hanging on to every word as the guards walked the server room for what seemed like an eternity, their flashlights crisscrossing, occasionally forking through the grill cover, piercing the darkness of her conduit.

"Well, this room looks fine, too," the first guard said before the static of a radio cracked in the room, followed by, "Server room clear. Tell Dr. Salazar."

And a moment later they were gone.

Angela hesitated, not certain which way to take. Behind her was the server room and a clear shot back out, assuming the guards returned to the front of the building, where she hoped Dago and his guys were causing a loud distraction to draw attention.

"Art, do you really know where this duct is leading?"

"Ah . . . it looks like it connects to another room . . . a lab of some sort."

Damn, she thought. She didn't need to go to any labs. She needed to get the hell out of there.

Slowly, she turned back around and pushed the cover open, sliding out, before closing it back up, and taking thirty seconds to reinsert the screws and tighten them by hand.

Stretching, rolling her head twice, Angela walked cautiously to the door and placed an ear against its cold surface, frowning. The guards were chatting just outside the door.

Stepping away from it and hiding in the rear, she said, "Art, I'm going back the same way I came in. Tell Dago and his guys to get off their bikes and fake a fistfight, maybe rattle the front gate. I need them to cause a serious uproar out there to get these guys off my ass."

"Hold on, Bonnie."

Angela waited, her shoulder aching with tension as every passing second closed her escape window. When the electricity came back up, she'd be stuck in this place.

Suddenly, static cracked and she heard someone shouting in the radio, followed by the guards running toward the front.

She exhaled, slowly inching the door open and peering in their direction, watching them disappear beyond the door at the other end of the long corridor.

"They're gone, Art."

"Hurry, Bonnie."

She stepped back out to the dimly lit hallway and scrambled for the rear double doors, reaching them seconds later, swinging one open, and running into the loading—

"You! Hold it right there!"

Shit!

Angela risked a backward glance, spotting a security guard dressed in black emerging at the other end of the corridor. He was tall, athletic, his face tight with anger, a radio in one hand, while the other reached for a weapon in a belt holster.

"*Stop!* Stay where you—"

The heavy metal door closed behind her, cutting off his warning.

Angela sprinted from the building, kicking her legs with all her strength, jumping from the loading dock, landing in a crouch, and hurtling toward the fence.

The wind, the night, and the adrenaline coursing through her veins all blended in a blur as she pushed herself, her vision tunneling on the rear gate, the one she had left open, the one she had to reach to—

"Stop!" the voice echoed from behind, followed by another voice from her distant right.

A second guard!

Angela didn't bother looking.

She could feel them converging on her like a pack of wolves, her eyes locked on the foot-wide gap in the gate, pointing her momentum toward it, kicking as hard as she could, gulping air through her mouth.

Twenty feet.

The shouts were closer now, almost on top of her, mixed with the noise of Harleys, with more shouting coming from the front of the building.

But she couldn't look, couldn't take her attention from her target, from the gap, aching with anticipation of a hand yanking her neck, taking her down.

So she pushed even harder, her heartbeat rocketing, almost drowning her other senses as the gap grew, as she reached it, going through, scraping a shoulder, banging an ankle against a post, the pain streaking up her leg as she winced, nearly losing her footing.

"Last warning!" a voice thundered behind her. "*Stop!*"

Screw you, she thought, cutting left, then right, like Jack had shown her, making herself a harder target, buying time to reach the forest, the tree line, where she could—

She heard a loud electric spark an instant before an invisible force stabbed her back with paralyzing strength.

Colors exploded in her mind as her limbs seized, fingers stretched to the night sky, before contracting into fists. Her vision narrowed as her legs turned to putty, giving out from under her.

Angela collapsed, her back on fire, as if someone was hitting her repeatedly with a two by four, pounding her into the ground with animal strength.

Shadows shifted about her as she thrashed on the ground, beaten, her thoughts vanishing to the periphery of her consciousness.

And then it stopped—the arresting pain, the spasm, the pressure on her back.

Instead, Angela just stared at the stars, at the cosmos above her, feeling the evening breeze caressing her face, soothing her quivering skin, before someone loomed into view, blocking the night sky, her heart sinking at the realization that she had been captured, that Hastings had managed to take her.

But she wasn't finished.

She needed more time to investigate, to analyze, to theorize.

Angela needed to find Jack.

But the face. It belonged to the enemy.

His lips were moving, but Angela couldn't hear anything, couldn't feel anything but the anger boiling inside of her at the thought of being captured by these bastards.

And like a wounded and cornered animal, Angela tried to lash out, tried to raise a hand and scratch his face, tried to lift a knee and kick him in the groin— anything to fight back, to inflict pain, to make them pay for what they had done to Jack, to her, to Olivia.

But Riggs's hands pinned her wrists against the ground, like a pair of steel clamps, unyielding, immobilizing her as he tried to tell her something, as his lips moved fast while looking over his shoulder, as Angela grew light-headed, dizzy, her tired mind starting to capitulate, to give in, to accept the fact that—

Another face materialized next to Riggs, shifting to the center of her tunneling vision, framed by a sea of bright stars.

Pete?

It was her friend—Jack's best friend.

But it couldn't be.

Pete was with Riggs.

And Riggs was the enemy.

She tried to speak, to shout, to scream that she didn't understand, that she needed answers, that she just wanted to find her husband and disappear forever.

But Pete remained there, floating a foot from her.

Smiling.

She watched him through her tears before passing out.

Angela and Layton lost him somewhere in the middle of gamma rays, particle collisions, quantum physics, and string theory. But he had grasped the basics of the discussion, as the scientists filled the white board with formulas, drawings, and mathematical proofs and theorems.

In the end, Jack had become what Layton called *energy loss*. That is, energy that existed in one dimension but was lost to another dimension as the byproduct of an unprecedented particle collision.

To Layton's knowledge, only CERN had been able to achieve such energy losses but at the subatomic level, when comparing the energy levels of particles before and after a collision, and theorizing that the difference had gone somewhere beyond this Earth, had crossed some sort of string or membrane as defined in string theory speak.

Jack looked out through the window blinds at the parking lot under glowing yellow lights.

Energy loss, he thought, shaking his head, in a way empathizing with those lost particles, vanishing from the world, floating in some sort of universal limbo, making him feel like he was indeed truly lost, slipping farther and farther away from his world, from his life.

From his wife.

But Angela was right there, in the flesh, as alive as ever, focused, direct, beautiful.

And quite passionate.

He closed his eyes, remembering, allowing himself a moment to reminisce, to fill his mind with her, with the way she had made him feel in that hotel room, the way she had taken charge in a very feminine way, controlling the pace, exacting her own pleasure while giving him the ride of a lifetime, only to be continued in the shower, which in the end had been bittersweet since his wife had never been a fan of shower sex.

Angela was the same but she was different, and that difference both kindled a hunger in Jack while also injecting him with a tranquilizing dose of guilt.

Bittersweet.

Jack took in a gulp of air and forced his mind back to the parking lot, to the problem at hand. Angela was doing her job with Layton and so he did his, too, keeping watch, making sure they were safe, recalling just how quickly they'd found themselves surrounded, how fast they'd almost taken her from him.

We need to be more careful, he thought, scanning the periphery of the parking lot, of the corridors connecting it to the academic quad, for a moment catching a glimpse of something by those palmettos, before he saw him, a shifting shadow in the corridor, there one instant and gone the next.

Jack narrowed his gaze at the potential threat, spotting him again, standing at the edge of the dark corridor, not far from where he had disabled that first mercenary.

He checked the rest of his field of view, peering beyond the windshields of every parked vehicle, looking for sudden changes in shadows, in coloration, in anything that suggested additional surveillance.

So it's just you, he thought, feeling slightly better since it probably meant they didn't know Jack and Angela were holed up here, otherwise he would have expected many more operatives, especially given the way Jack had handled the first three.

He looked over at Angela, entangled with Layton in some formula taking up half the board, each armed with a black marker, taking turns adding to it numbers and symbols that might as well be Greek or Chine—

There.

Jack spotted another operative, a shadow moving inside a parked car. But a moment later he realized it was just a young couple making out in the front seat.

Get a room, kids, he thought, grinning, before resuming his hunt, peering into every vehicle again while checking back with his first mark, verifying he was still in place, and again, finding no one else, deciding that Pete must have deployed men to cover every section of the campus after the disaster two hours ago.

And while that made this location safe for the time being, it would make their getaway a little—

"Jack?"

He glanced at her across the lab, a somber look on her face.

"Yeah?"

She stretched an open hand in his direction. "Come on."

"You guys finished?" he asked, walking over and taking her hand.

"For now," said Angela, staring at him in a way that almost made him feel uncomfortable. "We . . . we think we got it."

"You figured out how I got here?"

She looked at Layton, who smiled and slowly shook his head.

"What?"

"Jack, we solved that an *hour* ago," she said, her eyes suddenly filling.

"Then what, Angie? What did you—"

She hugged him, stretching a finger at the incomprehensible scribbles on the large white board, before whispering in his ear, "Jack . . . we think we just figured out how to get you . . . home."

Pete had to restrain her the moment she came about and her gaze landed on Riggs.

"What's that bastard doing here?" she asked, staring at the large man across the room while Pete held her from behind.

"Easy. He's on our side."

"On *our* side? He held a fucking gun to my head! He's Hastings's pit bull, Pete!"

"I'm a federal agent, Dr. Taylor," he said matter-of-factly, sitting with his legs crossed in a corner chair in a strange living room, hands on his lap.

Angela just stared at him for a moment before mumbling, "Are you *shitting* me?"

Riggs shook his head. "No games, doctor."

"You're ... *FBI?*"

"I've been undercover for almost three years trying to dig up evidence on the general's operation."

She looked at Pete, who slowly released her while saying, "It's true, Angela."

She took a deep breath, wincing in pain when trying to stretch her back.

"What happened to me?"

"Taser," Pete said.

"Damn," she replied, staring at the bruises on his face. "And what happened to you?"

He looked at Riggs, who shrugged.

"Let's just say that we beat each other up before Riggs decided to mention that he was a Fed."

"So now you're working together?" she asked.

"Something like that," replied Riggs.

"Where are we?" she said, looking around the small living room facing the woods.

"FBI safe house near Orlando," replied Riggs. "We're isolated and secure here. Closest neighbors are almost a half mile away."

"Where are my guys?" she asked.

"Your hacker friend wanted to take off when he found out that Riggs was FBI. He was mumbling something about not working for The Man."

Angela tried to suppress a smile.

"But anyway, Dago convinced him to stay. He's in the next room plugged in to his computer."

"And Dago?"

"Taking a nap in another bedroom."

Angela processed that for a moment, her mind trying to catch up. She looked outside and noticed it was still dark. "How long have I been out?"

Pete checked his watch. "About four hours."

"FBI safe houses have any water?" she asked.

Riggs stood, went to the kitchen, and returned with bottles for everyone.

Angela twisted the top and nearly drained half before asking, "How did you two hook up?"

Pete took a minute to bring her up to speed, starting with Hastings figuring out that Angela and her ragtag crew were operating out of his house.

"How did you track me down?"

"Riggs and I followed Hastings's people to Olivia's house. Somehow the general figured out that you had followed her there and sent a termination team. You were lucky to escape alive."

"What about her daughter? Did Dago's guys—"

"She's somewhere in Miami with his biker friends," Riggs said. "I wanted to bring her into protected custody but Dago said it would be up to you."

"I made a promise to Olivia that I'd look after her daughter," Angela said.

Pete and Riggs exchanged a glance before looking at her in silence.

"And I don't break my promises. I'm going to keep her hiding in Miami for now. At least until I can trust the FBI," she added, before taking another swig of water, swallowing, and asking Riggs, "Did you say that you've been undercover for three years?"

"Yes, doctor," he replied.

"Good. When are you arresting Hastings?"

Riggs looked at Pete before standing. "It's not that simple. We need proof. Evidence."

Angela cocked her head at the oversized man. "You mean to tell me that after *three* fucking years you still haven't gathered enough evidence against the man?"

Pete was about to intervene but Riggs raised a hand. "It's okay, Pete," he said before spending a few minutes giving Angela an overview of Hastings's mode of operation, which in many ways resembled that of organized crime, with several layers of buffers between him and his illegal activities, from embezzlement of government funds to kidnapping, blackmailing, and assassinations.

"It took me almost two years before he trusted me enough to run his private detail. But I still couldn't go beyond that . . . at least officially."

Angela bit the corner of her lip. "What does that mean?"

Riggs looked over at Pete.

"It was my idea, Angela," said Pete. "The Feds have to follow protocol. They're bound by a set of rules that prevents them from gaining traction fast enough, especially against someone as slippery and well connected as Hastings. But it's pretty obvious that you and your guys—and I for that matter—don't like to play by those rules."

"Like what you did tonight in that compound," Riggs said.

"Art told us," Pete added. "It was a brilliant move."

"And very gutsy."

Angela looked at Riggs and said, "My family's on the line. I don't have a choice."

"Well, doctor. That's the reason I'm here instead of at the FBI. My family—my wife and son—are under protected custody at the moment, but Pete brought up a good point. Hastings owns people everywhere, including the FBI."

"So you think . . ."

"I can't afford to take any chances. My handler's keeping their location off the system for now, just in case Hastings decides to get back at me. But Pete's right. Eventually the general may find a way . . . so, that puts my family on the line, too."

Angela slowly nodded. "I'm sorry . . . for being such a dick."

Pete looked down, failing to suppress a smile.

"Can't say I blame you, doctor."

"It's Angela, please."

"Very well, Angela. Now, where do we start?"

Angela considered that for a moment, before walking to a window overlooking the ocean. She stared at it long and hard, once more trying to think like Jack would.

As unfortunate as Riggs's situation was, it had presented Angela with the first lucky break since Jack had vanished into thin air. Officially or unofficially, she now had the FBI on her side plus Pete's connections in the government.

Slowly, she turned around to face her audience of two and said, "Strap on your seat belts, boys. Because the ride's about to get a hell of a lot more exciting."

12

THE BIG KAHUNA

Dictatorship naturally arises out of democracy, and the most aggravated form of tyranny and slavery out of the most extreme liberty.

—Plato

His legacy began in the American Civil War, where his great-great-grandfather fought valiantly for the North. Private Theodore Hastings had been young back then, barely seventeen when he first witnessed the horrors of war at Shiloh, tasting bitter defeat on the bloody banks of the Tennessee River, walking among thirteen thousand Union soldiers killed and wounded and another ten thousand Confederates—more dead than in all previous American wars combined.

But young Theodore had been spared, had survived to fight again at the Second Battle of Bull Run, where once again Union forces were defeated, retreating to Washington. It was there, during a short one-week leave, that Theodore married the daughter of an affluent attorney, consummating the marriage before he was called back to face what became known as the bloodiest day in U.S. military history: Antietam.

Theodore fell that day on September 17, 1862, among the twenty-six thousand dead, wounded, or missing. It was never clear if he had died on the battlefield or from his wounds, but his commanding officer awarded him the Medal of Honor for extreme courage under fire—an award delivered to his young wife, who was already with child, giving birth eight months later to George Washington "GW" Hastings.

GW grew up among the aristocracy of the nation's capital in those post–Civil War years as the nation healed, attending the finest schools, educated by the best teachers money could buy. But his heart belonged to the battlefield, like his father, eventually making his way to the United States Military Academy at West Point, and kicking off the first long-term military career of the Hastings family, fighting alongside Roosevelt's Rough Riders in the Spanish-American War before birthing seven daughters and one son, Ulysses, Hastings's grandfather.

Unlike Theodore, GW lived to the ripe old age of sixty-three and took joy in watching his only son graduate from West Point, marry, and give him three grandsons before shipping off to Europe to fight in the War to End All Wars. But it seemed that the young Ulysses didn't possess his father's luck in the battlefield, perishing in the death fields of Europe shortly after the first American troops landed in France in June of 1917.

GW looked after his grandchildren when news of his son's death reached his estate in Maryland, but only the oldest boy, Michael, survived the devastating Spanish Influenza epidemic of 1918. His brothers perished among the five hundred thousand casualties of the worst single U.S. epidemic, which also took the life of Michael's mother. GW raised the boy until his death in 1926, when Michael was just seventeen, but old enough to enroll in West Point and continue the legacy.

Like GW, Michael became the second member of the family to enjoy a long military career, earning the Medal of Honor for his courage under fire in Omaha Beach, driving his platoon inland and securing the area for the following waves of the American fighting forces of Operation Overlord.

Hastings remembered his father with respect. Brigadier General Michael Hastings had not only fought in World War II, but he had also served his country in the Korean War as a senior officer under General MacArthur, retiring in 1961 as a one-star general, the highest ranking in the Hastings family.

Until now, he thought, staring in the mirror at the two stars adorning his shoulders.

Hastings had come a long way in his military career, serving four tours in Vietnam with the 101st Airborne Division. He had been a "Screaming Eagle," making a name for himself, earning promotion after promotion, award after award, until the Pentagon brass realized his potential and pulled him from the battlefield, planting him in the middle of its inner circle, where his power and influence grew year after year, administration after administration.

Until he became his own universe, master of his destiny, controlling the actions of hundreds of legislators, politicians, lobbyists, and policy makers, never afraid to make the hard decisions, to bend the rules—even break them—to return his country to the glory of yesteryear, when America was *America*, feared by many, respected by all.

And they will respect us again, he thought, watching technicians install the salolitite modules into the next batch of Orbital Space Suits.

SkyLeap was his baby, his creation, America's future. He had envisioned it, funded it, staffed it, drove it, and protected it from short-sighted politicians, from leaders who lacked the vision and conviction of Theodore Roosevelt, of JFK, of Reagan. He had seen the once greatness of NASA, leader in every aspect of technical innovation, brought to its knees through lack of funding, lack of executive support, and lack of a long-term strategy.

Don't they realize that whoever controls technology controls the world?

Hastings crossed his massive arms and frowned, amazed at the inequity of elected officials, and more so at the sheer stupidity of those who voted them into office.

But the general wasn't about to let idiots elected by idiots define the future of his nation. His family had fought too damned long and hard to pass on not just the gift of freedom, but that of world leadership, of respect and fear, from generation to generation.

And I'll be damned if the trend's broken on my watch.

So he did what he had to do, call it vision, investing for the future, or embezzlement. Hastings took tax money and placed it in the hands of the scientists, of the innovators, of the visionaries. But not to innovate for the sake of innovation. That was for academic prima donnas. Hastings wanted to innovate to control, to rule, to leapfrog the technological advancements of the Chinese, the Germans, the Koreans, even the damned French. To reverse the unthinkable trend of American astronauts using Soviet-era Soyuz technology to reach space, or worse, Chinese rovers paving the way for control of the moon.

But to do that he had to change the rules of the game. He had to compartmentalize his operation, shielding it from the public, the politicians, and even the foreign powers determined to never allow American innovation to lead again. Hastings had to protect his vision at all cost, nurturing it, allowing it to take root, grow, and blossom. He had learned from the masters, from world leaders who had managed to unify their nations and transform them from the ashes of failure, financial deficit, and unparalleled unemployment. He had studied their approaches, their strategies, their successes and especially their failures, the iron fist with which they had to rule to succeed. He had analyzed their tactics—often brutal and unsavory—to incubate an idea, a concept, a vision, until the time was right, until it was ready to be unleashed.

And the time has come, he thought, as Dr. Salazar walked up to him.

"We're almost done for this week, sir."

Hastings barely acknowledged him, his eyes on the suits being transported around the assembly line, where a mix of technicians and robotic arms handled the delicate process of creating hardware capable of jumping to other dimensions, to other points in space. And he knew that was just the beginning of the almost-magical possibilities that salolitite had enabled. His army of scientists, like Salazar, were hard at work to allow jumps to other worlds, other galaxies, bridging the universe. And if the laws of space travel could be bent—or even redefined—so could the laws governing time.

"So everything's back to normal at your facility, Doctor?"

Salazar nodded. "Yes, sir. IT has gone through the network. We're clean."

"Check everything again. Dr. Taylor was seen leaving your building, Doctor. She did *something,* and you need to figure out what it was. I don't care if you need to tear down that building brick by fucking brick. I want to know what that bitch did. Clear?"

"Yes, sir."

"Good," he said, before walking over to the other side of the lab, past the glass accelerator, to take a look at the ISS module. Salazar silently trailed along behind him.

"Still on schedule?" Hastings asked.

"Two weeks," he said. "Then we move it to the Cape for launch preparations."

"No more mistakes, doctor," he said. "I mean it."

"Yes, sir," said Salazar, visibly shaken.

Hastings left him like that, in fear, and walked out of the facility and into his waiting SUV, settling in the rear seat before getting on a conference call with his security team, ripping them a new asshole for failing to silence Flaherty and Dr. Taylor at Olivia's house. Plus he added Riggs to his special list of bastards who belonged six feet under, along with his family.

Hastings pinched the bridge of his nose in silent anger, having a very difficult time accepting the fact that Riggs had turned out to be FBI. The thought burned a hole in his stomach, making him question every damn member of his inner circle, from investors, mine owners, and politicians to his key scientists and military officers. Everybody was now a suspect in his mind. Everyone needed to prove to Hastings that they were worth keeping their families alive.

I can't let up for one moment, he thought, making a fist and staring at it.

An iron fist. He understood then why every successful dictator had to take the same unyielding approach. There was no other choice. He had let his guard down for a moment and ended up with a damn FBI agent as head of his personal security.

But I'll make them pay.

His people were already probing through the FBI database to track down the whereabouts of Riggs, Flaherty, and the crafty Dr. Taylor, and it was only a matter of time before he learned where the Bureau had hidden them.

They think they're safe. But I'll find them. And when I do . . .

Hastings tightened his fist until the knuckles turned white. There was a time when he would have done the deed personally. But these days, it was in his best interest to remain isolated from his security team, who also didn't get their hands dirty but managed independent teams of mercenaries, hired guns, and contractors—professionals who would kill their own mothers for the right price, and who, if caught, wouldn't be able to incriminate his organization, much less him.

Hastings stared out the window, his thoughts drifting to those aged and yellow photographs in his father's study. He remembered their battlefield faces, marred in dust and blood, recalled the awards, the medals, all carefully arranged in sealed shadow boxes on the walls, and those priceless vintage rifles and pistols behind the glass of humidity-controlled cases.

And one day all of it became his to own, to cherish, and eventually pass on to his own son. But Hastings never had time for a wife, let alone a family, always too focused on his career, on his vision.

He slowly shook his head, imagining the conversation at the family dinner table. *Honey, how was your day? Today I had breakfast with drug dealers from Juárez, spent the morning with the Russian Mafia transporting illegal minerals into the country, and the afternoon blackmailing politicians—could you pass the bread, please?*

Besides, Hastings never actually came across a woman he considered worthy of his seed, someone with that unique combination of strength, courage, conviction, and intelligence to enhance the Hastings's unique gene pool, to create the right specimen to carry on his legacy—someone who wasn't afraid to fight the good fight, who would never surrender, even when confronted with seemingly insurmountable obstacles.

Hastings realized that what he needed wasn't a family and the burdens and obligations that came with it. He didn't need a wife or a home or a fucking Thanksgiving dinner. GW had raised Michael Hastings after Ulysses perished in World War I. GW hadn't needed a wife or a family to continue the legacy. He had just needed one strong boy, the one who survived the Spanish Influenza epidemic while his siblings and his own mother perished. GW had simply needed someone he could shape into his image, could instill the code of honor passed down from generation to generation.

As his mind recalled all of those medals and awards, from Theodore, GW, Ulysses, and Michael, he realized that what he needed was just a strong kid, someone whom Hastings could guide, coach, develop into his successor. And to do that all he needed was a disposable female host with the right attributes, from strength and intellect to unparalleled courage under fire—the key characteristic of his distinguished family tree.

He needed a female host who would never shy from fighting the good fight, someone who simply didn't know how to quit, how to capitulate, even when facing appalling odds.

And that's when the thought came to him.

Hastings shook his head at the simple and devious elegance of his solution to creating an offspring.

He quickly contacted his security team and said, "Kill everyone . . . except Angela Taylor. I want to be very clear about this. I need her . . . unharmed."

Getting out unharmed proved challenging.

Jack had spotted one sentry still standing by the palmetto thickets lining the corridor at the edge of the parking lot, which he had to cross to get to his truck.

But what he hadn't realized was that the couple who had apparently been making out in the car hadn't been just a pair of hormonal college kids.

They were actually operatives, who wasted little time exiting their vehicle the

moment Jack stepped out of the building, where Angela and Layton would remain hidden until he could fetch the truck and pick them up.

The mercenary by the palmettos remained put, like a lookout, while the
couple moved in swiftly for the kill.

Jack pretended not to see them as he went straight for the weathered truck,
drawing them in, but always keeping at least one row of cars in between as he
cut back and forth, forcing them to split up, before dropping out of sight, rolling under an SUV and retrieving his SOG knife.

The male operative appeared first, making the mistake of not wearing combat boots, which would have protected his Achilles tendons when Jack slashed
the steel blade out from under the vehicle, severing the sensitive ligaments on
the right foot.

The operative fell, screaming in Russian, his pronounced Slavic features tight
with obvious pain, fingers reaching for the wound while Jack rolled out, surging
to his feet and kicking him across the left temple.

One down.

The woman came at him like a jungle cat, silently, swiftly, agile, short blades
protruding in between the index and middle fingers of her fists. Her long hair in
a tight ponytail swinging around like a loose whip, her eyes, as dark as her hair,
focused on him as she pivoted on her right foot while bringing the edge of her
left foot up at an impossible angle, catching Jack by surprise, smacking him
across the face.

He shifted back, momentarily stung, but glad that she didn't weigh much
more than Angela, meaning less mass behind her strikes. Had that round-
house been delivered by a large male operative, Jack probably would have been
knocked out.

But what she lacked in strength, she more than made up in speed as she pivoted again, like a deadly ballerina, with grace, speed, and a ridiculous stretch
that signaled she was double-jointed.

He focused on the blades and her torso, and this time he was ready, blocking
the incoming roundhouse kick with his left forearm while palm-striking her sternum, knocking her light frame toward a parked van.

He risked a quick look toward the palmettos, spotting the operative now
running toward them as she bounced against the fender, fell, rolled, and was back

on her feet before Jack could follow up. Her eyes, glistening with anger and pain, matched her compressed lips as she charged again, hands crisscrossing fast, the blades glittering, reflecting the streetlights, aimed for his throat.

Damn, she's quick, he thought, dropping to a deep crouch to get away from those sharp edges while pivoting on his left leg, swinging his right one just a foot off the ground in a wide and fast arc, striking her calves, knocking her legs out from under her.

She yelled and fell, landing hard on her back.

He was about to kick her across the temple, too, when she rolled away, her legs scissoring as she pivoted to her feet, her hands still clutching the knives, coming at him again.

She definitely gets an A for effort.

Jack stepped back, avoiding the slashes before stepping in, stiffening the index and middle fingers of his right hand, like a viper's tongue, stabbing her eyes, shocking the optic nerves before driving the heel of his right palm against her nose at an upward angle.

She instantly dropped the blades, falling to her knees, before collapsing on her side just as the third operative stopped ten feet away, a hand reaching inside his jacket.

Jack threw the SOG knife on instinct, the blade slashing through the space separating them, flickering in the dim yellow light, its scalpel-sharp tip piercing the mercenary just below the chin, slicing through his windpipe.

He fell to his knees, hands reaching for the blade, trying to pull it free as he drowned in his own blood, as Jack reached him an instant later, gripping the handle while kicking him in the chest, yanking out the blade and stepping back as blood spurted from the wound.

The operative tried to speak, but Jack knew it was futile. Their eyes locked for a moment before he rolled on his side in convulsions.

Jack left him there and rushed to the truck, getting in, and drove it around to the front of the building, where he bumped the horn twice.

Angela rushed out of the double glass doors and climbed in, followed by Layton, who hauled a leather briefcase.

"What took you so long?" she asked, scooting over on the bench seat, sitting shoulder-to-shoulder.

Before he could reply, she added, "What happened to your face?"

"Bumped into someone," Jack said, stepping on the gas, wishing to get the hell out of Dodge before word got out.

"Jack?"

"There are three less mercenaries looking for us now."

"Oh," she said, understanding, putting a hand on the side of his face. "Are you okay?"

"I'm good. Really. Don't worry."

She kissed him on the cheek. "It's my job to worry."

"And it's my job to keep us safe, which means we need to get away from here. So, where to?" he asked, steering the truck.

"First to Orlando International," she said, taking a closer look at the spot right in between his right temple and his eye where the woman had landed that kick.

He appreciated the gesture but was starting to get annoyed, though he didn't let it show as he asked, "Why the airport?"

"We're dividing and conquering, Jack. Jonathan's headed for Cambridge to meet with one of my former MIT colleagues, an astrophysicist who just agreed to help us work out the details of your upcoming jump."

Jack processed that before asking the obvious question: "What about your classes, Jonathan? Isn't that going to signal back to Pete that we're up to something?"

"I'm close to retiring," Layton replied while leaning forward to look at Jack. "I don't keep a regular schedule, plus I have a staff of junior professors and grad students handling most of my academic load. No one's going to miss me for a couple of days."

"Besides," Angela added. "I'm sure by now Pete's wondering if Layton knows something. Too many disabled operatives in the area, especially the ones following him last night. It's probably good for Jonathan, and for us, if he left town for a few days."

"Okay," Jack said. "What about us? Where do we go after we drop him off?"

"Daytona Beach," she said.

"Why?"

"Jonathan's brother is a New York lawyer. He has a beach house there he rarely uses, and where we shouldn't be disturbed while we work."

"Work on what?"

"On your new suit."

Jack turned toward the highway, constantly checking his rearview mirror, having had some time to think about a way back and realizing just how difficult it would be, even if he had a functional suit.

"Okay, Angie, assuming we can build a new OSS...how are you planning to get me high enough to be able to use it?"

"That's the thing, Jack. We think you may not need to go as high. Just enough to achieve the desired trans-dimensional harmonic."

Jack thought he remembered hearing something about that when Angela and Layton were scribbling those incomprehensible formulas on the whiteboard.

"And that's what I need to work out," said Layton. "But I require access to MIT resources, including the supercomputers, to run some calculations."

The ride to the airport took less than forty minutes, time Angela and Layton spent engaged in a deep discussion of theoretical physics combined with astrophysics and computer engineering. Jack tried to keep up for the first minute but soon gave up as the conversation quickly went beyond his pay grade. Instead, he left them to their discussion on the semiconductor chip embedded in the purple glass and its connection to solar energy while his thoughts drifted to his wife back at home, wondering not just how she was managing in his absence, but how his vanishing was being handled by NASA. After all, the whole world had been watching his jump.

Jack was pretty damn sure that Hastings and his gurus knew exactly what had taken place, but that didn't mean that the rest of NASA had figured it out.

But if someone could, he was certain it would be Angela.

Following that train of thought, however, it meant that if Angela did indeed suspect that Jack had not burned up on reentry, if she had somehow connected the dots and realized that he had gone someplace else, and tried to go public with it, then she was in obvious danger because Hastings would likely go to any length to protect his secret.

Which made it so much more imperative that he find a way back.

Before he knew it, they had reached the airport, and Jack silently chastised himself for having gone on autopilot, immersed in his thoughts while half of Pete's posse could be right on his tail.

I need to be more careful, he thought, resuming his scan, once more becoming aware of his surroundings, checking the traffic behind him as he took the exit for the airport. He circled it twice, making sure they were clean, before heading for departures and dropping Layton off by the American Airlines check-in.

"Let's touch base in a couple of days," he said, walking away, briefcase in hand, disappearing beyond the automatic doors.

Angela once again snuggled against Jack's arm as he steered the truck back toward the turnpike, hugging his right bicep.

"So," he said. "Want to bring me up to speed?"

"It's a recording device, Jack," she said.

"What do you mean?"

"The chip embedded in the glass token. It not only controlled the type of harmonic required to achieve a jump, it also recorded the event, including your vitals during the entire event, plus the energy levels of the accelerator and the speed of the particles."

"Why?"

"Our best guess is that Hastings and his gurus were using the jump to collect data, to learn, to even understand the physiological effects. That's why they hid the token in the suit. They wanted to gather information on their miniature particle accelerator while you fell out of the sky. The token became active the moment it was energized by solar gamma rays as you dropped from sixty miles high. And this also explains why Hastings had insisted on Alpha-B, which would have narrowly missed the desired trans-dimensional harmonic, keeping you just on the edge, between worlds, while still providing them with mounds of data in the token's memory. We think that if your wife had left Alpha-B in the jump profile, per Hastings's instructions, you would have certainly seen some strange colors around you, like that purple halo, but continued on through a normal reentry, landed as expected, gone home a hero, and never known that the real mission objective was data collection."

Jack thought of the roller coaster that had been his life since jumping, and for a moment wished that was the way it had played out. But that would have meant letting Hastings get away with it, and the man had to be stopped.

"But they never got the data," he said.

"Well, we think they did, up to the point that you vanished. The token used an encrypted channel in the TDRSS link to also send telemetry, but not to

NASA. So while the folks at Mission Control kept tabs on you through one TDRSS channel, someone else was also following your jump but gathering a different set of parameters through a second, and well-hidden, channel."

"Incredible."

"And because of the descent profile change, Hastings and his gurus also got a clear signal that their technology works when you achieved the trans-dimensional jump."

Jack reached the highway and headed north, toward Daytona Beach.

"About the suit . . . how are you planning to build one?"

She leaned the side of her head against his shoulder while patting him. "Building you a pressure suit isn't the hardest part. Dago and his guys are already gathering the materials."

"Then?"

"The token was connected to a power source, Jack, and from what we can tell, it was on the underside of that Velcro cover. The residue we found on the token suggests that it was made of the same material as the token but designed to be some sort of solar antenna, to capture gamma rays. The bad news is that we left it behind with the outer shell."

"So . . . my old buddy has it," he said, checking his rearview mirrors as he accelerated onto the entrance ramp.

"Yep," she said. "And we're going to have to get it back."

"We're going to have to get it back in order to put it all together," Dr. Gayle Horton said, pointing at the display above her microscope. "Here are the connectors where the energy is channeled to the missing component."

Pete nodded while staring at what had to be the single most important discovery of the century.

"What really amazes me," she continued, "is the energy level of this material. Just to put it in perspective, a liter of regular unleaded gasoline has the energy equivalent of thirty-five kilo joules. The handful of experiments I have conducted so far have yielded the equivalent of thirty *million* joules. And there's still plenty of energy stored in it."

Pete inhaled deeply, trying to process the orders of magnitude. A joule was the traditional unit of measurement for energy in the metric system, which was the force of one newton acting through one meter. In electrical power terms, one watt was the power of a joule of energy per second.

He sat back. "This is . . . unreal. What have you learned about its composition?"

She grabbed the tablet next to the microscope and browsed through a few graphs. "I've confirmed the presence of armalcolite. The full composition is a strange combination of germanium, armalcolite, and dolomite."

"Dolomite?" he asked, trying to remember what that was.

"It's a crystal that's used on a number of applications, from furnaces to controlling the pH in saltwater aquariums, but the most interesting one is in particle physics, where detectors can be built under layers of dolomite to enable detection of exotic particles. Dolomite is particularly good at insulating against interference from cosmic rays. In this case it looks like the three compounds fused at an extremely high temperature. I'm firing up one of the furnaces we used to test shuttle tiles to try to reproduce it."

Pete liked hearing that. If they could reproduce the material, it would put him one step closer to a complete solution. He was already engaging two more scientists to develop a prototype version of the damaged suit, including a new helmet. With luck, they might be able to reverse-engineer the individual components in a few weeks and create a working prototype a month later. And that, combined with the jump profile he had extracted from the black box, would give him most of the pieces of the puzzle.

Except for the missing component, he thought, before thanking Gayle and walking back to his office.

His scientists were doing their part, but he couldn't say the same for his operatives. The field reports were not encouraging.

Six professionals had been brutally disabled—one even killed.

Pete had read the encrypted message on his phone and nearly thrown it out of his office window an hour earlier.

The only good news was that the mercenaries were quite adept at cleaning up after their own mess. Aside for unconfirmed reports of fistfights, the FIT campus was pretty much undisturbed. No bodies were found. And of course, there was no sign of Angela or Jack, or even Professor Jonathan Layton, one of the key assets he had under surveillance.

So they've gone after her academic contacts, he thought, pretty much deducing that his former girlfriend was digging, and given her level of technical brilliance, it was just a matter of time before she connected the dots.

But Pete needed her on *his* team, connecting *his* dots, helping him unlock the apparent marvels of this game-changing technology. Unfortunately, any chance of doing so peacefully had ended when he'd arrived at her house in Humvees packed with armed soldiers.

He looked out his window at the Launch Complex 39 and the ocean beyond it, having forgotten just how damned skilled Jack was, and combining his operational talents with Angela's mind only made them that much more formidable.

They had managed to escape his initial attempt to take them at her house, in the process neutralizing a dozen soldiers. Then they had deceived him—along with the Coast Guard and Homeland Security—with that ocean explosion stunt, before making fools out of a professional Serbian surveillance team in South Miami, and once again at FIT, where Jack had apparently disabled two independent professional teams, one Russian and the other Canadian.

But everyone had a weakness, something that could be exploited.

And then it suddenly came to him, as he stared at the distant ocean.

It couldn't be that easy, he thought, rubbing his chin, considering the concept, realizing that the best plans were often the simplest.

Follow the technology trail.

And he began to make calls, to dispense instructions, orchestrating a new plan that neither Jack nor Angela would see coming for a while.

Until it was too late.

And this time there would be no mistakes.

They reached the beach house just past midnight, punching in the code Layton had given them to gain access to the gated community, before driving up to the house, where Jack got out, and entered another code by the keypad next to the double garage doors, which began to lift.

Angela drove their truck inside and Jack immediately closed the doors, hoping no one had seen them this late at night. One thing he'd learned about living in Florida was that the majority of residents were retirees who usually went to bed in the early evening hours.

The place was a classic vacation home, with a gigantic main room connecting the kitchen, dining room, and living room with panoramic windows facing a silvery ocean under a bright moon.

He entered the alarm's security code before checking the place while Angela unloaded the groceries they'd gotten on the way, stocking up the refrigerator and pantry since they planned to be here awhile.

Jack walked into every room, inspecting closets, testing windows, making sure the place was secure, before returning to the kitchen, where she waited for him with a pair of Coronas.

They held hands while walking out to the covered back porch overlooking a private beach, which, like the rest of the neighborhood, was deserted at this late hour.

A half-dozen Adirondack chairs of different colors flanked a large covered Jacuzzi spa.

Angela set her beer on the arm of one of the chairs and walked over to the spa, lifting one end and testing the water.

"It's warm," she said, before lifting the cover and pushing it aside.

"What are you doing?" he asked, leaning against the railing while sipping his beer.

She ignored him, inspecting the touch controls before pressing a button. The unit came alive with bubbles and a soft blue light.

Taking charge again, Angela removed her T-shirt and jeans, before slowly stepping in with feminine grace, under Jack's stare, as he stood there holding the longneck. This version of Angela had the innate ability to constantly leave him at a loss for words.

"You may be gone tomorrow, Jack," she added at his silence. "But tonight you are in my world . . . where you're *mine*. Remember?"

Slowly, he set the drink next to hers and made his way to the side of the Jacuzzi, where he also undressed before climbing in, sitting on a bench, the bromine tickling his nostrils as he scooped water and splashed it on his face, inhaling deeply, relaxing.

Angela leaned back, wetting her hair before approaching him slowly, the water barely covering her breasts, her eyes looking right into his, her chocolate freckle hovering over those amazing lips.

She scooped water and washed the bruise on the side of his face, before kissing it gently.

He just closed his eyes, letting her do whatever the hell she wanted, unable to resist—unwilling to do so as she mounted him at once, her hips taking charge, doing all of the work, arms around his neck, fingers running through his hair while Jack embraced her, pressing her against his chest, her breath on his neck as she gasped, taking him away from the madness of mercenaries, of operatives, and space jumps.

They remained embraced after they finished, the side of her face once again on his chest.

"We start bright and early, Jack," she whispered as his breathing steadied.

"I know," he replied in the darkness, his mind foggy again, confused, emotions broiling, overcoming logic. "Though at this moment I'm not so sure I ever want to leave."

She hugged him tighter, before finding his lips, kissing him, hands framing his face.

"I know, baby. I know. But as much as I enjoy you being here, it isn't natural. It isn't right. This isn't where you belong."

Jack placed his hands on her face as well, staring into her eyes. This was Angela, the one he had fallen in love with long ago, the one who used to make him feel just like she did at this moment, passionate, alive, allowing him to forget about everything.

"I know I need to go," he said. "She needs me now probably more than ever."

"She does," Angela said. "And tomorrow we start, as soon as Dago gets here. Divide and conquer. I'll start working on the suit and you and him will take care of securing the components."

Jack nodded, remembering her plan to get him back up to the ionosphere, even if it sounded a bit far-fetched, but choosing to trust her just as he had trusted his wife by getting inside that suit and jumping out of that pod.

"So you think that's going to work?"

"As long as the model holds," she replied. "Jonathan should be at MIT by now. It shouldn't take more than a few hours to run the simulation and confirm our calculations."

"And as long as we recover that solar antenna from Pete."

"I get the feeling that you'll have no problem handling that."

"I'm actually looking forward to it."

She looked at him and frowned. "Just promise me you won't kill him, all right?"

He wasn't expecting that. "But . . . *Angie*. He's been trying to kill us for the past two days."

"No, Jack," she said, with a slight grin. "He's been trying to kill *you*. I don't think he ever meant to harm me."

"But—"

She put a finger over his lips. "Trust me, Jack. Okay?"

He paused, taking a deep breath, before asking, "What's going to happen to you after I leave?"

She smiled, the freckle dancing over her lips before she tapped him on the nose. "I know how to take care of myself, Jack. I did it long before we met and long after you were gone. Plus I have Dago and his gang looking after me."

"But—"

She kissed him again, drawing him in slowly, descending gently, glaring into his eyes as she did.

"Never forget me, Jack," she whispered, closing her eyes.

Jack didn't respond. He couldn't even if he had wanted to, hands dropping to those magical hips, clasping them, going another round, before once again collapsing on each other.

"Never forget me," she whispered again, a hand on his cheek while pressing the side of her face against his chest.

The key was to follow the money.

Angela had heard once from someone that if you tortured the numbers long enough, the truth would eventually emerge.

So they did. She tortured one financial stream while Art-Z tracked another one under the spellbound admiration of Riggs, Pete, and Dago.

"You should have stayed with the Bureau," said Riggs, standing behind them as the hackers sat side by side at the dinner table clicking away.

"Really? And miss all of this fun I'm having?"

Art-Z looked at her. "Nice job in that server room, Bonnie. The hack works like a charm."

"Sure," she said, her back still aching from those damned Taser probes as she deployed a small army of bots to follow the myriad global transactions from

Hastings's deals, channeling funds from Pentagon accounts into a large number of subcontractors, including the ones retained to provide components for Project Phoenix. Angela knew all of them quite well, having spent countless hours codeveloping the modules that made up the Orbital Space Suit. But what she was really interested in were the contractors supporting Project SkyLeap, and in particular the mining operations sourcing minerals, including armalcolite, germanium, and dolomite to the facility where she had installed Art-Z's hack in the server room.

"They're making something called salolitite. What's that, Bonnie?" he asked, pointing at his laptop.

Angela looked over to Art-Z's screen, read the compound's name, and made a face. "What *is* that?"

"I asked first," the hacker replied.

She stared at the strange formula on the screen. "Pete? Any clue?"

"Never heard of it."

"Well," Art-Z said. "Whatever salolitite is, it's being produced in large quantities in the materials building, and in two varieties; one is called just *modules* and the other *solar antennae,* and they're delivered daily to the SkyLeap building to be incorporated into the Orbital Space Suits."

"What the hell is Hastings up to, Riggs?" asked Angela.

"Sorry, doctor. Like I told Pete, I was never allowed past the lobby of either building."

"Whatever it is, it costs a hell of a lot of money," said Angela, reading down the screen.

"Yeah," said Dago. "My fucking *tax* dollars."

"That's one source," said Art-Z. "Over here it looks like the general's also associated with the Mexican cartel down in Juárez and Nuevo Laredo."

Everyone gathered around his screen, reading through the bank transactions.

Riggs spoke first. "That explains those strange meetings in Mexico. I never knew it at the time because he kept his security detail outside the meeting rooms, but it's obvious now. The general uses his contacts in the DEA and Border Patrol to provide planes and services to drug lords. In exchange, they make deposits for him at a number of overseas banks, money that he then also uses to finance his technological endeavors."

"That's right," she replied. "And look at these ridiculous mining costs. This stuff is more expensive than diamonds."

"Wow," Pete mumbled. "And I thought Project Phoenix was expensive. The OSS development is mice nuts compared to these payouts."

Angela sat back, thinking. Whatever salolitite was, it had to be what made Jack vanish. Nothing else in that space suit could have done anything remotely close to what she saw in those video frames. And that also explained the lack of alarm from Hastings, Olivia, and Salazar in Mission Control. They knew exactly where he had gone. And if they knew that, they should also know how to get him back. All she had to do was create some negotiation leverage, something to incentivize Hastings and his gang that it would be in their best interest to return her husband back to her unharmed.

"Say, Art," she said. "Now that we can see the bank transactions . . . can we change them?"

"Change them . . . how?" asked Pete.

"Well, Hastings's operation is a pretty serious black market endeavor. He's secretly acquiring materials and services from a host of shadowy organizations, including overseas mining operations, which are getting paid under the table from either drug money or through funds illegally taken from American coffers. And he's getting those materials—and those drugs—into this country by using our own planes. My point being that the people he's dealing with have to be the worst kind."

"Good point," said Pete.

"I can weigh in on that," said Riggs. "The reason my team existed was for the personal protection of Hastings. I attended many meetings where the general met with very unsavory people, like those who own mines in foreign countries as well as people in the drug business. Like I said, I was never allowed inside the actual meeting rooms, but I got to hang outside along with the bodyguards of the people that Hastings was meeting. I'm not easily intimidated, but some of these folks were pretty scary characters. The kind you don't want to cross."

"Good," Angela said. "I wonder how they would react if they suddenly didn't get paid? If in their eyes, Hastings wasn't living up to his end of the deal? What do you guys think?"

"I love it, Bonnie," said Art-Z.

"Brilliant," said Pete.

"It's definitely going to get his attention," commented Riggs.

"Fuck him," said Dago, standing behind them, his huge arms crossed.

They spent the following thirty minutes taking control of Hastings's primary accounts, mostly in the Cayman Islands, Hong Kong, and Geneva, plus, ironically enough, bank accounts in Laredo, El Paso, and San Diego—all set up to pay off a myriad of suppliers and carriers, including the planes used by smugglers to bring all of the goods inside the country.

"All right, Bonnie. Moment of truth. Ready when you are."

Angela stared at the arrangement, realizing that once she nodded, there would be no going back. But then again, there had been no going back since the moment Jack had vanished from those monitors. Hastings had played his cards and it was now time for her to play hers, to trump the general's hand by kicking him where it hurts.

"You guys good with this?" she asked while turning around to face the trio behind her, and she received a unanimous thumbs-up.

It took all of thirty seconds from the moment they issued the changes. All of the funds allocated to pay dozens of contractors, a total amount of nearly eighty-nine million dollars for services rendered in the past thirty days, were withdrawn from sixteen separate accounts in four countries and transferred into seven of the twelve regional Federal Reserve Banks located in cities across the nation—minus a fee for pain and suffering, which Angela shifted into an account in the Bahamas.

Riggs checked his watch. "It's three in the morning. By nine A.M., there's going to be a hell of a lot of confused people in Washington."

"This is what I call shitting in the general's Cheerios," said Pete.

Art-Z smiled. "This is what I call sticking it to The Man."

13

GOOD ENOUGH

Any damn fool can figure out a better way to do it . . . get it good enough, and get on with it.
                              —Bob Parks, aeronautical designer

Wiley Post built the first successful pressure suit in 1934, with financial support from the Phillips Petroleum Company. It was quite crude by today's standards, made of a rubber pressure bladder protected by an outer layer of parachute fabric. He wore pigskin gloves attached to the arms of the suit, rubber boots, and an aluminum diver's mask with a removable faceplate.

But it was good enough.

The suit got him to an altitude of fifty thousand feet and back down to Earth safely aboard a weather balloon.

His success inspired a large effort in the United States to develop the technology for pressure suits during World War II, although no actual suits were produced until after the war, when increased funding in aviation led to the S-1 and T-1 flight suits developed by the David Clark Company to be used by X-1 pilots.

By 1951 David Clark developed an improved version, the Model 4, first worn by USMC aviator Marion E. Carl, setting high-altitude records aboard a Douglas Skyrocket jet. The effort was continued by B. F. Goodrich, culminating in the Mk IV, which was adapted by NASA for Alan Shepard's historical suborbital flight, kicking off America's space program.

Over the following years—and decades—space suits evolved in safety and sophistication, culminating in Angela's OSS.

But the basic principles never changed. A suit had to provide a stable pressurized environment, some level of mobility, a supply of breathable oxygen, and temperature regulation. Those were the four essential features. Nonessentials included a communications system as well as a means of collecting solid and liquid bodily waste.

Angela focused her priorities on creating something that would meet the four essentials.

The concept of a space suit could be broken down into basic layers, starting with an inner, skin-tight layer that not only increased comfort for the wearer by reducing contact with the outer sections, but also provided some form of thermal control. Angela was glad she already had such a layer in the undergarment Jack wore beneath the battle dress during their initial escape. All she needed was a way of providing regulated pressure to the thousands of gel-filled capillaries lacing it.

Next was the pressure container, an inflatable, man-shaped bladder that could be pressurized. Angela chose to use an off-the-shelf diver's dry suit for this since it was made of very tough neoprene and nylon and was already airtight, making her job easier.

On top of that was the restraining layer, which as the name implied, prevented the pressure layer from ballooning or changing shape when pressurized.

And covering everything would be a few layers of aluminized Mylar for midsuit thermal insulation before finishing the design with a heat shield made of flexible insulation material for reentry protection.

So she began with the restraining layer, using basic white nylon canvas, which Dago had brought over to their secret hideout in Daytona Beach in the form of a long sheet, along with an industrial-class sewing machine and a spool of Nomex thread, which she would use for the entire suit not only because of its strength but also because of its amazing heat-resistant properties. In addition, she had requested inch-wide lanyards made of the same nylon material, which she would use to reinforce sections of the suit.

Dago and his gang had done an amazing job of obtaining her initial shopping list.

Angela laid out the one-piece undergarment on the dining room table and used it to take measurements of what would become the restraining layer, which she would cut out in three sections, the upper torso, the arms, and the legs, before sewing them together into a one-piece suit. The gloves and helmet would come from a dealer in Orlando that specialized in selling used space gear, American, Russian, and even Chinese. Once she secured those items, she would use Dago's shop to make the interfaces match the locking mechanisms, in particular the metallic rings for the gloves and the helmet.

Using a tailor's measuring tape, Angela took exact measurements before increasing them by 25 percent to allow room for the battle dress and the pressure layer.

She worked slowly, methodically, measuring everything three times, before carefully using tailor chalk to transpose the measurements onto a six-by-six sheet of nylon canvas stretched on the floor, which she cut with a pair of heavy-duty scissors.

She did this alone, after sending Jack and Dago on more errands, her mind needing the silence to stay focused on the task at hand, carefully stacking the sections on the other side of the table, by the sewing machine, taking almost four hours to complete the measuring and cutting phase.

Angela stretched her sore back and checked her watch. It was past seven, and Jack and Dago still weren't back.

Time for a break.

She grabbed a Red Bull and walked onto the covered back porch facing the private beach. Jonathan Layton lived the frugal life of a college professor, but his brother seemed to enjoy the opposite end of the spectrum, owning multiple residences funded by the insane salary of a senior partner in a successful New York law firm.

Angela grinned while looking at the Jacuzzi spa before sitting on an Adirondack chair to stare at the ocean for a while.

She went over the next steps in her mind, carefully going through the upcoming detailed assembly, from the position of ventilation and air pressure hoses to the correct placement of zippers and reinforcing straps. As in everything else in life, the devil was in the details, and she needed to be alone to consider every single feature that would have to be incorporated to keep Jack alive for what she estimated would be a five-hour ascent phase via a weather balloon—assuming Layton could get the physics to work—followed by a ten-minute fall.

Angela spent the next hour thinking through every detail, her mind cataloguing the actions without having to write anything down, stepping through every requirement from the moment Jack would leave the ground, through the required pressurization above twelve thousand feet as he entered the physiological-deficient zone, which was marked by a number of critical transitions. The first above thirty-four thousand feet, when an oxygen-rich breathing mixture was required to approximate the oxygen normally available in the lower atmosphere. The second was above forty thousand feet, when that oxygen-rich mix had to be delivered under positive pressure. A third inflection point occurred above sixty-three thousand feet, also called the Armstrong limit, when fluids in Jack's throat and lungs would boil away unless the suit transitioned to a pressurized 100 percent oxygen environment. All the while, the suit had to manage his body temperature as outside temperatures plummeted with altitude, as the balloon carried him through the stratosphere and into the mesosphere.

She finished her energy drink, gave the Jacuzzi another glance, and headed back in.

Next came the integration phase, sitting behind the industrial-class sewing machine, where she had already run the Nomex thread through the heavy-duty needle.

She started with the arms and legs cutouts, carefully stitching them before moving onto the torso, sewing heavy-duty zippers along the front, from groin to neck so Jack could put it on and take it off without assistance. She connected the arms and legs onto the torso, creating a one-piece coverall large enough to accommodate not only Jack in his battle dress and pressure suit but also the hoses and cable to power his ventilation and temperature control systems.

She continued by cutting out the access points on the chest for the oxygen, pressurization hoses, and thermal control hoses, reinforcing the edges with sections of lanyard before installing the ionized fittings, running the threaded end through the opening before smearing all edges that made contact with the lanyard with heat-resistant glue, and finally securing them in place by inserting large ionized washers from the inside followed by matching ionized nuts, which she hand-tightened before using a ratchet.

It was almost midnight by the time she finished stitching strips of heavy-duty lanyard to strategic sections of the restraining layer for added strength as well as to increase flexibility, fastening not just the edges of the strong nylon bands but also the center section by going over each of them a second time using an X pattern, especially around his torso, where the lanyard formed the basis for the attachments to a parachute for Jack's final descent—similar to the one on the OSS but more rudimentary.

But good enough, she thought, hearing Jack and Dago coming in through the garage.

She went up to meet them, giving Dago a hug and Jack a kiss, before helping them carry her shopping list into the living room, including an extra-large fire-proof suit made of flexible insulation material, similar to the one in the OSS but worn by firefighters, and which she would modify to fit over the restraining layer. To her surprise, they had also purchased a used Russian space suit from the dealer.

"Suit's too small," Jack said, "but the helmet and gloves will work. Plus I thought that maybe we can cut out the interfacing locking rings and use them in my suit."

Angela slowly nodded. "Good move, Jack. That makes the job a lot easier. I may be able to cannibalize a few more items."

Dago dumped a large box with wires, hoses, aluminized Mylar sheets, and even a home aquarium pump next to the dining room table and went straight for the kitchen, snagging a few beers from the fridge and passing them around while heading to the back porch to look at the moon.

"To your journey, Jack," said the large biker, raising his longneck, clacking the bottle with his friends.

Angela drank but suddenly felt a hole in her stomach, realizing that she had spent all day working on a suit that would allow Jack to leave her for the second time in her life. But she had occupied her mind with the technical aspects of the project, the scientist in her locking out emotions, focusing on what had to be the most critical project of her life. Jack wouldn't get a second chance up there if she made a mistake, if the pressure suit deflated, if the thermal control failed, if the oxygen delivery system malfunctioned.

If...

She stayed outside with them, looking at the ocean while Jack and Dago did most of the talking, engaged in a game of looking for differences between his world and this one—which she found a bit disturbing.

"Angie? You okay?" Jack asked after a while.

Angela managed a nod while sipping her beer and staring at the ocean, even though she was actually as far away from okay as one could imagine, as the re-alization of losing him again descended, twisting her insides, in a way even mak-ing her wish he had never shown up at her doorstep. After all, she had managed, albeit quite painfully, to get over him, to start a new life and develop feelings for someone else—even if that someone turned out to be an asshole.

And now, the realization of having to go through that again sent a sudden wave of depression through her.

But then another voice echoed inside her head, mixed with the sound of breaking waves and the whistling sea breeze: *put on your big-girl pants and suck it up.*

Sitting next to Jack, Angela placed a hand over his, interlacing fingers, also realizing that for the longest time she had prayed to hold him just one more time. She remembered quite clearly the many, many nights she'd spent crying, hugging her pillow, wishing like crazy that it was Jack, willing to trade everything for just one more night with him, for just one more moment of intimacy to say good-bye.

So rather than sitting there feeling sorry for herself, Angela did the only thing that made sense. She stood up, said good night to Dago, who raised his beer at her and winked, before taking Jack by the hand to the master bedroom.

Later, after they were finished and spooned naked under the covers, as she felt his steady breathing caressing the back of her neck, Angela slowly came to terms with the bittersweet hand she had been dealt.

Jack would only be here for a little while longer. He would warm her bed for just the days or maybe even the week or two it would take her to secure the items and get him ready for his return home.

And then he would be gone.

For better or for worse, that was all that fate was offering.

And it would have to be good enough.

The team moved through the woods swiftly, using the cover of darkness to make their advance near invisible, like shadows shifting in the night, moving single file.

Davis was in front, guiding his men, using this opportunity to prove his leadership not just to the team he had inherited from the treacherous Riggs, but also to Hastings, who had issued orders to bring Angela Taylor to him alive.

Everyone else was expendable.

Hastings had been very clear, and even someone as experienced and battle-hardened as Davis, having not just survived but actually thrived through three tours in Afghanistan, felt his stomach twist at the thought of disappointing the general.

Back in Kabul, Davis had fought for his country knowing quite well that win or lose, his family back home would always be safe.

That wasn't quite the case operating under Hastings's rule.

But Davis didn't have a choice. Opportunities for returning veterans were slim, and when his young son was diagnosed with a strange form of leukemia, and the best treatment was beyond his reach, Hastings had stepped in, providing his family with the resources to put the toddler under the care of the finest professionals in the business, pushing the cancer into full remission within a year.

But now Hastings owned him.

Davis's family continued their daily life, enjoying the benefits of his new employment, but unaware of the dark consequences of failure.

Tonight the general had been furious, and whatever it was, Davis noticed it had been serious enough for Hastings to appear visibly shaken, which was definitely a first, at least for the Afghan vet.

The general had left town within the hour and jumped on a plane to somewhere, but not before reiterating his orders.

Focus, he thought, momentarily looking over his right shoulder at his team. All six wore black uniforms beneath the protection of flexible body armor layering their chests and shoulders, also black, capable of absorbing the impact of rifle shots and shrapnel without impairing movement.

They continued, gloved hands gripping M4 carbines fitted with sound suppressors, finally emerging from the woods surrounding the property, crossing the short meadow, reaching the back of the one-story structure, shown in hues of green as painted by the Generation IV night-vision devices strapped around their heads, designed to reduce image noise over prior generations while also allowing operation with a luminous sensitivity nearly twice that of its predecessor, translating into sharper images.

Davis ordered his men divided into two teams of three, one to cover the front and the other the rear. He remained with the latter while watching the former rush around the corner, toward the front, signaling thirty seconds later that they were in position.

He checked the luminous dial on his watch, counting down the seconds before starting the next phase of the mission, when his team would flush the occupants toward the waiting arms of the men covering the front.

He inspected the metallic surface of the rear door, making his decision.

"Now," he whispered into his throat mike, and a moment later one of his men, almost six-five and weighing close to three hundred pounds of solid muscle, removed the battering ram strapped across his back, clutched it in both hands, and swung it back once, his neck muscles pulsating as he shoved it with all his strength right into the center of the door, just above the lock while also stepping in the direction of the blow to increase the momentum.

The heavy door creaked and caved in, but it didn't open.

"Again," he whispered, getting behind him as he swung it once more, delivering a second strike, ripping the door off its hinges, and sending it crashing into a hallway.

"Move, move, move!" he whispered, leading the charge, rushing across the hallway and into a deserted living room, his M4 up near his face, his goggles peering through the sights into every corner, looking for movement, for any sign of occupancy, his shooting finger poised over the trigger, the adrenaline heightening his senses.

But a moment later those same senses told him something was seriously wrong.

"Check the bedrooms," he ordered, going into the kitchen, staring at the dirty dishes in the sink and the empty pizza boxes on the counter, opening the refrigerator and noticing the cans of Red Bull and Budweiser Light.

"Bedrooms clear," one of his men reported.

He checked the front room again, looking under sofas, behind curtains, going into the utility room and then the garage, noticing it was empty. No bikes. No cars.

Not a fucking thing.

Slowly, Davis lowered his weapon and returned to the living room, confused. The tip had reached him just twenty minutes ago. He had literally accomplished nothing short of a minor miracle by deploying a team in such short notice, running a textbook operation.

Except the intelligence had arrived too late. The house was empty.

And as he stood in the middle of a living room he knew had just been abandoned, he had the strangest feeling that—

Davis turned around, hearing a faint mechanical noise, looking up to the far corner in the living room, near the foyer, where the walls met the ceiling.

A security camera.

And it was moving, following him.

For the love of . . .

Davis paused in front of it, making sure the bastards at the other end got a good look at his dark figure, before giving them the finger, aiming his M4, and firing once.

"Whoa," said Art-Z, blinking at his tablet computer when the wireless video feed went blank as they hid in the woods to the east of the house. "Not a happy camper, that one."

"No shit, *amigo*," said Dago, kneeling next to him in the knee-high shrubbery lining the floor of the forest.

"See, Bonnie. You can't trust The Man even when he's supposed to be on your side."

Angela frowned while standing behind Art-Z and Dago, also looking at the screen, before shooting Riggs a look that could grind the pine trees surrounding them.

"So much for your fucking safe house."

The large FBI agent was about to reply when Pete put a hand on his shoulder and slowly shook his head.

Riggs looked away while mumbling, "Oh, God."

"It's okay, man," Pete said. "At least your handler was able to give us a little head start to get the hell out of Dodge."

"It's not that," he said. "It's . . . my family. If Hastings can find us this easily, he can also . . ."

"Where are they?"

"Atlanta. My handler's moving them to another location. But apparently nothing's beyond Hastings's reach."

"Wrong," she said. "His operation relies on the good guys following the rules. He knows how the system works and has created a way to operate within it by taking advantage of the established processes at the FBI, the CIA, and the other agencies. But we're hackers. And he's having a hard time figuring out how to handle us."

"So, what are you suggesting? Should I go get my family? Maybe hide them somewhere not even the FBI knows?"

Angela regarded the agent while frowning.

"What?" he asked.

"Before I answer your question on what we do next, I have a . . . delicate question for you."

Riggs crossed his large arms. "Shoot."

"Hastings found our hideout. What makes you think he hasn't found your family already?"

He blinked and hesitated, before saying, "I just got word that they're safe . . . just got moved to another location."

"Word from whom?"

"My handler."

"This is the same handler who told you we were safe in there?" She pointed at the house beyond the woods.

He looked away. "So what are you saying? That I forget about them?"

"Of course not. I agree with your thought to get them off the system, like we did with Olivia's daughter. No FBI handlers. No FBI safe houses. And bring them down here, where we have options. I completely believe that if we continue operating this way, Hastings won't find us because he doesn't have any moles planted in our little group, so he's probably pretty frustrated since he's used to getting his own way all the time. I'm just questioning the timing given that we were almost caught. Do you think it is safe to go get them now?"

"I don't have a choice," he said. "I have to try. The longer I wait, the higher the chances of Hastings finding out the location of their new hideout."

Angela patted him on the shoulder. She understood of course. Family was family, and Riggs was willing to do whatever it took to ensure their safety just as she had done from the moment Jack vanished off the screens.

"You do what you need to do," she finally told him. "Just be careful. There's a chance he could be using your family as bait."

"I know. I will."

"Then I'm going with you," Pete said. "In case you need backup."

Angela looked at both of them, her stomach souring at the thought of them walking right into a trap, but again, she couldn't argue with rescuing family. "Atlanta's a seven-hour drive," she said. "If you leave now you can be there before noon and be back in the evening."

Angela watched them drive away, before turning to Dago and Art-Z.

"Ready to turn up the heat?"

* * *

She had already anticipated the heat he would be experiencing during a fitting session and had lowered the thermostat to sixty degrees, turning the beachfront into a meat locker.

Jack wore the undergarment plus the battle gear underneath the dry suit before stepping into the one-piece restraining layer, which she zipped up to his neck while Dago sat in the corner, wrapped up in a blanket, his massive hands holding a cup of steaming coffee.

"How does it feel?"

He walked around the room, stretching his arms, moving up and down and to the sides, before slowly dropping to a crouch and standing back up.

"I can move in it," he said. "At least before pressurization. And it's lighter than the OSS. Is it going to hold?"

"It'll do the job," she said in a reassuring tone. "Plus it's still missing layers and most of the plumbing."

She made adjustments, took measurements, tucking this and that, working the neck, stiffening the edges that would meet the helmet's base with stainless steel wire, which she looped multiple times around the opening, leaving enough space for Jack's head, before folding the nylon over the wire frame and hand-stitching a seam all around using Nomex thread, careful not to stab him with the curved needle, going over it several times until she felt it was sturdy enough.

She reinforced it with a circle of half-inch-wide nylon lanyard, again hand-stitching it before turning her attention to the sleeves, also getting them ready to accept the Russian gloves.

"All right," she said, holding a measuring tape and tailor chalk to mark the locations where she would insert the rubber restraint joint mechanisms to help localize air displacement.

Jack knew exactly what she was doing, having been through this more times than he cared to remember. The concept was to place those rubberized structures so that bending one joint, like an elbow or a knee, didn't result in another joint being forced to move due to the air pressure inside the suit.

Angela applied marks to the elbow areas as well as the knees, shoulders, and upper thighs, before also marking the spot across the shoulders where she would fasten perforated metal ribbons to keep the upper section structurally sound to allow Jack freedom of movement during the jump. The ribbons also formed the foundation for the heat shields.

It lasted close to two hours, and Jack was glad to be out of it probably as much as Dago, who had bailed on them and waited out back, sitting in one of the Adirondack chairs watching the waves. Jack joined him after helping Angela lay out the suit on the dining room table.

"Too cold for you, man?"

"Brrr," the biker replied. "I'm a south Florida guy. Don't get how people live up north."

"I just reset the thermostat. Should be back to normal in a little while," Jack said, sitting down next to him.

"I gotta tell you, Jack, these have got to be the most bizarre days of my life. What a mind fuck."

"Yeah," he said. "Especially for Angie. She's still in there working on the suit I'll use to leave this world. I don't think she's slept much in the past couple of days."

Dago crossed his arms. "She did that before, you know."

"What do you mean?"

"After you . . . died, she spent time down at the shop."

"I didn't know that."

The biker kept his gaze on the breaking waves. "Getting her hands dirty somehow helped her process her loss. She would work for days on end overhauling engines, rebuilding transmissions, welding frames—doing anything to keep from thinking about you."

Jack stared at him.

"And I'm afraid she's doing it again in there. She's already began her mourning process . . . even before you leave."

"Yeah. Assuming I *can* leave. We still need to get that solar antenna from Pete," he said, before pointing a finger at the sky. "Plus find a way to get me back up there."

Jack headed back inside after a while and helped Angela cut the aluminized Mylar panels, deciding that three layers should be enough insulation buffer from the outer layer of flexible insulation material. As expected, the latter was the hardest to manage because it was so bulky, but together they marked it and cut it, before stressing the sewing machine during stitching.

By mid-afternoon the suit had all of the layers it would need, and it was time for another fitting, which ran Dago out of the house.

Jack got dressed layer after layer, doing it by himself, starting with the undergarment and the battle dress, followed by the dry suit, the restraining layer, which had the Mylar layered over its surface, and finally the outer shell.

"What do you think?" she asked.

Again, Jack walked around, feeling the weight, deciding that he could still manage by himself. The suit was certainly bulkier than the OSS, and that was before pressurization. But he gave her a thumbs-up.

Angela helped him out of it, but told him to keep the liquid-cooled undergarment on.

"Time for a little test," she said after they took the suit back to the dinner table.

"What kind of test?"

"Stand still, Jack," she ordered, taking a few minutes to connect a modified aquarium pump to the manifold built into the garment at waist level.

She plugged it in and the pump began to circulate the thermal liquid, which was distributed over four quadrants, two symmetrically for both the upper and lower body. No active heating would be incorporated into the closed system, but Angela felt that the parasitic heat transfer from Jack's body should be enough to keep his temperature reasonably comfortable as long as the outer layers—especially the Mylar and outer shell—did their jobs.

Temperature control would be critical during the ascent phase, and Angela planned to use a pair of car batteries connected to an inverter to generate the required AC current to drive not just the aquarium pump but also the pressurization and oxygen delivery system.

Once he jumped, however, Jack would be at the mercy of a small oxygen canister to deliver air until he reached normal atmospheric conditions.

"Seems to be working," she said, walking around Jack to inspect the entire garment. "I don't see any leaks. Circulation looks nominal."

"Good," he said.

She unplugged him and he changed back into jeans and a T-shirt.

"Tomorrow I'll work on the plumbing," she said, returning to the table and taking more measurements. "While you and Dago fetch me the last components."

Jack nodded, grabbed two beers, and headed back outside.

"Here you go," he said, handing one to the biker, still staring at the ocean.

"Thanks, Jack," he replied, tipping it toward him before sitting down.

They drank in silence, listening to the sea, the evening breeze whistling.

Jack gazed into the dark horizon, letting his eyes get used to the darkness, like he did in his SEAL days, scanning the ocean beyond the breaking waves, remembering the training at Coronado, the insertions, the missions, the—

Dago stood, walking up to the short railing. "It's peaceful out here," he said.

But Jack had stopped listening, his eyes trying to focus on a shadow just beyond the break and the silvery surf.

Squinting, he leaned forward, staring at it through the bottom of the railing, catching the sudden glint of glass flashing from the middle of the shadow.

"Dago! Get down!"

But the large biker didn't, his hands gripping the top of the railing as he jerked, a circle of blood forming on the back of his denim vest by his left shoulder.

Instincts took over.

Jack grabbed the biker by the waist and yanked him down to the deck as a round splintered a post, followed by another one hammering the steps leading to the sand.

Jack stayed low, reaching the door, crawling in, dragging Dago behind him as the biker groaned, a hand on his wound, his face twisted in pain.

Angela looked up from the table. "What the hell?"

"Pack up everything," he said, turning off the lights in the living room, before scrambling to his feet. "Hurry."

"Why? What's going—"

"Now, Angie," he said, reaching in one of the duffel bags and extracting a field dressing before kneeling by Dago and tearing off the vest with the SOG knife.

"Don't move," he hissed, pressing it hard into the wound to stanch the blood, before securing it just as he had done countless times in places he'd rather forget.

"It went through clean, man. You're lucky," he added.

"Th—thanks," Dago replied, breathing heavily, clenching his jaw, taking the pain.

Jack turned to Angela and said, "Put everything in the back of the truck but do *not* open the garage door."

She stood there, in apparent shock at Dago getting shot as Jack helped him to his feet.

"Angie! Now! Everything! Except for my bags and the battle dress."

14

RISKS AND COSTS

There are risks and costs to action. But they are far less than the long-range risks of comfortable inaction.

—John F. Kennedy

He never liked surprises, especially coming from his primary contact in the Department of the Treasury, who was approached discreetly by the vice-chairman of the Federal Reserve system making an unofficial inquiry about a set of large deposits made from numbered bank accounts in the Cayman Islands, the Bahamas, Switzerland, and Russia.

The accounts could never be traced back to him, according to his financial team, who had set them up to belong to front companies that didn't exist beyond brick-and-mortar facades—companies that were erased from the face of the planet an hour ago.

Hastings hung up the phone after spending thirty minutes trying to calm down his Treasury associate, assuring him that those accounts and their respective foreign corporations were dissolved the moment they were breached, and no amount of probing would yield anything.

He then returned to the more pressing matter of covering that loss. Services had been rendered by dozens of suppliers and payments were expected.

On time. No excuses.

Hastings spent the next hour in a meeting in the rear of his C-17 with his financial and IT wizards, trying to unravel what had happened. He remained calm, though he knew this had to be the work of Dr. Taylor and her hacker friends. She had managed to change the descent profile, hijacked his phone, hacked into SkyLeap, and did who-knew-what to Salazar's facility.

She was brilliant indeed, and quite the fighter, certainly possessing the gene-
tic makeup to enhance the Hastings family tree.

But she also needs to be stopped.

Although this was nothing more than an annoyance for Hastings, whose team
discussed options and solutions that would have the problem solved within
the hour, Dr. Taylor and her little scruffy—though highly effective—team were
starting to get too deep into his business, into his master plan. Today she had
scratched him. Tomorrow she could deliver a fatal blow to his operation.

As his people worked the problem, he decided that the time had come to
activate a new option—one he had been unwilling to trigger because of undesir-
able side effects. But given the circumstances, he saw no other alternative. His
security continued to come short every time they dealt with her, even after the
FBI tip, missing her by what appeared to be a few minutes. On top of that, he'd
just gotten word that Riggs's family had vanished from protected custody in
Atlanta, and that Olivia's daughter had disappeared from school.

That had been the final motivating factor.

He walked away from his team and dialed a number he had committed to
memory long ago.

The general had used him in the beginning, when Hastings had needed his
help to break in, recruit, train, and establish a beachhead.

Over the years, the general had repeatedly engaged his services whenever a
problem came up that required skills beyond the reach of his operatives, from
incentivizing—or eliminating—certain figures in cartels, organized crime, and
foreign governments, to motivating the occasional Washington politician who
couldn't be persuaded to bend through conventional means.

But Hastings hated using him simply because he didn't own him.

No one did.

Meaning he couldn't be fully controlled.

And Hastings hated not having full control.

But at the moment, it came down to choosing the lesser of the evils, selecting this option and its associated costs and risks for the sake of eliminating a
much larger risk.

"*General?*" the man's deep voice said at the other end in a thick Latin American accent, also pronouncing the *G* as an *H.* "It has been a very long time, my
friend."

"It certainly has, Javier," Hastings replied, closing his eyes. "It most certainly has."

Jack had to assume that the threat would come from all angles and in larger numbers than the last time.

Pete wouldn't make the same mistake again.

And that meant Jack would need a new approach, a different way to counterattack.

"Front still looks clear," Angela said inside the dark house, peeking through the blinds in the foyer. Dago was already in the truck, happily sucking on a Fentanyl lollipop.

"Trust me. They're out there," Jack said, reloading the M32 grenade launcher with a mix of armor-piercing and incendiary rounds, strapping it across his back before loading backup rounds on the utility belt around his waist.

"Looks like a lot of firepower."

"That's because it is," he said, latching a twenty-round box magazine to the MK11 sniper rifle and chambering a round before securing two backup boxes to the Velcro straps on his abdomen, right above the belt, and hauling the rest of the gear into the back of the truck.

"All right," he said. "Get in and wait for my signal."

She hesitated, before opening the door and looking at him.

"*Wait* for my signal," he repeated. "No matter what you hear out there."

"Jack," she started, putting a hand to his face.

"I know," he replied, closing the door before rushing to the rear door, the place where no one would be expecting him after that initial attack. That yacht was the flush team, working the rear to force him to the front, where he knew would be an even larger force waiting for him.

But he couldn't get out through the back just yet, not while that vessel had at least one sniper trained on the rear porch, ready to put a bullet in his head.

Jack needed a distraction, a way to even out the playing field long enough for him to reach the sand, to get himself away from the house and blend with the dunes leading to the ocean.

The answer was the MK79 Mod 0 flare gun.

Jack slowly inched open one of the living room windows just enough to squeeze the hot end of the cylindrical signaling device through, angling it toward the vessel, now visible beyond the break, a long shape swaying in the waves.

The snipers had to be using nightscopes to have any chance at accuracy in the darkness separating them from the beach house, which Jack estimated to be around five hundred feet—give or take. And that meant someone looking through a device that magnified the amount of photons from all natural sources, like moonlight or starlight.

But like anything else, night-vision scopes had a weakness. A sudden increase in light, such as an incendiary grenade or a flare gun—or even a fork of lightning—had the nasty effect of flashing right into the user's pupils, momentarily killing night vision.

Jack adjusted the MK79, before firing the flare, which arced over the railing and the beach, detonating high above the surf, over the boat.

He rolled away from the window and pushed through the door in a deep crouch, the MK11 leading the way, scrambling down the steps, the spring-action soles of the battle dress pointing his momentum toward the safety of the sand, below the immediate line of sight from snipers he knew would be rubbing their eyes right about now, as the flare hovered above them.

Jack felt the sand beneath him as he zigzagged, dropping in front of two low dunes, placing the long barrel in between them, resting it on the Harris swivel-based bipod.

He trained the crosshairs on the vessel, painted in flickering hues of crimson and yellow-gold by the suspended pyrotechnic.

Jack used the Leupold rifle scope to locate the three figures on the top deck, aligning the crosshairs with the closest one, and exhaling while pressing the trigger.

The bullet found its mark an instant later, and the figure dropped from sight just as his companions turned to look in their fallen comrade's direction.

Jack used that distraction to switch targets, scoring a second hit before the vessel's captain gunned the engines, accelerating into the night, cruising away from the vanishing red glow.

Jack watched its silvery trail on the water before rising to his feet, blending with the surroundings, dashing around the back of the property, moving swiftly but measuring his strides, remaining within the obscure confines of the corridor-like path between the houses, scanning his narrow field of view but not in a single sweep.

Aware that the human eye had surprisingly low acuity in any part of the visual field not at the very center, Jack shifted his eyes by just ten degrees every five seconds, allowing the center of his gaze, the fovea, to pierce the darkness, letting the high density of cones in the retina do the heavy lifting, letting the millions of receptive fields in the ganglion cells search for any shapes that didn't belong, any movement that would telegraph the presence of more—

There.

At his ten o'clock.

Protruding through a row of waist-high bushes across the street, under the shadow of a towering magnolia, protected from the glowing streetlights, Jack spotted two barrels, long, with bulky silencers screwed at the end.

I see you.

He dropped to the ground slowly, remaining in the shadowed recess by the front corner of the building, systematically probing his surroundings one narrow arc at a time, spotting a third operative on the roof across the street, his high-powered rifle trained on the garage doors.

This time around Pete wasn't bringing a boatload of soldiers but had chosen to take them covertly, to keep this from the authorities, to avoid another public Charlie Foxtrot, military-speak for a clusterfuck.

And that played in Jack's favor as he surveyed the street once more, finding only three marks, and looking up and down the street yielded no additional targets. He spotted no parked vehicles that suggested additional mercenaries.

But this can't be it, he thought, especially after the way he had disabled so many soldiers at the—

The answer came a moment later, when a vehicle turned onto the street, headlights off, driving slowly toward them. A large black van with dark windows, followed by a second matching vehicle.

That's more like it.

But it really didn't matter.

There was a reason why only a microscopic percentage of U.S. fighting forces made the cut to be a SEAL. It was a hard thing to explain, but somewhere along the way during those weeks of unparalleled training, during the inhumane drilling, the mental abuse, the unprecedented harsh treatment, and the even more brutal missions, the world suddenly seemed slower to a SEAL. Everyone else appeared to move in slow motion, in ways that made their actions predictable, easy to counterattack.

And it was happening now. As Jack watched the incoming threat, as the vans made their way toward the house, everything suddenly slowed to a crawl.

Except for Jack, who reached for his M32 grenade launcher, his eyes on the approaching vehicles, lining them up in the reflex scope, before releasing two armor-piercing rounds in rapid succession, one per vehicle.

Switching targets, he popped one more at the shrubs with the barrels and a fourth one on the roof across the street.

BOHICA, he thought, shrinking back in the recesses, the age-old acronym echoing in his mind: Bend Over Here It Comes Again.

The first two ear-piercing blasts boomed in rapid succession, one after the other, deafening, lighting up the street, shaking the ground, shattering windows.

The vans turned, crashing into trees, catching fire as the well-placed rounds punctured the frame before magnesium cores incinerated anything in a five-foot radius.

Occupants screamed, some jumping out, their clothes on fire as they rolled on the grass as a third explosion tossed bodies in the air across the street along with rifles, just as a fourth detonation on the roof disintegrated the sniper in a ball of flames, and debris running down onto the pavement.

Jack followed that with four smoke grenades, which he tossed at twenty-foot intervals starting right in front of the house and continuing down the street to cover their escape.

"Now, Angie," he spoke into his voice-activated throat mike as blue smoke filled the street, diffusing the pulsating flames, mixing with smoke boiling from the vans, from the charred corpses littering the street.

He rose to his feet, the M32 in his hands housing his last two rounds, the smell of burnt flesh assaulting his nostrils, bringing him back to Afghanistan and Colombia, his fallen comrades, the death and destruction marking so much of his military career.

The garage door opened and the truck leaped onto the driveway, fishtailing as she turned left, toward him, driving through the smoke like a black ghost.

Jack took off, ignoring the screams, the flames, the smoke burning his eyes, jumping into the open bed, landing on his back, weapon ready on instinct, narrowed eyes peering through the haze, searching for any survivors.

She accelerated, burning rubber, swerving around the wrecks, sending him tumbling inside the bed, banging his shoulders against the sides, whacking the side of his head.

"Jack! Up in front!"

He stood with difficulty, his head on fire, his eyes watering from the smoke, from the blow to his right temple, managing to run his left arm under the roll bar over the cabin to brace himself, to keep his footing as he spotted a third van at the end of the block, a couple hundred feet away.

"Keep going," he said, centering it on the reflex scope before loosing his fifth round, listening to it pop out of its housing, arcing toward the vehicle trying to block the way, its parabolic flight landing by the front bumper, skittering underneath.

The explosion momentarily lifted the van off the pavement at a sharp angle, reminding Jack of the initial seconds of a launch, as tongues of fire swept across the street from under the van, flickering in the night, the magnesium flash spreading its incinerating wave toward the surrounding lawns, setting shrubs ablaze.

Angela veered around it like a pro, steady, in control, even driving up on the sidewalk to miss a man jumping out, his back on fire.

Jack took a good look at him, large, bulky, dressed in civilian clothing, like the operatives he had disabled at—

A round pierced the back of the bed, like a hammer. Followed by another.

Jack tried to drop from sight when a powerful force punched him in between his shoulder blades, like an invisible fist, tearing into him, shoving him against the back of the cabin with savage strength.

Damn!

Jack fell to his knees as Angela turned the corner, rolling to his side, heaving, trying to breathe, his back on fire, his hands trembling, branches and stars rushing overhead as she accelerated.

"Jack, you okay back there?"

He heard her through the earpiece while forcing his drifting mind into focus. He'd just been shot, but the battle dress had once again protected him, saved his life.

He knew he'd been lucky, even if his aching spine and the near-paralyzing pain shooting down his limbs contradicted the thought.

Breathe.

He forced air into his lungs before exhaling through his mouth, slowly, and doing it again and again, imposing concentration, reaching for his weapon and sitting up, his back against the cabin, his eyes slowly regaining focus, looking at the street behind them.

"Jack?"

"Still . . . here," he replied, hands clutching the MK11 sniper rifle, fingers automatically working the weapon, getting it ready but keeping it out of sight from any onlooker as Angela drove them toward the—

And that's when he spotted it, almost three blocks away, headlights piercing the darkness separating them.

Jack considered switching to the grenade launcher again, but there were people in the streets, so he stuck with the MK11, trying to look through the Leupold rifle scope as the truck sped down the street.

He was used to firing from moving platforms, from Chinook or Blackhawk helicopters to Combat Rubber Raiding Crafts and everything in between, but it was still a challenging task.

The trick was to relax, to not force the alignment, to hold the crosshairs in the vicinity of the target and wait for it to come to you instead of the other way around.

Jack kept the heavy rifle trained on the vehicle, which he now recognized as a fourth van, black, like the others, gaining on them.

He breathed in and out, the butt pressed against his right shoulder, ignoring the stabbing pain, pushing his body to deliver one more time, his shooting eye peering through the advanced optics, depicting his target clearly under the streetlights.

But he still didn't fire, biding his time, waiting for the right moment, which came as the vehicle closed the gap to just over half a block, the driver coming into view behind the windshield.

Jack exhaled slowly and fired.

The 7.62mm NATO round pierced through the windshield, but was off to the left, missing the driver's head, nicking the shoulder.

But it was enough for him to lose control. The van veered to the left, then the right as he struggled to center it, but ran into a light post, crashing through it and into the side of a building.

Jack lowered the weapon as Angela continued driving, unaware of what had just transpired. But Jack was very much aware of everything, his senses on edge from the adrenaline rush, which he knew was dulling the pain streaking across his back.

"Angie, the highway," Jack said into his throat mike.

"Got it. North or south?"

"South," he replied.

Jack was sick of running, tired of dodging team after team, knowing that eventually one of them would get lucky. It was just the odds, and he hated playing them here as much as he did during his last mission in Colombia.

But he hadn't had a choice in that jungle. The gear had malfunctioned, telegraphing his position, killing his options.

Not here, he thought, deciding to stop hiding and strike back like only a SEAL could. Jack needed to do the unexpected and regain the element of surprise, like he had done in so many missions, striking fear in the heart of the enemy, turning the hunter into the hunted.

To do so, he would need to change tactics, do the unforeseen, and take the fight right back to its source.

Right back to Pete.

They didn't even put a chink in his armor.

Angela and Art-Z sat back and just stared at their screens in a roadside motel in Vero Beach while waiting for Pete and Riggs to return from Atlanta. Dago was out getting food and drinks.

"I don't get it," she said. "We took forty-seven million dollars from his accounts—his own fucking accounts—and deposited them into Federal Reserve banks and there's nothing there."

They'd read every scrap of news from dozens of outlets trying to see the effect of their work.

At first they had expected a major story in Washington, but it soon became evident that Hastings had orchestrated amazing damage control, to the point that there wasn't a single mention of anything even remotely related to General George Hastings or the money that suddenly appeared in government coffers.

It simply didn't make any damn sense, especially with the way the U.S. Government went after anyone screwing with its money, including public officials caught embezzling or misusing tax dollars. The list was even larger inside the Pentagon, where cases of selling military equipment in black markets resulted in hundreds of millions of dollars and tons of indictments.

Yet, there was nothing in the news.

Her only hope—and she knew it was a stretch—was that although publicly their plan had apparently not yielded any results, under the covers Hastings could be scrambling to cover his losses. After all, the money taken was meant to pay for shadowy jobs, secret services, and smuggling operations.

You're reaching, Angela.

She shook her head, accepting the hard reality that their attempt to expose him had been fruitless. And the irony was that she was the one hiding in this flea motel, on the run instead of Hastings.

And what made matters even worse was that she hadn't heard from Pete or Riggs, who should have been back a couple of hours ago from their trip to Atlanta.

Where are they?

She had thought about calling them but resisted the temptation. If somehow they had walked into a trap and got caught, calling them wouldn't accomplish anything but risk giving away her location.

She exhaled heavily, starting to get a bad feeling but deciding to stick to her own plan. Pete and Riggs would call when they returned to the Orlando area, where the FBI agent would pay cash for a motel room like this one and leave his family there, before Angela would tell them how to get here.

She returned her focus to the screen, pointing at the passwords they had gathered, at the back door she had installed. "It looks like they haven't found our little gadget yet."

"For now," he said. "Do you want to go after more banks? Maybe crash his network again? Slow down production?"

She shook her head. Art-Z was thinking too much like a traditional hacker, and Angela wasn't so sure that would be the best way to move forward. "Perhaps we need a different approach."

"What do you mean?"

Angela stood. For the first time since Jack vanished, she began to wonder if she was in way over her head.

But what choice did she have?

She had to continue, had to keep pushing, learning, dissecting Hastings's web of deception. But she needed a new tactic. The definition of insanity was doing things the same way and expecting better results.

"You heard Riggs," she finally said. "The general has too many buffers, too many layers of protection. There's a reason why even the FBI can't touch him. Bastard owns too many people in too many damn places to come at him indirectly, like we just did. As brilliant and gutsy as that move was, all we accomplished was letting him know that we're on to him. But if we really want to hurt him, we need a new strategy."

"What do you have in mind?"

Angela walked over to the windows overlooking a parking lot. Nowhere near as glamorous as that lovely FBI safe house in the woods—but certainly a hell of a lot safer.

Once more she tried to think like Jack would. How do you stop someone who seems unstoppable, who didn't even blink when they stole tens of millions of his blood money and deposited them into the Federal Reserve system? How do you go up against a network that had its tentacles everywhere, who even the mighty FBI couldn't bring down?

She pinched the bridge of her nose and closed her eyes.

Hastings had created the perfect machine, controlling all of the angles, striking the perfect balance in his operation, not only owning apparently enough people in the government but also forging allegiances with criminal networks. And he had also devised an internal security apparatus straight out of the Third Reich, governing his operation with an iron fist, preventing anyone from gaining too much power, from ever becoming a threat to him.

Angela crossed her arms, staring into the distance. Strengths always had the potential to become weaknesses when overused. This was a fundamental truth everywhere, from science and religion to politics—and even criminal networks.

By becoming overly zealous in controlling every aspect of his operation, in his obsession for security, for a Gestapo-like internal police, for refusing to let anyone know the entire picture, Hastings had unknowingly created a huge weakness.

She turned around and looked at the master hacker. "We go for the head, Art."

"The head?"

She ran the tip of her thumb across her neck. "We need to chop it off."

"*Literally?*"

"That's the only way to bring down his massive house of cards. That's the weakness in his operation: it can't survive without him. There's no number two in his scheme. No one's ready to take his place because he's set it up precisely to *keep* anyone else from gaining power over him. That's the reason Riggs couldn't get close enough to make a difference."

Art-Z considered that before saying, "That's . . . brilliant, Bonnie . . . except . . ."

"Except?"

"How are we going to get close enough to take him out?"

She crossed her arms and smiled. "We won't have to."

"What do you mean?"

"I mean we're not going to try to get to him."

Art-Z made a face. "I'm not following."

"We're going to make him come to us."

They reached his street and drove up and down twice, making sure it was clean, before pulling up his driveway, which went around the side of the house, leading to a four-car garage. They parked the truck there, out of sight from the street.

Dago needed a little help getting out but was able to walk on his own, the field dressing having worked its magic, plus he had been fortunate that the bullet hadn't only gone through clean, it had also missed major arteries or bones.

"You sure about this place, Angie?"

"He's a workaholic. He's never here when things are normal. Now who knows when he'll be back. Plus I have a way to keep tabs on him."

"How?"

"You'll see," she replied, as they approached the front.

Angela reached under a rock beneath knee-high shrubs framing the entrance, producing a key.

"And you know his alarm code?"

"Unless he changed it in the last few days, which I doubt. Like I said, the man's never here."

The key worked and they stepped into a foyer leading to a large open area that combined the living room, dining room, and a massive gourmet kitchen. It all overlooked a beautiful swimming pool backdropped by the Indian River and what Jack recognized as a fifty-eight-foot Sundancer, a Sea Ray sports yacht moored by a dock next to a couple of WaveRunners perched on their individual lifts.

"I guess it pays to be a bad guy. Your boyfriend ever cooked for you in there?" Jack asked, pointing his chin at the kitchen.

She punched him lightly on the shoulder before stabbing the alarm keypad with an index finger. "He can't even boil an egg."

Jack inspected the entire house, going through every room followed by Angela, stopping to inspect his workout area, looking at the heavy punching bag hanging from the ceiling on a chain as well as another one in the shape of the upper body of a flesh-colored rubberized sparring mannequin atop a heavy black base. Both looked quite worn out, signaling heavy usage. He also eyed the free weights, bag gloves, and even some trophies.

"Is he still boxing?"

"More like mixed martial arts," she added. "He's actually pretty skilled."

"Good to know," Jack said.

Satisfied that the house was clean, they took Dago to the master bathroom, where Angela went straight for the medicine cabinet and changed his bandage, applying generous amounts of antibacterial cream to both sides of the wound.

After leaving him sleeping in Pete's king-size bed, Jack and Angela retrieved their gear from the truck after parking it in the empty spot in the garage, next to a Porsche 911, a BMW SUV, and a shiny Harley Davidson Fat Boy.

"The Mercedes sedan is missing," she said.

Jack slowly shook his head at the bike. "The Pete I know never rode a day in his life."

"I seem to have that influence on my men," she said.

Jack didn't like that answer, but shrugged it off, focusing on the gear, which they hauled to the dining room. But instead of picking up where they had left off at Layton's place the night before, Angela powered up Pete's home computer.

"What are you doing?" he asked.

"Jack, do you really think we're going to stay here without keeping tabs on . . . what did you call him . . . oh, yeah, my boyfriend?" She winked at him.

He grinned. "All right, I deserve that one. What are you doing?"

"Scoping things out in my old stomping grounds."

"You're hacking into NASA?"

"Well, I don't have an account."

"How are you going to do that?"

"Please, Jack. The only reason you're here is because I . . . because your wife hacked the descent profile. She did that through a back door into the network that she installed when no one was looking. I did the same thing back in the day."

He sighed and watched her work. It didn't take her long, invoking a back door she had programmed eons ago. Suddenly, the screen divided into nine windows, each depicting a different view of the Cape as she accessed the security system.

"There's Pete's car," she said, pointing at a silver Mercedes in the top right window, fed by one of the security cameras from the KSC Headquarters building on NASA Boulevard.

"Where do you think he's hiding the OSS?"

"Good question. If we run with your theory that he's playing this one close to his chest, then I'd guess he's taken the suit to a building that's not being used at the moment, but where he could still analyze it, perhaps even bring in a handful of his most trusted scientists."

"The Project Phoenix building was at the intersection of A Avenue and Fifth Street," Jack said. "In the southwest corner of Industrial Park."

She looked at him. "That's the same location we used. When we canceled the project, we stored all of the gear there, including the prototype suits."

Angela spent just fifteen minutes in the site, browsing through most of the security cameras, peeking inside buildings, in labs, in conference rooms, getting a feeling for the security, counting the number of guard stations, before injecting a link into the security camera covering Pete's car.

"Now we get an alert the moment that car moves," she said, getting up and stretching. "Ready to finish your suit?"

"I thought you'd never ask."

They worked from memory, running the tubing and wiring required for thermal control, pressurization, and oxygen delivery, spending the next few hours connecting, sealing, and sewing, before shifting to the Russian suit.

They spent another two hours removing the locking rings for the large helmet and gloves before integrating them into his suit, securing them with plenty of Nomex stitching, running each layer, from the pressure vessel and up into the grooves of the titanium rings, creating airtight seams that Angela believed would hold. Along the way, she was able to harvest additional components from the Russian suit, including wrist gauges for pressure, oxygen, and altitude, which she secured to the left sleeve.

"Time for a pressure test," she said, connecting the hoses for oxygen, pressure, and thermal control into the anodized receptacles on the front of the suit, before zipping up the empty suit and locking the helmet and gloves in place.

Angela turned on the small pump connected to a pair of car batteries with an inverter to generate the required AC current, delivering pure oxygen under pressure through the hoses.

Jack stood next to Angela and checked the gauges on the suit's wrist. Had this been the real thing, pressurizing high up in the atmosphere, the suit would have stopped at 4.3 psi—pounds per square inch—or around 0.29 atmospheres, the typical NASA pressure for spacewalks. But since they were at sea level under a normal atmospheric pressure of 14.7 psi, or 1 atmosphere, Angela pressurized the suit to just below 30 psi, before shutting off the pressure pump and looking at her watch.

He kept his eye on the pressure needle, which remained steady at the 30 psi mark for the fifteen-minute test while Angela checked all around the suit, using tailor chalk to mark any areas that were ballooning more than normal, meaning the restraining layer wasn't holding back the pressure vessel strongly enough. But besides those areas where she might need to add more nylon lanyard to reinforce the container vessel, the suit was holding quite nicely.

"Good job, Angie," he said as she slowly relieved the pressure, deflating the suit.

If the seams could hold at 30 psi, they shouldn't have any problem at 4.3 psi up in the stratosphere.

Leaving Dago asleep in the bedroom, Jack got in the truck while Angela jumped on Pete's Harley. They headed to a large storage facility located just south of the Cape, where NASA stored obsolete equipment.

It was almost midnight by the time they parked a block from the only entrance to the chain-link fenced storage facility protected by a pair of graveyard-shift guards inside a glass booth just beyond the gate.

"You know where to go once we get inside?" he asked.

"Yep."

Jack surveyed the place again, spotting security cameras covering pretty much every angle of the facility and likely feeding monitors inside the guard station. Beyond it was a windowless building two stories high with a flat roof.

"Ready?" he asked her, donning an empty backpack.

She nodded, starting the Fat Boy, which rumbled to life. "See you on the other side," she said, driving off in her jeans and a halter top. No helmet.

Jack tested the fence, just eight feet tall and lacking any other security feature, like barbed wire or electricity.

He watched Angela reach the gate and gun the Harley, prompting the guards to look up from whatever they were doing, exchanging glances, before stepping outside.

Lock and load.

Jack went over the fence in ten seconds, landing on his feet and taking off in the direction of the guards, who seemed entertained by Angela's little biking display, her halter top flapping in the breeze as she winked at them.

The guards never saw him coming, his approach masked by the deafening noise.

He palm-struck their necks almost in unison, shocking their vagus nerves, dropping them in seconds before removing a remote control connected to what he guessed was the facility's master key. He used it to open the gate for Angela, who drove through before he closed it and dragged the guards back inside the guard station.

Angela went ahead while Jack removed the DVDs from the monitoring system, pocketing them before closing the door and rushing down the short driveway to the building's main entrance.

He used the master key to get inside, closing the heavy metal door behind them, removing all evidence of their attack from anyone driving by.

"Six minutes left," Jack said. He had allowed ten minutes for the entire operation and they had already consumed almost four.

The interior of the building was open to the roof, like a classic warehouse, with two-story rows of shelves packed with a variety of gear on wooden pallets.

Angie ran to the rear of one row, stopping by a set of boxes labeled PROJECT PHOENIX.

She skipped the first three before rummaging through the fourth one and began handing Jack plastic bags filled with cube-shaped reinforced carbon-carbon tiles each roughly an inch square and a quarter of an inch thick.

He placed them in the backpack while she went through five more boxes, finding tubes that he recognized as high-temperature cement as well as cans of a pasty material commonly referred to as gap filler, made of alumina fibers to fill in any apertures between tiles, especially around the leading edges of the shuttle such as the nose cap, windshields, and wings.

"How do you remember where all this stuff was?"

"I just do," she said, closing all of the boxes and placing them back in their original position. "Some things are hard to forget. Project Phoenix was one of them. I packed this myself shortly before my resignation. Never thought I would need any of it, ever."

"Time," he said, tapping his watch.

They made their way back to the door, where she jumped on the bike while he locked the warehouse, opening the gate for her to leave before closing it and dropping the remote and keys inside the guard cage, where the two men lay unconscious.

Jack left the compound in the same way he had gone in, over the fence, landing in a deep crouch by the truck just as Angela pulled up on the Harley.

He thought about driving the stolen truck back to the house and decided he had probably gotten as much use out of it as he should. So they ditched it several blocks away.

Angela donned the backpack and rode in back, hugging Jack from behind while he steered the bike off the curve, accelerating into the night, the breeze sweeping his face as he enjoyed her embrace, the side of her head pressed in between his shoulder blades.

They reached Pete's house fifteen minutes later, closing the garage door and walking back into the living room.

Dago was still out.

Although it was close to two in the morning, they decided to press on, cementing RCC tiles to the helmet and shoulder pads and using the gap filler to create a continuous surface, finishing the job just before 3:00 A.M.

Angela stood, stretched, and headed into the kitchen, returning with two Coronas, handing one to Jack before they held hands and walked outside, sitting by the pool to look at the stars.

"Are you ready to go back?"

That was one hell of a question, and Jack wasn't sure he could answer it truthfully. A growing part of him had gotten used to this version of Angela, affectionate, passionate, even a little naughty in the bedroom, or the shower, or even the spa. She was simply adorable, with her long blond hair, her magical chocolate freckles, and her innate ability to leave him at a loss for words, like she'd just done.

Instead, he just hugged her, kissing the top of her head.

"It's still so surreal," she added.

Jack raised his eyebrows. That was one word to describe the past week, and he could think of many others that would fit the very, very strange sequence of events since he had jumped from that pod.

"I don't want to leave you," he said.

"But you have to," she completed for him.

"I know."

"And I understand that, Jack. You need to go back not just for her or for you, but also to stop whatever it is that Hastings is trying to do with this technology. The more I think about it, the more terrifying the scenarios that play out in my mind."

Jack didn't need to add anything to that comment. Angela, as usual, was spot on. This technology in the hands of Hastings was nothing but bad news. And Jack could only hope that his wife back home had found a way to at least stay alive long enough for him to return.

Angela's disposable phone vibrated once.

She looked at it and said, "Layton," before reading the text message and adding, "He's confirmed three altitudes. Forty-eight kilometers, sixty kilometers, and seventy-two kilometers. Any of those will hit the right harmonic of twelve."

"So we're going to need that high-altitude balloon that Dago's guys secured after all," he said, glad that they had narrowed down at least one altitude reachable with a balloon—forty-eight kilometers or around twenty-nine miles, which would make the jump much less complicated than if they had to get him into a rocket.

"And a place to launch it."

But before they could do that, Jack would need to pay a little visit to his former best friend.

15
REAL FEAR

The only thing we have to fear is fear itself.
—Franklin D. Roosevelt

Pete blinked to clear his sight as he sat in the corner of a warehouse-like room, zip ties securing his limbs to the arms and legs of a heavy wooden chair bolted to the concrete floor, a strip of duct tape over his lips as he was forced to watch the horror show.

Riggs hung naked from his shackled wrists in the middle of the room covered in cuts and bruises as the man who called himself Javier walked around him armed with an X-Acto knife.

A bit shorter than Pete, which made him look even shorter standing by the tall and muscular FBI agent, Javier smoothed his beard, regarding him with indifference, almost as if he was just a pig being slaughtered.

That was the thing that had chilled Pete the moment he first saw the Hispanic man who had ambushed them on the way out of Atlanta: the detachment in his eyes, in his dead stare, almost like the eyes of a shark, dark, lifeless.

Pete tried to control his breathing. Everything had happened too fast. One moment he had been pumping gas at a station outside of Atlanta, and the next, he had a bag over his head and was bouncing inside the trunk of a car with his wrists tied behind his back.

And next thing he knew he woke up right here a moment ago, in this windowless building strapped to this chair while Riggs swung from shackles on a meat hook at the end of a long chain bolted to a rafter, his feet hovering inches from a metal pan on the concrete floor collecting his dripping blood.

Javier slashed his skin, though never too deep, just enough to make him bleed a little, as Riggs tensed, jerked, squirmed, briefly groaning in pain, his tight fists fighting the heavy shackles, before exhaling and going limp again.

Pete sat against a heavy wooden table a few feet from the hanging agent, metal shackles anchored to its rough surface at both ends.

He slowly looked about him, gazing at the disturbing metal objects on shelves, at the furnace in the corner. This was no ordinary building or warehouse, resembling some sort of medieval blacksmith shop.

And what was even more disturbing was the video camera on a tripod angled to capture the table as well as Riggs.

"You and . . . Hastings can go . . . fuck yourselves," Riggs hissed, coughing, his bloody lips twisting in anger.

Javier smiled. "You are so brave, my friend," he said in his thick accent. "But the only ones getting fucked tonight are you . . . and your family."

Riggs's arm muscles throbbed as they stressed against the iron restraints. "Don't you dare . . . fucking bastard . . . don't you dare . . . lay one of your greasy hands on them."

Javier pressed the tips of his right index finger and thumb against the corners of his mouth and let out a near-deafening whistle.

A door slid open and two large Latinos, as big and muscular as Riggs, dragged Riggs's wife into the room. She also had duct tape over her lips and had been crying, her cheekbones smeared with mascara. Pete had met the tall and slender brunette, who went by the name of Susan, when they'd arrived at the FBI safe house the day before. But at least she was still dressed and seemed unharmed.

Pete inhaled deeply in relief.

"Leave her . . . out of this," Riggs hissed. "This is between Hastings and—"

Javier punched him hard in the solar plexus. The FBI agent gasped for air while swinging from the meat hook.

"*Colgarla al lado de él.*"

The men shackled Susan's wrists and hung her from a second meat hook adjacent to Riggs.

"Look at that," Javier said with a grin. "Husband and wife about to die side by side."

"Okay . . . wait . . . I'll tell you everything."

Javier rubbed his bearded chin. "Oh, will you, now?"

Riggs looked at Pete who shook his head.

Don't do it, man! They'll kill us anyway.

"Yes. Just don't hurt her. Please," Riggs said.

"Very well, my friend," Javier said, pointing at the camera.

Riggs began to talk, telling them how they were supposed to contact Angela after reaching Orlando and setting up his family in a hotel. He even gave them her phone number, told them about Art-Z and Dago, and how they had masterminded the banking transactions.

"You speak the truth, my friend?"

"Yes . . . I swear it."

Javier pressed his lips together and nodded solemnly at him. "I believe you."

As Riggs exhaled slowly, Javier turned to his men and ran the tip of his thumb across his own neck while shifting his gaze to the terrified woman.

"Wait!" Riggs pleaded. "I told you everything that—"

Javier kicked him hard in the groin.

Riggs groaned, twisted, and screamed, before nearly passing out, his eyelids fluttering as one of his men slashed her throat.

Pete watched as she thrashed about, moaning, eyes wide open in shock, the duct tape muffling her screams.

Riggs went crazy, screaming, jerking against the metal restraints, howling at the top of his lungs, cursing, swearing.

Javier laughed before punching him in the gut, sending him swinging again.

Pete closed his eyes, unable to see this, wanting to shout, tugging at the zip ties.

"Bastards . . . you fucking . . . bastards. I . . . told you . . . everything," Riggs hissed, his bruised chest expanding and contracting as Susan stopped moving, hanging limp from her restraints, eyes staring into the distance.

Javier walked over to Riggs, who was breathing heavily, his face twisted in pain.

"Take a good look at her, my friend," Javier told him, reaching for his face, forcing him to stare at his dead wife, before shoving the ends of his thumbs into the base of his eyes, gouging them.

Riggs screamed, lurching against his restraints to no avail.

Javier ripped them out of their sockets and threw them in the bucket, before producing a switchblade and castrating him, letting him bleed out.

Riggs howled, blood streaming from his face and groin as his back bent like a bow, tight fists fighting the restraints, before slowly going limp.

Pete shrunk back in his chair, his throat dry, his mind in turmoil, the coppery smell of blood filling his nostrils.

Slowly, a door slid open and General Hastings stepped in.

He pointed at the video recorder and one of Javier's men turned it off and walked away with it.

Hastings took a moment to inspect the bodies.

"I see you haven't lost your touch, Javier."

"*Gracias*, General."

Slowly, he turned to Pete and approached him.

Pete tried to control his breathing, his rocketing heartbeat, his mind still trying to comprehend what he had just witnessed.

Hastings stood in front of him awhile, looking larger than life, and finally said, "Riggs didn't have a choice, Flaherty. But you do. I could use someone as talented as you and Dr. Taylor in my operation. Now, are you finally ready to talk?"

He came in from the water.

Under the cover of darkness.

Like a SEAL.

He had used one of Pete's WaveRunners to get him close enough, before ditching it and diving the rest of the way, using his compass to hold a course of one seven zero, heading south for two miles in the Banana River, which bordered the east end of the Kennedy Space Center's industrial park, at a depth of just ten feet, letting the SeaScooter do most of the work.

Jack relaxed in the pitch-black waters, the battle dress keeping him comfortable, enjoying the ride, surfacing only once to check his position, spotting the NASA Parkway bridge in the distance, which connected the Industrial Park to the launchpads by the Atlantic Ocean.

He went under again for another fifteen minutes, surfacing for the last time by a narrow bay that curved inland from the main river, leading to Tenth Street, the southeast corner of the Industrial Park.

Jack followed it, reaching the marshes a few hundred feet beyond, stopping by a narrow sandy path that sneaked up to the street past a narrow forest.

He remained immersed, except for his eyes and ears, which surveyed the sur-roundings under a star-filled sky, listening for several minutes, examining the terrain beyond the protection of the water.

The place was quiet this time of night. Jack removed his tanks, masks, fins, and BCD, leaving them partly hidden in the marsh alongside the SeaScooter, before reaching the waterproof pouch strapped to his left thigh, removing his Sig Sauer 9mm semiautomatic, a sound suppressor cylinder, and four spare clips. He screwed the suppressor to the end of the muzzle and slipped the extra clips in elastic pouches on his battle dress. He also secured three fragmentation grenades and three M84 stun grenades, which he hoped he wouldn't need to use tonight.

Before heading out, he put on a black bandanna, reapplied camouflage cream on his face, donned a pair of skin-tight gloves, and hooked up his throat mike.

"In position," he whispered.

"Read you loud and clear, Jack, but I can't see you on any cameras," Angela said from Pete's house.

"Good. That means they can't see me either."

"Starting the loop now," she said. "Give me a second."

Jack waited. Angela had recorded an hour's worth of video footage for each camera in the Industrial Park and was now launching an algorithm that would replay them so anyone watching wouldn't see the live feed for sixty minutes—the time he estimated he would need to complete this mission.

"It's done," she reported.

"What's the guard situation?" he mumbled.

"Looking now," she replied. "Pretty dark out there."

Jack crawled out of the water, staying low in the thick forest separating the marsh from the road, like a predator in the jungle, reaching the gravel by the edge of the trees, peering beyond it, inspecting the street, devoid of any traffic this late at night.

Jack followed the tree line east, for almost a half mile, using the forest to shield him as he reached the intersection of Tenth and F Avenue and quickly crossing it, entering another narrow forest in between E and F Avenues, and continuing north for five more blocks, arriving at the west end of Fifth Street, where it met D Avenue, and telling Angela where he was.

Again he paused, listening, observing, measuring his approach. His eyes, long

accustomed to the darkness, probing deep beyond the edge of the woods, searching for figures, for shadows, for anything that would break the natural pattern
of the—

Jack held his breath, his ears picking up the sound of soles crunching gravel.

"I just spotted a guard by the edge of the parking lot."

"Taking a look now," he mumbled, inching forward, peeking around the corner of the waist-high grass separating the woods from the parking lot, spotting
the guard's silhouette fifty-some feet away, dark against the streetlights on C Avenue at the other end of the parking lot, walking at the edge of the tall grass in
his direction.

"I see him," he whispered.

Beyond the parking lot rose the main set of structures making up the heart
of the space center, including its headquarters, labs, office buildings, processing
facilities, and, most important, Building M7-1345, the old Project Phoenix location, where Angela guessed Pete was hiding the damaged OSS.

The guard, armed with a standard-issue M-17 SCAR-H rifle, patrolled the
edge of the parking lot, focused on the perimeter, scanning the top of the grass.

Jack frowned. Angela was right, as always. Pete and Hastings had certainly
turned this place into a military facility.

The guard continued his assigned route, moving methodically, in Jack's direction, slowly, his eyes probing the woods.

Jack waited, blending with the tall grass, his eyes on his prey as the man's
left boot came into view.

He surged from the grass, surprising the guard, their eyes locking for an instant, as Jack chopped him in the neck before clapping his hands over his ears.

"Jack, the guard just fell."

"Not quite," he said, dragging him into the marsh.

"Oh, I see you."

He removed the guard's jacket and rifle, pretending to be him while crossing
the short parking lot, while ignoring a pair of guards posted a few hundred feet
away at Gate 2F, which led to State Road 3—ironically the way Angela and he
took to reach their house in Cocoa Beach.

The guards glanced in his direction and one even waved at his dark figure,
and he waved right back.

"Jesus, Jack," Angie said.

"It's okay," he said, walking up Fifth Street and reaching an alley, dumping the rifle and jacket. "All right. Which way?"

"There are guards at every intersection down Fifth. You just can't see them because they're around the corners on B, C, and D Avenues. So take a right on D and a left on Fourth street. I don't see anyone there now."

Jack complied, rushing down for a block on D Avenue, stopping short of the intersection and peeking around the corner, looking down Fourth and verifying it was clear.

"On Fourth now," he said.

"Yeah, I see you," she said. "Coast looks clear."

Jack rushed down the street, stopping at every corner, before crossing intersections, quickly making his way to the southeast corner of the KSC Industrial Park, reaching A Avenue, his eyes—

"Hold it right there."

Jack stopped, feeling the muzzle of a barrel pressed against the middle of his shoulder blades.

"What the hell do you think you're—"

Instincts took over.

The human brain, as amazing as it is, has a key flaw: it delays physical reactions by a second or two whenever the subject is talking, which allowed Jack to pivot on his right foot while also sweeping his right forearm, shoving the gun out of the way and palm-striking the guard, driving the heel hard up his nose, shocking him as bone and cartilage pressed against the brain's prefrontal area.

Thank God for amateurs, he thought when the guard dropped the gun as his legs gave out from under him.

Jack caught him and the rifle, keeping his counterstrike silent as he dragged him into a recess between buildings, knocking him out completely with a chop to the neck, stressing his vagus nerve system.

"Just got surprised by a guard," he said into his throat mike.

"Oops. Sorry. Hard to see clearly in the dark."

Jack sighed, realizing he would have to be more careful. Angela's ability to use the security cameras was limited to areas illuminated by streetlights.

"But it looks good to the target," she added. "And by the way, Pete's car is parked in front of the building."

Jack peered beyond his hideout at the street leading to M7-1345. He could see its worn-out facade, which looked the same as when he saw it a week ago, when Angela and he had arrived to meet up with Pete the night before the jump.

"I have eyes inside the building, Jack," she said. "One camera in the lobby and another one upstairs, in the hallway."

"Guards?"

"Two in the lobby and two more on the second floor, standing by a door near the stairs. All four have rifles. I'm guessing that's where Pete's hiding the OSS."

He narrowed his gaze.

Pete Flaherty.

It was time to pay his old friend a little visit.

Pete crossed his arms while looking out the second floor of the old Project Phoenix building, trying to decide if he would bring Hastings in on his discovery.

The general was due in from Washington in the morning, and as much as he hated to admit it, Pete's multiple attempts to secure his runaway friends had only resulted in more disasters.

The body count, between his own soldiers and mercenaries was close to twenty dead and twice as many wounded.

Damn it, Jack, he thought, once more chastising himself for having underestimated his former friend, and perhaps wondering if he should have done the deed himself. He certainly had the training to put him down. Maybe then he could secure Angela and the missing component from the suit.

But first I need to locate them again.

And that's where Hastings might be able to assist.

But Pete needed to be careful on a number of fronts. First, coming out with a way to spin this to the general to avoid pissing him off for having left him out of it for nearly a week. Second, doing so in a way that Pete could still retain control over the project. And third, getting Hastings over the first two fast enough to stop Jack and Angela before they somehow managed to reverse the tables on him—something he knew Jack was quite capable of doing.

He checked his watch.

Seven more hours before Hastings's C17 transport landed on the runway a few blocks away, the same runway used by the shuttle for so many returns from space.

His gaze landed on the suit, which Gayle Horton and three more of his trusted scientists had dissected to the core, extracting the information they would need to reproduce it—except, of course, for the missing module.

He'd had them lay out the disassembled suit across three lab tables, including the small membrane-like solar antenna, which Gayle had left for him on its own table ready to be activated by a pair of LEDs in case he wished to put on the show for Hastings.

Pete yawned. He was tired. No, strike that. He was downright exhausted, having not returned home since getting that call from Angela in the middle of the night, which meant sleeping in his office in KSC's headquarters for the past several nights.

And with Hastings arriving on an early morning flight, it meant yet another night with little or no sleep, especially if he planned to have everything ready to break the news to the general about his discovery.

And it also meant he needed to decide how he would present it to his boss.

Pete walked away from the windows to face the tables, gazing at the various components, at the damaged helmet, the outer shell, the boots and gloves, amazed at how much more advanced it was from their last prototype.

We were certainly busy in that other world, he thought, wondering how much time it would take them to catch up.

He stopped when reaching the last table, where Gayle had set up the stage for the membrane. Everything was there.

Everything except for the membrane.

What the hell?

He first thought it was a shadow shifting in the corner of his left eye, perhaps the reflection of streetlights diffusing through the lab's large windows.

"Looking for this?"

Pete turned around and froze. Standing in front of him, looking larger than life, was his former friend, Jack Taylor. And in his hand he held the miniature solar antenna, which he stowed in a pocket of what looked like a very advanced version of the same battle dress he had worn on that ill-fated mission in Afghanistan a lifetime ago.

Jack observed Pete from a short distance before shifting to the right, though not fast enough to avoid telegraphing his position. In an ideal world, he would have preferred doing this SEAL style, sneaking into his office while Pete was looking away, stealing the membrane, and getting the hell out of Dodge before he even knew it was gone.

"Jack!" Pete said, facing him just as he was about to walk out the door. "Wait. I can explain."

He didn't reply, measuring Pete up as he approached him slowly.

"That's far enough," Jack warned, remembering all of those trophies in his house, before reaching for his sidearm and leveling it at Pete.

"Jack? Who are you talking to?" Angela asked through his earpiece.

"Pete," he replied.

Pete looked at him funny as he stopped a few feet from him and raised his hands, asking, "Who are you talking to, Jack?"

"Your old girlfriend," he replied.

"Who?" asked Angela.

Jack shook his head, said, "Hold on, Angie. I'm having a little chat with Pete."

"Please don't kill him," she said.

Jack sighed. He could end it right here so damn easily. But a promise was a promise. Although he truly didn't get it, he still had to respect her wish, however irrational it seemed at the moment.

"Turn around slowly," he said.

Pete complied.

Jack got right behind him and was about to knock him out when Pete dropped to a deep crouch an instant before Jack realized his mistake. In making him turn around, Pete faced the large windows and saw Jack behind him in the reflection.

Jack stepped back, but not fast enough.

The turning roundhouse kick landed on the side of his face, right behind his left ear, striking him in the exact spot still tender from that female operative kick three days earlier.

Stunned but conscious enough, Jack rolled back into the hallway, his head throbbing, his eyesight blurring as he stood, taking a step back, tripping on the bodies of the two guards he had disabled before sneaking into the lab.

"Jack!" Angie screamed into his ear now that she could see him on the security camera in the hallway.

"Get up!"

He stood with difficulty, realizing that he no longer held the Sig.

Pete rushed into the hallway clutching the 9mm semiautomatic.

"He's got the gun, Jack!"

Realizing he had a second, maybe two, before Pete turned the gun on him, Jack sprung into action, rushing across the few feet separating them, his left hand sweeping the space in between them in a semicircle, striking the shooting hand with the edge of his palm, pushing the gun out of the way just as Pete pressed the trigger.

Jack's left arm stung, but the battle dress deflected the shot, punching a hole in the wall next to him. He ignored it, following the chop with a palm-strike to Pete's sternum, which he blocked with his right hand just as Jack grabbed the shooting hand, twisting the wrist, forcing him to drop the Sig.

Pete pulled his arm free and turned sideways to Jack, recoiling his left leg, faking a low kick and spinning toward him, bringing his right leg up in a stretch that reminded Jack of that same female operative at FIT, agile, lightning fast.

This time Jack was ready, shifting back and sideways, missing the round-house kick by inches, feeling the air in front of his face as Pete's foot rushed past him.

Angela screamed for an instant, before the earpiece popped out of his ear, dangling from its coiled cord behind him as Jack stepped in, connecting a palm-strike to his sternum, pushing him back.

Pete fell, rolling away, scissoring his legs, landing on his feet, hands in front, pivoting to the right, the left, the right again, faking with his left fist before swinging his right hand at his temple.

Jack barely had time to duck, the hand caressing his bandanna before he shifted to his right, recoiling his left leg, extending it toward Pete's midriff, heel high, toes pointing down.

Pete drove his right elbow down, driving it into his attacking ankle, connecting at the same instant as Jack, pushing him into the door to his lab.

Still recovering from that first strike to his temple, Jack blinked, retrieving his throbbing leg, wincing in pain, thankful for the battle dress, which cushioned the elbow counterstrike, and surprised again at Pete's nimbleness, at his ability to move so fast and precise.

Both men reached their striking poise again, eyes narrowed, hands in front.

Pete lunged first, spinning, hands slicing the air like a cyclone, whirling, feigning to go high before extending a leg and driving it toward the side of Jack's left knee, aimed at the anterior cruciate ligament that controlled rotation and forward movement of the tibia.

Jack jumped at the last second, saving his ACL, getting out of the way, before stretching his left leg, striking a perfect jumping sidekick to the side of Pete's face, between the jawbone and the chin. He felt it crushing bones.

Pete rolled away, a hand on his cheek, his mouth bleeding, his feet staggering as he tried to force control.

Jack landed and spun, closing the gap, swinging his right arm around to deliver a finishing blow to the back of his neck, to knock him out by triggering a vasovagal episode.

Pete shifted back like a ghost, avoiding the blow while delivering a painful palm-strike to the same side of Jack's face, exactly where his first kick had landed, shocking Jack's auriculotemporal nerve, the branch of the mandibular nerve that ran with the superficial temporal artery providing sensory input to the side of his head.

Jack nearly collapsed, his legs trembling, but he somehow managed to roll back, to get away from the next two strikes, as Pete followed him down the hallway, trying to finish him, kicking, spinning, throwing blow after blow.

Jack shifted, ducked, and jumped, forcing savage control to ignore his pounding head, the crippling headache that almost made it impossible to even keep his eyes open as his jaws suddenly contracted from the extreme pain, as the stressed nerve system prevented him from moving his mouth, forcing him to breathe through his nose.

Jack continued retreating, avoiding what would certainly be a final blow as Pete kept coming at him, hands and feet swinging with precision, each attack carefully aimed at disabling him, like a professional.

But Jack had something few people did: years of training, of abuse, of conditioning in the unprecedented Basic Underwater Demolition/SEAL Training course, in the harshest environments, developing a physical strength deep in his DNA to earn the coveted trident, his ribbon of honor, his ticket into an elite class of warriors who performed best under duress, under severe stress, even while in extreme agony.

And it was this training, as the world slowed down around him, that allowed him not only to avoid and block, but also to counterstrike, to hit back, hard, unexpectedly, delivering an uppercut the moment Pete spun into position to deliver a front kick, nearly ripping his head from his shoulders.

Jack spun, adding momentum to his turning kick, snapping his leg straight, driving the heel deep in Pete's solar plexus, shocking the radiating nerve fibers just below his sternum, where renal arteries branched from the abdominal aorta, momentarily collapsing his diaphragm, inducing spasms.

He watched Pete fall, retreat, crawl back toward the lab.

Jack considered his options as he grabbed the Sig and aimed it at Pete while inserting the earplug and looking at the security camera covering the hallway.

"Your call, Angie."

"Shoot the bastard," she said.

Jack aimed the pistol at Pete's head when he felt a hand grabbing his ankle, almost making him lose his balance.

One of the guards he had disabled was coming around, blood dripping from his mouth as he tugged at Jack's battle dress, his other hand reaching for his holstered sidearm.

Jack kicked him across the temple, knocking him out before returning his attention to Pete, but he had made it to the lab, closing and locking the door behind him.

Damn.

"Get out, Jack!"

He hesitated, staring at the locked door.

"Jack! Get the fuck out!"

He did, sprinting toward the exit, reaching it a moment later, scrambling down the stairs, flying through the double glass doors, where a second pair of guards still lay there unconscious.

And that's when alarms went off across the Kennedy Space Center.

Alarms blared in her head as she hung up the disposable mobile phone and stared at it awhile.

"What's wrong, Angela?" asked Dago, standing by his Harley next to her Triumph at a large gas station off of IH-95, sunlight reflecting from the mirror tint of his large sunglasses. Art-Z was inside getting drinks from a machine while they fueled the bikes.

"Not sure. Pete sounded . . . strange."

"What do you mean 'strange'?"

She looked over at the traffic on the highway. "First he's over twelve hours late calling and when he does . . . well, he sounded a little weird. He even called me Angie. No one calls me that except for Jack."

"You think they grabbed him and Riggs?"

She exhaled heavily, a knot forming in the pit of her stomach at the thought. "I have to assume that, for now."

"So what do we do?"

"We pretend to stick to the plan," she said. "And in the meantime, we'll light a fire under his ass that's so damn hot he won't have a choice but to come after us . . . and just to be sure he follows, we'll leave a little trail of cyber crumbs."

Art-Z returned with two Red Bulls and a Coke.

Dago took the soda, popped the lid, and took a swig before saying, "Ready?"

She looked at her watch. "Yeah."

Art-Z hopped behind Dago and they started their bikes, heading toward the Vero Beach motel, where she had told Pete to meet up with them, getting off the interstate at Highway 60 East, which turned into Twentieth Street as it reached downtown Vero, steering the bikes into the crowded parking lot behind a restaurant a block from the motel.

Angela walked off alone, leaving Dago and Art-Z by the bikes. She reached the front of the restaurant and was glad to see people waiting to get to their tables, many sitting in the patio in front of the building.

She gave the hostess a fake name, was told it would be around twenty minutes, and blended in with the two dozen waiting patrons, her eyes gazing across and down the four-lane street, waiting.

But she didn't need to wait long.

Two white Ford vans with tinted windows rushed down the street a few minutes later, pulling up in front of the motel.

Four Hispanic-looking men got out of the lead vehicle. Three large and muscular and a fourth one who looked half their size and had a thick beard, and who appeared to be in charge. He sent two men around the back before signaling the second vehicle. The side door slid open and Pete stepped out flanked by two of the men, before all four went inside.

Oh, Pete, she thought, not even wanting to think what had happened to Riggs and his family.

She returned to the parking lot, tears filling her eyes.

"Bonnie? You okay?"

She slowly shook her head while getting on her bike. "They got them," she finally said, strapping on her helmet. "Bastards got them."

"They're there already?" asked Dago.

She nodded. "And they have Pete."

"What do you want to do?"

"There's nothing we can do for him here," she said.

Dago understood and started his Harley. "Ready to come home?"

She nodded, wedging the kick-starter pedal against the sole of her riding boot before using her weight to drive it down. The British bike came alive, idling to a low rumble.

Angela clenched her jaw, angry for not listening to her gut, for letting Pete— and Riggs—walk straight into a trap.

Get out of here.

Angela listened to the same inner voice now. She most definitely needed to get away, to put some distance between her and Hastings's posse.

She needed to head home.

To South Miami.

The area where she grew up, where they would have options, friends, and most important, a place to stay that was truly off the reservation.

A place where she could plan out her revenge and hopefully figure out a way to help Pete.

16

RUNNING MAN

The only easy day was yesterday.
                           —Unofficial U.S. Navy SEAL motto

He moved quickly but soundlessly, remaining in dark recesses, like a shifting shadow, using his knowledge of the area to get away, to escape, just as he had done in Colombia, anticipating, avoiding, hiding, striking only when required, as he just did, when he spotted a guard in his way.

Jack had disabled him easily, before running away again, making it down Fourth Street while sirens blared, while security personnel rushed to their posts, as all access bridges lifted, gates closed, emergency procedures were activated, and this militarized version of Cape Kennedy performed an emergency lockdown.

"I lost you, Jack! Where are you?"

"On Fourth and C," he said, spotting a pair of guards running in his direction a block away down C Avenue.

He ignored them, just as he ignored the helicopters taking flight in the distance, turbines screaming, blades biting into the air, their reverberating sound drowning the alarms.

"Stay on Fourth."

He did, reaching the edge of the road at Fourth and D Avenue, and dropping to a crouch when immersing himself in woods surrounding the southeast border of the industrial area.

Jack heard their shouts behind him, heard shots fired, though none in his direction as helicopters took flight, searchlights piercing the edge of the woods.

He focused on the terrain ahead, on the darkness beyond, listening to their sounds as the guards reached the woods.

"Jack, they're following—"

"I know," he said, scrambling through thick vegetation, his mind flashing back, remembering Colombia, the jungle, the cartel's militia, the threats, which he now heard again, as Pete unleashed every asset at his disposal to track him down, to take back the one thing in this world that Jack needed to get home. He required that membrane, needed its almost-magical ability to generate the power required to achieve his dimension jump.

So he ran, sprinting away from the incoming threat, the battle dress protecting him from razor-sharp palms, tree bark, and branches swatting around him like invisible whips.

He heard them behind him and he now also detected them from his far right, as Pete deployed his forces to flank him, to cut off his retreat.

He needed to get to the water before they did, needed to reach his gear and—

He spotted them straight ahead. Two of them, their silhouettes clear against the light diffusing from the other end of the forest leading to the marsh, to the narrow bay, and safety.

Jack dropped to a deep crouch, clutching the SOG knife in one hand and the Sig in the other, pointing his momentum directly at them as they swept the forest searching for him. But he had the advantage, the dark woods behind him, shielding his figure, masking his approach as he narrowed the gap to ten feet. One of the guards whipped his head toward him, finally noticing him.

Jack fired once just as the guard swung his weapon around, unable to loose a single shot before the bullet found its mark. Switching targets, Jack fired a second time, but missed, the guard seeking shelter behind the wide trunk of a towering pine.

Bark exploded as he fired again to keep him trapped as he rushed to the tree, dropped to a deep crouch, and swung around the wide trunk, surprising the guard from beneath, driving the SOG's blade upward, from groin to sternum, gutting him while pressing a hand against his mouth.

The guard trembled, going into shock, entrails hanging, before his legs gave. Jack let him fall in place and took off toward the tall grass beyond the woods just as bark exploded to his left, then his right.

Damn.

He ducked, hearing a third round buzzing just past his right ear before he raced around a tree and squinted back, realizing that the tables had just been turned, that he was now the one exposed, the one backlit by the light streaming from the clearing beyond the trees.

He needed a distraction, something to level out the playing field if he expected to cross the final fifty feet of jungle unharmed.

His back pressed against a tree trunk as the incoming guards plastered the pine with bullets, trapping him, giving him a taste of his own medicine, Jack holstered the Sig and the knife and removed two fragmentation grenades, removing the safety pins as he heard them approach his tree, before flinging them in a cross pattern over his left and right shoulders.

He dropped to the ground, counting, waiting, eyes closed.

The blasts came a moment later, deafening, blinding, followed by cries and shouts.

Jack jumped to his feet and scrambled away, this time reaching for an M84 stun grenade, turning around for an instant to throw it back at the forest with all his might, before continuing his escape, putting as much distance from it as his legs would allow, finally reaching the waist-high grass swaying in the breeze just as the grenade went off, reverberating in the woods.

His feet sunk in the sandy terrain, his mind focused on the approaching shore, on the narrow bay leading to the river.

"Talk to me, Jack."

"In the marsh," he said, the sound of alarms deafening as searchlights crisscrossed each other around him. He kicked harder, pushing himself, realizing he only had a minute, maybe less before more guards converged on his position.

He heard the sound of approaching helicopters, could see their searchlights looming above the treetops just as he reached his gear and dropped to the sand and rolled into the water, dragging his equipment.

"Get to the extraction point," he said into his throat mike before taking a deep breath and immersing himself in the dark waters as searchlights glowed across the marsh, almost overhead, as he used the weights in the BCD to keep him submerged in the waist-deep water.

Get outta here, Jack, he thought, powering the SeaScooter, gripping it with one hand while holding the rest of his gear with the other, letting it take him deeper, farther, until he could no longer feel the bottom.

In total darkness, Jack donned his BCD with ease, thanking his BUD/S instructors for the relentless drills, for the physical punishment that allowed him to keep calm while the world above him exploded in a rainbow of colors from search beams and flares.

But he heard nothing in his underwater realm as he shouldered the dual tanks, clearing his mask with a burst of compressed air and putting it on, taking a deep breath and holding it for as much as two minutes before exhaling slowly to minimize bubbles while the SeaScooter dragged him away at a depth of ten feet.

He heard propellers in the water, sudden, loud, signaling patrol boats.

Jack focused on the task at hand, forgetting about guards, about alarms, about explosions and helicopters, his eyes glued to the compass on the back of the Sea-Scooter, pointing the way out of the bay, toward the river and the safety of deep waters.

He forced his body to remain almost still, minimizing oxygen consumption while disciplining his breathing, watching the second hand of his watch mark two minutes before he allowed himself to exhale very, very slowly, taking another deep breath, wishing for his SEAL Draeger rebreather unit.

He kept course and depth, deciding against going deeper because that meant a higher oxygen demand, which then meant shorter intervals between releasing bubbles.

Jack sensed the current pushing him south the instant he cleared the bay and turned to one eight five for twenty minutes, only breathing nine times, his heart rate slowing, his senses dulling as the early stages of hypoxia set in.

But he persisted, conditioned to operate this way for long periods of time, forced to become one with the water by his Coronado instructors, until the sea became his home, the place where he could hide from a world above the surface intent on terminating him on sight. He knew that was the order given, the instructions that Pete had shouted at his men as they found him beaten inside his own lab, as alarms reverberated across the complex.

Minute by minute, breath after agonizing breath, Jack slowly, painfully, got away from the kill zone, from the searchlights, flares, and patrol boats, reaching the middle of the river and going farther south, toward the tip of Merritt Island, where the river ran just west of Cocoa Beach.

He turned off the SeaScooter and just drifted with neutral buoyancy ten feet under, waiting for the signal, which came about ten minutes later.

He heard the propellers of a nearby boat revving up from idle three times in rapid succession, his cue to come up.

Slowly, with caution, he did, eyes just breaking the surface, avoiding any ripples, performing a 360 scan before locating the Sundancer, Pete's yacht.

Despite the way he felt—tired, bruised, and even a little cold—Jack couldn't help a small grin.

Slowly, he made his way to it, reaching the rear swim platform, where Dago helped him in. The biker had a bandage on his shoulder but he was a big strong man and after a good night's sleep, he had woken up this morning ready to cause some trouble, shouting orders to his team in Miami to make the final preparations for Jack's upcoming launch, for the next phase of his return home.

Pete sat in his office contemplating his options while rubbing his aching chest. Jack had vanished, and with him any hopes of retrieving this amazing technology.

He got on the phone and ordered his men to expand the search, to comb every last square inch of river between here and Vero Beach. Jack had escaped by water, like a SEAL, of course, but that also meant an extraction somewhere by some sort of vessel.

He dispatched dozens of helicopters and once again reached out to Homeland Security to divert drones to the area. Al-Qaeda, he claimed, had struck the Kennedy Space Center, and he wanted the terrorists terminated on site.

The first piece of news came ten minutes later, when his IT manager informed him that the security cameras had been hijacked during the intrusion through an old backdoor account set up by none other than Dr. Angela Taylor.

The second piece of news arrived fifteen minutes after that, when the Coast Guard reported a large yacht abandoned by a rocky beach near the Pineda Causeway, ten miles south of the Cape.

The third piece of news arrived five minutes later, when the IT manager informed him that the hack had originated from Pete's own IP address.

But the most shocking news came within a few more minutes, when the Coast Guard identified the yacht as a fifty-eight-foot Sundancer registered to one Pete Flaherty.

They ditched the yacht by the Pineda Causeway, where Dago's gang waited for them with trucks and bikes to take them to a remote farm on the edge of the Everglades, arriving just past four in the morning.

The plan was simple, devised by Angela and executed by Dago and his Paradise shop team. In reality creating a platform to house Jack and his life support system during the ascent phase had been simpler than building a custom chopper.

They had selected an aluminum frame, light, but strong enough for Jack to sit in comfortably plus enough space for the car batteries and the pumps that would keep him pressurized for the three to four hours she estimated would take him to reach the first option altitude of forty-eight kilometers.

The key was keeping the weight down.

A few years earlier, aviation pioneer Felix Baumgartner ascended inside a capsule that weighed close to three thousand pounds, requiring a helium balloon that weighed an additional 4700 pounds and that at launch actually stood taller than Seattle's Space Needle, requiring almost thirty million cubic feet in capacity. By contrast, Jack's total weight would be far less than eight hundred pounds, including the balloon.

He remembered enough of the physics from the many high-altitude jumps he performed to test the OSS components. At launch, most high-altitude balloons were thin and long, but as they ascended, the helium expanded in the thinner atmosphere, slowly stretching the balloon into a round shape. This process continued until the balloon either reached what was called the float altitude, where its lifting ability balanced out with its payload, or when it burst due to the expanding helium in increasingly thinner air.

Dago backed a stolen helium truck next to the weather balloon—the largest that his guys could secure from the NASA contractors, designed to carry a payload of five hundred pounds to an altitude of forty-five kilometers. Angela had estimated that by keeping his total weight below three hundred pounds, they would be able to get him at least to the option altitude of forty-eight kilometers before reaching a maximum altitude of about fifty-three kilometers, where either the density inside the balloon equaled the density of the surrounding atmosphere and stopped ascending, or where the expanding helium would stretch the balloon beyond its limit, bursting it. Angela wasn't sure which would come first.

It took four people to start the long filling process, as the balloon slowly rose from the ground.

Angela worked a tablet computer, confirming the number of cubic feet required to strike the delicate balance between pumping enough helium to achieve

the desired ascent rate and option altitude, but not so much that the expanding helium would prematurely stretch out the fabric to its limit before reaching the OA.

Jack watched them work while using one of the oxygen delivery systems he
and Dago had secured at a medical supply store to conduct his one hour pre-
breathing of pure oxygen to eliminate the nitrogen from his blood and tissues.

Almost forty minutes later, as the first traces of orange and yellow forked
skyward across the eastern horizon, Angela had Dago cut off the helium as it
reached the calculated number of cubic feet, watching the balloon assume its long
and thin launch shape, reaching almost seven stories high, just over ten percent
of the height of the Baumgartner balloon. But then again, Jack's total weight was
also quite lower than that successful jump.

Dago had already rigged the connecting mechanism using five Kevlar and
nylon ropes to anchor Jack's platform to the five metallic grommets at the
bottom of the balloon, which rose quickly to an altitude of fifty feet, stretching
the ropes while four men kept the crate secured with chains connected to the
backs of three pickup trucks. Below the aluminum structure hung three weights,
each fifty pounds, representing his ballast to keep his initial ascent rate below
1500 feet per second to avoid expanding the balloon too fast. As he reached the
lower stratosphere and his ascent rate decreased, Jack could release them indi-
vidually should he require additional lift to reach the OA before his oxygen
supply ran out.

It would be cramped quarters, with Jack occupying the center of the aluminum seatlike frame, flanked on one side by three oxygen tanks and the pressurization pumps and on the other by three sets of car batteries inside an airtight
vessel connected to the inverter that would power the pumps. It was rudimentary but effective, again providing the essentials for his survival beyond the
protection of the lower atmosphere. On top of that, Jack kept his SOG knife, a
side-arm, and his trusty M32 grenade launcher loaded with a mix of fragmentation and incendiary grenades to have something to defend himself upon returning to his world. This time around he planned to land with more than his knife,
especially since he had a very strong feeling that his sudden return would not be
welcomed by General Hastings.

But first he had to jump.

And that meant it was time to suit up.

Angela read out the checklist on her tablet as Dago helped Jack get into the suit while continuing to breathe pure oxygen.

Jack stared at the heavens for a moment, as the indigo skies fought the dawning sun's wan light.

He donned the inner thermal layer before once again putting on his trusted battle dress, which although not required for the jump, would provide an additional layer of thermal insulation.

Next came the suit, already incorporating the glass token and the membrane, which Angela had positioned just as she had found them in the original OSS.

Dago held it up while Jack backed into it, working both feet down the built-in boots before running his hands through the bulky sleeves.

Dago zipped him up and folded the airtight flaps over the zipper, securing them with a Velcro strap.

Angela reviewed the procedure on the tablet one more time as she paced around him, checking every item one last time, tugging here, pulling there, before standing in front of Jack and testing the firmness of the ceramic tiles on his shoulder pads. The jump would be from a lower altitude than his last one, meaning much less heat, but he would still need some protection.

Walking on his own to the crate already floating two feet off the ground, held in place by the chains, Jack gave the towering balloon a quick look, watching it sway in the breeze while Angela and Dago strapped on his parachute harness, securing it to the rear of the suit in six locations. Finally, they fastened a narrow canister to his right thigh, which would provide him with oxygen during the jump.

Sitting down in the crate, he closed the simple lap belt, similar to the ones in airliners, easy to open, even with the Russian gloves, which locked in place just as they had during the pressurization test.

Next came the helmet, which Angela held in her hands.

And that's when it hit him.

He was leaving her.

Just like that.

And just as it had happened many times before since meeting this amazing version of Angela Taylor, Jack found himself unable to speak.

Leaning down, she removed his portable oxygen mask and kissed him one last time as they stared into each other's eyes.

She put a hand on his face, a tear running down her cheek, before the scientist took over and lowered the helmet, her eyes never leaving his.

She locked it in place and flipped on the pumps in the lowest setting to start the flow of oxygen and to keep him from overheating until he reached colder temperatures.

Internal pressure quickly reached 4.3 psi, which didn't cause the suit to inflate because outside pressure was still at sea level, or 14.7 psi. But as the air thinned and external pressure dropped during ascent, the suit, like the balloon above him, would slowly stretch out.

Listening to his own breathing now, Jack forced his body to relax, checking the four key instruments on his wrist: altitude, outside temperature, oxygen level, and internal pressure, before giving his small launch party a thumbs-up.

And with a final wave and kiss that Angela blew at him—and just as the sun loomed over the horizon—they released the chains.

Jack felt the familiar upward tug, as the balloon pulled him away from the ground quickly, at a projected rate of one thousand feet per minute.

He watched her wave at him as the world shrunk beneath him, as Angela turned into a tiny dot in the otherwise green and brown expanse of marshes making up the Florida Everglades, making up this very strange world he was leaving.

And he was alone again, even more so than during prior jumps.

He had no one to talk to. No CapCom. No Mission Control.

Jack's breathing, the hissing oxygen and the whirling pressurization system were the only sounds as he rushed above twelve thousand feet, as the nylon and Mylar layers began to creak when the suit slowly inflated in the thinning atmosphere at twenty thousand feet, then thirty thousand.

His hearing became hypersensitive again, a primary sense as he listened to every sound this rigged suit made while keeping tabs on the atmospheric lapse rate, which marked the temperature decrease of roughly 3.5 degrees Fahrenheit for every thousand feet of altitude for the first ten kilometers, until he reached the edge of the troposphere, when the temperature stabilized for a while, before it would slowly warm back up through the middle of the stratosphere, above the ozone layer.

The balloon reached a maximum ascent rate of almost 1400 feet per minute somewhere near forty thousand feet or around twelve kilometers, as OAT, or outside air temperature, dropped to negative seventy degrees Fahrenheit.

He kept scanning his pressurization level as well as listening to the smaller pump circulating the fluid through his thermal suit, stabilizing his body temperature.

Jack continued to rise, watching the Earth's horizon become curved, dotted with white clouds above expanses of greens and blues as the tip of Florida resolved beneath him, angling ever so slightly to the southwest by the collection of islands making up the Florida Keys.

He kept his gaze on the horizon, watching for any sign of aircraft deployed by Pete to shoot him down.

"We just got an FAA report of an unidentified object climbing above forty thousand feet, sir," reported one of his men while Pete sat in his office, where he had spent the past three hours deploying every possible resource to locate Jack. "The radar signature suggests a high-altitude balloon drifting north of the Everglades."

Pete slowly made his way to the windows, arms crossed while staring at the dawning skies, wondering if it was actually happening, if Jack was indeed trying to perform a high-altitude jump to return to his own world.

"Did you check with NOAA to make sure it isn't one of theirs?" Pete asked, referring to the National Oceanic and Atmospheric Administration.

"Yes, sir, and it isn't them. Plus the radar return is quite large, suggesting a larger object than one of their standard weather balloons."

"Get me Patrick Air Force Base on the line," he said after a moment to consider his options.

Jack started to relax when he reached fifty thousand feet. The ceiling of most American fighter jets was sixty-five thousand feet, which at his current ascent rate meant he would be almost out of their reach in another six or seven minutes.

He felt the M32 strapped next to him, deciding that if the time came, he could easily reach it in a few seconds. On the ground, he had practiced dry firing it with the bulky Russian gloves. The hardest part had not been squeezing the trigger but actually holding on to the weapon as it recoiled against his right shoulder.

He checked his gauges. Fifty-four thousand feet, OAT at a steady negative sixty-five Fahrenheit, pressure at 4.7 psi, and oxygen supply at eighty-seven percent.

He had already consumed thirteen percent of his supply in the first forty-five minutes of his ascent, which continued at around 1300 feet per minute—according to his mental math.

"Nice suit, Angie," he said to no one, breathing in pure oxygen that smelled like plastic and his own sweat while staring at the thinning atmosphere as he continued to rise, alone, his life in the hands of his wife's expert work, on the tens of thousands of Nomex stitches, on the multiple layers of carefully selected materials that continued to creak under pressure. At this altitude, a breach of his pressure vessel would mean unconsciousness within ten to fifteen seconds and death a minute or two later. There would be no blood boiling as portrayed in movies, nor would he instantly freeze. Death would come rather anticlimactically, with Jack passing out.

Fifty-seven thousand feet.

He did a quick mental calculation and came up with 18.3 kilometers or just over eleven miles. OAT still holding at around negative sixty-five degrees Fahrenheit.

He checked all the pumps, including the smaller one removing his exhaled carbon dioxide to keep his blood properly oxygenized. The system wasn't nearly as sophisticated as the one in the OSS and lacked any kind of gauge to monitor its performance, but it seemed to be doing its job, otherwise he would have already blacked out from carbon dioxide poisoning.

Jack glanced at the battery meter connected to all three power sources and watched it pointing to the seventy-five percent mark.

"KSC this is Phoenix," he said to himself, once again feeling the need to speak to someone. "All systems nominal."

He didn't get the response he quite expected.

Major Benjamin Kelly, USAF, entered the coordinates provided by the FAA and punched through Mach two while rocketing to sixty thousand feet, before leveling the Lockheed F22 Raptor and engaging the autopilot, which flew the plane better than any human at this critical altitude, just below the fighter's operating ceiling, where the thinning airflow over its control surfaces rendered the fighter a bit sluggish and prone to stalls.

He scanned the horizon. According to the coordinates, as well as his radar, the target should be just a hundred miles ahead and climbing.

Kelly's orders were to force the balloon down, ideally by encouraging its oc-cupant to vent helium and return to Earth. But if all else failed, he had approval to shoot it down.

At his current speed, he closed the gap within two minutes, spotting the bal-loon at his two o'clock, high.

Disengaging the autopilot, he banked the fighter by ten degrees in its direc-tion, careful to avoid brusque maneuvers in the thin atmosphere.

Jack first noticed the glint of glass against the dawning easterly skies. It rapidly grew as a fighter, which he quickly recognized as an F22, coming up beneath him, leveling off just as Jack reached sixty thousand feet, which he guessed to be pretty darn close to the Raptor's service ceiling.

The fighter jet circled him twice, close enough for Jack to see the pilot sig-naling him to head back down.

Major Kelly tried every frequency in the book to make contact with the balloon operator, but all he got in response were a few friendly waves.

Damn, he thought, not relishing the thought of taking out what appeared to be just some yahoo wearing a suit that looked homemade strapped to a similarly made contraption.

"Base, Red Leader."

"Red Leader, Base. Go ahead."

"Red Leader has target in sight. No response to my attempt to commu-nicate."

"Red Leader, Base. Did you use hand signals?"

"Affirmative. He . . . he just waved back. Looks unarmed, sir. I think he's just up here having a good old time. Permission to hold at a lower altitude until he comes back down."

"Permission denied. Your orders are clear, Red Leader. He either comes down on his own, or you shoot him down."

Kelly frowned inside his oxygen mask, his eyes watching the balloon rise above his service ceiling, approaching seventy thousand feet. Pretty soon, this guy would be beyond the range of Kelly's 20mm guns, and he really didn't want to take him out with one of his two AIM-9 Sidewinders or his even more powerful and radar controlled AIM-120 AMRAAM missiles, of which the Raptor carried six.

"Roger that," he replied, breaking his circle and heading out for a few miles to accelerate, before entering a shallow climb, coming back at the balloon from beneath while caressing the trigger of his gun system.

The Raptor trembled in the thinning air, making it difficult to lock the target in its crosshairs as he exceeded his service ceiling, the twin Pratt & Whitney F119-PW-100 engines wrestling with the nearly depleted air molecules.

Jack knew he was in trouble the moment the F22 broke away in a wide circle.

Gun run, he thought, his heartbeat skyrocketing while he checked his altitude, realizing that the fighter had to be struggling to remain airborne.

And that gave him an idea.

The Raptor came at him from the west, gaining altitude, approaching fast.

Jack gauged the distance, realizing that at this close proximity the pilot wouldn't be using a Sidewinder but just his guns, meaning he would have to get even closer, almost as if he were engaging him in a dogfight.

He waited, as the distant grayish shape grew against morning skies staining the atmosphere in hues of red and yellow-gold.

And just as the fighter got within a couple thousand feet, as Jack's SEAL sense decided the pilot was about to open fire, he pulled the lever, releasing all of his ballasts at once, feeling the sudden upward surge tugging at him as he shot up to a rate of nearly three thousand feet per minute. He watched the fighter jet open fire, its traces shooting through the altitude he had just crossed a second before.

Bastard isn't screwing around, he thought as the altimeter read sixty-seven thousand feet and continued climbing awfully fast.

Kelly pressed the trigger for a couple of seconds but stopped the moment the balloon soared away from his crosshairs, almost as if attached to an invisible rocket, a mix of surprise and relief sweeping through him as he broke his run and descended to fifty-five thousand feet.

"Base, Red Leader."

"Red Leader, Base. Go ahead."

"Ah . . . the target has climbed beyond the range of my guns."

"Hold, Red Leader."

"Roger," he replied, entering a ten-mile holding pattern while maintaining 350 knots centered beneath the runaway balloon.

The order came a minute later. "Red Leader, you are approved to use a Sidewinder. Repeat. Shoot the target down with a Sidewinder. Acknowledge."

"Roger that, Base. Acknowledge use of a Sidewinder missile to shoot down unidentified and unarmed civilian balloon with one soul aboard," he replied, wanting to make sure his ass was completely covered on this one since he had a really, *really* bad feeling what he was about to do would trigger a media shit storm for the Air Force.

He broke off from the holding pattern, dropped to fifty thousand feet and engaged the afterburners, placing the Raptor in a steep ascent while arming one of two Sidewinder missiles.

So sorry, pal, he thought as he waited for the heat-seeking head to latch on to the weak but still relatively warmer signature of the crate beneath the balloon, now over ten thousand feet above him, but well within the missile's range.

He achieved lock a moment later.

"Fox one," he said as the F22 released the missile from its left bay just as his altimeter indicated sixty thousand feet, watching it ignite and hurtle skyward while he cut power and nudged the stick forward, dropping back down to a safer altitude.

Jack knew what was coming next, as the Raptor broke off the climb an instant before releasing a missile, which rocketed toward him.

Clutching the M32 grenade launcher, Jack fired two shells in rapid succession, watching them drop beneath him in long arcs, detonating in a burst of flames as their magnesium cores heated the surrounding air to incandescence, creating a much hotter signature for the Sidewinder's heat-seeking head, drawing it away from him, exploding almost a mile under the crate.

He exhaled in relief as he watched the brief fireworks display, though he wasn't certain how many more times he would get lucky as he topped seventy thousand feet or twenty-one kilometers, as his oxygen level dropped below seventy percent and battery power was reduced to two thirds.

And I still have another twenty-seven kilometers to go, he thought, for the first time starting to wonder if he was actually going to make it as he watched the F22 circling below him, finally losing sight of it as his altimeter read eighty thousand feet.

"Patrick, Red Leader. Missile failed. Repeat. Missile failed. He released flares."

"Flares?"

"Affirmative."

The channel went silent for a moment.

"Red Leader, engage target with AMRAAMs."

Kelly checked his altitude and the altitude of the target, before he said, "Ah, target's above twenty-four kilometers, Base, well above the AMRAAM ceiling. But he eventually has to come back down. Requesting permission again to hold until he does."

More silence, followed by, "Hold approved, Red Leader."

United States Navy Captain Ray Rodriguez, commanding officer (CO) of the USS *Roosevelt*, an Arleigh-Burke Class Destroyer patrolling the waters south of Daytona Beach, put down the radio after receiving the strangest of orders, which he asked to be confirmed twice, finally getting it directly from Admiral TJ Perry, commander of Task Force 20, which operated in the Atlantic Ocean from the North to South Poles, and from the Eastern United States to Western Europe and Africa.

He glanced over to his executive officer (XO), Lieutenant Commander Tricia Moore, almost ten years his junior, and frowned.

"Pretty fucking strange, sir," she said.

He almost laughed and shrugged at the number two officer aboard a vessel he had commanded for almost three years. "Like they said in the *Charge of the Light Brigade*, Commander, 'theirs not to reason why.'"

Moore relayed the order to the RIM-174A missile operator, arming one of the *Roosevelt*'s primary strike weapons, a two-stage surface-to-air missile with a flight ceiling well over 110,000 feet and a range of 240 kilometers.

"Range to target?" she asked while Rodriguez observed her in action.

"One hundred and seventy kilometers. Altitude of . . . one hundred fifteen thousand feet."

Rodriguez frowned again, shaking his head. "That may be a bridge too far."

"What happened to 'theirs but to do and die,' sir?" she said, smiling.

Now he finally smiled. She was right, of course, even if it meant wasting a five-million-dollar missile.

With a single nod, he gave her the order to fire.

Jack regulated his breathing as the altimeter climbed above 120,000 feet or thirty-six kilometers, the altitude where he had vanished on the way down over a week ago. OAT had increased to almost negative ninety-five degrees Fahrenheit as he got above the ozone layer, smack in the middle of the stratosphere.

He had already consumed well over half his oxygen and battery power had decreased to forty-five percent as the pumps continued to hold pressure and body temperature.

Jack was in the middle of doing some mental math again when he noticed a flash of light well below him, probably several kilometers, although it was hard to tell this high up, as he could see almost two-thirds of the Earth's curvature projecting around him.

Now what? he thought, as he spotted a distant speck growing by the southern tip of Florida, followed by another flash, much closer than the first.

And that's when he understood.

A two-stage rocket.

A missile.

Jack watched it rise up toward him, almost in slow motion, its second-stage booster glowing.

"Fuck me," he hissed, right hand reaching for the seat belt strap, while his left clutched the hoses tethering him to the crate, ready to disconnect them.

The rocket continued its skyward trajectory, its booster glowing bright orange against the darker surroundings, backdropped by a spectacular view of planet Earth.

But an Earth in which he didn't belong.

The missile grew in size, probably just a few miles below him.

Jack stopped breathing, tightening his grip on the hoses as the index finger of his bulky Russian glove reached under the seat belt release latch.

But he stopped when the incoming warhead, gray with green stripes, suddenly slowed down, its propellant firing intermittently, before going out.

Jack stared at the missile in disbelief, no more than a thousand feet away, floating in space, before slowly dropping back to Earth.

What are the odds of that? he thought, as he continued rising, passing the forty-kilometer mark or 131,000 feet with 32 percent oxygen left and 30 percent battery power.

He tried to relax, lowering his breathing rate, conserving the cold oxygen hissing inside his faceplate as the balloon began to slow down to around 750 feet per minute, as he watched his digital altimeter inch toward his option altitude, approaching the upper boundary of the stratosphere.

Almost there.

He forced himself to relax, to imagine his fall, the skydiving profile he would need to adopt as he reentered the atmosphere, as he went supersonic, though he had no way to gauge that. He just had to trust the physics that Angela and Layton had worked out.

Kilometer 46
Oxygen level 16%
Battery power at 12%
Ascent rate 550 feet per minute

Jack glanced at the heavens, momentarily surprised at the size of the balloon at the other end of the ropes. It was almost round in shape, massive, the expanded helium stretching the silvery fabric, in sharp contrast with the long and thin shape during launch.

It's all in the physics, Jack.

He managed a smile.

Jack was definitely going to miss her.

Kilometer 47
Oxygen level 12%
Battery power 9%
Ascent rate 400 feet per minute

Jack unstrapped the seat belt and set the pressurization pump on high, increasing pressure to 6 psi to give himself a safety margin before untethering the hoses providing thermal circulation and pressurization.

From this point on he would rely on the suit's hermeticity to hold internal pressure and hope the G-forces of the jump didn't stress the multiple layers to the point of losing pressurization below 3 or 4 psi before he reached a safe altitude. He would also now be at the mercy of the multiple insulation layers to keep his body at a reasonable temperature for the duration of the jump.

He watched the altimeter tick off the last remaining feet before he disconnected the oxygen hose from the crate and turned on the valve of his portable oxygen canister.

And as the altimeter read exactly forty-eight kilometers—and without hesitation—Jack dove head first into the abyss.

Pete slammed the phone and stood up, turning his hands into tight fists.

Jack had managed to escape, and the irony was that he did it all under his damned nose, using Pete's own resources against him.

He closed his eyes, hoping like hell that when Jack jumped from that balloon, somehow he would just fall back the same way he went up, landing in the waiting arms of a dozen helicopters and a pair of circling F22s, not to mention the dozens of soldiers he had deployed to southern Florida to grab him the moment he—

There was a knock on the door.

He turned around and before he got a chance to say he was busy, Pete stared at the bulky figure of General George Hastings standing in the doorway.

"Pete? Do you mind telling me what in the world is going on?"

17

BLINDED BY THE LIGHT

Darkness cannot drive out darkness; only light can do that.

—Martin Luther King, Jr.

It began slowly.

A frozen bank account here, a canceled credit card there.

Then it picked up momentum.

The private accounts of his contractors were hit, tens of millions in funds vanishing overnight.

It became critical when shipments were intercepted by anonymous tips, when his supply chain came under attack, crippling his ability to coordinate his operation, to sustain the production of his suits, when the delicate formula to process salolitite was corrupted, sending Salazar and his team into a tailspin.

Then he lost access to the digital video files, to the real power he held over his people. He thought that those servers were secure, beyond the reach of anyone but him.

But General Hastings had underestimated his enemies.

Standing and walking over to the windows overlooking the peaceful meadow surrounding his salolitite production facility, while Salazar and the rest of his scientists worked feverishly to stabilize the operation, Hastings stared at the eastern skies, at the looming sun breaking the horizon with blinding shafts of orange and gold, staining the indigo sky, washing away the darkness.

A new day.

Hastings thought of those who came before him, of Theodore Hastings, of the legendary GW, of his own father. He would not let them down. He would find a way to survive this attack and continue his legacy.

And I will do so with Dr. Taylor, he thought, after giving the order to Javier and

Davis to follow the digital trace that Raj from SkyLeap had detected in the most recent attack.

In their obsession to destroy him, the hackers had gotten careless, leaving behind a path, a trail for his people to follow in the cyberworld, converging on an IP address that would lead them to a physical location.

Hastings watched the rising sun, squinting, momentarily blinded by the piercing light, his mind already at work outlining the required damage control, which albeit more painful than the first strike, was still manageable.

But his coordinated defense would soon be followed by a carefully choreographed offense the instant Raj and his team provided him with an address.

And this time around, as he continued to stare at the amazing sunrise, he would make sure there would be no tricks.

No mistakes.

No decoys.

Only results, including transporting Dr. Taylor, completely unharmed, to his secret compound deep in the mountains of West Virginia.

Jack didn't sense downward acceleration for some time, as he seemingly glided in the outer reaches of the atmosphere, like a wing, the nylon and Nomex webbing stretched between his torso and arms and also between his thighs, increasing stability.

But his altimeter told a different story.

He was most certainly falling.

And fast.

Lacking a vertical speed indicator, he did quick mental calculations to determine his speed based on time and lost altitude, determining that it had taken him four seconds to travel one kilometer, meaning he was falling just under the speed of sound.

When he reached kilometer forty-two, Jack assumed a near-vertical profile and sensed a light buffeting in his legs as he closed them, locking the rare-earth magnets Angela had sewn to the sides of his boots.

The buffeting increased, shaking him, forcing him to stiffen his muscles, to keep from tumbling. Jack clenched his jaw, trying to keep it together as he gained speed, finally reaching the sound barrier.

And just like that, the turbulence vanished.

Another calculation confirmed that he had just covered a kilometer in under 2.9 seconds.

I'm supersonic.

He slowly brought his arms to the sides of his suit, controlling his acceleration just as a purple glow materialized around him.

Hello there, he thought, watching it dance about him as solar gamma rays began to charge the glass accelerator embedded in the suit.

Speed increased to the neighborhood of Mach two as he counted seconds in his mind, outside temperature beginning to climb, but not nearly as much as his last jump, when he had reentered the atmosphere at a much faster speed, meaning less energy transfer from vertical speed to heat.

But the air finally heated to incandescence several seconds later, though Jack could no longer tell where he was because it would mean breaking his descent profile to lift his left arm and look at his altimeter.

He frowned at this unfortunate flaw in Angela's design, unlike the OSS, which had a faceplate display providing him with relevant descent telemetry.

So he did the only thing he could do: continue counting seconds in his mind, working under the assumption that he dove roughly through one kilometer every two and a half seconds.

And with air molecules heating around him, sound returned to his world in the form of the ear-piercing growl of an atmosphere fighting back, slowing his descent, like an invisible shield.

Holding his profile and trusting the physics in Angela's calculations, he watched the lavender glow increase about him as the pressure from deceleration and the accompanying heat tore into his ablation shields, as he began to feel the temperature rise through the insulation layers.

Damn, he thought, finding it difficult to concentrate, realizing that he wasn't only pulling multiple Gs but lacked the ability to apply pressure to his legs and force blood back to his upper body.

Somewhere in the following seconds, as his tired mind guessed he had reached the vicinity of kilometer twenty-eight, the blinding purple light around him began to pulsate, slow at first, but with increasing intensity.

Squinting, his facial muscles tight, his jaw locked from concentration, Jack felt the rocketing temperatures permeating beyond the flexible insulation material, reaching his inner layers, beneath the aluminized Mylar and the nylon suit.

He tried to see beyond the glowing sphere of fire surrounding him, trembling with hues of purple, barely able to breathe, to force cool oxygen into his lungs as the pressure on his chest rocketed, as thoughts once again began to drift to the periphery of his mind.

But he couldn't afford to pass out.

Not now.

He lacked an autopilot, the means to maintain his descent profile during this critical period, where he had to keep the blunt shape of the reinforced carbon-carbon tiles facing the inferno, shielding the rest of his suit from certain incineration as he dropped through the atmosphere like a meteor.

Jack pushed himself, fighting the growing light-headedness, his rising body temperature, his inability to deliver enough oxygen into his bloodstream.

And he persisted, reaching deep into his core, into his training, into the discipline instilled in him by his relentless BUD/S instructors to never give up, to refuse to surrender, to ignore staggering odds and forge ahead, to stare death in the eye and wait for it to blink.

The only easy day was yesterday.

Jack forced the thought into his mind, letting it flash as bright as the purple light converging on him, alive with sheet lightning, entrapping him, swallowing him through the incandescence, the heat, and the deafening noise.

He tried to breathe to inhale, but the heaviness on his chest became overpowering, unbearable, gripping him like a scorching vise, squeezing him.

The only . . . easy day . . . was yesterday.

Jack summoned all his strength to inhale again, just one more time, holding his breath for as long as he could, knowing that each passing second brought him closer to his goal, his target altitude, and to the harmonic that would magically arrest his fall, cheat the laws of physics currently trying to crush, incinerate, and tear him apart.

He wanted to scream but that would require the oxygen he could no longer deliver to his system as the weight on his chest pressed harder still, as he opened his mouth but couldn't fill his collapsing lungs, his caving chest.

Lightning gleamed again, bright, violet and green and blue, its ear-piercing thunder crushing the reentry uproar, the billons of air molecules blazing a quarter of an inch from his blunt shields.

The light intensified, blinding him, forking into his helmet through the heat shield and the sun visor, through his eyelids, stabbing his mind.

And then it suddenly stopped.

The pressure, the furnace, the glaring light.

Jack filled his lungs for the first time without effort as he opened his eyes, staring at the vibrating membrane surrounding him, laced with color, writhing with flashes of light, but also soothing, comforting, insulating him from the harsh conflagration of a moment ago.

But he was still falling, once more inside this colorful chute that Angela had managed to calculate with impressive precision.

Jack risked a glance at his altimeter, locked on twelve kilometers as he dropped fast toward the bottom, alive with jagged lightning, its surface rippling, awash with sparks of static energy.

He quickly regained focus, became aware of his surroundings, recalling the last trip down.

Here we go again, he thought as he dove into the bottom, crashing head-first, feeling the familiar elasticity as the chute's floor stretched, giving under his downward momentum, thinning as it extended, as lightning cracked around it, flickering with energy just before it burst, releasing him into bright skies.

Jack squinted again as he free fell, checking his altimeter, realizing he had lost exactly 1.2 kilometers, emerging at 10.8 kilometers or 35,000 feet.

Thank you, Angie.

He transitioned into a traditional skydiving profile, once more stretching the fabric between his arms and legs to adopt a winglike shape as his eyes scanned the rapidly approaching ground, trying to get his bearings from this altitude, recognizing the tip of Florida, the Keys, locating the large metropolitan area of Miami off to the west.

Twenty-seven thousand feet.

He controlled his descent easily, just as he had done for so many years in the SEALs performing high-altitude low-opening insertions into hostile territory.

And that's precisely how he had to view the world below. Hostile.

Twenty-two thousand feet.

He searched for highways, for roads, for any semblance of civilization, and shifted his arms to glide in that direction. West. Toward the greater Miami area.

Angela was raised there. And Jack guessed that would be precisely where she must have gone when in trouble, where she would have options, help, people willing to help her.

Seventeen thousand feet.

Jack selected his landing site. A grassy field close to a two-lane road that fed into a larger road running east-west, disappearing into the distant Miami metropolitan area.

Thirteen thousand feet.

He slowly opened a valve on the front of his suit to equal pressure with the atmosphere, feeling his ears ringing for an instant, before probing his target again, confirming his choice, free of trees or fences, the grass swaying gently toward the west providing him with wind direction as he dropped below nine thousand feet.

He reached for the rip cord handle secured with Velcro under his left arm and held it tight, waiting.

Six thousand feet.

Forty-five hundred feet.

Jack watched the ground rising rapidly toward him, but he waited just a bit longer, determined to reenter this world by the book, like a SEAL, hitting his selected site with precision.

Twenty-seven hundred feet.

Twenty-one hundred feet.

Fourteen hundred feet.

Nine hundred feet.

Jack waited just a couple more seconds, a hand on the rip cord handle, pulling it hard the moment he read five hundred feet.

The parachute performed flawlessly, blossoming above him with a hard tug, quickly arresting his fall, slowing him down to a gentle glide a hundred feet from the ground, allowing Jack to land with a slight wind drift.

He rolled the moment his feet touched the grass, letting his cushioned body absorb the impact, before sitting up against the wind, the parachute collapsing behind him.

The helmet came off first, and Jack took a deep breath of fresh air, filling his lungs, briefly closing his eyes as he once more thanked Angela for building something that, albeit not perfect, had been more than enough to do the job, to get him back in one piece.

The gloves came off next, before Jack unfolded the airtight flaps over the main zipper down the front of the suit and zipped it down his waist.

He walked out of it with ease in his skintight battle dress, which this time he would wear under a pair of loose jeans and a long-sleeve T-shirt that Angela had secured for him to the bottom of the parachute compartment.

Last time he hadn't had a choice, venturing into the world in his futuristic suit. This time around he wanted to blend in right away, to minimize attracting attention, but still without giving up the protection of this bulletproof piece of engineering.

He got dressed and tucked his Sig in the small of his back, covering it with the T-shirt and kept the SOG knife in its ankle sheath.

He looked around, selecting a cluster of trees separating the meadow from the road to hide the parachute and suit, covering them with branches before heading for the road, feeling the front right pocket of his jeans, where Dago had tucked in a roll of twenty-dollar bills.

Jack grinned, deciding that if anyone would know the whereabouts of his wife, it would be her old biker friend.

The road was Highway 41, which framed the north end of the Everglades National Park, meaning he hadn't drifted significantly during the entire ascent and subsequent jump. And based on the sun, he estimated it to be mid-morning.

This time around, however, he had little luck hitching a ride, walking for almost thirty minutes before reaching a large gas station that had a convenience store and a large restaurant.

He bought a couple of bottles of water and some snacks, consuming them at a picnic table at the edge of the parking lot while watching the patrons come and go, biding his time, waiting for the right opportunity, which came about ten minutes later.

An elderly couple in an old Chevrolet convertible pulled up to one of the pumps, fueled up, and then parked just twenty feet from Jack, not bothering to put the top up before walking into the restaurant.

Thank you, he thought, waiting for them to go inside before jumping in and reaching under the dash, locating the right wires, bypassing the ignition, taking less than thirty seconds to hot-wire it.

He steered the vintage car, which was in impeccable condition, out of the gas station and headed west on the highway, checking his watch, deciding that unless someone alerted the couple, it would be at least thirty minutes before they came out, and probably even longer before a cop arrived and added it to the stolen vehicle database.

But Jack remained vigilant, keeping to the speed limit, trying to look relaxed, just another Floridian enjoying a morning ride on a sunny day. He even put on the owner's Wayfarer sunglasses left on the console.

His right hand on the wheel and his left elbow resting on the door, Jack covered the thirty miles to Miami in fifteen minutes, turning south on Highway 997 and west on 296th Street, near Homestead Air Reserve, reaching the shop in another thirty minutes.

He drove past the building, noticing it was closed, which was strange for a weekday, and headed to the corner to go around the employee parking lot in back.

That's when he spotted it. A white van with tinted windows parked across the street a block away from the shop's entrance. Two men were inside. Jack pretended to ignore them while driving around the block, noticing another white van at the edge of the empty parking lot with two more men.

Hastings had this place covered front and back, and the fact that it was closed meant that Dago, his gang, and probably Angela were somewhere else.

Maybe even with Pete.

As he was about to drive off, the van in the parking lot sprung to life, accelerating toward him. Jack went for his gun, but the driver simply swerved around him, taking off, turning the corner and heading to the front, obviously not interested in him.

Jack's instincts screamed at him to follow, and he did, also turning the corner just as the van in front also drove off, following the first one.

Where are you guys going in such a hurry?

They reached the farmhouse at one in the afternoon and spread across the front and back, covering the gravel entrance connecting the main house to the road, the path from the back porch to the large orange grove, and even the trail off to the left leading to a duck pond.

Davis decided to be thorough, to do this by the book, securing the perimeter first before tightening the noose.

The place was secluded, accessible only by a narrow road that wound its way to the northwest corner of the Everglades National Park.

There were no neighbors for miles. No witnesses.

Just the group who'd made a fool of Davis and his men two days ago.

But not today, he thought, each of his four team leads confirming their positions, getting a visual on the motorcycles parked outside, as well as the satellite antenna providing the Internet access that the general's IT staff, assisted by none other than the NSA, had used to track a series of hack attacks to this location.

Davis inspected the one-story structure once more with suspicion. The farmhouse looked quiet, peaceful.

Almost too good.

But Hastings had been clear: raid the place and hand over its occupants to the men waiting on the access road just beyond the edge of the woods in a pair of white vans parked behind his team's SUVs.

The general's Hispanic friends, he thought with a frown and a heavy sigh. The ones he had summoned after Davis had failed to raid that FBI safe house fast enough, allowing them to escape.

"Move in," he spoke, leading the assault team himself, stepping out of the woods and rushing across the grassy meadow followed by three of his men, single file with a ten-foot separation, reaching the front in thirty seconds, glancing at the bikes, before motioning to one of his men to break down the door.

The figure, dressed in black and wielding a silenced Heckler & Koch MP5 submachine gun, collapsed the moment Jack chopped him behind the neck.

He eased him down next to his fallen comrades—all three of them making up one of four teams converging on the farmhouse.

Jack inspected them briefly, deciding that they were guilty by association with the men in the white vans he had followed here from Dago's place. But it was the Harleys parked in front of the farmhouse that had justified his attack on these strangers.

Is Angie hiding there?

Grabbing the silenced MP5, he scrambled through the woods, approaching the next team, four more men standing by the edge of the woods looking toward the meadow—as they were ordered. But a better trained team leader would have posted at least one of his men facing the woods, their six o'clock, to prevent precisely what Jack did next.

From a distance of just ten feet, he fired, aiming for the back of their heads, where their fancy Kevlar vests wouldn't protect them. Only the last man managed to turn around and return fire, which Jack was glad to see was from a silenced MP5 just like the one he held.

But it was a futile attempt.

Jack placed his final two shots on the side of his head, and he collapsed next to his team.

Dropping the empty MP5 and stealing one with a full magazine from one of his victims, Jack continued his hunt, rushing to the third team a couple hundred feet away, also under orders to watch the house, cover the exits, and keep its occupants from escaping.

Amateurs.

Slowly, Jack got ready to disable the last lookout team.

Davis reached the living room first, a sinking feeling descending on him when he found it empty. His men quickly separated, covering the bedrooms, the garage, the dining area, even going up into the attic.

But as had been the case less than forty-eight hours ago, the place was empty.

"Damn it," he hissed, staring at the sofas facing a large fireplace and an even larger flat-screen television hanging on the wall. "How is this *possible?*"

The hackers had managed to elude him again, and Hastings would *not* be pleased.

Putting down his weapon and reaching for his mobile phone, he pressed a button on his speed dial. Hastings picked it up on the first ring.

"You've got them?"

"Negative, sir. The place is empty."

Silence, followed by, "But I thought you said there were bikes parked in front."

"There are, sir. At least someone's bikes. But they're not here. No one is."

There was a heavy sigh and Davis closed his eyes, not relishing being the deliverer of bad news, especially when Hastings had a reputation for shooting the messenger. But fortunately for Davis, the general was back at his compound in West Virginia, where he had decided to weather the storm.

"Regroup with Javier and wait for my orders," Hastings said, hanging up.

Davis stared at his phone and slowly shook his head before switching to his radio.

"All right, people, the package isn't here. Repeat, the package is *not* here. Back to base."

He frowned when no one responded.

"Damn it," he hissed, clicking the radio off and back on. But he still got no response.

And that's when he saw Jack, standing in the foyer, one of his men's MP5s in his hands.

"I . . . I thought you were dead," Davis said.

Jack motioned the team leader, whom his men called Davis, to his knees, hands behind his head, before sitting across from him with the MP5 pointed at his head.

"Where's my team?"

"Some dead, some knocked out."

Davis didn't reply.

Jack tilted his head at him. "I remember you. The night before the jump. You were there with that other asshole . . . Riggs."

Davis slowly nodded. "He turned out to be FBI."

"*Really?*" Jack said, leaning forward. "Well, he had me fooled."

"He had us all fooled."

"Good for him."

"Not really," Davis said. "The general caught him, along with your friend Pete Flaherty."

Jack didn't like that. "And?"

"Last I heard, Riggs got the double-T."

"The *what?*"

"Traitor treatment. He got to watch his family get . . . brutalized, murdered before they gouged out his eyes and castrated him."

In spite of all the horrors he had witnessed in his life, Jack blinked. "You . . . *saw* this?"

"No. But Hastings has a thing for videotaping those . . . Hallmark moments and showing us clips for . . . motivation."

Jack exhaled, then asked, "What about Pete?"

"Don't know," he said. "And that's the truth."

"Where's Hastings now?"

"Look, they have my family, man," Davis said. "Please understand I have no choice."

"Everyone has a choice," Jack replied. "And my choice right now is to kill the son of a bitch. So, where is he?"

Davis considered that for a moment before he said, "Would you please make it look like I fought back? That's the only way to protect them."

Jack considered that for a moment and said, "You got it."

Davis slowly nodded. "All right. Apparently, your wife and some hacker and biker friends of hers have created a financial mess for the general, stealing bank accounts, freezing assets, disturbing factories, his operations, injecting his networks with viruses. If it can be done with a computer, they've sure as hell done it."

Jack tried not to beam with pride. "Continue."

"Anyway, we got a tip that the latest hack attacks had originated from this location. But it was just like the last time."

"The last time?"

Davis looked down, apparently embarrassed. "Yeah. We got a tip to raid another place—an FBI safe house. And same thing. Missed them by a mile. And not only that, but the bastards watched us through Webcams they'd left behind."

Jack was trying to process all of this. "So where's Hastings now?" he finally asked, before checking his watch, deciding that it was time to move out. Although he had disabled fifteen soldiers in thirty minutes, there was always the chance of anyone he hadn't killed waking up and bursting in here guns blazing. Or perhaps Davis had backup standing by in the vicinity, like those four guys in the white vans waiting up the road.

"He has a compound in West Virginia, off of IH-68, by Cheat Lake. Been there a couple of times. The place is off the reservation . . . so to speak. Can only get to it by boat, sea plane, or helicopter," Davis said, giving him the actual directions.

"Anything I need to be aware of?"

"He's got lots of cameras covering every angle in the place, plus a lot of guards," Davis said, taking another minute to give him the details of the compound's defenses that he recalled seeing.

Jack took it all in before asking, "What about the men in the white vans parked by your SUVs?"

Davis shrugged. "Some associates of the general. We were supposed to hand over anyone we captured in here. But my guess is that they're gone after I reported to Hastings that the place was empty."

"Anything else?"

Davis slowly shook his head. "Please make it look good."

Jack got up and walked behind him.

Everyone has a choice.

He pressed the muzzle against the back of his head and was about to pull the trigger, when he said, "There's another way."

Davis looked back at Jack. There were tears in the man's face as he mumbled, "How?"

"By helping me kill the bastard."

"I . . . can't take that chance. Others have tried, and they all ended up in the same place as Riggs."

"I won't fail," Jack said. "Your best chance is with me."

"I . . . can't. I've seen what he's done to their families. I . . . just can't."

Jack took a deep breath, hating to put down someone who looked like a good soldier caught in an unfortunate situation.

"And please don't just knock me out," Davis said. "This makes my second time disappointing the general. He's probably going to kill me anyway. That's the risk I took by accepting his offer."

"All right. Get up. Turn around," Jack said.

Davis did, facing Jack, who took a few steps back before leveling the gun at his face.

"Thanks," the veteran soldier said, a tear rolling down his camouflaged cheek. "I hope you stop him."

Jack clenched his jaw, hating having to do this, but failing to see any other way. He had given Davis every chance he could think of, but it was clear that the general's fear campaign was working as designed.

"Look, man," Jack said, trying to give him a final chance. "Join me. We can beat Hastings."

"I . . . I can't risk it. Do it for my wife . . . for my kids."

Jack frowned and took a deep breath.

"Please. I'm begging you. It's the only way to be sure."

Well aware that he would hate himself for doing this, Jack finally squeezed the trigger. The silenced round hit Davis in between the eyes, killing him instantly.

Slowly, he knelt by the body and put a gun in his hands, firing it a couple of times into the ceiling to make him look like he went down fighting like the soldier he was.

Jack stood there a moment, trying to find the right words, angered at himself for having killed him, for failing to convince him to join forces, to take a stand.

Everyone has a choice.

And Davis had certainly made his, for better or for worse.

And so had Jack, who would now have to live with—

A strange noise behind him made him swing his weapon in its direction while dropping to the ground.

But there was no one there.

Confused, he got up to one knee and surveyed the living room, spotting a camera, which turned in his direction.

Standing and facing it, he understood.

And waving at it he said, "Honey . . . I'm home."

18

TAKE ME HOME, COUNTRY ROADS

Victory at all costs, victory in spite of all terror, victory however long and hard the road may be; for without victory there is no survival.

—Winston Churchill

He went to the address he had written on a piece of paper and shown to the camera in case they couldn't hear him.

It was an old watering hole in South Miami by the name of El Habanero, and ironically not far from where Dago had met him and Angela after stealing that Tiara yacht in another world.

Jack drove one of the Harleys he found parked outside the farmhouse since the police were probably already looking for the convertible he had stolen earlier.

He continued down the picturesque Tahiti Beach Island road, the wind in his face, the sun in his eyes as he steered the bike past opulent mansions, manicured lawns, and beautiful parks, all backdropped by the Atlantic Ocean.

The oceanfront bar, one of Dago's favorites from the old days, had two floors of decks overlooking the water plus a large parking area that ran along both ends of the establishment as well as on the street side, where Jack steered the bike into a corner spot facing the exit, ready for a quick getaway should anything go south.

El Habanero glowed with neon lights in every pastel color imaginable, even in the middle of the afternoon.

He walked toward the glowing structure slowly, with caution, searching for—

"Jack! Over here!"

He turned to his right and saw her a couple hundred feet away, down a row of parked cars, waving her arms frantically.

Behind her was Dago and a short and slightly overweight guy with an unkempt beard.

Angela took off, running toward him.

Jack found it hard to breathe, unable to believe he had actually made it back
to her, back to his wife, and he owed it all to the Angela he had left behind, the
one who had sacrificed everything to get him back here, to this moment, as "his"
Angela ran toward him.

But a white van pulled up behind her, tires skidding on the pavement as it
came to an abrupt stop just as the side door slid open and two large men jumped
out and grabbed her from behind.

No! This can't be happening!

Jack rushed toward them, adrenaline surging, heightening his senses as Angela fought them, arms and legs lashing out, kicking, punching, but she was too
small, too light, and just one of the men was able to handle her while the other
stood in the way.

Jack spun, bringing his left foot up, striking the man across the temple with
a turning kick. But he was large, strong, and the kick only made him shift a little
before he reached for Jack, trying to grab him, succeeding in wrapping both arms
around his waist, squeezing him in a deadly bear hug.

Jack winced in pain as the man's oaklike arms tried to crush him, finding it
hard to breathe, watching in horror as the other man threw Angela in the back
of the van.

Stiffening his hands, Jack clapped hard into the sides of the man's head, into his
ears, driving a powerful shockwave through the ear canals and into the brain.

The man released him, trembling, hands on his face, shocked, blood
dripping from his nose.

Jack ran around him, scrambling after the van, as the door slid shut, as the
driver punched it, engine roaring, tires spinning, kicking up gravel, fishtailing
into the street.

He started to go for his bike but the Hispanic man wasn't quite ready to fall
yet, blocking his way. Jack went after him again, spinning like an angered
cyclone, hands and feet stabbing the air. But the man, albeit bleeding from his
nose and ears, was still able to shift out of the way, missing his strikes, before
trying to punch Jack in the solar plexus.

Jack brought his right forearm down, hard, deflecting the incoming fist, shoving it out of the way before palm-striking his nose at an upward angle, planting his entire body behind the blow, mashing bone and cartilage, forcing him to his knees.

Cupping his hands, he clapped them over the man's ears again, and he finally collapsed on the pavement.

Jack looked toward the street, ignoring the people stepping out of the bar, some of them on phones, spying the tail of the van vanishing around the—

"Jack! Over here!"

He turned around. Dago was waving him over, already on his Harley and pointing at Angela's Triumph.

He ran to the bike, climbing on, kick-starting it, ignoring the bearded man sitting behind Dago as the bike rumbled to life, and he throttled it, shifting into gear and popping the clutch, lurching forward, reaching the street.

But the van was out of sight.

Jack steered the bike into the direction of his last sighting, twisting the throttle, revving up the engine, accelerating, his eyes frantically searching, his mind refusing to believe that he could have come this far, this close, and then lose her like that.

Where are you, Angie?

He continued down the same avenue, slowing down at intersections to look in both directions, and continuing on, but the van was nowhere to be found.

Jack persisted, crisscrossing the streets, expanding his perimeter search, block after block, but after twenty minutes he stopped, pulling over, jumping off the bike, a hand on his forehead.

Think, dammit. Think!

Dago pulled up behind him and also jumped off.

Jack was about to get back on the bike and continue the search but Dago put a hand on his shoulder.

"Get off me!"

"Wait, Jack! Listen to me!"

He turned around, facing the large biker, who looked downright identical to the man who had helped him and Angela so much for the past week, even down to the bandanna and open denim vest.

But he was barely listening, unable to contain a fury growing deep in his gut, a consuming anger that threatened to strip away his sanity, his logical mind at the precise moment when he needed it the most.

Slowly, breathing deeply, once more invoking savage control from years of training and discipline, his focus finally shifted to the biker, who was trying to tell him something while pointing at the bearded man still sitting on the back of the Harley.

"Art knows where they're taking her! In West Virginia!"

And that's when it came to him, Davis's words, the warrior who had chosen death to protect his family.

He has a compound in West Virginia, off of IH-68, by Cheat Lake.

Jack kept breathing, kept listening to Dago, to this hacker who went by the name of Art, someone whom he vaguely remembered Angela mentioning a time or two in the past—someone who confirmed what he already knew.

Slowly, as traffic continued up and down the avenue, as the sun started to set in paradise, as vacationers returned to their hotels after a day on the beach while others headed for the nightclubs and bars to party under the stars, Jack began to plan his revenge.

He watched the helicopter fly in from the east as the sun rose, skimming the lake, circling the fenced perimeter twice before hovering over a large patch of grass downhill from the main building, next to a deflated windsock, softly touching down.

Javier got out first, followed by two of his muscular bodyguards flanking a small figure wearing a hood.

Welcome, Dr. Taylor, he thought, a surge of confidence boosting through his system not only by her presence but also because the cyberattacks had stopped the instant his contractors had snagged her right off the streets of South Miami yesterday afternoon.

The plan, masterminded by Javier himself, had required the sacrifice of Davis and his team, sent to the location that his IT guys had pinpointed as the origin of the hacks.

But Hastings knew better.

Fool me once, shame on you. Fool me twice . . .

"They're here, general," his aide said, holding the door to his office partially open.

"Yeah. I got eyes, too," he said, pointing at the decelerating blades above the helicopter and the foursome walking up the steps from the helipad. "Throw her in the same cell with Flaherty for the whole day. Maybe that will encourage her to cooperate."

"Yes, sir."

The basement room was dark and humid, with a small, barred window near the tall ceiling, out of reach. The walls and floor were made of concrete, rough, unfinished. But it was the stench that assaulted her as they had pulled off the hood and threw her inside, slamming the heavy door. It was a brew of urine, disinfectant, and the coppery smell of blood that triggered a wave of nausea.

And that's when she heard the low cry coming from the far corner, like a whimper, agonizing, heartbreaking.

Angela walked slowly, letting her eyes adjust to the darkness, her skin goosebumping, converging on the origin of the noise.

"No ... more ... please ... no ... more ..."

She paused, listening to his voice, darkness slowly resolving into a naked figure, curled on its side, like a baby, hugging himself, shivering.

"Pete?"

The man rocked himself slowly, his legs tucked against his chest, visibly shaken, his skin covered in bruises and cuts.

She knelt by him, put a hand on his shoulder.

"Pete?"

He shrunk away at her touch, trembling, his face a mess of bruises, swollen, one eye completely shut, the other bloodshot, gazing at her, before blinking recognition.

"Pete, it's me. Angela."

Slowly, he came about, realizing he was naked, scrambling to cover himself with his hands.

"It's okay. Let me help," Angela said, removing her leather jacket and wrapping it around him.

Pete pointed at a bottle of water on the floor, near his feet, and she brought it to him, helping him take a few sips.

Bastards, she thought as he drank, as he took a few deep breaths. She looked around the concrete cell, at the small hole in the middle of the room where he had to relieve himself.

He couldn't believe that in the two days since she had seen him from a distance at that motel, Hastings and his guns had turned him into this.

"What happened?" she asked, sitting by his side, letting him rest his head on her thigh as she tried to comfort him.

He hugged the jacket, obviously cold, shuddering, having lost a lot of blood from all of those cuts, not to mention the impact of the bruises, which were everywhere, from his head to his broken toes.

"Riggs . . . they . . . killed him and . . . what they did to his wife . . . God . . ."

He slowly shook his head and started to weep. She held him tight and just let him vent while she closed her eyes, trying not to think about what sort of horrible things Hastings's people had done to the federal agent and his family—and to Pete, for him to be this shaken up.

"And now . . . they've got you," he said. "I'm sorry . . . Angela . . . so sorry."

"Don't be," she replied.

It took a few minutes, but slowly, Pete regained his composure and managed to sit up, taking another deep breath, color slowly returning to his face as he leaned toward her and whispered, "We're . . . being watched . . . middle of the ceiling."

She looked up and spotted a camera trained on them, and proceeded to give them the bird.

Pete managed a half laugh before wincing while holding on to his rib cage. "Bastards," he said, coughing. "Broke my ribs."

She leaned over and whispered in his ear, "Jack is back."

He looked at her with his one good eye while slowly shaking his head, before mouthing, *"How?"*

She shrugged, gave him a smile, and said, "He found a way, Pete. He just found a way."

Hastings returned to his desk, where he had been in the midst of performing his latest round of damage control, of shifting money from safe accounts to cover losses, to pay for services, to buy loyalty, discretion, and even assassination—to remind those he owned to look the other way, to ignore the firestorm of problems that would soon disappear. His IT guys had managed to recover most of the missing videos, the real power he held over his people, and stored them in a new location guarded by the world's most complex firewall. His scientists had restarted production, cranking out orbital suits. His people in the press had squashed any semblance of a story from field reports. His people in Washington—even in the White House—would focus on pressing issues in the Middle East, as well as the economy, the unemployment level, and even the latest battle with OPEC on crude oil prices. In another day or two, this would be in the past, and he could concentrate on the future.

Hastings looked about his massive office, filled with inspirational icons from his past, from his family's legacy. He stared at the vintage guns, at the medals, the awards and commendations, the handwritten notes from Abraham Lincoln, Douglas MacArthur, Teddy Roosevelt, JFK, and even LBJ. The last one addressed to him personally for his service in Vietnam.

The past is the springboard for the future, he thought, as he returned to his computer. First, protect the cash, then maintain the relationships, and third, continue to instill fear in his subordinates. Reward loyalty but be ruthless to punish treason, using the likes of Riggs and his wife to show others what could happen to them and their loved ones if they crossed him.

In the old days, governments had used public executions as a way to deter, to set an example, making those who were on the fence about committing a crime to think twice. His method was similar, highly effective, and even more so when he got those under his employment to perform the executions, the tortures, incriminating them, forever owning them and their families.

He spent the entire day at his desk, eating a small lunch while completing his tasks . . . dispatches, conference calls around the world . . . his damage control, finishing at seven in the evening and summoning his aide, ordering dinner for him and his very special guest.

The dining room was modern, with a long wall of floor-to-ceiling windows facing the tranquil waters of Cheat Lake under a full moon. Two waiters stood by while Hastings, in Army dress blues, sat at one end of a glass table facing his guest, who had yet to touch her food.

"Had this especially prepared for you, Doctor," he said, cutting into his prime rib.

"I've lost my appetite, General," she said, "especially after seeing the way you've treated Pete, who told me about Riggs and his wife."

Hastings looked up from his food and raised a brow. "That was most unfortunate, doctor. But necessary."

"It was necessary to torture and kill an innocent woman, General?"

Hastings cut another piece of prime rib and chewed it slowly, before taking a sip of an amazing pinot noir that his wine steward had managed to find during a recent trip to Australia. "Like I said, doctor. Unfortunate but necessary."

"Necessary for what?"

"Necessary to make sure no one else decides to be as stupid as Riggs. Frankly, doctor, he brought it on himself. He knew the risks and decided to cross me anyway. What choice did I have?"

She regarded him with a look that could cut through the tempered glass surface of the table, and that pleased Hastings immensely. She obviously came from great stock, unwilling to display the fear he knew she had to be feeling at this moment, especially after seeing Pete and learning about Riggs and his wife. Yet, here she was, as defiant as the first time he'd laid eyes on her the night before the launch, when she had attacked his scientists.

Feisty, that one, he thought. *And damned smart.*

And that just made him want her even more. Jack Taylor had been one lucky son of a bitch indeed, but he was gone, forever lost since that other Earth lacked their technology. In a way, he even felt sorry for Jack, arriving to a world like that, practically naked. But him being gone presented Hastings with the solution to his dilemma. He needed a son, perhaps two to carry on his legacy, to rule the world he would leave behind after he was finished securing its future, making damn sure that the United States of America would never again face the financial uncertainty created by the fools elected into office these past decades.

The woman sitting across from him represented the future, his future. She was certainly worthy of his seed, of his family's gift. She had been smart enough to not get caught right away and to fight back in ways that even came close to hurting his operation, and that was quite impressive in itself. She had outfoxed his finest operatives, his best scientists, and top IT talent, and done so while on the run, hunted, operating with scarce resources.

Hastings couldn't even begin to imagine what she could do if properly funded, given anything her brilliant mind required, convinced to work with his engineers, taking his breakthroughs to the next level.

"What do you want from me, General?" she finally asked, reaching for her cup of wine and taking a sip, before raising her brows. "This is actually quite good."

He nodded in approval. "Only the best for you, Dr. Taylor. Only the best."

This time around he used only the best equipment available, including a Draeger rebreather, which he wore like a vest, secured to the waist of his battle dress with a heavy strap. Most of the critical equipment was in front, where he could reach it, including the flexible breathing tube projecting up at chest level into his full-face mask with integrated goggles. The oxygen tank was strapped horizontally at the bottom of the unit, just above his waistline, and would inject small amounts of oxygen into his breathing mix after the absorbing canister removed his exhaled carbon dioxide, eliminating bubbles.

Dago was with him in the small rented boat, which they had steered close to the middle of the lake, as close as Jack felt comfortable getting to the compound before going under, which he did, after giving his biker friend a thumbs-up and whispering, "Relax, buddy. I'll be right back."

And the familiar darkness engulfed him as he adjusted his BCD to compensate for his weight as well as that of his heavy waterproof duffel bag at the end of a short lanyard, and dove to a depth of just fifteen feet, which was plenty deep, especially at night and without releasing bubbles.

He powered up the SeaScooter and used its luminescent compass to steer in the direction of the compound, which the GPS measured to be just over two miles away.

Jack focused on the task ahead, having forced himself to sleep most of the way up from Florida while Dago and Art-Z took turns driving nonstop, taking just under twelve hours to get to here after making a pit stop at his Cocoa Beach house, which he was glad to find unguarded, confirming his hunch that with Angela and Pete captured and Jack presumed dead, Hastings had no need to post guards there, allowing him full access to his favorite SEAL equipment.

The lake was cold, even with the wetsuit he wore over his battle dress, as he glided under the water, the constant hum of the single propeller tugging him at a constant five miles per hour as he managed his breathing, relaxing, conserving his energy.

He went over his insertion plan, which he had memorized from the satellite images that Art-Z had provided from who knew where. After watching him work for an hour, Jack had lost interest in the endless lines of indecipherable code as he hacked into a number of sites to reach the high-resolution imagery that he downloaded to a tablet computer.

The compound was certainly fortified, but not in the traditional sense.

Hastings, who had difficulty trusting people, relied more on gadgets than on guards to secure this secluded retreat, which played directly into the expert hands of Angela's bearded associate from her hacking days.

Jack checked his depth and his oxygen supply, verifying his direction, forward speed, and distance to target, slowing down as he got within a thousand feet of the shore, finally shutting down the unit a couple hundred feet out before surfacing slowly, barely breaking the waterline, his eyes surveying the grounds sloping up from a long deck with a number of moored vessels, including a pair of sailboats and three power boats.

He swam slowly, without making any ripples, like a predator, his gaze on the lone figure standing just beyond the shoreline, an arm resting on the stock of his rifle, the other holding a cigarette between his index and middle fingers, smoke coiling skyward.

While keeping his body immersed, Jack floated under one of the docks, out of direct line of sight from the guard as his feet touched the lake's sandy floor.

He removed the Draeger, the face mask, and unzipped the wetsuit, letting it all fall to the bottom, next to the SeaScooter, before pulling on the lanyard and retrieving his gear, taking another five minutes to secure all of his ammunition to the battle dress.

Jack reached down for his Heckler & Koch MP5SD submachine gun, similar to the ones Davis's team had used, but developed specifically for the U.S. Special Forces, including an integral wet-technology stainless steel sound suppressor, which, due to its ported barrel, didn't require the use of subsonic ammunition for tactical sound reduction, and which was capable of single shots, three-round bursts, and full automatic fire.

Finally, he strapped on the throat mike and earpiece and connected them to the tactical radio secured to his battle dress, before tapping it twice to test it.

"Hear you loud and clear, Jack," said Dago from a motel across the lake. "Ready when you are."

Quietly, he floated out from under the dock, his eyes converging on the smoking figure as he lifted the MP5SD, aiming it at the guard's head through the Prismatic scope while his finger shifted the ambidextrous selector lever from its safe position to single-shot.

He checked his watch, waiting for the second hand to reach exactly ten o'clock, the time when Art-Z would take control of the compound's security cameras while replaying an hour of taped video to fool the guards monitoring them, basically repeating the same trick that Angela had done with the NASA surveillance cameras.

He tapped his throat mike again, but three times, signaling his readiness.

"Art's in. You're clear."

Slowly exhaling through parted lips, Jack pressed the trigger.

The 9mm round left the muzzle silently, impacting the guard's head a fraction of a second later, dropping him from view.

Jack waited, raising his head out of the water, listening, hearing nothing that alerted him, before crawling out of the water by a bed of rocks, slowly standing before donning his night-vision goggles, which amplified the available light, painting the terrain in hues of green.

The main house stood two hundred feet up a gentle slope of trees and waist-high shrubs, which Jack began to cross, avoiding the main path, ignoring the surveillance cameras atop every fourth or fifth tree trunk, red lights blinking, signaling their active status while Jack hoped like hell that Art-Z had control over them.

The terrain leveled off as it neared the mansion, where he spotted three more guards standing by the steps leading to a rear observation deck, just beyond a helipad housing a mid-size helicopter, its blades tied down to the ground with black ropes.

Jack took a knee and pressed his right shoulder against a tree for stability as he aimed the MP5SD, aligning the first figure in the crosshairs while setting the selector lever on full automatic fire.

The guards faced each other, making it impossible to kill one without alerting the other two, leaving him with no other choice but to perform an aim-and-sweep technique first developed by Israeli commandoes with the venerable Uzi submachine gun.

Here we go, he thought, lining up the rightmost guard while using his right hand to grip the barrel hard to counter the gun's natural upward motion when firing multiple rounds.

Making a final adjustment to his stand, Jack exhaled and pressed the trigger while slowly shifting the barrel to the left.

The MP5SD released twelve rounds in the two-second sweep, and all three guards dropped to the ground.

"Talk to me, Dago."

"Three more guards on the right perimeter fence and another two on the opposite side. We're also seeing four guards up in front, drinking coffee by the front steps. No alarms yet."

"Any sign of Angie?"

"Still looking. The man's got hundreds of cameras in this place, Jack. We're prioritizing the ones relevant to you now. Art's going to start browsing the interior cameras in a moment."

He waited, listening, and once again hearing nothing, confirming Dago's report, he moved around the side of the house, spotting the three guards by the perimeter fence looking out, like they should, expecting the threat to come from the outside.

They made easy targets, and Jack removed them quickly with another aim-and-sweep strike that consumed his first thirty-round magazine.

He removed it and let it drop to the ground by his feet, grabbing one of five magazines he had strapped to his chest.

Jack clicked it in place and chambered a round, resuming his hunt, going around the back again and up the other side of the mansion, a light breeze cooling his camouflaged face as he listened to insects clicking nearby.

He spotted the other two guards just as Dago had reported, also looking out through the fence.

Slowly, he dropped to one knee and set the MP5SD back to single-shot once more, lining them up in the Prismatic scope and firing twice in rapid succession, watching their figures drop to the ground before advancing to the front, where four more guards stood, drinking coffee from paper cups. Two of them were smoking.

They looked relaxed, comfortable, feeling safe behind the electrified perimeter fence and the dozens of surveillance cameras.

Jack frowned, recognizing one of the guards, the muscular Hispanic who had abducted Angela.

Hello, asshole, he thought, switching to fully automatic fire while dropping to one knee, lining him up first, and once again doing an aim-and-sweep routine, taking them all down before they knew what had hit them.

And that's when he heard shouts from around the corner.

"Shut it all down now," he spoke into his throat mike. "I need total darkness."

"But we lose the cameras, Jack."

"Now, Dago!"

Hastings finished his meal and stood, regarding her with a stare that signaled something more than interest in her scientific mind.

Up to now, the general had made his case over dinner to get her to not only join his scientific team, but to lead it, to help him exploit the untapped potential of salolitite, to go beyond dimensional jumps and turn Einstein's theories into reality.

But now, as he stood across the table staring at her, she began to wonder what other ideas this crazy bastard had floating in that sick mind of his.

She considered her options. After all, something that came with prime rib was a sharp steak knife, which she hadn't touched, along with the rest of her food, finding it difficult to stomach eating anything after seeing how they had treated Pete, and even worse, knowing the horrors they had done to Riggs and his wife.

She smiled at him as he got near.

Cut off the head and the rest of his house of cards will come crumbling down.

And just as Hastings was about to walk over and do whatever it was he intended to do, just as Angela planned to grab the steak knife and do as much damage as she could before the waiters could stop her, the lights went out.

Jack moved quickly, the night-vision goggles allowing him to see two more targets by the front of the house, green figures shifting in the night, trying to navigate in the darkness.

They were easy marks, taken down in single-shot mode one after the other, as he made it to the front steps, pushing open the double front doors and storming into the foyer, rolling once, twice, before rising to his feet and searching for hostiles, finding none.

He started at one end, going room by room, in textbook urban warfare fashion, reaching a large office, its walls full of medals and cases of old rifles and pistols.

A short, bearded man stood by the window, looking out, apparently trying to figure out what was going on.

The man slowly turned around, squinting to see in the darkness.

Jack recognized him as the driver of the white van yesterday in South Miami.

Hello, asshole number two.

He stared at him for another moment before shooting him in the head, spraying half his brain on the glass, watching him collapse on the desk.

Giving the office a final glance, he moved on to the next room, clearing the right side of the mansion, disabling everyone he spotted, from two more guards to the kitchen staff—a half-dozen men in white uniforms which he forced into a large meat locker and closed the door.

He heard shouts coming from the adjacent dining room, just as the emergency lights came on across the compound.

Angela shifted aside in the twilight of the room after slashing the steak knife at Hastings's larynx, but she underestimated the distance and barely nicked the skin.

The general stopped, put a finger to his throat, and grinned.

The waiters started to approach, but Hastings held out an open hand. "Stay back! This is between Dr. Taylor and me."

Angela remained calm, the blade protruding from the bottom of her left fist, just as Jack had shown her.

Hastings moved on her again.

Angela shifted her gaze between the waiters and the incoming general, stepping sideways to him, resting most of her weight on her rear leg while slashing the knife at him again, keeping him at a safe distance.

The general paused to remove his jacket, wrapping it around his right forearm as he started to circle her.

Angela kept her gaze on Hastings's torso, which she knew from Jack would telegraph his intentions.

The general faked a punch with his right fist before pivoting on his left foot while extending his right foot in a semicircle inches from the floor to sweep Angela's legs from under her.

But she had stepped aside an instant before, when Hastings's torso had betrayed his attack, leaving him standing in front of her for the single second that it took Angela to kick him in the groin.

Hard.

Hastings winced and staggered back, but to Angela's surprise, he remained standing.

She pressed on, rushing toward him, slicing the air with the knife.

Hastings blocked with his padded forearm, striking her wrist.

She managed to hold on to the knife and slashed it outward again, the tip of the blade grazing his throat a second time.

Hastings ignored it, following the sweep of the knife, grabbing her wrist with his right hand.

She tried to pull free but he managed to seize her neck with his left hand, squeezing, picking up her light frame off the ground, shaking her.

"Who do you think you're fucking with?"

Angela found it impossible to breathe, her legs swinging wildly under her, trying to kick him again. But Hastings's long arm kept her at bay as he began to twist her wrist, forcing her to loosen the grip on the knife.

As her vision began to tunnel, she heard spitting sounds behind her, listened to bodies fall on the floor.

Someone just shot the waiters.

Angela used the distraction to palm-strike Hastings's sternum with her free hand, pushing away, landing on her feet, the knife still in her hand as she stepped back while the general looked past her with surprise.

Capitalizing on the distraction, she lurched forward, closing the gap while slashing the knife at him with all her might, feeling it cut through his larynx.

Hastings shifted back and reached for his throat, blood gushing through his fingers, eyes wide open but still focused behind her just as a bullet hit him smack in the middle of the forehead, in between his eyebrows.

She turned around, bloody knife in hand.

"Hey, it's me," Jack said, lowering the weapon and lifting his goggles, letting them rest at the top of his forehead.

She froze, dropping the knife, staring at him in sheer disbelief.

"Dammit, Jack," she said, rushing to his arms. "What took you so long?"

Jack loved her embrace as she jumped on him, wrapping her arms and legs around him, burying her face in his chest.

He hugged her back while looking around the room, making sure they were alone, briefly closing his eyes, kissing the top of her head, before cupping her face and kissing her, then hugging her, and kissing her again.

"I knew you weren't dead," she whispered, her lips brushing his. "I just knew it."

"It's a long story," he said. "But first I need to get you out of here."

"Good, because I'm done here," she replied, jumping off him.

"You killed Hastings," he said, staring at his still figure on the floor, blood pooling around him.

"Didn't like the way he looked at me," she replied.

He raised his brows. "Remind me never to piss you off."

"Just don't vanish like that again. Gave me a fucking heart attack."

He almost laughed, then said, "We're not out of the woods yet." Tapping his throat mike, he added, "Found Angie."

"Give her a hug from us."

Jack grinned. "Dago and Art say hello. They helped me get here."

"I owe them everything," she said, before adding, "Now let's go get Pete."

"Here," Jack said, handing her the Sig Sauer. "Try not to shoot me."

Angela made a face and took the weapon, making sure a round was chambered before saying, "Ready when you are, Mr. Navy SEAL."

He lowered the goggles and led the way, finding two more guards in the basement, where Angela told him they would be, before reaching Pete's room.

It took him a moment to get over the weirdness of the moment. His nemesis in one world was his best friend in the other.

And this Pete had been beaten into a pulp. He was unconscious but had a pulse. While Angela stood guard, Jack dressed him quickly in one of the uniforms, then threw him across his shoulders, just as he had been trained when extracting wounded soldiers from the battlefield.

Once again leading the way, Jack went out the back, down the steps leading to the helipad, past the guards he had killed, and straight to the docks, selecting the smaller of three speedboats.

While Angie worked the lines, untying them from the cleats, Jack got under the dash and hot-wired the boat, engaging the engine.

A moment later they were off, cruising across the lake.

And as Angela sat next to him on the bench seat, running an arm around his bicep and pressing her head against his shoulder, as the wind blew on his face and the moon and the stars looked down on them, Jack Taylor felt that everything was suddenly right with the world.

EPILOGUE
NEW BEGINNINGS

There can be no thought of finishing, for "aiming at the stars," both literally and figuratively, is a problem to occupy generations, so that no matter how much progress one makes, there is always the thrill of just beginning.

—Dr. Robert Goddard

The destruction of his empire happened rather quickly, just as Angela had predicted.

The IT guys figured it out first, as they regained control of the security cameras and noticed that General Hastings was dead along with his security detail, including his South American colleagues.

The exodus from his operation was nothing short of dramatic, as scientists, politicians, security personnel, accountants, bankers, merchants, and military leaders tried to put as much distance as possible between them and the imploding operation, especially after the wave of cyberattacks, exposed bank accounts, shadowy financial deals, and clear evidence of money laundering and embezzlement reaching not only the desks at the *New York Times*, the *Washington Post*, and a dozen other news outlets, but also going viral on a host of social networks.

In the end, the president had to step in and bring some sense of order to the madness, appointing a congressional panel to investigate the matter and bring those responsible to justice.

Jack and Angela Taylor, plus Pete Flaherty, were among those who spent countless hours behind closed doors with a panel of congressmen and scientists going over their observations, their firsthand accounts, documenting the incredible discovery of an amazing source of energy, and the disturbing plot to use it for global domination in the hands of a madman.

And shortly after that the arrests began, and not just across the nation, but across the world, as U.S. law enforcement collaborated with the international community to tear down every aspect of Hastings's operation. The goal was to root it out, to drown it all, leaving it no chance of reigniting under another madman. The president, assisted by his congressional panel, and a team of advisors, which included Jack, Angela, and Pete, wanted to make sure that they would not be fighting this battle again in the future while also ensuring a safe and responsible way to harvest the benefits of salolitite, a clean energy source with the potential to realize the dream of forever moving away from fossil fuels.

And the evening when they returned home from their month-long trip to Washington, the three friends toasted to that future while enjoying a blazing Florida sunset.

Pete left at around midnight. Tomorrow was his first day back at work, back at the helm of not just Project Phoenix but of NASA after a grateful president appointed him director of the space agency under the applause of both sides of the House.

Jack and Angela could also have gotten pretty much anything they wanted, but they just chose each other and their home in Cocoa Beach. Tomorrow would also be a special day for them, and not just by returning to NASA and continuing to pave the way for space jumps while also exploring the potential of salolitite to realize Einstein's theories, but also because they would get a very special visitor.

Angela had made one request to the president: she'd asked for full custody of Erika Wiltz.

After all, a promise was a promise.

She was as determined as ever to get her marriage back on track, and she never did push much trying to find out exactly what had taken place in that other world for those couple of weeks with someone who Jack described as her twin, beside learning that she had built him another suit. Perhaps some things were best left alone. Jack was with her now, and that was all that really mattered.

And it was him who had suggested a few new rules for their relationship, including always being able to speak their minds in front of each other, never going to bed angry, and never, ever, sleeping in separate beds again.

But late at night, long after they'd made love and fallen asleep in each other's arms, he would sometimes get up and walk outside to gaze at the stars.

She never asked him why and he never offered. He would just spend a few minutes staring at the heavens, before crawling back in bed to hold her in a way he never had before, tight, tenderly.

And there were other things, like the way he now liked to step in the shower with her, or that new hot tub he ordered, or the way he let her take control in bed.

She knew it reminded him of the woman at the other end of that dimensional jump.

But she didn't care. It was that same woman who figured out a way to return him back to her.

And Angela even began to appreciate the way she'd somehow changed him in such intimate ways in such a short time, how she'd made him care just a bit more, which in turn made her care a bit more.

Little by little, in just a couple of short months, Angela found herself in the middle of a great marriage, full of passion, love, joy and laughter, just like in the old days, making her believe once again that they might be able to go the distance, giving her a solid foundation to start the next phase of their marriage, adopting a wonderful little girl in need of a loving family.

And it was all because of her, the woman beyond the stars, who'd made them both realize that forever meant forever.

The frame took forever to complete.

It had to be light but strong, ready to receive a chrome-glistening engine that looked more like an elaborate work of art than the deliverer of 150 horsepower to the extra-wide rear wheel.

Wearing a pair of greasy coveralls, welding goggles and gloves, Angela stepped back to admire her creation in the making. There was still much work to be done, but tonight a set of aluminum pipes had been painstakingly transformed into a thing of beauty.

Mickey Valle would have been proud.

She removed her protective clothing and left them hanging next to the frame, before starting to shut down Dago's shop at just past five in the morning.

She loved the late shift because that meant she had the shop all to herself to work on Dago's special projects, the ones commissioned to Paradise by a growing list of discriminating clients to whom money was secondary to their pursuit of one-of-a-kind toys. And this one was certainly starting to look like another unique master creation.

Stepping back, she took another moment to enjoy what would likely be her last project before the fall session started up in Melbourne. Where she would be back to her old routine.

Well, her old routine minus one Pete Flaherty.

She frowned, still furious at him for having reacted the way he did, for letting greed take over his senses. She had agreed to meet him a week after Jack's departure, but only on her terms, down in Miami with Dago's full staff in attendance.

He had managed to keep his job at NASA after selling Hastings the Taliban lie while also announcing that his team had managed to locate and rescue Angela Taylor down in Miami.

She had reluctantly agreed to the lie, letting him take credit for rescuing her in exchange for the safety of Dago and his gang—plus getting NASA to foot the bill for the repairs of her home and a new boat. After all, the glass accelerator was gone, and with it any chance of reproducing it.

And then she told him she never wanted to see him again. Ever.

That was almost two months ago.

Angela grimaced and put a hand on her belly.

She was nauseated again. The third time this week.

Reaching in the refrigerator next to Dago's office, she grabbed a can of ginger ale and sipped it slowly while turning off the lights, walking out the back, activating the alarm system and closing and locking the heavy metal door.

She climbed on the Triumph and put on her helmet and lowered the goggles before kick-starting the bike, twisting the throttle to rev it up when the engine caught. But she had to shut it down when her stomach contracted.

Leaning over, she vomited right onto the pavement, splashing her riding boots. *What the hell?*

She stared at it for a moment, as the feeling passed just as soon as it had started.

Angela sat there, on the Bonneville, alone in the parking lot under a blanket of stars, which always reminded her of Jack, of the short time they'd spent together, which now almost felt like some sort of dream, an escape from the loneliness that had been her life for the past five years.

But Jack had returned to her, if only for a little while.

They had laughed, and talked, and rode together, and they even had—

Angela froze, trying to remember the last time she got her period.

Oops.

She kick-started the bike and rode to the nearest twenty-four-hour pharmacy, grabbing the first instant pregnancy test she could find and not even bothering paying for it before rushing to the store's ladies' room.

It didn't take long before she stepped back out, holding the results in her hand, walking aimlessly up and down the aisles, her mind going in twenty different directions, before somehow she found the cashier, an elderly lady who gave her a puzzled look as Angela stood there with the small test wand in her hand.

"Where's the box, honey?"

Angela blinked, staring at the results again, before mumbling, "Back there . . . in the . . . bathroom."

The woman's wrinkled face shifted, becoming warm, soft, beaming with motherly pride as she said, "Well, that's perfectly all right. You just had to know, dear. Now, let's see what kind it is."

Gently, she reached across the aisle for Angela's hand and slowly turned it over to look at the brand and model, also noticing the results.

"How much do I owe you?" Angela said, reaching for her cash.

The lady gave her a smile and said, "Nothing, dear. This one's on the house. Congratulations."

She thanked her and walked back out to the bike and sat there awhile, before riding to the ocean to look at the sunrise, just as she had done every night since deciding to accept Dago's summer job offer while her house was rebuilt up in Cocoa Beach.

The stars were starting to retreat when a streak of burnt orange forked skyward, as the eastern horizon became alive, dotted with distant vessels.

A new dawn.

Where she suddenly didn't feel alone anymore.

Angela left the bike, pulled off her boots, and walked barefoot on the cold sand, listening to seagulls, to the sound of the ocean, and the smell of the sea as the looming sun stained it with hues of yellow-gold, marking the start of a new day, of a new life.

She dropped to her knees, hugged her belly, and watched it through her tears.

* * *

He heard them come in the middle of the night.

Like they always did every full moon for as far back as he could remember, especially after the headaches subsided.

They came to purify him again, just as his wounds started to heal.

But this time it was different.

They had waited too long.

Perhaps they'd lost track of time after so many years. Or maybe the helicopters he'd heard flying overhead or the artillery thundering in the distance for the past several weeks had distracted them.

But they had eventually returned.

The door resisted, as it always did every time they tried to open it. The hinges were old, rusted, like the heavy metal door they connected to the concrete wall. But they gave with a loud creak, and he heard their footsteps as they walked in. Three of them. Always three of them. Waiting by the entrance with their leather straps.

None of them spoke, which was part of the ritual, as was their insistence for total silence. He wasn't allowed to make a sound, especially during the purification.

He did once, in the beginning, and the punishment had been so severe, he couldn't walk for nearly six months, according to the crude calendar he kept on the far wall, in the dark, where only he could see.

Turning around slowly, pretending to be hurt, signaling that his ribs, wrists, and ankles had not fully healed, he used his loose clothes to hide the slim muscles he had built through rigorous—and highly secretive—exercise for the past several weeks.

They seemed to relax at his visible weakness, as he staggered slowly toward them, hands trembling, his gaze on the stained concrete floor.

One of them, the older one who went by the name of Atash, grabbed him by the arm and began to fasten one of the leather straps they would use to snap his wrists.

In a single fluid move, he spun on instinct, yanking the three-foot-long leather belt from the startled Afghan and used it like a whip, smashing the heavy buckle into Atash's head while kicking the second man, Fahran, in the solar plexus. He collapsed gasping for air next to Atash while the third man, Jawid, reached for the AK-47 hanging from his broad shoulders.

But his hands never touched it before a palm-strike pushed his nose deep into his brain, triggering seizures.

He paused, staring at his captors in disbelief before looking at his own hands, not certain how he had moved this way or even where he had learned to do so.

But a deep desire to end the purifications had seized him, making him kick each of them across the temple with a force he knew would be hard enough to kill. And again he questioned how he knew that.

He checked their bodies, removing two daggers as well as a sash to holster them before picking up the Kalashnikov, marveled as his hands moved automatically, with trained precision, checking the safety, making sure a round was chambered even though he couldn't recall ever holding such a weapon.

Fascinated by his hidden skills, he walked out of the cell and made his way across a compound he'd never seen before even though he'd been imprisoned here for longer than he could keep track.

How long has it been?

Three years?

Longer?

He wasn't sure, just like he couldn't remember his name, or why he could kill so easily, but at the moment those skills could help him stop the pain.

Taking a deep breath of cold and fresh air while glancing at a star-filled sky, he instinctively began to look for guards, for sentries, for any sign of threat. But he found none in this small courtyard-like place, feeling cold sand in between his toes as he walked toward what looked like the only gate.

Where is everybody?

He didn't understand at first, but then realized it was very late, probably in the predawn hours, but the same voice told him he didn't need to understand why.

What *did* matter was taking advantage of the opportunity to unlock the gate and inch it open just enough to squeeze his slim frame through, before quietly closing it.

And just like that he was free, the mountains projecting skyward at the edge of the short valley.

He strapped the AK-47 across his shoulders and broke into a run, leaving the small village behind, feeling the wind in his face, once more gazing up at the stars, confused at the strange thoughts filling his mind—thoughts of falling from the heavens, vague memories of the Earth rushing up to meet him, of a parachute blossoming above him.

Reaching the thick vegetation beyond the narrow valley that led into a thick forest, he slowed down, his body automatically dropping to a deep crouch while his hands once again clutched the Kalashnikov, noticing how his shooting finger automatically rested on the trigger casing, feeling quite at ease surrounded by the woods.

His eyes drifted to the south, to the source of those helicopters and artillery rounds that he believed had given him the critical weeks to heal since the last purification.

Continuing up the side of a mountain, using the sporadic breaks in the thick canopy to check the stars for navigation—yet another thing that he just knew—he maintained a steady pace, making it down to a ravine that led to a pond fed by a narrow stream glistening under the moonlight.

Dropping to his knees by the sandy shore, he washed his face before getting his fill of cold water, breathing deeply, staring at his reflection in the rippling water.

He saw his hollow cheeks, his sunken eyes, touched his unkempt beard, his mind flashing images of a clean-shaven man in a strange suit surrounded by other men in lab coats tending to him.

But the images vanished as quickly as they appeared, like flashes of lightning, glimpses of his mysterious past, there one moment and gone the next, replaced by other disjointed images, other memories that also made no sense—memories that had grown vaguer with each purification cycle.

He stood and studied the stars again while scratching the side of his head, where his cranium had a slight indentation, the source of the headaches that had driven him almost mad in the beginning. Hair eventually grew over that old wound—a wound that like so many other things, he couldn't remember getting.

But a voice deep inside of him told him that the clues were all there, locked deep inside, and just as his muscles remembered, his mind would soon follow. He just needed to trust it, like how he now trusted his hands clutching the AK-47 and his legs bending halfway as he walked mostly on the balls of his feet, devoid of all noise, using the big toe of his leading foot to feel the terrain ahead in the darkness before shifting his weight forward.

As the first beams of light pierced the eastern sky to his far left, he spotted the compound in the vast valley below him, watching the large camouflaged helicopters beyond the tall chain-link fence.

Slowly, with caution, he spent a few hours following an old goat path veering down the southern face of the mountain, reaching a gravel road that snaked its way around boulders and clusters of trees toward the gated entrance of the compound, now thriving with activity under a mid-morning sun, as helicopters took off and landed, as troops moved about the place, some on foot, others on Humvees.

He hesitated leaving the protection of the woods, choosing instead to inspect it for some time from a safe distance, watching the men guarding the gate, all armed with U.S Army standard-issue M-17 SCAR-H rifles. And again, he had no idea how he knew that.

But somehow he knew he might want to approach them, though he wasn't certain when it would be the right time to do so. A part of him dreaded losing his newly acquired freedom, feared walking right into another cell, into another group of captors. And more purifica—

The shock wave from the sudden explosions pushed him back, and he landed on the ground, confused, momentarily stunned.

He heard cries, shouts, and alarms as the compound came under attack from an unseen enemy, at least not visible from his vantage point.

Helicopters exploded, men ran to their battle stations to return the fire, aimed high, at the cliffs to his far right, blocked by the forest protecting him.

The battle raged, buildings caught fire, attack helicopters took flight, swooping above him, their downwash swaying the forest canopy. Soldiers jumped on Humvees and scrambled out of the compound, their engines roaring as they sped by the road just fifty feet from him in the direction of the threat. Other soldiers remained inside fighting back, their machine guns reverberating, echoing across the valley.

The same voice that had urged him to find a way to stop the purifications now screamed at him to get back into the forest.

Slowly, he did, walking away from the intense battle, losing sight of it as he obeyed the voice, immersing himself in the woods, where he would be safe, where he would have time to think, to remember, to piece together the fragments of his obscured past.

Perhaps he would recall where he came from, who he was, why he ended up here, and maybe, just maybe, even remember the name of the woman who would sometimes visit him in his dreams, the one who would tell him to go on, to be strong, to never give up and find a way back to her.

The one who called him Jack.

ACKNOWLEDGMENTS

Peter Wolverton, editor in chief of Thomas Dunne Books, and Brendan Deneen, head of Macmillan Entertainment, came up with the idea for this book, developing it into a terrific synopsis about a man who jumps from the uppermost reaches of the atmosphere and vanishes during reentry, landing on an alternate Earth, where he died five years earlier. What a wild ride! I was spellbound by the outline, thrilled to be tapped to write the book, and honored to have worked with such pros. Thanks for taking a chance with me, guys. A special thanks goes to Brendan for your continued support and confidence. Every author should be so lucky.

Matt Bialer, my super agent at Sanford J. Greenburger, who discovered me over a quarter of a century ago. Thanks for sticking by my side ever since, for your unflagging support and guidance, for sharing your amazing artistic talents—from watercolors to photography and poems—and for getting me connected with Pete and Brendan.

Nicole Sohl, Associate Editor at Macmillan Entertainment, for your diligence and consideration during editing and production. It is much appreciated and recognized.

Bob Gleason, although not involved with this project, for teaching me what it means to be a novelist while pushing me to hammer out the best books I could for over two decades.

Dr. Cameron M. Smith, professor of anthropology at Portland State University, who in addition to digging for fossils in Africa and launching solo voyages in the Arctic, actually built and tested a DIY functional space suit on a shoestring budget. Your adventurous life and your efforts to democratize space travel are an inspiration. Thanks for taking the time to review the manuscript and for your very insightful feedback.

The hero of the story, Jack Taylor, is a former U.S. Navy SEAL. Special thanks go to a retired U.S. Navy SEAL who prefers to remain anonymous, for your candid feedback when I got it wrong and for doing your best to keep me honest.

Many thanks go to my personal proofreaders, Linda Wiltz, Michael Wiltz, and my wife, Lory.

Last but not least, a tip of the hat to my son, Cameron. Your dad is very proud of the man you have become.